"Don't you believe in the devil?" he asked, almost teasing her.

"Well," she cleared her throat trying to come up with the right answer, as if there was one. "The good book says…"

"Do you believe in God?" he quickly cut into her reply.

"Well, yes, I do," she both thought to herself and said out loud at the same time.
"Yes. I do believe in God."

"Then you must also believe in the devil," he added.

"Do you believe in the devil?" she hesitantly asked him.

"Yes." The killer's smile started to disappear as his eyes looked directly into hers and pierced deeper into her heart. "The devil is in this room."

BANG-BANG YOU'RE DEAD

JOE JANOWICZ

Editor: Elly Stevens
Cover Design and Formatting: Megan J. Parker

Printed in the United States of America
by NewField Publications

For Romeo
My beloved "chug" dog. My shadow, my
companion, my friend.
Who sat beside me, or on my lap as I wrote
this story.
2007-2018

The itsy-bitsy spider went in the old folks' house.

Heard were the shots that scared the old folks out.

Out came the blood that left the dead behind.

The itsy-bitsy spider went off to kill again.

CHAPTER 1

NO ONE HEARD THE FIRST GUNSHOT.

Dorothy Paine loved her bedtime tea. Not only did it relax her and get her mind ready for another night of what she always said was the "best sleep she ever had," but it also helped bring back the fondest of memories from her 93 years of life. So, just as she was about to take her first sip, a happy smile came across her face. Life here in the Sunny Side Up Retirement Home wasn't so bad after all. Yes, she fought it at first, not wanting to leave her lonely condo after the sudden passing of her husband and 66 years of blissful marriage. But she quickly adapted with all the new friends she met, and the new activities that kept her busy throughout each passing day. Dorothy had all the luxuries she needed here, in what her family and friends called her "golden years."

Apartment 101 was "just the right size" for Dorothy: A small bedroom with a 3-drawer dresser that held all the unworn, tucked-away clothing she received from her family each holiday. A living room with an old sofa, and a brown antique English sitting chair with extra padding for her thin, wrinkled behind. A small breakfast nook, whatever that was, with a half-sized refrigerator and microwave that she always had trouble working. "Damn electronics!" she told her laughing family members when they watched her fiddle with it. A bathroom with a special padded toilet seat to help relieve her hemorrhoids, and a walk-in bathtub-shower combination with enough jungle-gym-type handles to prevent even a monkey from falling down in it. Plenty of wall and table space for all the many (and there were so many) family pictures of her children, and the grandchildren they gave her. And, of course, her slightly faded wedding picture, when she looked so beautiful, and he looked so handsome. They were both 20 years of age in a world that was so simple and different from all the bad things she now saw on her new Hi-def (whatever that meant) TV, and what she read in the ever-shrinking newspaper she still looked forward to every day. And, most importantly, just enough floor space for her trusty and sturdy walker she kiddingly named the "Silver Express."

Yes, Dorothy was a very happy, very content, and very well-liked person in these, her "golden years." She had so much to look forward to. Each day was a blessing to her, as she knew her lifetime calendar was coming to an end. And, now, as it had become a nightly ritual, it was time to take that wonderful sip of that wonderful tea she so enjoyed each night. It had been sitting, cooling, and waiting for her on that fine old antique wooden end table next to the chair she sat in. It was the perfect table for her to keep her latest issue of *Reader's Digest*, the TV remote she could never work right, and just a little bitty space left for her nightly cup of tea.

So, as she did each night at about the same time, her somewhat shaky hand gently and slowly brought that warm tea closer to her lips. The aroma filled her nostrils with a heavenly feeling of "Can't wait." Her smile broadened even more. *"Ah, this is the life,"* she thought to herself. Or, should we say, "this was the life," as a bullet suddenly went right through Dorothy's head.

It happened so fast. She didn't even see it coming, not that she'd want to. The bullet entered the back of her head just above her ears, and quickly travelled through her brain, filled with those wonderful memories, and then straight out the front of her smiling face, right between her eyes. Probably a good thing she didn't have her hearing aids in. The sound of the bullet would have startled her, and she probably would have dropped the hot tea on her brand-new nightie that she recently received as a birthday present. That would have made her very upset. But, be as it may, the speeding bullet cut through her brain matter that controlled her well-worn reflexes and she dropped the tea cup anyway, and it spilled all over her brand-new nightie, as the blood poured from the still-smoking hole in her head. At least she didn't burn herself, or, if she did, she certainly didn't feel it, because she was already dead. "Really dead. Deader than a doornail." Just like the silly old expression she sometimes laughingly used when she killed a pesky fly or mosquito that just bit her. Old people sometimes use a lot of silly expressions. But right now, there was no silly expression to describe what happened to her next. It just happened.

Dorothy's frail body fell forward, almost in slow motion. After all, she only weighed 100 lbs. At her age of 93, her appetite was diminished, so she didn't eat a lot anymore, and she was secretly fighting a slow, untreatable cancer. Yep, no silly expression from that smiling Dorothy as she fell. Just the accompanying sickening sound of her bones shattering, breaking, or just coming apart as she hit the floor. Maybe if it were a more expensive carpet with soft, plush padding that you pay extra for, her landing might have been more comfortable. But it was a cheaper, thinner grade of carpet that the owners bought to save construction costs. Such a shame that it was also a light-colored carpet. Dorothy had even expressed her concern to the management that it would be hard to keep clean. Now, for sure, it would have to be replaced from the enormous amount of blood that poured out from the freshly made hole in her head.

As she lay there motionless, it almost looked like

one of the several garish garage-sale reproduction paintings on her wall that she had brought with her when she moved. Quiet and peaceful – bubbling brooks and huge waterfalls that didn't move, or snow-covered landscapes that never melted. Yes, they were the running joke in her family since no one was going to lay claim to inherit these magnificent phony paintings.

From the growing river of the rich, red-colored blood that poured out of her head, it was apparent that she wasn't just 100 pounds of skin and bones. She had a lot of blood; it was like someone forgot to shut the faucet off, her bleeding seemed to never end. And that really happy smile, which was on her face as she was about to sip that warm tea just as the bullet entered her head, was still there, and would remain there forever. Frozen in time, like the majestic garage-sale paintings on the blood-splattered walls that surrounded her.

In her position on the floor, caught forever in that wonderful smile, it became apparent that she had no teeth, having taken them out shortly before. Yep, Dorothy was toothless. As part of her nightly ritual, her pearly whites were nicely placed in that half-filled glass of water on the end table next to where she had prepared her tea. And that two-thousand-dollar set of choppers was only two weeks old.

As her blood flow turned into a trickle, Dorothy's killer stepped from the shadows behind her. Cautiously, her killer walked around her crumpled body, as not to get any of her dirty old blood on his sneakers. They appeared to be the type of sneakers that a man would wear, a size 10 or maybe a size 11.

Besides, bloody footsteps would only mess up the carpet more.

With his face in shadow, the killer stopped beside the end table next to where she had been sitting. As if being watched from Dorothy's perspective, not that she can see, 'cause she's dead, he reached for the half-filled glass of water that held her dentures. The killer's hand was young and smooth, not old and wrinkled like hers. Holding the glass carefully, he turned it left, then right, looking at it curiously, like it was a toy being examined for the first time. Slowly, her killer brought the glass upwards towards his mouth, stopping just before it reached his lips. Only his eyes seem to glow through the darkness which hid his face from view. An eerie glow, as if he were the devil himself.

All we know, or what we think we know, is that this is one very bad, very, very bad individual. After all, who would commit a murder as heinous as this? Putting a bullet through a smiling, frail, 93-year-old woman's head wearing a brand-new nightie and without teeth. Maybe someone who had a shady past, or maybe a lifetime filled with terrible abuse, or maybe an escaped convict, or maybe some psychopath who Dorothy would hear about on the nightly Hi-Def TV news, or maybe read about in her morning paper. Maybe. But whoever, whatever, this person is, he is a very, very bad person. And now, this killer, this maniac, this psycho, this evil, sick person with a twisted mind, was going to drink the water from Dorothy's glass that was holding her dentures. Just another indication of how very bad this killer really is. A "sicko," as Dorothy declared out loud as she watched or read those news stories about a person like this. A "sicko" – her favorite phrase that she told her children, or even her grandchildren, as she described the very bad people in the world she lived in. A very, very bad person is nothing else, but a sicko.

And so the killer was, as he drank from the glass of water containing her brand-new dentures, quenching whatever thirst for death he had.

As quickly as the glass was emptied, it was returned to the end table. As quickly as the bullet had smashed through poor Dorothy's 93-year-old head, the killer turned to leave. As quickly as everything happened, it stopped. The killer paused, then turned back to look at her crumpled body on the bloody carpet. Without any indication, without any further warning, he pointed his gun and pulled the trigger again, suddenly putting another bullet into poor, dead Dorothy's head.

"Bang-Bang. You're dead," he whispered out loud to himself, and maybe to Dorothy wherever she was.

Like a hammer smashing an egg, this was not a pretty sight to see. Exposed bone, wrinkled remnants of droopy skin, bloodied scalp hair from that first fateful bullet, and maybe even part of a 93-year-old ear, blended together and flew "through the air, with the greatest of ease," like "that daring young man on the flying trapeze." Another favorite silly expression of once-alive Dorothy, who loved going to the circus in her long gone and forever forgotten childhood years. As quickly as this whole horrid scene took place, it came to a final, jarring end.

Before he left, the killer stopped in front of a

small antique mirror on the wall next to the door of her apartment. Yes, the image of Dorothy's twisted, broken, bloodied, dead body on the floor was now displayed in the mirror, like one of her gaudy garage-sale paintings hanging on the wall beside it. And yes, facing the mirror, the killer finally revealed his face to dear, dead Dorothy. Yes, it was the face of a very, very bad person, a murderer, a crazed, seasoned killer, a monster, a demon, the devil himself, or as Dorothy would say, a "sicko." A soulless, evil person. Yes, the devil himself.

And in that mirror, the killer's face is revealed – it is the face of a ten-year-old boy. Smiling and lovable. Neatly groomed. Neatly dressed. A ten-year-old boy who looks like he belongs in the Boy Scouts, or maybe on the honor roll in his 6th grade class. A ten-year-old boy who has just killed a 93-year-old woman named Dorothy Paine.

He stood smiling in the mirror, with a gun in his hand, preparing to kill some more.

Turning off the room light, he departed, leaving her dentures abandoned in the now empty glass.

CHAPTER 2

SOME GUNSHOTS ARE MEANT TO BE SILENT.

"Bang-Bang. You're Dead!" exclaimed 10-year-old, brown, bushy-haired Timmy Jameson. His year-younger brother Ryan artfully dodged an imaginary hail of pretend bullets by running behind a gnarly, old dying elm tree. The summer air they played in was rich with all the scents of life and growth. An old, red, wooden barn blocked the view of their adjacent farm house where they lived.

"Cops and robbers." "Cowboys and Indians." Whatever game they played, it always had the same ending, "Bang-Bang. You're Dead." Kids will be kids, and a harmless game such as this was just another way to pass away the long, fading summer days before school would start again.

"My turn," yelled Ryan.

For a 9-year-old baby brother, he was almost as tall as Timmy, had the same color hair, and tried to emulate everything his big brother did. Ryan looked up to his older brother, idolized him, and wanted to be everything like him. But there were some differences. Timmy excelled in school sports; Ryan had trouble catching a baseball. Timmy was friendly and cool around people of any and all ages; Ryan was shy and quiet. Timmy had an "eye" for the young classmate girls who were developing "boobies," as he joked with his friends; Ryan had no idea what "boobies" were. They were different as brothers could be. Yet, Ryan did everything he could to make them appear so much alike. Ryan mimicked his brother's mannerisms all the time – sometimes too much. Their father would tell him sternly, "It's okay to be like your brother, but you also have to be like yourself." Not that Ryan totally understood this. After all, he was only 9 years old, and like any 9-year-old kid, not everything made sense. Maybe later in life, but not always now. But no matter what their differences as brothers were, or maybe would be, the most important thing that bonded them was that Ryan and Timmy were best friends. Best "buds" as Ryan jokingly referred to them.

But it wasn't always fun and games around their house. Their dad was a former military man, in something called "special ops," and sometimes he even commanded his two sons like they were part of a military squad. There were rules to be followed, chores to be done, and then there was "practice time." Target-practice time. Mr. Jameson taught both how to load a gun, aim a gun, and shoot a gun. Timmy and Ryan enjoyed this a lot. Shooting real-life guns with their father was much more exciting than using their fingers.

Living on a rural, northern Wisconsin farm with no close neighbors – just big, spooky woods behind them – no one could hear the sound of guns as they did their target practice. It was almost as if their dad was "preparing them."

It was their special time.

And it was their special secret. Their dad mentioned that to their mother one night in a conversation they overheard. They didn't quite understand what he meant. Maybe you had to be in the military to know that. Their dad did a good job of keeping all the guns, and there were many of them, all different types, locked safely in their house. Had to. That was the law, and that's how he was trained – keep the guns safe, keep the guns ready. But the boys knew where the hidden key was, as all boys know where their parents hide things.

But now, it was just after supper, and they were just having fun, using their fingers as guns. But the game had lasted a little too long.

"I'm tired of this, Ryan. I want to go in," Timmy said, a little out of breath, since he was recently diagnosed with asthma.

"Just one more game, please," begged his brother.

"Come on, Ryan, we've been playing for a long time. We've played it all summer. You know, we're getting too old to be playing this. Let's do something else," Timmy replied, while taking a quick puff of fresh air from his pocket-sized inhaler.

"But I like this game. We're not too old. I don't want to grow up," Ryan pleaded back to him.

"Well, like it or not, we all have to grow up," Timmy said matter of factly, blended with a boyish sigh, and then a sneaky smile.

Suddenly, Timmy turned and surprised his brother.

"Okay, you asked for it. Bang-Bang. You're Dead!" Timmy yelled, as two imaginary finger guns were aimed at Ryan.

And just as suddenly as Timmy had aimed and shot, Ryan fell to the soft, freshly mowed lawn beneath his feet. Timmy slowly walked over and stood over Ryan, his finger guns at his side.

"Gotcha. Game over. You're dead!" Timmy proclaimed loudly after a triumphant and surprisingly imaginary win.

"End game!" he added in a smug and final exclamation.

Blowing away the pretend smoke from his finger guns, and then putting them away in two twin imaginary holsters on his belt, that it was the ending to their fun. And it was. It truly was. End of game. Except this time, the game had a different ending. This time, his brother Ryan didn't immediately jump up and say, "Okay, it's my turn. I want to shoot you." No, this time, there was only silence...dead silence.

Timmy looked down to what he assumed to be his "playing dead" little brother, and there appeared to be no movement. It was only natural for a youngster like Timmy to tell his brother to get up. Not once, but twice, and maybe even a third time. But this time, unlike all the many times before, in all the many shoot-'em-up games they played, this time, his brother didn't respond. Maybe, maybe he was really, really, doing his best bluffing act. You know, holding his breath, trying to fool his brother. Maybe even scare him. You know, just like any precocious 9- and 10-year-old kids, especially brothers, would do. Scare each other.

But no, this time, it was different. Ryan didn't jump up jokingly, laughing as he would sometimes do. No, this time he didn't give himself away with releasing the breath he was holding in to the very last moment. No, this time he wasn't pretending to scare his brother. No, this time was really different. This time...he was dead. Like "really dead." Like really, really dead, as if a cop shot a robber dead, or a cowboy shot an Indian dead. Brother Ryan was dead.

And, in that moment of understanding, he knew that his brother was not fooling him. Not playing a joke on him. Not messing with him. Timmy sometimes said that Ryan was "annoying" and "messing" with him. Not this time. For suddenly, as suddenly can be, he realized that his brother was no longer going to play the game of cops and robbers with him, or cowboys and Indians, or any other games. Nor was he going to go to the movies together with him and their dad anymore. Their dad loved cops-and-robbers movies more so than cowboys-and-Indian movies. No, there would be no more of any of this, or other things they used to do as brothers, best friends, or...just being kids. No more. Ever. Little brother Ryan was really, really, dead.

And in Timmy's still-developing child brain, he felt, truly felt, and he believed, truly believed, he had killed his little brother. He had become a killer. He was the cause, the fault, the one who made his little brother dead. The one who took away his little brother's young life all because of "Bang-Bang. You're Dead." Yep, it was all his fault, and only his fault. Not knowing, or ever believing, or even understanding, the eventual coroner's report that it was a simple brain aneurism that ended his young life; just that, nothing more. Just happened, just like that. A brain aneurism. Painless, quick, and right at the most fun part of "Bang-Bang. You're Dead."

Timmy didn't know of any such thing as an aneurism, nor did he care. All he could think about over, and over, and over again, was that he was a killer. A killer of his own brother. And now, with that painful thought filling his head, all he could do was kneel next to the lifeless body. He knelt in the fresh evening dew, dirtying his brand-new after-school pants. Pants that he had been told to never get dirty by an always complaining mom. Now, he was, for sure. He dirtied those pants as he began to gently rock back in forth in the grass, holding little brother Ryan's limp, freshly dead, but still warm body in his arms.

And then there was the blood he got on his hands that slowly flowed, then trickled, from the back of his brother's head. Of all the luck. Not that there was any amount of luck involved here. When Ryan fell backwards on to the ground, a sharp, jagged rock that was stuck in the soil cut into the back of his head. Not a deep cut. Not a lot of blood. Just enough. Didn't matter, he was already dead from the aneurism. All he knew, all he believed, is that he had his brother's blood on his hands.

Timmy remained kneeling on the ground with Ryan in his arms for a long time. He did this until the evening darkness began to fill the sky. His parents were probably wondering where he and Ryan were, but it didn't matter to him, because all he thought about, over, and over again, was that he killed his brother. He was a "killer." He was a bad person. He was an evil person. He was what his mother would refer to this type of bad person as "a sicko." Anyone who killed another family member and showed no emotion was definitely a "sicko." That's right, and she was probably right. Had to be true, just like his mother said. Timmy never shed a single tear as he began to rock back and forth, holding his dead brother's body, which turned from warm to cold throughout the passing time, to the coming of twilight. Never flat-out cried, as a normal child might. No emotion. Nothing. He just rocked back and forth, getting his brand-new pants dirtier and dirtier, from the damp evening dew forming on the ground he knelt on. And as he rocked back and forth, he made no sound. He kept his eyes closed. He just continued to rock faster, and faster, and faster, until he could rock no more. Until his brother's body was so cold, it began to stiffen. Timmy had rocked so much, he wore a slight hole in his new pants from where he knelt on the ground. The cold ground that matched his cold, dead brother's body, that matched the cold from the approaching nightfall.

And then, suddenly, without purpose, or maybe intent, or whatever goes through a "sicko's mind," he stopped the rocking. His arms opened, and he dropped the lifeless form he had held for so long onto the ground next to him. And he smiled. A strange smile; not a happy smile, but a sardonic smile. And although no one could hear him, or would want to hear him, he could hear himself, as he whispered the words, "Bang-Bang. You're Dead." Not once. Not twice. But over, and over, and over again.

CHAPTER 3

NOT ONE BULLET, BUT TWO BULLETS.

"Twins!" exclaimed a shocked Margret MaGoo as she sat propped up on a doctor's table with her legs spread open.

"Yes, Margret, twins. And everything looks fine, and it should be a normal, non-eventful delivery," Doctor Monroe replied with an assuring smile. He was approaching 70 and retirement and knew a thing or two about babies, having delivered most of them in the past 50 years of medical practice in the small town of Brentville, Wisconsin.

"Non-eventful," she thought to herself. She had just turned 40, had three previous miscarriages,

divorced, out of work, and had become a devout Christian with a whole lot of praying every night to the Good Lord upstairs for a blessing. *"But two?"*

"Look at it as a blessing," he replied with a nod or two.

"Twins." She repeated it to herself almost in a whisper of disbelief.

And three months later, twins it was. But not quite the blessing the good doctor had forecasted. Neither did he forecast the heart attack that killed him two days prior from being part of this historical delivery.

The MaGoo sisters came into this world as very unique sisters, having been born at the exact same time, 11:11. Now, someone might ask what's so unique about being identical twins, but note once again that they were born at the exact same time. The MaGoo sisters were conjoined twins, attached together at the hips, born premature, tiny, and both sliding out head first, at the same time. It was a hard birth, an exhausting birth, but a successful birth. All the parts and organs were in the right places. That doesn't happen every day. You could even call it historical.

And because this happened so long ago, there weren't any records of it happening at all. But it did. So the story goes.

Saint Mark's Hospital birth records weren't quite sure which one gave a cry of life first, as the doctors, the attending nurses, an exhausted mom, and the possible dad, were all surprised. Actually, very surprised. Okay, shocked. All the preliminary pregnancy tests pointed to two babies, but this?

Well, let's just say it was quite the talk of the hospital and the local town gossip for days to come.

Both were beautiful babies, and each was named after one of the mother's favorite movie stars, Joan and Bette, as in Joan Crawford and Bette Davis. The planned separation had to wait a few months for the babies to get stronger. In the meantime, Joan and Bette both showed their similar characteristics from day one. They waved all four of their tiny arms, and all four of their chubby legs at once when they cried. They bobbed and weaved their twin little heads and pooped their twin wrinkled butts simultaneously as they sought motherly milk to appease their constant hunger. And boy, oh boy (or should we say, girl, oh girl), they drank a lot of it. Poor Mrs. MaGoo, she went from a size Double D to a size A in a matter of days. Thank goodness there was a local dairy store nearby to supplement their nursing needs.

When the attached twins were finally deemed strong enough for separation, the operation went exactly as planned. The only distinguishing feature to tell them apart after surgery was the long scar each had on the side of their baby hips where they were separated. Baby Joan had a scar on the right side of her hip, while Baby Bette had a scar on the left side of her hip. Other than that, they were still identical.

Life "sort of" became normal as they grew together through the years not only as identical twin sisters, but identical best friends. As time passed, their mom and dad, and some uncles and aunts, began to feel, or recognize, or surmise, that there was another uniqueness to them, besides their exact time of birth.

An unsettling uniqueness. Joan and Bette seemed to be able to know what each other was thinking.

For example, young Bette would ask a question, "What time is it?"

"It's 2:05," Joan would reply at the exact same moment.

In other words, one would give the answer at the same time the other asked the question. This alone would make a good horror-movie plot (if written with an evil intent), but what they felt, or what other people felt about this, had a medical term, "memorization identification." In plain and simple layman's terms, because they were with each other so much from infancy, they mimicked and memorized each other's movements and expressed feelings, and had a tendency to think alike, resulting in knowing the correct response at the same time. Maybe there was more to this, but for now, that's all there was to know.

However, it's important to understand that, as Bette and Joan reached their early teens, they each took sharp turns in their personalities. The medical term for this as exhibited in normal case studies of conjoined twins is "differential realization." Again, in simple layman's terms, as they matured in their differences, one was becoming a "good girl," and one was becoming a "bad girl." One was the "Yin" to the other one's "Yang." For example, if one would lie and cheat, the other would be honest and forthcoming. But the interesting thing about all of this was that neither of them would ever tell on the other. When it came to punishing the bad one, no one could tell them apart, and they always inherently protected each other, no matter what the circumstance. So that made a punishment, whether it was "go to your room" or "you're grounded," all the more difficult. Of course, their mom could check the scar on their hips. But, with time, and a lot of aloe vera crème, their tell-tale identification scars became less and less distinguishable.

In their later teen years, things became even more troubling. While one wouldn't kiss a boy because that was "wrong and had to be saved only for marriage," the other began sleeping with every Tom, Dick, and Harry in town. It was even rumored, and sometime later proven true, that the bad one "did it" with the entire high school basketball team one night after a rousing home game. A real gang-bang as gang-banging goes. In other words, she certainly showed a lot of "team" spirit that night.

Now, all of this is important, because with the insatiable sexual appetite Bette had, sometimes bad results happened. And it did. Bette got pregnant and had an illegitimate child. Living in a small town, in those long-ago days, this was a no-no. The bastard child was immediately put up for adoption and later turned out to be...well, let's not get ahead of ourselves, as all that comes out in the wash, or should we say, in the police report, later.

Both were attractive looking from day one, and both aged gracefully through the years. Tall and slender with wispy, flowing blonde hair. Friendly and exuding an air of confidence. They always wore trendy and matching wardrobes without letting the other know what they were wearing that day. They just did. Polite, kind, good-natured girls, and they always had the same smile when they smiled. Perfect smiles that showed perfect pearly white teeth. Didn't even need braces. They could have been in TV commercials if they lived in a bigger city, but in Brentville, population 25,000, they were just known as the attractive, quiet, twin MaGoo sisters, nothing more, nothing less.

But there was more. A hidden, almost secret "more." As the years quickly passed by, the rest of Joan and Bette's lives was split between being a "storybook life and a horror show." Their different personalities became more extreme. Although they seemed to drift apart in their lifestyles, they couldn't accept being physically apart from each other. They even lived in a similar looking two-story house next to each other.

Living so close, the twins saw each other quite often. Almost too often, according to the neighborhood gossip. Joan had what appeared to be a Cinderella-type marriage with the local Prince Charming. Actually, he was more than a "Prince"; he really was a "King." "King of the local used-car-sales TV commercials," that is. And Bette, well, Bette lived by herself, and just kept whoring around, even with Joan's husband, even though Joan knew about it and even felt it.

It was even rumored that sometimes when they were alone, they could be overheard talking to themselves, as if they were talking to each other. Kind of weird and spooky. Especially when they were overheard answering themselves. Probably good candidates for *The Jerry Springer Show* on TV. Neither one had any more children, except for one little bastard that was conceived behind the bleacher stands surrounding the basketball court, and the baby quickly disappeared after birth many years ago.

So now, today, in their golden years, with Joan's Prince Charming being killed in a freak car accident (how appropriate), and the unmarried sister Bette still having affairs with every son of the original Tom, Dick, and Harry she slept with in her youth, they too, like their now-dead neighbor Dorothy Paine, ended up in the Sunny Side Up Retirement Home. Joan and Bette were alone, but always together.

They had a somewhat quiet life here. A peaceful life, interrupted only by a few strokes, seizures, heart attacks, back operations, and knee and hip replacements. You know, the normal things old people endure.

Here at Sunny Side Up, they shared a nice two-bedroom apartment, with a mixture of modest and inexpensive furniture. Each of their bedrooms was decorated identically. They even had the same fake acrylic painting of an evening scene in Paris. They never went to Paris, but always dreamed of going to Paris. The only difference in the two bedrooms was that Joan had a Bible next to her bed; Bette had a box of condoms. Figures.

The adjoining living room was as neat as could be, with two identical walkers placed side by side, next to their apartment door. They never quarreled or squabbled over whose was whose.

The MaGoo sisters kept to themselves for the most part, hardly going to any of the retirement home's planned activities. The only visitors they had were on every other Sunday when the few remaining family members, mostly nephews and nieces, came. Fortunately for Bette and Joan, these visits were always short and uneventful, and they couldn't wait for these boring "people," as they referred to them, to leave.

Bette's illegitimate child was rumored to have visited them once. Turned out that she was a drug addict and came looking for something she demanded as an inheritance. Needed to feed her habit. She got nothing, not even a hug or kiss goodbye. Sadly, she was found dead a few days later in an abandoned car where she had lived – a needle in one arm, while holding a picture of herself as a baby. At her small and hastily arranged funeral, only Joan, her aunt, showed up. She placed a picture of Bette in the coffin next to her. Kind of weird, spooky, and strange.

And now, as Joan and Bette prepared for their end-of-day sleep, attired in twin, matching, light blue nightgowns, they spoke silently to each other in their usual, unusual, shared thoughts. Whatever they felt was personal, and only they understood. They never shared their feelings with anyone, only themselves. Sometimes one would smile. Sometimes the other would frown. Sometimes one would laugh. Sometimes the other would cry. Whatever connection they had, it had remained lifelong and truly special. Truly unique. As slow and arthritic as they had become with the wear and tear of the passing years, they were still well connected spiritually, and now physically, living together. Almost like being joined at the hip.

Together, they shared dreams and relived the wonders of their lives. The pleasures, the pain, the good, and the bad moments. The memories they made, the lifetime they experienced.

"Goodnight, Joan."

"Goodnight, Bette."

They hugged each other with an everlasting love as their smiles cracked their wrinkled faces.

"I'll see you in your dreams," they both said simultaneously.

As they closed the doors to their individual bedrooms, it would be the last time they would see each other alive. They had come into the world together, and now, they were about to leave the world together, as they would become victims number three and four of the young killer, who quietly entered Apartment 102 and put a bullet in each of their heads.

CHAPTER 4

STICKS AND STONES MAY BREAK MY BONES, BUT BULLETS HURT EVEN MORE.

The large brown ball swooshed through the worn basketball hoop just as the game buzzer went off.

The overflowing crowd of spectators jumped to their feet and cheered wildly.

"And he scores! He scores the winning basket with no time left on the clock. Oh my God, Brentville High wins! Brentville High wins!" the high school sports announcer screamed over the gymnasium loudspeaker, joining the screaming 500 people in attendance.

It was mass pandemonium as players, families, and friends all raced out onto the school gym floor and held their star player, 17-year-old Miles Patchwork, in the air while the crowd chanted his name.

"Miles! Miles! Miles!"

"Miles Patchwork gets the game winner! Brentville High is going to the state championships!" the radio announcer repeated over and over.

It was a night to remember. A miraculous come-from-behind win by a team that had never been to the basketball championships in their entire school history, nor would they ever again. But now, it was finally going to happen. All thanks to Miles Patchwork's last moment game-winning jump shot. Yes, the state championships. They were finally going.

And, so they did, but not with star high school basketball player Miles Patchwork. That was 58 years ago.

The first Sunny Side Up Retirement Home shooting, or should we say murder, happened at 10:10 p.m., exactly 18 minutes before poor old Dorothy Paine took one in the head, becoming what police referred to as "Victim Number 2." It was also 58 years later, to the day, and almost to the exact time, from that memorable night at the Brentville High School gym just 4 miles away from Sunny Side Up. It was an unexpected, expected killing, and was destined to happen, as the lone evening security guard, Miles Patchwork, happened to be in the wrong place at the wrong time.

"Patch" was short for his last name, or that he had a patch over one eye. In any case, he was loved by all the Sunny Side Up residents. How he originally lost the one eye is quite the story. How he lost his second eye is even more of a story. If he had survived the retirement home shootings, he would have been called "Patches," because the killer's knife went through his one good remaining eye and almost out the back of his head. But that really didn't matter, 'cause when the knife went through that one and only good eye, Patch was already dead.

So now, on this fateful chilly late fall night, as Patch made his usual rounds, it seemed to be just the same as it always was. Up one corridor, down another, making sure that no residents were wandering the hallways, and that they all were in their rooms. Being a 76-year-old security guard, Patch was actually more of a babysitter. He was a kind, friendly, gentle man. He knew everyone by their first and last name, but always greeted them as "mister" or "missus." It was how he was brought up to show respect for his elders, even though he was nearly as old as the residents.

At six-foot tall, even though he had shrunk an inch or two with age, he still had an athletic build, and got quite a few looks from the single and lonely women here who had lost their husbands. He was a polite and quiet man. Never missed a night's work, never had a bad word for anybody. His only drawback was that he had a bad limp which made his nightly rounds even longer to finish. But he never complained, nor ever told anyone how he got the limp. Some thought it must have been from his service in the army. He looked like someone who would stand up and defend his country; but he never had that opportunity.

Miles Patchwork had his humble beginnings as the oldest in a family of eight kids. They had just relocated into a rundown neighboring big city not far from Brentville. His whole family was crammed in an older, inner-city, decaying apartment building. That's how it was for a lot of black people who relocated from the South with a promise of jobs in the growing manufacturing companies in the North. As a young black child in a mostly white world, Miles saw it all, and understood it all. He was called "nigger," a common word for people of color back then. He was without a dad, who was in jail, and his momma managed to watch over and take care of eight kids.

In school he was remembered as an average student who always paid attention in class. But growing up in a racially divided world, Miles was more "street smart than book smart." You had to be, in order to survive. The 1950s was an era struggling with racism and discrimination. Because of his color, he wasn't allowed to participate in many school sports. He spent most of his free time playing hoops with the few other local colored boys in the inner-city playground. From early on, one could see that he had a certain gift, as he completed his throws from all angles of the asphalted court with the old, rusted basketball pole and hanging torn net. And he was good at it, real good at it. He hardly ever missed his shot.

Because sports were still mostly white dominated, he could only dream of playing in the newly refurbished school gym in the school he attended. With segregation and integration locked in street and court battles, the 50s were changing, and Miles was finally given a chance to try out for the high school team. Even though the coach didn't want to play him, he was forced to, because Miles was the best player. No doubt about that. But it wasn't easy, especially with all the typical racial slurs aimed at him by the other teams and many of the local prejudiced parents.

"Get the darkie off the gym floor," or "Go home, nigger boy," voices would call out from the schools he played against. And sometimes from his own classmates.

But Miles learned to be tolerant and blocked the hurtful words.

"Sticks and stones may break your bones, but words will never hurt you," his momma would tell him.

And that became his mantra, as he closed his ears to the cruel and hateful remarks and concentrated on his skills. He owed a lot to his momma. All her life she tried to teach her children to be responsible and to be respectful, and she prayed one day that boys and girls of all colors and all nationalities would be accepted. It was a shame she died at an early age in a cross fire of bullets as a victim in a random street shooting. Her untimely death gave Miles all the more reason for being a better person in the world he disliked and that disliked him. He knew his only ticket out of the neighborhood would be through sports. This made him practice more, and he got better and better, and without a doubt he became the best player on his high school team and all throughout the county. Winning game after game, people became more accepting of him. Not everyone, but slowly and surely, people were starting to cheer him on as the Bob Dylan song would soon reflect, "the times they are a-changin.'"

Miles Patchwork, before he got the nickname Patch, had one dream. He just wanted to be the best high school basketball player, get a scholarship to a prestigious basketball-playing college, go to the pros and make lots of money for himself and his family, get married and retire happily ever after in a really big house with a really big indoor swimming pool. Although Miles didn't know how to swim, not that he cared, it would just be so cool to have that "big ol' indoor swimming pool." That was his goal. No more Momma struggling to raise eight kids; no more sharing a small cockroach-filled bedroom with his many brothers and sisters. He'd have a big bedroom all to himself, and, because he would be rich, super rich, life would be everything he wanted, dreamed of, and more. That was his plan, but plans don't always work out the way you want them to, do they?

So, that night, when up-and-coming basketball superstar, and potential sports scholarship winner Miles Patchwork scored a school record-breaking 45 points, and was the game winner at the buzzer, it was truly going to be one for everyone to remember. That night was even written up in the out-of-town newspapers. That night, when the team celebrated its homecoming high school victory, Miles Patchwork had one hell of a celebration victory to remember the rest of his life. At 17 going on 18, Miles "Superstar" Patchwork, on his way walking home, was hit suddenly by a drunk driver – a white male driver who swerved his car on purpose, so they say, to hit that "black boy" on the sidewalk and chalk up "two points" in a foolish racist game. A game that crazed drunken drivers played when they saw someone they didn't like.

How Miles survived was a story in itself. A witness said she saw Miles airborne after he was hit at 50 miles per hour by a souped-up Chevrolet.

"Just like a dunked basketball," she told the police, recalling how "he flew through the air with the greatest of ease." High into the air, his body twisted and turned, finally striking a big old maple tree next to the street, face first.

And as luck would have it, that one, lone, twisted tree branch, which had just lost its last row of leaves in the ending autumn days, impaled Miles' left eye. It left him impaled on it, unconscious, eight feet above the ground. Eight feet and two inches, to be exact, from the ground below. And one of his nice, new basketball shoes, which he had received from his high school coach for this important game, just plain fell off his big, black, size-13 foot, and laid beneath him, with his blood dripping on it.

Amazingly, that one, lone, twisted tree branch went through right through his eye and eye socket and stopped millimeters from his brain. Millimeters. No brain damage here. Miles Patchwork was one lucky boy...if you could call it that. He would still be able to read and write, but basketball? The verdict at that very moment was still out.

Witnesses said what a "sight" it was. No pun intended, but a horrible, gruesome sight. Miles was stuck on the tree branch like fresh road kill, squashed on a street. He hung there for what seemed an eternity, his head tilted sideways on that sharp branch, blood oozing out of that no-longer-there eye. Miles body just remained there, arms to his side, slipping in and out of consciousness, until his body weight finally snapped the tree branch. With a sickening thud, he fell to the ground, breaking both legs at his ankles, resulting in a lifelong limp, and for sure, no more basketball games ever. Oh, and no sports scholarship, and no superstar pro basketball salary, and no big house with his own bedroom, and forget the built-in swimming pool. No, all that was gone now, and all that remained was a "one-eyed boy with a two-step limp," as they called him behind his back. And a nickname "Patch," for the patch he would wear over his empty eye, as a reminder of that memorable and horrible night.

And so, "dear ol' Patch," as people in the Sunny Side Up Retirement Home referred to him, lived his years doing menial jobs, never graduating from high school, never marrying. After all, who would marry a one-eyed gimp without a diploma, never becoming anything that he dreamed he would become. Yes, dear ol' Patch ended up, at age 76, guarding, or as some said, babysitting what he referred to as his workplace "family." The people he knew by first and last name, the people he had come to like and even to love. A family he protected each night as it was his job and duty to make sure they were safe in their sleep. Just like the packed school gymnasium that cheered him on as he made the winning shot 58 years ago to this very night, the Sunny Side Up Retirement Home was his court, his playground, his place that he protected from any and all evil.

Unfortunately, in the next few minutes that were about to unfold, his "family" wouldn't be there to cheer him on as he became a star player in his final game. A game of death. Destiny plays cruel and funny games with all of us in one way or another. Miles Patchwork's destiny tonight was to be "Victim Number 1" in the most unexpected, expected way.

CHAPTER 5

"I SEE YOU, BUT YOU CAN'T SEE ME."

Just as Miles Patchwork completed his rounds before returning to his little office next to the first-floor back stairwell to watch his favorite TV show, he saw something that caught his eye, that is, his one eye. There, in the hallway, just a few yards ahead of him, was a young fella, as he referred to the young ones...a young fella carrying what looked like a gun.

"Jeezuz Christ," he muttered out loud to himself, "a gun?"

And there in the back of the boy's belt, holding up his khaki pants, was a large hunting knife seen from beneath his jacket.

Again, Miles muttered out loud to himself, "Jeezuz Christ, and a big knife!"

Without trepidation, Miles approached him from behind, but not before the young boy turned to face him. *"Damn squeaky shoes,"* Miles thought to himself. *"Never liked them from the day I bought them."*

The boy stopped and smiled. He was about 10 years old, brown bushy hair and half the height of the towering security guard. On his face was a "big-ass" smile, as Miles would say to his cousin Duke when they were kids hanging out reading the funny books, you may know as comic books. That expression always brought a smile to Cousin Duke's usually stoic face. After all, Duke was said to be a bit touched, being born premature and dropped on his head by an alcoholic neighbor who helped in the birth delivery. Yep, a big-assed smile that surprised Miles and stopped him in his tracks.

"Hello, Mr. Patch. I was looking for you."

"Looking for you?" The question ran through Miles' mind like a slap on the back of his head. Just like a slap his momma would give him as a youngster when he repeated a question she asked. *"What the heck does he mean by that? He was 'looking for me'?"* And, *"Who is this kid?"* Miles began to think out loud as he tried to put the kid's face and voice together.

"How did you know my name? And how did you get in here?" Miles asked with a puzzled expression on his worn and tired-looking face.

"Your picture and name were on the wall by the front entrance. You're the security guard," the young boy replied.

"Well, now, just a minute, it's after visiting hours. I don't know how you got in here, and why you're here," he replied back with a voice of authority. After all, he was the security guard.

"I'm here to see my grandma," the young boy casually replied.

"Really? At 10 o'clock at night," Miles said to himself. Miles decided to play along and find out what this kid was actually doing here at this hour. And Miles was also concerned about the gun and knife the kid carried. Were they toys or were they real? He decided to proceed cautiously until he found out more.

"Visiting your grandma. Well, that's really nice of you. And just who is your grandma?" Miles asked politely.

"She's the nice old lady who lives here," the youngster replied, as if he had rehearsed the answer ahead of time for a moment just like this.

"Right, the nice old lady who lives here; any one of 50 of them," Miles thought about this while processing the kid's reply. With a pause in his voice, he cocked his head a bit so he could see more out of his one lone eye. Miles refocused his attention on the gun the kid was carrying in his hand. *"It looks like a real gun, but then again, it has to be a toy gun,"* he

thought to himself. *"The kid is about 10 years old, he couldn't have a real gun, could he? But what if it is?"*

"Jeezuz Christ, is that a real gun you're toting?" Miles blurted out his words, while losing his patience, and looking for an explanation to this whole strange situation.

The young boy's big-assed smile grew even bigger, and with a shake of his head he politely replied, "Why no sir, it's just a toy. Grannie gave it to me for my birthday and I wanted to show it to her."

Miles knew a thing or two about kids, and what they said, and what they meant, and how they sometimes lied. He remembered all that from his role as a big brother to seven younger siblings. But he knew he had to be careful here, so as not to cause a confrontation, or a commotion, and disturb or wake the residents.

"Well, it sure looks like a gun to me. You better hand it over now, you hear, and you better follow me to my office. We gotta call your folks. It's after hours. You shouldn't be here, Jeezuz Christ," Miles replied with a stern voice of authority.

The boy just stood there and stared at him.

"Do you know Jesus, Mr. Patch?" the young boy asked in a serious tone that slowly wiped away his big-assed smile.

"What?" Miles replied, caught off guard, and then questioning the boy's question.

"You're always referring to him. I thought maybe he's your friend." The boy's voice was very calm, very deliberate, and sounded much older than one would expect of his age.

Miles didn't answer the boy's question, probably because he didn't know how to answer it.   After all, it was just an expression he used, an expression he used most every day when he was at a loss for other words. Not that he wasn't a religious man and couldn't find some way to explain why he used the expression. Miles did go to church every week, and sometimes twice on holidays, but no, he didn't actually know "Jeezuz" Christ. He might have felt some connection to Jesus Christ in his feelings, his thoughts, his prayers. It was just an expression he used. Miles also didn't know he was going to meet Jesus Christ very soon. Well, if He really existed, that is.

"Hmm. Now you listen up, boy, and follow me to my office where we're gonna call your folks before you get in any more trouble here, but first give me that toy gun." Miles tried to be both polite and stern with his request. He also showed his response with a straightening of his slumped posture, while cocking his head again to peer at the young boy through his one big eye.

"You didn't answer my question, Mr. Patch. Do you know Jesus Christ?"

"No, I don't know Jeezuz Christ, for Christ sake. It's just an expression," Miles shot back, showing a slight sign of anger in his voice that he hadn't shown for a long, long time.

After all, why would he get angry here at the quiet and friendly Sunny Side Up Retirement Home where he was surrounded by a bunch of old people that he watched over each night. They were kind and nice to him. Even gave him candy, and he had one hell of a sweet tooth when it came to candy.

"And my name is Mr. Patchwork," he quickly added while getting his temper back under control.

"Now give me that gun before someone gets hurt," Miles demanded.

The boy hesitated for a moment, if a moment can be measured, and then that quizzical tone he had used turned back into that big-assed smile. "Would you like to meet Jesus Christ, Mr. Patch?"

Now it was time for Miles to hesitate for a moment, however long that moment might be.

"Now just give me that gun," Miles repeated in a calmer voice than before.

And without any more moments, even though the clock on the wall kept ticking those moments away, the young boy handed the gun to Miles without hesitation. And as his hands closed around it, Miles was shocked once again.

"Jeezuz Christ! This ain't no toy; this is a real gun!" Miles exclaimed out loud.

As quickly as the words came out of Miles' mouth, the young boy pulled the large 7-inch knife from his belt behind him and suddenly thrusted it deep into Patch's lower stomach.

"And this is a real knife, Mr. Patch," the young boy added. "Jesus is my friend, and I want you to meet him."

With the unexpected stabbing of the knife into Miles' belly, the boy flashed that big-assed smile even more.

"Jeezuz Christ...you stabbed me!" Miles exclaimed with pain and horror, exemplified in his widening eye of disbelief.

"No. Jesus Christ didn't stab you. I did." And, as if those words were his cue, the young boy started to turn and twist the sharp blade deeper into Miles' stomach, cutting through his stomach lining, into his liver, and ripping his bladder and kidneys, immediately causing Miles to wet his pants.

Looking down at the knife protruding from him, Miles reached for the boy's hand that still held the knife tightly in him. For a moment or two, their hands touched. Their eyes looked deep into each other's soul. Miles is, was, and will ever be remembered as a "good man." The boy's eyes reflected a monster within.

Suddenly, the young boy pulled the sharp blade out, and then without a word, just that big-assed smile, he plunged the knife back in again. In and out of Patch's blood-covered flannel work shirt. He poked it in and out quickly, just like a cook putting a sharp cooking instrument into a piece of meat to see if it was done. And yes, Patch was just about done.

As the boy's smile grew even bigger, if a big-assed smile could, he finally stopped the repeated stabbing, and slowly, deliberately, pulled the sharp knife out of Miles' blood-gushing wound.

But he wasn't done yet.

Again, he stabbed Miles in the stomach, and again he stabbed Miles in the stomach, and again he stabbed Miles in the stomach. Repeatedly. A lot of times... A lot, a lot... of times.

As Miles' hands intuitively tried to stop his bleeding wounds, he fell to his knees, and his one lonely, one-and-only eye widened with complete shock.

Miles, aka Patch, the once tall, almost superstar high school basketball player, no longer towered over the young boy. Now on his knees, in an amazing amount of speechless pain, he and the young boy were about the same height. Now he was in just in the right position for one more thrust of the boy's bloodied knife, right smack into his one, lonely, remaining eye.

And as it happened, the knife plunged deep into the eye and entered a part of Miles' 76-year-old brain. What part, doesn't matter, but let's just say that it was a part that stored a memory from a long, long, time ago. The time that Miles Patchwork, while walking home from the last basketball game he would ever play, was hit on purpose by a car, and "flew through the air with the greatest of ease" and as luck would have it, landed face first, or eye first on that one long, lonely branch of the tree that seemed to be waiting for him, just him. "Yes, siree, Bob," as cousin Duke would say when he was done reading those funny comic books way back when, "this is really funny." But actually, it wasn't; but actually, it kind of was. Think of the odds of this happening. Make the bet, roll the dice. Miles, at this moment, this unmeasurable, excruciating, pain-filled moment, some 50 years later to the exact day, and guess what, at the exact time he lost his one eye, now had this long, sharp, hunting knife sticking out his one lone, now-gone eye. How fucked up was this?

As if adding more icing to the finished cake, Miles fell face first, silently onto the blood-splattered floor, pushing the extended knife even deeper into his head. And that was the end of this sudden sequence of an unexpected meeting, and not so good meeting, between Miles Patchwork and a young boy whose name he didn't even know. If things had turned out differently, Miles would have said, "I remember him now; I see his face." But things hadn't turned out differently. They turned out just this way, as Timmy, who put that sharp 7-inch hunting knife into Mr. Patch, as he called him, so many times – countless times – now stood over his bloodied dying body.

So, no more late-night rounds of making sure everyone was safe asleep for Miles Patchwork. Nope, no more going back to his little office watching reruns of his favorite old-time TV shows while collecting a salary of twelve dollars an hour. Nope. It was curtains on the final act of Miles Patchwork's interesting and very sad, and very tragic life. The once promising basketball player who could have become a superstar, could have made lots and lots of money, could have bought many fancy cars, and could have lived in a big, beautiful mansion with an indoor pool. Nope, none of that now or ever, not even in his last dying thoughts. All Miles could think of this moment in his scrambled mind before it was "lights out" was about his dumb cousin Duke, with a big-assed smile that matched this kid's smile. Dumb cousin Duke, who made a young Miles smile and laugh when he yelled out loud, "That's all folks!" as the Looney Tunes cartoon ended. And at this very moment (let's not even think of measuring it nor how long it actually was), with his last breath, as the pool of blood grew around his lifeless body, Miles' grip loosened on the kid's gun he still held. It fell from his outstretched hand. Yep, "that's all folks," at least for Miles.

A fading echo of a voice long ago drifted with Miles' soul into the oblivion of death. "He scores! Miles scores the winning basket!"

Silently and swiftly, the boy picked up his gun. With one foot, he turned over Miles' body into the pool of his blood. He reached down and slowly pulled the knife out of Miles' eye as blood squirted outward from it like a hole in a water balloon. Wiping it on Miles' plaid shirt, he returned it to the sheath beneath his coat.

He then reached into Miles' pocket and searched for, and pulled out, the magic keys that opened all the Sunny Side Retirement Home apartment doors. And as the big-assed smile left the boy's face as he stood one last time over the dead man beneath him, a different smile began to take shape. A very, very different smile. The smile of the Devil himself.

And now, the game was about to begin.

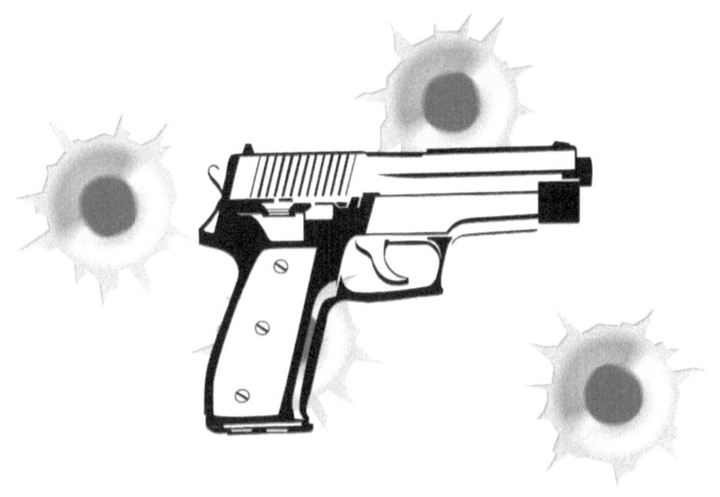

CHAPTER 6

THERE'S A CLUE UNDER EVERY ROCK.

Raymond McNail was the area's most honored, revered, and feared police detective. He was known for "nailing" the bad guy, time and time again. He had an uncanny sixth sense when it came to police work. He could figure out the most unusual of unusual cases, the most challenging and complex cases. Cases that were referred to as cold cases, colder cases, and even frozen cases, as some chuckled, after he figured them out. He made it seem so simple. And he was not even a relative or descendent of Sherlock Holmes, as some claimed him to be. If there was a clue still to be found, or no clue at all, that no one, and I mean no one – even teams of no ones – could find, leave it to Detective McNail – he'd find it. It was even written in the countless newspaper articles and numerous citations he received that, no matter what, he always found his clue. And that one clue would always lead him to get "his man." Maybe he really was, after all, that long lost, never discovered, actual relative of Sherlock Holmes.

Police Detective Raymond McNail was called the best. The "bestest of the best." That is, except for just once. Just once in a hundred, make that a thousand police cases. Just once, he came up empty. Just once. And it was in this very case. He didn't get "his man," even though we already know that the killer was a young boy. But it made no difference if it was a man or child, or, as the other police officers were overheard to have said, "It had to be the work of the devil himself." No, this time, Detective McNail failed. This time, he couldn't figure it out. This time, he had no answers. This time, the puzzle remained unsolved. This time, there would not be a clue that only he could uncover. This time would be the only time he failed, and this time would be the last time he failed, as this time, Police Detective Raymond McNail, the "bestest of the best," the possible heir apparent to the legendary Sherlock Holmes, this time, he was to become "a victim" and, this time, it was his time...to die.

Approaching retirement age with a receding hair line that he measured with a pliable, cheap, plastic ruler each year on his birthday, Raymond was not exactly a Don Juan TV-type cop. He had a double, or maybe a triple chin, big, odd-shaped ears from having been tugged on one too many times by his Catholic grade-school teacher when he disrupted the class, and he was extremely pigeon toed. Sort of walked, or waddled, like a penguin that you see at the zoo. But even with these awkward, non-Robert Redford characteristics, up to this day, looks didn't matter. What mattered was – he always got his man.

Ray got the emergency dispatch call at his quaint two-story home while having an evening-ending, illegal Cuban cigar. Yes, cops did smoke some of the "evidence" they discovered, even so-called good cops, like Ray, especially when the evidence was one of those hard-to-find Cuban cigars.

Sitting with his feet up on a hassock, with a late-night *Hawaii 5-0* rerun on his antiquated 25-inch TV, Ray always wondered what it would be like to live in a sunny climate versus the cold tundra of northern Wisconsin, which was his home for his entire life. Just as Ray took one more puff of that illegal cigar, and a sip of some illegal local moonshine (also found in a not too long ago case), the phone rang and broke his concentration.

"Gosh damn," he muttered aloud in a moment of unexpected surprise to himself.

It was his favorite expression. And everyone on the local police force knew it and kidded him about it. "Gosh damn," whenever he was bothered, perplexed, amused, or even confused.

Always "Gosh damn." Ray would never take the name of his Lord in vain, in fear of those memories of the Catholic nuns pulling on his large ears!

"Gosh damn, here we go again," he stated to himself, as he answered his landline home phone on a very cluttered end table next to where he sat.

"Ray, we have an ongoing situation at the Sunny Side Up Retirement Home," a female voice quickly blurted out.

As he sat on the phone in his two-day-old boxer shorts, he was surprised to hear that anything would be going on at the retirement home at 1:30 a.m.

"What's going on there?" he replied, trying to clear his head from that wonderful cigar aroma that had mixed with that wonderful sip of kick-ass moonshine.

"A resident called in. Heard noises like muffled gunshots – lots of them. Two patrol cars are on their way. Something big, very big. Something very bad is happening there."

"Gosh damn," he replied, as he abruptly hung up and hurried towards the door, almost forgetting to put on his pants.

As he drove through a light rain, he thought about what a gloomy and miserable day it had been. Almost two years ago his wife of 40 years had died of pancreatic cancer. It was a horrible, drawn-out illness that took its toll on both of them. It left him a lonely and sad 60-year-old man who would soon be facing his retirement alone. His two kids lived out of state and kept telling him to move to a warmer climate like where they lived. But his home and his whole life in Wisconsin had too many memories to just pack up and leave behind. He sometimes felt his wife's presence at night as he slept in the bed they had shared for 40 years of marriage. For a detective who always had the answer to everything he faced, he had no clues to his future and didn't even want to think about it. It just made him sadder. All he could think about now was what could possibly be going on at a quaint and quiet retirement home filled with a lot of old folks. Heck, he thought to himself, it might even be his home someday.

It was about an eight-minute ride at the excessive speed he drove. Had to be a bit careful with the wet roads – it had poured earlier, and of course, the moonshine was still sitting in his large, protruding stomach, which just about touched his steering wheel. He gently patted his stomach; he never did like exercise.

Ray could see the faint lights of the Sunny Side Up Retirement Home ahead. Already there were two other police cars, an ambulance, and a fire truck, all with flashing lights on. All of this made a bizarre scene as the rain became mixed with the persistent and chilling northern Wisconsin oncoming winter wind, almost as if it were beckoning a clue as to what he was about to see.

Lucy Johnson, lead Emergency Medical Technician (EMT), mid-twenties, attractive, big busted, and a "wanna be" doctor, greeted him as he slowly got out of his now finally warm car and set foot into the late-night cold air. She was a graduate of the local community college, a recent lab technician, and anxious to make a name for herself. Everything by the book, was her motto.

"The place is as quiet as a church mouse," she whispered to Ray, as if not to wake up the church mice, if there were any.

"We all just got here, waiting for your lead," she continued with a deepening and serious tone with each spoken word. "Sheriff Robach has been called and he's on his way from a family function in Broward."

On either side of her were two other police officers who arrived separately – Gary Miller, a veteran of twenty-plus years, very overweight, and yawning from the late hour, and Alonzo Gonzalez, Deputy Sheriff, who quickly inserted himself into the conversation.

"My gun's loaded, Detective. We should storm the place and catch the perp by surprise," Gonzalez stated.

Lucy gave the deputy a look of disdain. She knew he was in his position only because of the state law to hire as many minorities as possible in government jobs. Officer Miller paid no attention, swaying in the night wind, half asleep, still yawning, and probably thinking of the next donut he would eat.

Gonzalez was in his early thirties, short, very much into himself, and not very well liked by the members of this small-town police and fire department. Rumor was that he never took a written qualifying state-law enforcement exam. The whispered joke behind his back was that he couldn't read English, although it was probably true, and he probably couldn't write English either because he never filled out any reports. But he was the town's "minority" cop. Oh, but he could speak fluent Spanish, if it ever was needed. He was also quick on the trigger and felt police force was the best way to defuse a situation.

Lucy jumped back in to the conversation before Gonzalez could make a bigger fool of himself. Not that she really cared to protect him.

"The 911 call was from a Sally DiPonzio, one of the residents, who said she heard muffled gunshots. Then, while she was answering the operator's question, a loud noise was heard in the background and her phone went dead. Everything seems eerily quiet now. A lot of lights on for this time of night. We phoned the night watchman but got no response. It almost seems like a morgue."

From the way she maturely handled the situation, it was apparent that she'd be a better deputy than Alonzo. Alonzo glowered at her.

The northern Wisconsin air whipped up suddenly, and a strange howling noise came with it. Almost like a death wail – like in the horror movies, just before something bad was about to happen. But "bad" already happened here even as Ray, Alonzo, Gary, Lucy, and a few firefighters, called along with the police, stood looking at the Sunny Side Up Retirement Home, like it was going to somehow change their lives. And it would.

"Okay," Ray pondered with his mind and then finally with his voice. "It may be nothing; it may be something, but whatever is going on inside, we're gonna find out...but carefully."

"Gary, you stay here as backup. Leave your shoulder mic on and listen for any instructions from me."

Gary nodded, all too pleased to stay behind and maybe fall asleep on his feet. After all, as Ray said, this would probably amount to nothing. Then on the way home he could stop at the all-night Donuts Delight shop for one of them jumbo glazed donuts he so loved. Nothing like a nice fresh glazed donut to add to his ever increasing and extruding stomach. He patted it gently, thinking of it.

"Alonzo, Lucy, follow me." Ray gave the command and nodded toward the retirement home.

And with those cold words on a cold morning in northern Wisconsin, the three of them approached the building entrance.

With Ray in the lead, Alonzo two steps behind, and Lucy trying to get ahead of Alonzo with every step in the silent, breaking dawn, it was almost like a scene from a Three Stooges movie. The only noise to be heard was of their boots crunching the dead autumn leaves with each step.

Ray drew his gun first, then Alonzo. Lucy held her medical bag of wonders tightly in her hand.

"Okay," Ray again pondered first in his mind, and then again with his voice, as the cold breath mimicked his word. "Okay, I will go in first. Alonzo, you go to the back entrance. Lucy, you follow behind me."

Alonzo didn't like that Lucy would be next to the detective. He never liked her from the first day they met when he gave her the once-over, checking out every curve on her young 20-something body. Thinking of himself as a macho cop, it irritated him when she didn't even respond to his flirtatious looks. This was bothersome to him, setting the tone for their work relationship. Back in his hometown of San Juan, he was known as quite the stud, especially with all the young 20-something female cruise-ship tourists, who wandered the town looking for a special "vacation" adventure. So, Alonzo just silently nodded, slumped his shoulders, and walked away from them, going around the side of the building and out of their sight.

From where Ray stood, he could see into the main lobby. It was big and spacious, and intended to greet all the residents and their families as a happy place to live. Most of the lights were on throughout the entire front of the building.

"A bit unusual," he said to himself, as he went into "finding the clue mode," as others referred to his thought process. After all, he was the king of clues, and all the lights on at this time of night was certainly a bit unusual. The old folks at the Sunny Side Up Retirement Home were known to embrace their written motto on the doorway above the foyer entrance, "Early to bed, early to rise, makes a Sunny Side Up resident happy and wise," so, why were all the lights on?

"Okay." Again, his mind was processing things that only a top-notch sleuth would do. "Lights on, check," he stated, just loud enough so that Lucy would know he was in control of the situation, whatever the situation was.

The door was ajar and it opened easily.

"Unlocked for who knows how long, check. Look at the lobby entrance, left to right, right to left, check. Nothing. No one at the front desk; no one in the main lobby, check," he rattled off as he pieced together whatever clues all of this led to.

"And not a sound to be heard from within, check." His mind concluded that this was okay, and so did his next words out loud to Lucy, "Time to go in."

"Quiet. Dead quiet. Lobby secured," he whispered to no one in particular, but loud enough for Lucy to start positioning herself safely behind his bulky body.

Ray's detective mind had checked off all the things to get him, and now Lucy, safely inside the front lobby. There was a huge grand staircase ahead of them, which led to the second floor. All the nearby chairs and other lobby furniture looked in place, and undisturbed. Maybe there was nothing wrong here, maybe just a prank call. Maybe the lights were left on all night in case any of the "oldies," as Ray would refer to them in conversations with his few friends that he still had in his life, needed to feel more secure. Maybe this was normal. After all, he had never been called to the retirement home at 1:30 a.m. before now.

"Yup," he said to himself, *"Maybe everything is alright. They just forgot to lock the door. Right."* He thought this over in his analytical detective mind. The unlocked door, that was the clue. A puzzling clue. For Ray knew, if he ran the place, he would make sure to lock the oldies in every night. After all, you didn't want them wandering around the state of Wisconsin in their undies, like he almost did when he hurried out of his house. Not a pretty sight.

Ray and Lucy proceeded slowly through the main lobby past the closed entrance desk, and past the many wall photos of all the Directors and main financial contributors to the Home. They even passed the photo of Miles Patchwork, the on-duty evening

Security Guard. Under the photo was a small, engraved nameplate, "Employee of the Month."

Cautiously, they proceeded toward the first hallway, just a few yards past the lobby entrance sign-in desk. And that's where the whole situation immediately changed, and Ray realized that what he was seeing was something neither he, Detective Ray, the number-one clue gatherer, nor Lucy, the trusty ambulance technician, expected. And the only words he could say in that moment were his famous words that had become his, and his alone, "Gosh damn!"

The hallway was littered with bodies. The floor was a flood of blood. Blood was also splattered and still dripping off the adjoining walls. Bodies were laying in front of many of the apartment doors all along the length of the hallway. And the hallway was quite long, so there were a lot of bodies. A lot of dead bodies, maybe six, or eight, or maybe more. Hard to tell, at first shocking glance. But Detective Ray would not be able to get the exact count, or if he did, in that horrific moment of discovery, he would tally up all the dead, but would miss one – himself.

Without warning, suddenly out of nowhere, as if being observed from the moment he and Lucy entered, a lone, silent, gun sent a bullet propelling down the blood-covered hallway. It struck Detective Ray right smack in the middle of his throat. And, like someone squeezing a big, fat, plastic ketchup bottle, like the type you see and use at the state fair when you're pouring it all out on your jumbo dollar hot dog, a stream of his blood came spurting straight out. Ray's blood shot right out of his neck, as his flailing hands reacted either by choice, or as a result of being unexpectedly shot in the middle of his neck. His hands furiously clutched at his throat. Like the scene from that childhood story of the little boy who stuck his finger in the dam to stop the water flow, Ray's finger went right into the hole in his neck. But to no avail. Way too much blood pouring out. Way too bad of a wound for even Lucy to try to bandage. No, nothing more could be done. Ray's body collapsed straight down to his knees. He swayed back and forth like an accordion being compressed while he made weird and horrific gasping sounds. There, he teetered for a moment. A long, long, moment, as Lucy would recall. And with his last breath, he spoke just two, almost distinguishable, words. Those words, his words, the most fitting words to sum up this whole crazy nightmare that he just walked into, and was carried out of, eventually. "Gosh...damn," Ray mumbled in a whispery, blood-gurgling voice, as his body slumped forward face first onto the blood-covered floor. Although, it could have been, "God damn."

Detective Ray McNail was dead. And that was the missing body in his earlier body count. The one clue he missed, and never saw coming. His own death.

Lucy, terrified, dropped her medical bag, screamed, and ran faster than a speeding bullet back out the front entrance door.

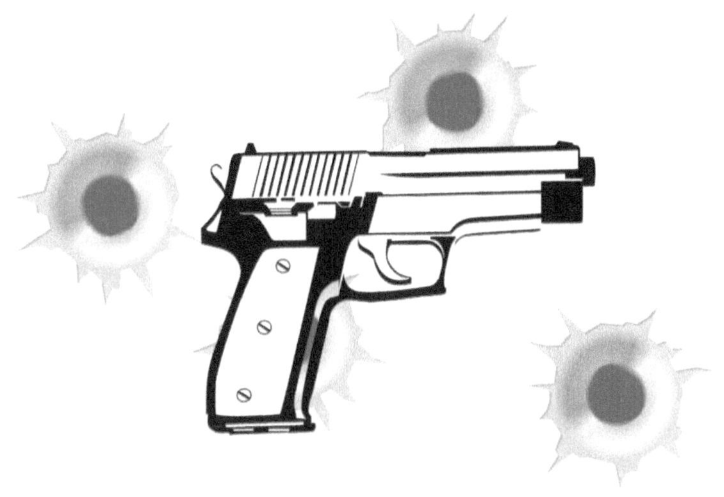

CHAPTER 7

HAIL MARY, FULL OF GRACE.

The first thing the young boy saw when he entered Apartment 104 was a life-size statue of Jesus. The second thing he saw was a naked man kneeling in front of the statue, praying.

"Dominus foe-bits com, Et com spirie too-too-oh," Father Novak proclaimed in a mumbled Latin to the heavenly ceiling above him.

In his 90-year-old mind, or what was left of it, Father William Novak, the Sunny Side Up Retirement Home's resident priest and "resident resident," was about to say his last prayer. Not that he knew it, for in his mind at that very moment, he was immersed in the long-gone days when his life was a spiritual pathway for so many people, including himself. In his memory, he relived the times his congregation completely filled the 20-plus rows of wooden pews before him, bowing their heads, mimicking his every movement together in a religious ritual. With his back to the boy who had now entered the apartment and closed the door quietly behind him, Father Novak raised an imaginary blessed silver chalice and Host of the Lord's Body high in the air.

Timmy raised the gun in his hand at the same time. He pointed it directly at the back of Father Novak's head, with his finger on the trigger.

Prayers. Our lives are filled with prayers, some meaningful, some forgotten. We all pray in one way or another, at one time, or no longer any more. Prayers are full of interesting words, and interesting symbolism. Take the Lord's Prayer for example. "Our Father, who art in heaven." If you examine the words, you find the symbols. The meaning of the first line is that the "Father," or let's just say the "Big Guy" upstairs, somewhere in the place above the iCloud, wherever that place is, is the one true Father of us all, and the words are acknowledging Him as that. So, if He's really #1, that makes every father here on earth, a step-father, not a real father. And if your step-father passed away unexpectedly, and your mother remarried, that would make your new step-father on earth a "step-step father." Interesting.

What you need to know is how Father Novak came to be a resident of the Sunny Side Up Retirement Home, and how he played an interesting role in this story. Not only in words, but in symbolism.

Born in the mid-1920s, William Novak was the third child of five, raised by an alcoholic step-father. Interesting. William, or, as his family would call him, Billy, felt destined for priesthood from an early age. He was a normal youngster, like most kids back then. His mother dressed him in the nicest of nice hand-me-downs from other relatives, his hair was always neatly combed, he ate his supper willingly, looked forward to doing his chores, and always said his prayers. Billy Novak was polite, very polite, very respectful. He was referred to as a "good boy."

When his family crammed into their 1935 Studebaker with over 100,000 miles and headed down to church in a weekly Sunday ritual, Billy didn't squirm in his seat or let his mind wander when the priest gave his very long sermon or rambled in some weird language called Latin. No. Billy sat there, hanging on to every word spoken. He would stare mesmerized at all the wonderful statues and ornaments of long-dead memorialized people who were either nailed to a wooden cross or crying and moaning in some sort of disturbing ceremonial scene.

Billy seemingly enjoyed all this. He actually looked forward to every week's visit to this elaborate, giant-sized, several-stories-high cavern called a cathedral. In Billy's imagination, this place of worship was so big, it actually touched the clouds. It may have even gone right through the iCloud before it was even discovered and named such.

While other kids his age played cops and robbers or cowboys and Indians, Billy fantasized what it would be like to stand on that grand stage called an altar in a colorful flowing robe, singing praise to the true Father above, while speaking in the strange language called Latin. Billy even tried mimicking it, not very well, as his older brother Jack taught him Pig Latin instead. Made no difference either way; it was all gibberish to him.

So, it was only natural that Billy would want to, and would become an altar boy. Here he would be closer to all the inner workings of this amazing and strange ceremony, helping the man in the robe. Here he would be able to touch, and feel, the countless statues adorning the altar, and stored in the backroom closet. In other words, he was on his journey. Billy was becoming closer to the "Big Guy upstairs," as his earthly stepfather in some drunken state of mind referred to the real Father up above.

And, by being an altar boy, Billy also got his first taste of wine, and, his first experience of sex. It had nothing to do with the open bottles of booze in his mom's kitchen pantry, or the well-read naughty books under his earth father's bed. Billy would never forget either moment. Even though it was hard for an inquisitive mind of a young boy to find the right words to describe what he experienced and witnessed, there certainly was some life-altering symbolism to the experience.

It was a sunny summer Saturday afternoon, when all his friends were playing baseball or enjoying other childhood pastimes, that it happened. Billy was spending some extra time in the church to help Father Murphy, the church's lone priest, prepare for that afternoon's scheduled confession.

Father Murphy was a friendly, or maybe even jolly, leader of this congregation for what was a long, long time, even before Billy was born into this world and baptized into the Church. He was somewhere in age between fifty and a hundred, had a warming smile, and was always full of amazing spiritual advice for everyone, both in and out of the confessional. He even seemed to have a direct connection to the Big Guy upstairs, his true Father, as he stated in his endless Sunday sermons. But this was rather a conundrum, 'cause if he really believed what he preached, that the Big Guy upstairs was the real Father, then he was, and should be called, Step-Father Murphy. It just didn't make a lot of sense, but not much did in the Church anyways, unless you understood Latin.

As Billy was left alone behind the altar one long ago Saturday afternoon, dusting, arranging, and touching the glorious statues that overflowed the small room, he spied a half-filled ornate cut-glass bottle that was filled with some sort of magic elixir that only Father Murphy could drink each and every time he did his presentation on the altar. One of the altar boy's jobs, his job, was to keep that bottle filled. It was only natural that Billy would be tempted to take a little taste of it. After all, he felt that by doing this, he could help himself move along his religious journey that he had mapped out for himself.

This special liquid was supposedly the Blood of Christ. Billy knew it would be just a little taste – no one would know; no one would miss it. Carefully holding the ornate glass bottle in both hands, Billy took his first sip. And in doing so, he felt a warm, tingling sensation like none he had ever experienced before. A sensation that he would never forget. And the sip became a longer sip, and even a longer sip, until half of the half-filled wonderful liquid in the bottle was now in his body. Smiling to himself, or maybe just displaying a big-assed-looking grin from sipping too much booze, he now had the holiest of holy Blood from the one and only true Father in his body. Billy didn't question this temptation to do what he did, but he did think for the briefest of moments, that the Big Guy upstairs must really be a big guy because every week he somehow kept putting more and more of his Blood in the bottle.

Having his first buzz, or religious moment, as he would recall it, Billy was now prepared to have another sip or two. But before he could, he heard the approaching voice of Father Murphy from outside the door to the backroom. Billy didn't want to be caught red handed with that magic elixir, still clutched in his hand, so he quickly hid behind the open closet door, squeezing himself between a 3-foot-tall statue of Jesus and another 5-foot-tall statue of Jesus. *"Must have been from different times in his life,"* Billy thought to himself.

Father Murphy entered the room leading a young and very attractive 14-year-old girl with him. Billy recognized her as one of the usual Sunday worshippers. He didn't know her name, but did recognize her pretty face and her pretty, large breasts. Hard to believe that she was only 14. Those were "pretty big boobs," he would fondly recall throughout the years.

Billy stood between the two Jesuses, quiet as a "church mouse." *"What a silly expression!"* he thought to himself. *"When are mice really quiet, and why only in a church?"* Didn't matter, 'cause his thoughts immediately left that silly expression to the unfolding situation at hand, or would be, *in* his hand.

Father Murphy guided the young girl close to another nearby large statue of Jesus.

"What a popular guy Jesus must have been to get all these statues," Billy thought to himself.

Father Murphy stood next to Jesus (the statue, that is), nodded to it, and then nodded to the big-boobed girl, and began to speak in a sermon-like fashion.

"As you behold the face of our Lord Jesus, the Forgiver of sinners, and the only Son of our Holy Father, as I told you in the confessional, your special penance for your sins is to prove your love and devotion to Him, and to your Church, by doing what I ask, I mean, what He, our Lord asks."

"Yes, Father. I understand that my penance is to do what the Lord commands. I am ashamed and feel terrible to learn that what I did to myself was wrong, and I want to wash my sin away," the young girl's shaken voice replied.

"And so, you will, my child," Father Murphy said with a strange, almost smug tone to his voice.

"As a gesture of my kindness, I will not tell your parents of your sin. Nor will you. It will be our secret between us and the Lord above. Now come here, my girl, and kneel before me and begin your penance," Father Murphy commanded.

"Yes, Father. I appreciate your kindness and not telling my parents of what I did, and I willingly accept my responsibility to the Lord," she answered in a trembling, but obedient voice.

"Remember, my child, your penance will wash away your sins, and whenever you have those evil thoughts again, those dirty, nasty, evil thoughts, you must come to me immediately and I will continue to cleanse your soul and make your heart pure again." Father Murphy's words reassured her as he put his hands gently, yet firmly, on the top of her head.

While all this was going on, young Billy continued to drink the magic elixir that he brought with him. He felt it would only bring him even closer to the true Father above, while Father Murphy, the true step-father, here and now, would make this bad girl good again. And boy, did he ever! Or should I say, she made him "feel good again" as he forced her head down into his groin while he moaned and prayed out loud. His gasping words sounded like a mix between Latin and Pig-Latin.

Since that day, the years passed quickly for Billy, as quickly as they pass for all of us. After graduating into priesthood, working around the world as a missionary, finally getting his own church and congregation, Billy returned to his hometown after Father Murphy passed in his sleep one night to the pearly gates above. Billy, that is, Father Novak, had a wonderful and spiritual life. He had become everything he wanted to be and was now in his golden years of priesthood. His life was perfect. Until that first of two fateful days.

On his 70th birthday, while performing Mass to a half-filled dwindling congregation, the "Big Guy upstairs" gave him a "not-so-pretty" birthday gift. Right smack in the middle of the Lord's Prayer, Father Novak had a stroke. His brain scrambled, and his words began to mumble, and the usual, overly long ceremony now became a bit longer.

"Hail, hail, hai, hai, hey, Mary…Mary, full, full, full of ofo of…" His words slurred in a straining voice that woke up the few sleeping Mass goers.

It was both horrific and amusing. Horrific to the older crowd who suspected something was wrong and amusing to the few young children who had been dragged there by their parents, and who thought he was performing a rap song. Anyway, Father Novak's days of drinking the Lord's Blood in a colorful flowing robe came to a sudden end. He was hospitalized, rehabbed, forced out of his parish, and placed in a nursing home for several years. Miraculously, he got better, somewhat, and was moved to an apartment at the newly opened Sunny Side Up Retirement Home. There, in his mind, he became the resident priest, and in the makeshift corner of one of the lounge rooms, he held Sunday Mass for the few residents who would show up and fall asleep. Happily serving the Lord and regaining most of his speech (most, not all, especially when nervous), he would live the rest of his God-worshipping days there until that "other fateful" day. Today.

So, as Father Novak, now a semi-retired priest, thanks to that godawful stroke he endured years ago, sat in his small one-bedroom apartment filled with statues of Jesus, his memory stuck in the replay of his life. He vaguely and clearly remembered that, while performing Mass on that very same altar, of that very same church where he was about to drink from that very same ornate bottle, something strange happened that changed his life. Maybe it was "meant to be," as he would try to comfort his parishioners after hearing their countless stories of lives filled with doom and gloom. But the effects of his stroke left half his brain a bit slow, along with a paralysis of his left arm and left foot.

Father Novak spent most of his days sitting in his wheelchair, with a wool blanket around his legs, and an open Bible on his lap. He could walk on a good day, or limp, as others saw him, but, for most residents at the Sunny Side Up Retirement Home, wheelchairs and walkers were "man's best friend" rather than pets.

Counting the days until he could one day make the next journey in his planned life to meet the Big Guy upstairs, he let his mind drift to bits and pieces of memories that he clung to. He grasped onto lots of jumbled memories, but one would always come back to haunt him, to taunt him. It was that memory of him as a 10-year-old altar boy, hiding in a church closet full of Jesus statues. It was that memory of watching that 14-year-old, "big-boobed," pretty girl make her penance to the true Father Almighty, and ordained step-father. Billy was a virgin then, and remained a virgin all his life, having chosen God over women. And, in that memory he began to question how different his life might have been. Unfortunately for old Father Novak, and for the once young Billy, those memories suddenly became interrupted.

"Aren't you cold?" Timmy asked, with a touch of curiosity in his voice.

After all, here was a naked 90-year-old man kneeling in front of him, spouting strange gibberish. Not exactly an Adonis type, or some buffed guy you wouldn't mind admiring on a nude beach, not that Timmy knew any of this. This was just a wrinkly, bony, old bag of flesh, with what looked like some sores, or big dimples, on his flat, naked, white ass.

"Why are you naked?" Timmy asked.

Father Novak turned to look at the intruder. His mind slowly returned from his church-like memories to the moment at hand. Father Novak had an aura of calmness surrounding him.

"I was ba, ba, born, into the world naked, and I am red, ready to leave da, the, world the same way," he stuttered out, trying his best to get the words right, even though he was not quite right, or would ever be again.

Timmy studied him curiously. He looked at the large Jesus statue that the naked man was kneeling before and quickly glanced around the room. It was almost like being in a church. It was filled with religious drawings and religious pictures on all the walls. There were very few furnishings other than a sofa, chair, and a small, wooden end-table next to it. A Bible was opened on the table and a few candles were burning, placed sporadically, throughout the room. His wheelchair was sitting next to him on the floor.

"Do you recognize me?" Timmy cut right to the point.

It was Father's Novak turn to study the boy curiously from his kneeling position.

"No, no, yes, way, way, wait, wait...from before. You're that...that ba, ba, boy, that boy from earl, earlier today?" Father Novak stuttered his reply with some sort of recognition as to who this kid was.

"Yes. I'm that boy," Timmy retorted, with a hint of rising anger in his young voice. "And I'm here to kill you. Are you afraid of dying?" Timmy continued.

"I, I, I'm a priest. I will be, be with my Father. I am not afraid," Father Novak replied in a calm voice.

Timmy paused, taking in the words of the priest.

"Maybe you should start your prayers."

"I'll pra, pra, pray for you," Father Novak replied, casually.

"Don't bother. I don't believe in God," the boy answered with a strange smile.

"I'm okay, okay; red, ready to go to heaven," Father Novak answered, as he looked directly at the gun pointed at him, while stretching his hands outward and upward to the waiting pearly gates above.

Timmy chuckled.

"After what you did? You're going straight to hell."

Without hesitation, or feeling, without anger or hatred, or even acknowledging that he respected, or disrespected those ordained of the cloth, Timmy just pulled the gun's trigger.

With a muffled sound from the silencer on Timmy's Glock 9mm semi-automatic gun, a shiny silver bullet flew quickly into Father Novak's body. A perfect shot. A perfect 10. Dead center into the naked priest's heart.

Without blinking an eye, or trying to stutter another word, Father Novak fell forward to the floor. His body quivered for a few moments. His one paralyzed hand and foot even tingled and sort of moved for the first time in many years. He didn't die immediately, although a hell of a lot of blood poured from his holy body. No, he lay there, face first with his outstretched body dancing spasmodically in the blood. In his last moments, his stuttering voice, the one that forced him to leave the priesthood, started to recite the Lord's Prayer in a mixture of clear and recognizable Latin and English. And, his last earthly thoughts before he believed he was to meet his Maker, the one true Father, were of that long ago forever-etched moment in his brain, when that 14-year-old, pretty, well-endowed girl performed her penance. In his fading thoughts he saw himself hiding behind a big Jesus, while spying through a crack in the closet door. He clearly recalled his moment of coming-of-age boyish wonderment, watching her willingly follow instructions of a necessary religious penance. He remembered taking that one last swig of magic elixir, the Big Guy's Blood from that ornate bottle, which he had to fill each week, over and over again. And he unleashed his hidden and forbidden thoughts of how he secretly and quietly let his hand slide to his crotch then, as it now found its way there once again. And he touched himself, as if it were meant to be.

Ninety-year-old, naked Father William Novak, Billy, rolled over, dying on the floor in the ever-increasing pool of his blood. His last spoken words were not as clear as the prayer he had just spoken before. His last words were stuttered. It was an interesting choice of words, for an interesting moment of, and interesting ending to, an interesting life. They were words filled with profound symbolism defining a profound moment of his life's end. His last word was not the expected word "Amen," nor was it the quote from Psalm 23, "Though I walk through the valley of the shadow of death, I will fear no evil." No, his last words were simply, "I'm commmmming."

He was truly prepared, and truly ready, to meet his true Father. In death, he orgasmed.

There was an eerie silence in the room. Timmy stood quietly and looked at the naked man in a bemused sort of way. A sardonic smile remained on his boyish face as he thought of one more thing he had to do. Attached, on the nearby wall was an ornate metal crucifix, about a foot high and six inches wide. It was quite beautiful as it seemed to radiate in the dim, flickering candlelight of the apartment.

Timmy walked over to it, studied it, then took it gently off the wall. He slowly walked back to where Father Novak lay dead on the floor in front of the giant blood-splattered statue of Jesus. Kneeling next to the body, Timmy was careful not to get any of the naked priest's blood on his pants. His momma always told him to keep his pants clean. Maybe it was her way of telling him, "Cleanliness is next to Godliness."

The young boy slowly knelt next to the old dead man, as if he were going to say a final prayer, in a final moment of a final horrific scene. Maybe it would be a prayer for his penance of all the sins he had committed already tonight, or the sins he was yet to commit. Maybe it would be a final prayer for the old priest, or maybe a prayer for his dead brother.

Or maybe it wasn't a prayer at all.

Instead, without a word, without a thought, he quickly thrust the metal crucifix he held in his hand into the forehead of Father Novak's dead, balding head. The old and weak bones in his skull made a strange snapping sound like twigs from a tree being broken by a curious child. Timmy loosened his hand, bringing it back to his forehead while making the sign of the cross. The metal crucifix remained embedded in what was left of the priest's smashed head. Father Novak's religious journey was now complete. He was crucified like the Big Guy upstairs.

CHAPTER 8

WHAT LEGENDS ARE MADE OF.

"Now hold it steady. Keep your eye focused on the target. Don't blink. Let a short breath out, and quickly squeeze the trigger," Mr. Jameson calmly directed his one son while the other patiently waited his turn.

Sunday morning target practice in the Jameson family was just as important as Sunday church service, which preceded it. As for 9-year-old Ryan and 10-year-old Timmy, this was a way to hone their shooting skills especially for their favorite game of cops and robbers. Although, in that game, they just pointed their fingers at each other, shooting each other with imaginary bullets. Not today. Not in practice. This was for real; and it was more than just fun, it was a training session for survival.

"And remember, make the shot count. Don't wound the person. Make it a kill shot. Or they'll kill you," Mr. Jameson concluded. He always concluded with those same words. "Make it a kill shot, or they'll kill you."

Their father was a towering figure of a man. Of course, he was a giant to them, because they were young and small, and he was tall. He also had a large voice that, when used in that angry tone every so often for whatever set him off, it was a loud, gigantic voice. There were other reasons, too, but it didn't really matter. He was a "giant" to them, no matter how they looked at him.

A retired Special Ops military man, Jesse Jameson had earned the nickname "Jesse James" during his six tours of duty in Iraq. He was given this name, his official code name in the Special Ops force, for shooting dead so many of who were referred to "as towel heads," a common slur. He was the "elite of the elite" in the inner circle of military sharpshooting snipers to which he belonged. Yes, Jesse James, Timmy and Ryan's dad, Mr. Jameson, was an honorary presidential Medal of Valor winner for killing or, what he referred to as "dispatching," a whole lot of the enemy under all sorts of circumstances. It was rumored he could shoot the wings off a moving fly at 200 meters in the dead of night. That's how good he was. But he was mostly a quiet man, a focused man. He made his call of duty just another "work day." It was a job, and he did his job well. On a mission, as it was called, he would walk into battle with both barrels a-blazing, just like in the old American West, but now it was in a very hot Middle-Eastern desert, no cowboys or Indians here, just a lot of mean, angry, "towel heads." If he were a woman, he would have been nicknamed Annie Oakley for his amazing shooting accuracy, and amazing dead body count that he left in the burning sands. But his code name suited him just fine: Jesse James, like the legendary cowboy killer of long-ago American folklore.

Now, eight years removed from his military patriotic duty, his new duty was to protect his family, and to teach his two sons how to protect themselves by learning how to shoot a gun. He called it his "American family" duty. And so, it was. Timmy and Ryan learned how to handle, maintain, quickly load, and accurately shoot a lot of different guns. It was their American family duty to learn all this. Rifles, pistols, shotguns, even one of those things called a bazooka, but that killing device was way too heavy to teach Timmy and Ryan to use because it weighed even more than they did.

With his mini arsenal stocked with countless legal, and not-so-legal guns, or "weapons of survival", as their dad referred to them, and the fact they lived in the rural area of the Lake District of Northern Wisconsin, they could shoot all day long, or all night long, and it would only be heard by the closest, or farthest neighbor, as the sound of firecrackers going off.

"Them crazy Jameson kids, playing with all them fireworks, gonna lose a finger one day," someone, or someones once said.

And it wasn't just Sunday practice for Jess and the boys. Fact is, they enjoyed their extra shooting time whenever Mrs. Jameson went shopping or visited a nearby friend or relative. The "James Gang," as they were playfully referred to by Mrs. Jameson, went out fully armed, like in one of those war movies seen on the small TV they had in the farmhouse they called home. The house was willed to them through Mr. Jameson's dad who died of cancer a few years back, while Jesse was away overseas fighting the enemy – a two-story, wooden farmhouse with plenty of privacy surrounding their quiet and kept-to-themselves life.

Here, they would go out behind the big red barn on their property and shoot for an hour at a time at the manmade target range Jess had built. And each of the targets – tall, thin, fat, short, and in the shape of a man – had a towel wrapped around its head. Kind of brought back memories to Mr. Jameson of the days when the targets were real, and the shooting was a matter of life and death. It was ingrained in the two brothers that they couldn't miss, nor would they ever miss.

"It was a matter of survival," their Dad would repeat each and every time they practiced. "A matter of survival. Make the shot count."

This was something they would never forget. And it was something very important for Jess to teach the two boys, in addition to becoming comfortable with guns and enjoying the "bang-bang" sound each gun would make. It was only natural that during the James Gang's many practices, the winner would be determined by who had the most bullet holes in each towel. And as their practice continued, there were so many holes; so many, many holes.

Now, you might ask why would a petite 5-foot, 3-inch woman, the now Mrs. Jameson, their sweet and somewhat shy mom, ever consider to marry a man who was a foot taller, sometimes quiet as a church mouse, sometimes louder than a loudspeaker, an experienced, trained killer, and a "borderline sharpshooting psychopath," as one army psychiatrist once put in Jesse's required yearly physical and mental exam file. And you might also ask why would she allow, or even encourage her two boys to learn to shoot with rifles and pistols at such a young age? The answer was simple. She was a hunter herself. Growing up in a North Dakota family, she was proud to be part American Indian, and her father taught her how to use a bow and arrow and a hunting knife from the age of 5 on. About the same age the boys began to learn how to handle a gun. And she was quite a "sharpshooter" herself, winning many archery contests in her school years and becoming known later in life as one of the most respected deer hunters in the yearly fall hunting season. With a skill like that, you would almost think she should have the nickname "Annie Oakley," but she was actually called "Robin Hood" instead.

So, it was known, and not known, that the James family were marksmen, and a markswoman. There were even stories, or tall tales, how they went to the Wisconsin State Fair each year and won every stuffed animal, or whatever toy they wanted in the shooting galleries where you paid one dollar and got three chances. Never missed a target. Didn't even need the three chances, or even two. The rich game-booth owners, who enjoyed taking dollars from the local yokels and giving them guns where the sights were a little off, never realized that it wasn't just looking down a gun sight to hit a target. It was more of a special skill, an inner skill, a passion, or perhaps a built-in belief of survival of the fittest, to make certain to hit the target, each and every time.

At the end of their yearly family outing at the State Fair, they always went home in their 15-year-old, 250,000-plus-miles driven Chevy, filled with teddy bears, Smurfs, stuffed toy pillow hearts, and whatever else was the "prized favor" of the game booth. And the interesting thing is that they never kept their winnings. They always drove straight to the local children's group home and gave away every stuffed toy to every needy kid who lived there. The Jamesons were good people. They were a good family. The "James Gang and Robin Hood" had a good legacy, as they were nicknamed and called by the local community. They robbed the rich game-booth owners and gave to the poor needy children. It was a great legacy they had built. But that warm and wonderful legacy was about to change.

CHAPTER 9

TIME FOR ANOTHER ONE.

"*I wonder how hard it will be?*" Dorothy Paine asked herself as she watched a confident 90-year-old Franklin Dixon walk past her with a quick wink to let her know it wasn't that hard...yet.

"I admire a man who wants to make it hard," replied her 85-year-old resident friend Gloria Alright, with a twinkle in her eye, as she thought to herself what it would be like if she did it, too.

"Do you think it's hard for him?" Dorothy Paine replied, half in concern, half with a smile.

"The harder the better, I heard him say once," Gloria said matter of factly. "At his age, I bet it's always hard," she concluded, shaking her head in a memory of a time long gone by.

"Well, if anyone can do it, it would be him," Dorothy answered back, as their eyes focused on Franklin Dixon's "to-and-fro" moving fanny, as he passed them in the main lobby of the Sunny Side Up Retirement Home.

He was tall, thin, with a leftover athletic body. Not bad for a 90-year-old man, who made most of the women at the home catch their breath whenever he smiled, winked, or stuck out his tongue at them. The smile and wink made them shiver inside; the tongue sticking out, well, it was an uncontrollable jaw reflex problem from an accident years ago that made it jump right out of his mouth without him even knowing it. But it was a long, long, tongue and all the women knew about it, and anxiously waited to get a glimpse of it.

When he reached his destination in the center of the main lobby, he paused and looked back at them. A smile, a wink, a flash of tongue sticking out, and he was ready. So were they. And so were all of the other early-morning residents who sat sipping coffee or tea, holding their small hard-to-read morning newspapers and waiting to see if he would finally do it today. It was hard for anyone their age to complete the task before him, but he was determined to be the first. And today would be the day, for sure, as the fawning women all smiled and winked in return. One of the overweight women even stuck out her tongue, as they all sat smiling at him on the lobby sofa and chairs watching him sort of bend over, sort of stretch, and sort of prepare himself for the "hard" journey ahead.

The Sunny Side Up Retirement Home was written up in the local advertisements as the "Place to Be"...before they went to the "Place to Become." Kinda catchy. Kinda dumb. Marketing an old folk's home where you probably would never leave, and would probably end up dead, is no easy task. But they got it right, 'cause a lot of Sunny Side Up residents would be dead on that fateful day, which would soon come like the looming winter. And, as to the phrase, a "Place to Become," we haven't quite figured that out yet.

Built just one-and-a-half years ago, it was a quaint set of nice looking two-story wooden buildings with lots of friendly colors for the old folks who still could see. Unfortunately, and most likely, their vision ultimately failed along with the rest of their aging bodies and most of those old folks didn't see well enough to enjoy the colors anyway. But, for now, for those who could still see, and wanted to see, a swaying fanny, a friendly smile, a casual wink and a long, long tongue, well, it was a bright, a really bright place – bright enough so that the oldies (as they were referred to by the young staff of college kids who cleaned their living quarters, cooked their meals, and took the residents on walks or wheelchair rides around the many long hallways) could see where they were going and what was happening around them, even though their failing minds didn't always comprehend it.

It was also a clean place, really clean – clean for them to live comfortably, and clean for them to be comfortable. That's because most of the residents wore diapers, the adult type. It prevented that "hurry-up, here-I-come, and I-can't-stop-it" accident that happens with the age. Thank God for the diapers, which kept them all, and the place, clean. But it did smell. Not so much from whatever was in their diapers, but from the fact that old people have a distinct odor. Let's forget political correctness, they stunk, or at least some, or most of them did.

The entrance to the Sunny Side Up Retirement Home was designed by an architect to give the place a very, very grand-looking feeling. It reminded everyone of entering a New York City hotel lobby from the 1930s – spacious, ornate, displaying cheap plaster Romanesque statues and an amazing, big – really big – fake-glass chandelier. The lobby even had a piano that played its own music. Scattered throughout the lobby were nice, comfortable chairs and couches with plastic covers to protect against soiling by the residents. And, of course, the centerpiece, the main attraction, as many would refer to it, was a majestically wide, but narrowing, fake cherry, wooden staircase, smack dab in the middle of the lobby, that went to the second floor, which no resident ever used – just the guests. It was a huge staircase, a focal point, but mostly for looks, as the residents used the elevator off to the side of the lobby.

Climbing those stairs for the oldies was like attempting to climb Mt. Everest. And so, "it had to be done." And, certainly, the conqueror would become a publicized legend, whose name would be whispered forever among all the residents.

Although this day was a long ago yesterday, it seemed like today. Retirement homes have no real reference to time. It just happens. And so, it did. As "hard" as it would be for Franklin Dixon, he didn't know the word "hard," not at this age; he just knew the word challenge. And a "hard" challenge it would be for anyone else, but not for 90-year-old Mr. Franklin Dixon – "Fearless Frank," as his nickname implied. This was his time. This was how legends were made.

Fearless Frank got his nickname from being a fearless thrill seeker in his early days, working at a traveling carnival. He was a stuntman who rode a "souped-up" old Harley motorcycle, jumping over 12 cars (actually 11, since he never made it over 12), and tragically breaking his hip for the first of several times. He was a daredevil at heart, who once jumped off a tall, rocky cliff with a parachute that barely opened and broke his hip again. He even filmed a movie stunt scene in a burning Hollywood building, but he fell on the way out, catching his pants on fire, and badly burning his hip. At least it didn't break, that is, until he fell off the ambulance stretcher onto the pavement in front of the hospital. Fearless Frank was a "legend in his own mind," and somewhat of a local legend to the retirement home residents.

At the age of forty, with bad and burnt hips, he became a marathon runner, and finally got an invitation to run in the Boston Marathon. He ran it five times in his life, but never won. And he didn't injure his hip, but he did twist his ankle on his final run and, eventually, had to have a toe or two amputated for some reason or other.

"Fearless Frank." Not afraid of any challenge even to this day, which was his 90th birthday. Happy Birthday, Frank. Yep, some residents still alive after that fateful day remember it like it was yesterday. Sadly, others have completely forgotten it, thanks to that thing called Alzheimer's.

The story goes that his family didn't want to care for him anymore, so they checked him into a first-floor apartment at Sunny Side Up right after the home opened a few months earlier.

He always used his walker to stroll down to that grand staircase. There, he looked up at the 21 steps that led to the second floor, or as some residents would say, the "stairway to heaven." He stood there for a very long time with a wide smile, crisscrossing his puppet-like face. Okay, he was wrinkled. Really wrinkled, and his face looked like one of those puppet faces. After all, his life was filled with a lot of unsuccessful stunts that left him a bit battered and worn.

This staircase, this 21-step-tall staircase that led "to heaven," would be the place where he would become a legend. And this is where he made his plans for his 90th birthday.

"This will be my greatest stunt ever," he exclaimed to himself, and to the few sleeping residents in the nearby soft, plastic-covered chairs.

Today, as he woke up 90 years old, he knew it was his time, his "place to be." And finally, after that long walk down the hallway from his apartment, without his walker, with just some smiles, winks, and some tongue, he stood there for the longest of moments, looking at the two-story staircase, from bottom to top, and top to bottom. He was determined to conquer it.

Dorothy, Gloria, and several others, who were in between awake and dozing off, recalled watching him as he prepared to do it.

"He wore a clean pair of dress pants and a nice button-down Hawaiian shirt with colorful pineapples on it," Gloria recalled.

"And the nicest of smiles," Dorothy added, happily.

If you would have asked him "why" he had to do this, he would have likened the challenge to one of his many stunts on which he tested himself in his younger years – a long, long time ago. The burning desire of a challenge such as this was foremost in his mind since the day he moved in. Especially today, on his 90th birthday. It would be his crowning achievement to a mostly injury-plagued and unsuccessful career.

Glancing back at his adoring audience of two or more ladies his age, he smiled, winked, and stuck out his tongue. And with the first step he took, Dorothy, Gloria, and the few other residents sitting in those nearby plastic-covered lobby chairs sat forward and followed his every move.

Three steps, four steps. He was on his way. No resident had ever attempted to conquer the grand retirement home staircase. This would definitely be one for the record books.

Five steps.

The lobby was filled with the excitement of silence. Six steps, eight steps. Upwards he went, and he wasn't even holding onto the stairway railing. He was smack dab in the middle of that giant, never before been conquered, majestic staircase.

On step number nine, Fearless Frank paused. He looked back, directly at Dorothy, who watched him, and who was said to secretly carry a torch or a flame for him (or whatever old people fantasize about for each other), and he smiled again. It was a special smile. Just for her. Dorothy knew it and could feel it in her heart. And she smiled back, but added a wink and just a little bit of tongue.

"This climb up the staircase is way too easy," he thought to himself. And so, he continued with an aura of increasing bravado surrounding each and every step.

He was on his way to becoming a living legend, for sure. Fearless Frank, the one, the only staircase-climbing champion of the Sunny Side Up Retirement Home.

Twelve steps up, fourteen steps. The staircase narrowed, but he remained in the middle. No handrails for this remarkable daredevil!

Sixteen steps up, eighteen steps, nineteen steps; just two more steps to go. Well, just two too many. Maybe Frank should have taken a rest along the way. Maybe he should have held onto the handrails. Maybe he should have slowed down and smiled some more at the residents who had yet to let out a cheer, although one had let out a snore or two. Lots of maybes. Didn't matter. It happened so quick. His heart attack. And it was one heck of a heart attack. The coroner's report said it "just blew up in his chest." Like an exploding army hand grenade. Boom!

And in that silent moment, because, even if there was a boom, or some sound inside of his tired, failing, old body, none of the nearly deaf residents would have heard it, nor did he; Fearless Frank just fell backwards. He fell backwards almost in slow motion, hitting his head soundly on step thirteen (lucky step thirteen), breaking his neck in four different places. Skinny legs went over his head, as he tumbled toward the bottom. Snap. Crackle. And Pop. Breaking one leg, a shoulder, and the hip that had been broken before (you know the story) and ever since then never worked right anyway, and "boom," landed at the bottom of step one. And there he lay, as the residents in the plastic-covered chairs just stared in silence, although someone reported that Mrs. MaGillicutty let out a half-assed, "Yay!"

In Fearless Frank's final moment between life and death (even though he was clinically dead, his body still lived on for a moment or two), he landed on his back, his terribly broken back, and within a brief silent pause, and after that lone cheering "Yay," he shit his pants. Should have worn his diaper. Unfortunately, that day he forgot. (Sometimes the memory goes at different times.) Sadly, it was a lot of shit. Maybe a lifetime of leftover shit. But even with a pantload of shit, he died with one heck of a smile. After all, that's what stuntmen are supposed to do.

Well, that was the only tragic death that ever happened at the Sunny Side Up Retirement Home. It happened about six months ago. The rest of the passings were just the usual – strokes, heart attacks, pneumonia, choking to death on a candy bar, or by a few minutes of very slow and awkward sex, or sex by oneself. No other tragedies until now, this day, this night, six months later, when Timmy entered Apartment 105 on the first floor, just down the hallway from that grand and majestic, and still unconquered, staircase in the lobby.

It was the apartment of Clive Rinaudo, an avid coin collector, and one-time owner of a coin and stamp store. Clive Rinaudo, who loved the Sunny Side Up Retirement Home. He told everyone that it was his "place to be," just like the advertisements said. Tonight, it would also be his "place to become," just as the advertisements also said.

Tonight, he would "become Victim Number 6."

CHAPTER 10

DEAD SILENCE.

"Hello."
"Anyone there?"
"I know you're there."
"Why don't you answer me?"
"I'm serious."
"Answer me! Now!"
"Answer me!"
"Don't play a game with me!"
"Answer me!"
"Please."
"Just say something. Say anything."
"This isn't a game!"
"I don't hear you. I don't hear you. I don't hear you!"

Voices. We all hear voices. Not just the day-to-day voices in the world we live, but those silent personal voices that we hear inside our head. Maybe, maybe it's just your own voice thinking. Or maybe you're saying something out loud without knowing you're saying something out loud. Or maybe it's your subconscious, the area that the psycho-babble doctors tell us is hidden somewhere beneath the conscious and unconscious. Right. Or maybe it is the Guardian Angel we all have who is watching over us and is talking to us in our head, helping to make us better people in a very bad world. Or maybe it's the devil. We all have a little "devil" inside of us, don't we? Or maybe it's none of these, or something we haven't even thought about, or want to think about. Maybe it's the voice of "God" we hear. The voice of our Maker, the voice of what some people have called the "Big Guy upstairs." Yes, that's what we are all probably hearing. The voice of God. But in the head of Timmy, there are none of these, nor none of those. Inside the head of Timmy there is no voice of God. There are no voices. None. Not since the day Ryan died. The day he killed Ryan. There are no more voices. There is only silence. Dead silence.

Life is like a puzzle. And we are all pieces of that puzzle, in one way or another. Whether connected, unconnected, or yet to be connected. As we put all the pieces of the Timmy puzzle together, we are trying to figure out what makes him tick. What a silly expression! Do you think he's a clock? No, a human time bomb, maybe. Waiting to explode. Waiting to kill. But now that we know his head is filled with silence, it's easy to rule out that he was driven to his madness by a voice, or a lot of voices. As the reader of this story, you now have in your head a voice that must be saying, "Aha!" because you thought you just figured it out. It was the silence that drove him to madness. Aha! Not his subconscious, not his Guardian Angel, not the Devil, and not even the Big Guy upstairs, God. Aha, it was his silence that drove him to madness, that made him the killing machine we have come to know and have yet to learn more about.

Congratulations. The defining moment in this story, the "Aha moment," gave you, the reader, a moment of satisfaction. You have figured it out, or maybe it has been figured out for you. Either way, now you know.

But, alas, you don't really know. Let's call it the "alas moment;" not the "aha moment." It wasn't the silence that drove him to madness. It had nothing to do with the silence. Shocker. Had you fooled. Spoiler Alert. No, that's not what made Timmy a killer, a "sicko," as poor "hole-in-the-head Dorothy" used to say about bad people before that hole in the head left her dead. No, it was all because of his brown-with-white-spots, playful, loving, caring, best friend of best friends, cocker spaniel dog named Butch. It was all because of Butch.

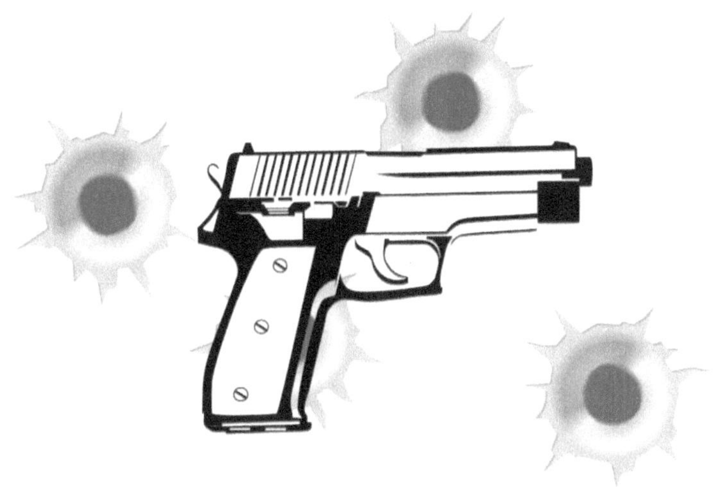

CHAPTER 11

AND THE ANGELS TRUMPETED THEIR HORNS.

Funerals are no fun. And the funeral for the young Jameson boy was certainly an example of that. For the steady stream of older folks who came by to pay their respects and to get a glimpse of such a boy in such a small casket, it was very sad. For the steady stream of classmates who came to their first-ever funeral to look at their dead friend, words cannot describe how they felt. They mostly didn't understand. They were too young, too new at this game of life and really had no understanding of death. For all who came, it was no fun.

For the Jamesons – Dad, Mom, and Timmy, it, too, was no fun. Mr. Jameson, the former trained killing machine, just stood there as expected from his military service days, coldly shaking everyone's hand, and repeating the same phrase over, and over again.

"Thank you for coming to my son's funeral." Nothing more, nothing less.

Mrs. Jameson was a complete 180. Tears constantly swelled in her eyes and then flowed down her face like lava from a volcano, leaving extra wrinkly lines in her caked makeup. She barely said a word. And when she did, it was more of a courtesy, telling the person or persons who stood sadly in front of her to make sure they got a cookie before they left, from the many baked cookies the townspeople brought. They were so neatly displayed, just a few feet from her dead, little son's small coffin. Ryan used to love cookies. Not that it mattered anymore.

As for Timmy, well, it was certainly difficult, and certainly will be difficult to paint a true and accurate picture of what was going through his childlike mind. Silence. Yes, that is true. But inside that silence, there was something else. That "something else" is what was most haunting.

Haunting, in the way he looked at you as he stood next to his grieving mom and dad. Haunting, in the way he stared at you as he was given condolences, which were words he couldn't really understand, nor cared to understand. Haunting, in the way he never spoke after receiving those sympathetic words. Haunting, in the way that he just stood there and smiled. Not a grin, a smile. A big smile. A strange smile. Sort of a "death-like smile." It never changed throughout the whole day. It was the same smile from the moment he looked at his dead brother for the first time in that little coffin. It was the same smile to the last moment when they closed the coffin top, leaving his dearly departed brother in darkness. Closed and locked shut, forever trapping his young body into that wood and silver, specially manufactured, tomb for dead children just like him.

Timmy's smile was enough to send a chill through each and every adult who paid their respects or each and every classmate who was there because their parent or school teacher told them they had to be there. A haunting smile that everyone who came to pay their respects, or just came to be part of this spectacle of death, would always remember. And when that adult or classmate moved on, before the next adult or classmate moved up in line to face him, Timmy would mutter to himself, or softly speak, so that only he could hear, the same words, over and over again.

"Bang-Bang. You're Dead."

CHAPTER 12

A PENNY FOR YOUR THOUGHTS.

When the locked door to Apartment 105 suddenly opened, you might have thought at this hour, sometime after 11 p.m., Clive Rinaudo would be in bed. The average bedtime for most of the residents of the Sunny Side Up Retirement Home was around 8 p.m. It was always 8 p.m., give or take a few minutes. But not tonight. Tonight, time seemed to stand still as if waiting for something to happen, something that would change the lives of so many people here. And it did.

After an early dinner hour, a game of cards, bingo in the clubroom, or playing solitaire on their personal computers, there was always a lengthy ritual of washing their saggy-skinned bodies before bedtime. It took time to get the dirt out of the wrinkled folds of flesh, especially when they often dropped their bar of soap due to the loss of hand-movement dexterity. No matter how the short evening would go, it was important for all the residents to clean up. You know the old saying, "Cleanliness is next to Godliness." Most of these oldies wanted to be "squeaky" clean to meet their Maker if they never woke the next morning. Little did they know that night, as they cleaned themselves up, that they would never wake up the next morning. They would all be dead. As to whether or not they would get their bedtime wish to "meet their Maker," who knows? But if they did, they certainly were clean.

Clive Rinaudo was an exception to the other residents living here. Most were friendly, happily medicated, or just too far gone mentally to know any different. The Sunny Side Up Retirement Home was just like being in kindergarten all over again, except they looked older – a lot older, and moved slower – a lot slower.

Clive hardly ever left his apartment. If he were Superman, this would be his Fortress of Solitude. The apartment was standard looking, cookie cutter, like most: a small eat-in kitchen; adequate living room with space for a modest-sized couch, chair, end table, and a TV; a bedroom with a twin bed, dresser, and closet; and a bathroom with a special, soft, cushy, toilet seat for all of the variations of hemorrhoids, or butt sores, old people have. And, of course, a big walk-in shower/bathtub combo. Gotta be clean.

Clive hardly socialized or cared to socialize. He never joined the other resident oldies in falling asleep on the plastic-covered lobby chairs next to the grand staircase. He hardly did anything with anybody. To most of the other residents, he hardly existed, and they hardly existed to him.

"Who is that?" Mrs. Smith asked repeatedly whenever she saw him in the hallway.

Actually, she said those same words about everyone, because of her dementia.

The only times that he would leave the apartment were to eat alone in the dining room and maybe to take the once-a-month bus trip to the nearby mall where there was a small coin shop mixed in with a collector's corner store.

That was something very important to him, to visit that coin shop. He had taken the trip earlier that day.

Clive just sat in his room and counted his pennies, day in, day out. Pennies. Jars full of pennies. Not nickels, not dimes, not quarters. Pennies. And every so often, while counting them, he would recall where he found, or bought them. Whether he found a penny on the sidewalk, or a store floor, or wherever he may have gone in his youth-filled days, or even the later years such as now, Clive remembered exactly where he found each one. Amazingly, Clive found a great many pennies because he always walked with his head looking downward. Didn't want to miss finding that penny, and he never did.

On a daily basis, he probably found five or six "homeless ones," as he fondly called them. And equally amazing, or somewhat oddly, that's all he would find – just pennies, no nickels, no dimes, no quarters, just pennies. It was as if they were meant to be his, and his alone, and they wouldn't be homeless anymore; they would be in a new home with him. That was important to Clive.

He had never married, had no children of his own, never had other brothers or sisters; he was basically alone. Except for his family of pennies. And over a lifetime of looking downward, he made a lot of homeless pennies his family. But in doing this 24/7, it also gave him a permanent crooked neck. Whenever you saw him and tried to talk to him, Clive never looked you in the eye. He couldn't. His neck was permanently damaged from looking for pennies.

Sitting in the middle of his living room with several open jars of pennies spread out on a rickety old card table, Clive, in a state of shock and confusion at Timmy's sudden entrance, tried to look up.

"Who are you? What do you want?" Clive said slowly, but with authority, as if protecting his prized pennies.

There was no immediate response from Timmy. He closed the apartment door behind him and silently walked over to the card table.

"You shouldn't be here. You don't belong here. Get out of my apartment," Clive commanded.

Clive spoke with a voice that an angry or irate parent would use to scold a younger child and show who's boss.

Timmy just stood there paying no attention to Clive's words. Timmy was more fascinated with the mountain of pennies that Clive had neatly stacked on the card table.

"Don't come any closer. These are my pennies. Don't touch them. Get out or I'll call security." Clive spoke quickly in a stern voice while putting his thin arms in a semi-circle on the card table protecting his pennies.

It was all very odd, the whole scene.

Clive sat in his wheelchair, only able to look at the many pennies before him because of his damaged neck. He never really could see Timmy's young face or even the smile that Timmy wore on it. Clive didn't even see the gun.

There was an awkward moment of silence.

Then Timmy put his left hand into his pants pocket and seemed to be fishing for something he knew was there. And then he found it. Out of his pocket, he held in his hand a penny. A fairly new, fairly worn, 1978-D penny, which he handed to Clive.

Clive slowly reached out his hand to take it. When their two hands touched, the penny was exchanged from one hand to another.

Clive held it in front of his face, held it close enough to examine it. His eyesight was still good for close-up, but not for far distance. Even on today's bus trip, he couldn't see much due to his eyesight. He saw his feet, mostly. Didn't really matter much to see distance; all that mattered was to see his penny collection. Seeing close-up was all that he cared about. He even took vitamins for his eyes. Had to have that close-up vision to study each and every one of his pennies. And that's exactly what Clive did each and every night, while most of the other oldies in the Sunny Side Up Retirement Home were playing cards, or bingo, or asleep with dreams of their youth gone by. Not Clive; all that mattered was his pennies.

Clive turned his new possession back and forth, looking at the quality of it. Studying it. In his mind, he started thinking to himself about the history behind the penny. Turning it from front to back, and back again, he wondered if it was given to the boy in some sort of change, or maybe he, too, found it on the ground like he had found so many of his.

"1978, copper, minted in Denver, common, four billion, two hundred eighty million, three hundred thirty-three thousand, four hundred made that year. Value of one penny." Clive spoke as if reciting from a dictionary, while looking closely at the copper coin. Clive knew his pennies.

In his forty-plus years of running a coin shop, he was a coin expert, even though no one really cared. Today, hardly anyone collected coins anymore. People just used their pennies to buy things, lots of junk things, that probably weren't worth the money they paid. Clive would never do that. Clive would never give up a single one of his family. Family of pennies, that is. No, never. Clive saved all his pennies. That's why his apartment had jars full of them.

Clive gently placed the penny on his card table next to the many stacks he had just counted, and had placed so neatly together. He leaned back in his wheelchair. Because of his crooked neck, it was the only way he could look upwards, if he leaned backwards.

"Even though it is a common penny, a penny only worth one cent, I have never found one of these, or owned one of these. This is worth a lot to me. How did you know I didn't have this one? Why are you giving me this?" Clive questioned the boy's motive.

"Are you here to complete my collection, or to steal my collection?" he asked, curiously.

An awkward silence surrounded them both, as if both were contemplating the true meaning between the questioning words, and the actual reason of the penny being handed to Clive.

Without a spoken or whispered reply, Timmy just brought his right hand upwards, pointed his gun at Clive's head, and without any expression, pulled the trigger. That, in itself, was the reply.

As the bullet discharged, the silencer on the gun again muffled the sound, as it had done several times earlier. And there was no responding sound or sharp cry of pain, or surprised exclamation from Clive.

Basically, the bullet that hit him in the middle of his forehead went quickly through some important nerve endings and tissues in his brain and amazingly, oddly, and miraculously, cured and straightened his damaged neck. Just like that. Clive no longer had to live a life of looking downward, although this miracle would have prevented him from finding more pennies so easily as he had done in the past. But that really didn't matter, because the one lone bullet that entered his head immediately killed him.

For Clive, there would be no more pennies to be found. There would be no more life to live. Clive's body teetered in the wheelchair in which he sat. With the chair's wheels turning from the force of the bullet, Clive fell backwards taking the chair with him, kicking his feet upwards, and knocking over the rickety old card table.

As his body hit the carpeted floor, so did the mountain of pennies.

Lying on the floor in a pool of fast-flowing blood, and having just ruined another of those Sunny Side Up Retirement Home newly installed carpets, Clive's lifeless old body was covered in falling pennies. Lots and lots of falling pennies. Neatly stacked mountains of pennies, which had been knocked over in his death fall. It was like a waterfall, except with no water, just pennies. Each and every one of these pennies that he had once found on the ground, over all the many years that he was so fortunate enough to find them, had all found him. So many, many pennies. If it were Las Vegas, the coins would be merrily coming out of a slot machine in a procession of winning. Coin after coin after coin. What seemed like an eternity was only a mere few moments. Finally, the falling pennies stopped. He was buried in his pennies.

Timmy stood there, taking it all in with a sense of childlike wonderment, mixed with an evil, devilish smile.

What appeared to be the last penny that had rolled off the table, wasn't. There was one more yet to fall. Alone, it rolled off the overturned card table and fell onto the floor spinning on the blood-splattered carpet, until it spun no more, and landing in Clive's outstretched hand.

How odd, or how coincidental, or how amazing that the last one, the last penny from the table that fell alone, spun on the ground, and now fell into Clive's outstretched hand, was the one Timmy had given him. The fairly new, fairly worn, 1978, copper, minted in Denver, common penny from the four billion, two hundred eighty million, three hundred thirty-three thousand, four hundred made that year, was to be the final penny in his collection. In Clive Rinaudo's death, his life was now complete.

Timmy turned to leave. Stopped. Paused. Thinking a moment, he then turned back to look at the dead man on the floor. Without another passing moment, Timmy walked over the dead body covered in pennies. Timmy bent over to reach for the penny that had landed into dead Clive's outstretched hand. His penny.

Timmy picked it up, looked at it, and put it back in his pocket.

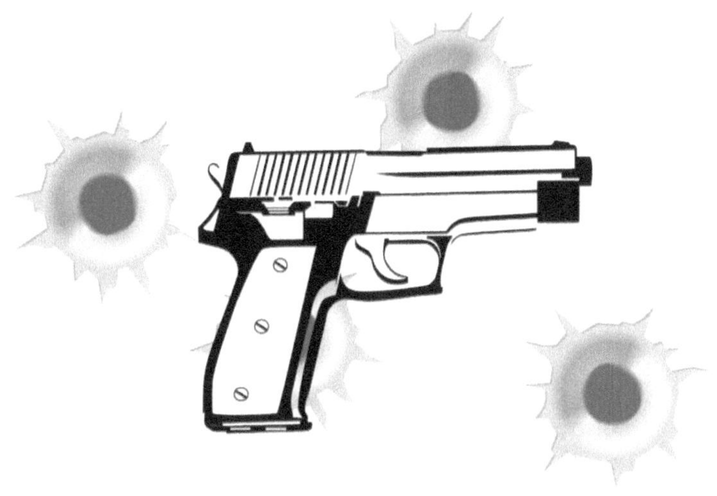

CHAPTER 13

SO WHERE DID HE REALLY GO?

"Do you think he's watching us?"

A curious question, from a curious boy, who didn't understand death like his father did.

"No. He's dead. The dead don't watch. They're just dead," Mr. Jameson answered without any display of emotion.

Mrs. Jameson just squeezed her son's hand tighter, too grief stricken to answer. Gentle tears flowed down her wrinkled cheeks. She was a believer in life after death; her husband wasn't. To her, death was a tragedy. To him, death was just an end to life.

The three of them followed the procession with the child-sized coffin through the cemetery. Four funeral home pallbearers walked slowly ahead, in unison, carrying the dearly departed body of their son towards an open grave.

It was mid-morning as a light rain began and continued for the remainder of the day. The Jameson boy was placed into his final resting home six feet under around 11:11 a.m. on that gloomy Saturday. The rain continued for some 20 hours straight after his burial and was even said to have left areas of deep water throughout the cemetery grounds for days to follow.

"It was the angels crying," Mrs. Jameson thought to herself, trying to find some semblance of comfort in this surreal nightmare for which she was unprepared. Children are supposed to outlive their parents, not die before them.

"From ashes to ashes, dust to dust." The local church priest droned on. A small clap of thunder from the approaching darkening sky seemed to punctuate the cleric's words.

All of the mourners stood huddled under their umbrellas. All but one. Mr. Jameson. He stood in the rain, wearing his retired military uniform. Still fit perfectly, just like the last time he wore it. He exercised every morning, just like when he was in the service. Had to stay fit, had to stay ready. That was his military motto, and he carried it in his heart and soul every waking day. He stood alone next to the deep, dark hole in the ground and saluted as his son was lowered into it.

Everyone remained silent, that is, almost everyone. As one brother was being buried, the other brother made a fist with one hand, then pointed a thumb upwards, and the first finger outwards, in the shape of a gun. He held it to his side, then placed it in his pants pocket. No one saw this, nor saw his smile.

The following day, as the Jameson family drove in silence to Sunday Mass, Timmy finally spoke his first words since the burial, and since the funeral parlor, while looking at his dead brother's body for the last time.

"Do you think Ryan is getting wet from all the rain?" he asked his parents, the same way he would ask a teacher in his school when he wanted to know an answer to a question he wasn't quite sure of.

The answer didn't come quickly from either of the Jamesons. Maybe they were trying to figure out the right words to use to answer him. After all, this was only the second time their young son spoke in two, going on three, days.

"No, he's not wet; he's in the comfort of the Lord our God in heaven," Mrs. Jameson finally replied.

There was a pause, a long pause, as Timmy contemplated the words and tried to find meaning in the answer. And, so he did, and maybe he didn't. It's hard to understand the mind of a young child, especially the mind of a future killer.

"Pah," as he referred to his dad, "Pah, how did Ryan get out of the ground and go to heaven?"

"Timmy!" Mrs. Jameson quickly shouted in a not too happy sounding voice to the very odd and disturbing question. But Mr. Jameson jumped into the conversation before his wife could say anything more.

"He's dead, Son. He's still in the ground where we put him yesterday. He'll always be right there in the ground, until he rots away to nothing. He's not in heaven, he's not in hell, he's nowhere but in the coffin. That's where he will always be. He's dead."

As unpleasant as it was, it was what Mr. Jameson believed to be true. He always faced the reality of truth, having lived with the haunting memory of the war he fought in – the memory of the dead bodies he left behind in the hot, burning Middle-Eastern sand or inside the crumbling, bullet-ridden or bombed-out buildings he fought in. These memories would never go away. How could they? They were etched in his brain like living nightmares. They had left him a different man than the average man, if there really was anyone such as that.

The young boy heard the words clearly. The words of his father came and went in and out of his head. And then they were gone, never to be heard again. He could hear people speak, but he could not hear himself think. Since the death of his brother at his hands, his mind had become a coffin too, forever shutting out anything and everything that a normal person might ask himself or would think about. He wasn't the same boy anymore. He was different. In between what he heard when someone spoke to him, his head was filled with silence. Empty silence.

There was no more conversation. His mother and father sat quietly, not speaking to each other nor to him. He sat quietly also, in the backseat of their car, and showed no emotion. Staring out the window of the car, he saw the large, looming church, their church, staring back at him as they approached it.

"His body may be in the ground, but his soul is with the Lord," Mrs. Jameson suddenly added.

Mr. Jameson said nothing more as the short conversation returned to silence. Jesse James, the trained soldier, who knew what "dead was" but couldn't accept what death really was, never spoke of his son's death again. To that very day, he never spoke about any of the many people he killed or saw being killed. Death is never a pleasant sight, especially when you are part of it. Maybe that's why he never showed any emotion when he found his son's cold and lifeless body. It was later that night when he went looking for the two brothers and stood watching his one son sitting on the ground holding the other in his arms while rocking back and forth as daylight turned to twilight. He knew immediately. No one had to tell him. He knew death, and death knew him.

Whether Mr. Jameson believed in a heaven or a hell, or whether he believed in a god or a devil, he never told anyone. Not his wife, not his priest in confession, nor even himself in the days before, during, or after this family tragedy. He just felt (if that's the right word) that what other people may have thought or believed or preached about the religious teachings of a life hereafter, meant nothing. Nothing at all to him. All he knew was that dead people, including his now dead young son, don't come back, don't go anywhere, don't become anything else. They're dead, and that's all there was to it. Dead. And eventually, they rotted away. Dust to dust, ashes to ashes.

When the car stopped in the half-filled church parking lot, Timmy's mom and dad got out together. Without looking back at him, or waiting for him, they walked toward the church. The rain, which started the day before at the burial of his brother, now suddenly stopped. A faint glimpse of a new day's morning sun peeked out of the dark clouds, which seemed to disappear.

Timmy looked at the large cross on top of the church, and a lone tear came from his eye, followed by another, and another. He sat there alone in the cavernous back seat of the family car and he started to cry. For the first time in a long time, a very, very, long time, he started to cry. Maybe for the loss of his brother, maybe for the sadness of his mom and dad and what they were experiencing. Or maybe because of what he knew. What he knew he was about to become.

CHAPTER 14

DO YOU BELIEVE IN MAGIC?

Casper Cosmo Merlinski was a magician – "The Great Merlin," as he was called in his Vaudeville performances when he was a young man of twenty-something. Handsome, six-foot-tall, 100-percent European, and with a small trademark mustache that seemed to have a life of its own when he smiled. It just went up on one side of his face, almost like a caterpillar raising its tail, if it actually had one. With a Slavic accent, and hand gestures as if he were a master conductor of a major orchestra, The Great Merlin was also a great showman. He had a remarkable theatrical style and unique flair for mesmerizing and making the crowd "ohh" and "ahh" during his magic act. And he was not only known as a great showman on stage, but he was also known in the tabloids as a "greater showman" after his performances. It was reported more times than were counted that he would bed some young lass in the back of the stage behind the main curtain, bending her over and making her say "ohh" and "ahh," just like the audience. It was also whispered among the other magicians that he had a very big magic "sword," if you know what I mean.

Now, long after his last professional magic act on stage, he was still performing another magical act with all the willing and lonely women in the Sunny Side Up Retirement Home. He was "the resident stud."

The widowed women swooned when he passed them in the hallways. He knew it. They knew it. He really was the resident stud. One woman, who will remain nameless but was killed earlier in the story, even passed out when he smiled at her with his mustache, giving her that little special wink. She fell right out of her wheelchair and broke her knee, but it didn't matter, for she had been one of those willing, sword-swallowing members during his private, in-room, late-night magical performances.

Yes, "The Great Merlin." (Let's just call him Casper.) Even though approaching the age of 90, Casper was genetically blessed with a wrinkle-free, movie star, handsome face. He was the "Romeo" to all the Sunny Side Up Retirement Home "Juliets." Even though his mustache had turned gray along with the remaining hair on his half-bald head, he still could perform with special magic in his sword.

Yes, he had it all; that is, had it all except the timing of tonight's fateful encounter. An encounter with a 10-year-old boy, who had just killed a half dozen of the neighboring resident oldies and was about to add another one to his list.

And so it was to be that Casper's sudden appearance in the hallway made him an early victim of the horrors of this night as our killer boy Timmy made his rounds from apartment to apartment. It was just his luck that Casper was leaving the recently widowed Gladyis Giltspur's apartment, situated directly across from Clive's, when he ran into Timmy. To say the least, the encounter caught both by surprise. Casper was standing in the hallway casually zipping up his pants. He had forgotten to do this after he finished the magic act he performed on Gladyis. Sadly, Casper was losing a battle with dementia. A lot of the residents there had the same battle, but it helped them hide the shame of what they did behind closed doors. Basically, they forgot. Casper was standing next to Gladyis' apartment door, fiddling with his pants zipper that sometimes stuck, when he heard Timmy approach.

"Hey, young fella, aren't you out a bit late?" Casper politely asked, as his frail hand finally gave up on the battle of the zipper.

Besides having trouble remembering things, like zipping up his pants, Casper also was losing his eyesight. He did not notice the knapsack that Timmy had on his back, nor the handle of the gun that was hanging out of his coat pocket.

They stood a foot or two apart, eyeing each other.

Being the ever consummate performer, Casper forgot about the zipper and instead put his hand behind young Timmy's ear and pretended to pull out a coin from it.

"What do we have here, a magic coin?" Casper exclaimed in his put-on showman's voice, filled with mystery and awe.

But there was no "ohh" or "ahh" from Timmy. He just stared at Casper and then broke a small smile. Casper handed the coin to Timmy, as he was accustomed to when he performed his act. That's when Timmy noticed that Casper was missing a finger, a middle finger.

"Oh, my finger, yes, it's gone, magically gone." Casper spoke both to the boy and himself as he held up his four-fingered hand, pretending to admire it.

"Lost it during one of my greatest performances," Casper continued, not waiting for a question as to how he lost it.

"I was sawing my lovely assistant, the bodacious Miss Elizabeth, in half. There she was in a wooden box, which looked like a coffin, with only her head and feet showing."

The word coffin suddenly caught Timmy by surprise.

"And there I was with my magic sword, and just as I was about to cut her in half, she sneezed. Sneezed real loud. The wooden box shook. Caught me by surprise, and I cut my finger right off. Lots of blood. I remember that, for sure, lots of blood. People thought it was part of the act. And so, it became part of the act. I had a fake finger put on, and cut it off every night, and reattached it every day. It was quite a trick but, somehow, I kept forgetting where I put the rubber finger and kept losing it. Had a whole box of fake fingers. My real finger – I kept it and tied it around my neck. Called it my lucky finger. Ha ha ha!" Casper chuckled, proud of his story, and proud that he remembered it. He also put his hand into his open shirt top and pulled out the finger. There it was, attached to a thin, gold chain.

"Never know when an extra finger will come in handy!" Casper added, laughing out loud while tucking the finger back into his shirt.

Nothing like a master showman, laughing at his own joke. But that was the only laughter in the hallway that night. Timmy didn't even let out a little giggle or a tiny, "Ha." He just kept staring at the missing finger. Never saw a missing finger on a hand before. Nor a real finger on a chain, either.

"It was my most famous act, the sawing of the lady-in-half trick. Houdini even stole it from me," Casper exaggerated, raising his voice, since the great magician Houdini was long dead before Casper was even born.

But that didn't matter, because that's how showmen talked. A big talk, for a big show. Always performing, always on, even here in the dimly lit retirement home hallway. Casper was reciting his show biz act lines, exactly the way he had spoken them so many, many times before. Whether it was an audience of a thousand, a hundred, or just one, just as it was right then and there, it was all part of the act. And Casper loved his audiences, and they loved him.

"Why, I even made an elephant disappear. Yes, a giant 22-foot, two-thousand-pound elephant!" Casper exclaimed with a big smile, and a big hand and arm gesture, as if indicating an imaginary elephant was there in the hallway with them.

"Made him disappear right off the stage. Of course, magically, I made him reappear moments later. No smoke, no mirrors, no tricks, Laddie, just the 'magic of my magic,'" Casper concluded, catching his breath before continuing. He didn't even give Timmy a chance to respond, no time for an "ohh" or an "ahh."

"I was the greatest magician of all time. I was The Great Merlin, and here I am before you tonight!" and with that, Casper took a stage bow.

The last stage bow, or call it a hallway bow, or a farewell bow, that he would ever make, as Timmy's hand reached into his coat pocket and touched the barrel of his still-warm gun.

What Timmy didn't know, what most people didn't know, was that The Great Merlin really could have been the greatest magician of his time, or all times, even bigger than Houdini. But drinking, and gambling, and womanizing with the wrong woman at the wrong time ended his rising-star career a bit too early. His own tricks, not the magical kind, the human-faulted kind, left him without a career – just a bunch of mixed-up memories and tall stories, and a pocket full of coins he could still pull out from behind a young boy's ear with only four fingers remaining.

In his 50s, Casper had been on a downward personal spiral for a few years before it all came to an end. Too much drinking, too much gambling, and too much womanizing. Casper had just finished a sold-out performance in Las Vegas when he wandered into a late-night casino card game in a smoke-filled back room. It was a room reserved for, and filled with high rollers, and some mean rollers, if you can imagine how mean they might be. Mobsters. "Mafia Robert DeNiro" types. Not really *the* Robert DeNiro, but the tough guys who looked like they just stepped out of a gangster movie.

Too much booze, and a cocky showman attitude, made Casper the focus of the high-stakes card game. With a four-fingered hand that could magically pull the lucky winning ace out of his sleeve, with the sleight of hand magicians had, it made him a big winner that night. But it didn't exactly make him a lot of friends. Just a lot of sore losers who didn't like losing their hard-earned, freshly stolen money from robberies, extortion, and counterfeiting.

In addition to not enjoying Casper's lucky streak, they also didn't like his Don Juan-like caterpillar mustache that seemed to wink at them when he smiled. The little "fucking mustache" was making fun of them, with each and every pot of cash Casper won. And, of course, where there's high-stakes gambling, there are always high-stakes dames – Vegas show girls with the low-cut, skin-tight dresses, and the so very, very nearly exposed beautiful, big breasts, just like the ones the bodacious Miss Elizabeth teasingly flashed in their magic show each night. Yes, big bosoms of the gangster's molls which seemed to have a life of their own, as they heaved so excitingly in response to Casper's life-of-its-own winking mustache.

So, as bad timing would have it that night, as much as it would be a part of this night, the one dame that he took up to his room on the 13th floor of the hotel above the casino, after the card playing ended, happened to be the mistress of Bugsy Carbone – FBI's #1 "most wanted." A real tough guy, who was a real bad guy. A real gangster guy, who did not like anyone messing with his woman, let alone a cheating card-shark magician with a winking caterpillar mustache that made his gal's breasts heave ho and who took his stolen money, too.

As it turned out, that night was the definitive end of The Great Merlin's great career. Just as Casper was about to perform his famous, private, in-bed magic act with his famous magic sword and a willing, busty, naked babe, Bugsy's #1 girlfriend, four very big, and very mean, and very ugly henchmen, or let's just call them thugs, entered his hotel room. They got a room key from the Security Officer, who was also on the not-too-happy Bugsy Carbone's payroll, to let them into Casper's room. They weren't there to watch Casper's "magic act," but they were there to do some acts of magic of their own. Before you could blink an eye or give out a few "ohhs" and "ahhs," they broke almost every bone in Casper's body, magically, if you want to call it that, leaving him alive. Alive, but unconscious, and in a month-long coma.

And if that wasn't enough, they took his sawed-off finger that dropped next to him on the floor. It had fallen off his naked body during the merciless beating. And if that wasn't enough, on top of the first if-that-wasn't-enough, one of the big, mean, and very ugly thugs unzipped his pants, and pointed his own "magic sword," letting a big stream of pee go all over Casper's unconscious and not-so-pretty (anymore), unrecognizable face, and directly on his caterpillar mustache. And if that wasn't enough, on top of all the other if-that-wasn't-enoughs, there was one more. The biggest and the meanest and the ugliest of the thugs stood over Casper's head, pulled down his pants, and squatted. Bombs away! He left a huge pile of shit on Casper's bloodied face. Better that than his feet in concrete. When the maid came in Casper's hotel room the next morning and found him, she stated in her police deposition that the shit had hardened across his face, like a fat mustache.

As you could probably guess, Casper never performed in Vegas again. He never performed in any other casino worldwide as the very vindictive gangster, Bugsy Carbone, was very well connected, and made it very well known that the "show was over" for the Great Merlin. The finger was returned in the mail to Casper with a very nice note, "Next time, uppa your ass, if ever you come to Vegas again." Not exactly the best and most proper English, but it certainly made its point.

In the following years after a lengthy rehabilitation from the coma, and a few facial reconstructive surgeries from the brutal beating, and learning to walk again, whatever was left of Casper moved to Wisconsin. Here, he lived his golden years in a run-down trailer owned by that "once-upon-a-time assistant with the bodacious big breasts" he used to saw in half, sort of. The best magic gigs they could get were at local family restaurants, or birthday parties, where they entertained kids and bored parents. Casper would never make an elephant disappear again, but he sure knew how to blow up balloons and make twisted-looking elephants appear.

As his lifetime wound down, and he was finally tossed from the rundown trailer by the now older and saggy, big-boobed, bored-with-him assistant, Casper became a resident of the Sunny Side Up Retirement Home.

There, he got a new lease on life. Casper became the resident Romeo, the sexy stud muffin, the dapper four-fingered Don Juan, who made the older women he passed in the hallways swoon with his winking caterpillar mustache and his, excuse me, still functional magic sword. Casper could still perform some of his old card tricks, but not as quickly as before because of the way his broken fingers healed, very crooked-like from that long-ago fateful night in Vegas. But once a magician, always a magician. He could still pull a coin out from behind a young boy's ear.

But tonight, bad timing continued to follow him. Casper Cosmo Merlinski, The Great Merlin, had his last performance, his last coin trick, his last stroll down his personal memory lane. His final curtain came down, as Timmy pulled the gun out of his pocket and put one bullet into Casper's head.

The force of the bullet at such close range pushed Casper's thin and bony body into the hallway wall. As he slowly slid dead downwards, a smear of his blood was left on the wall. Landing on the seat of his pants, his body rolled to the left, and fell sideways to the floor. An outstretched hand crumpled under him, as his body landed atop of it. The force of his body hitting the floor made Casper's finger fall off the cheap gold chain on his neck. It rolled away from him across the floor and stopped at Timmy's feet.

Curious, Timmy stooped down and picked up the finger. He had never held a real cut-off finger in his young life, and felt as if he had just won a carnival prize. A prize just like when he and his family would win after shooting so many bull's eyes in the carnival games. Timmy turned the lone, loose finger back and forth in between his own. Satisfied, he smiled, pocketed it, and turned away from his latest kill, towards another beckoning apartment.

Casper's dead body laid alone on the floor.

Damn his womanizing. Damn his drinking. Damn his magical sleight-of-hand card cheating. And, goddamn, his missing finger was gone for good.

CHAPTER 15

SIT. ROLL OVER. PLAY DEAD.

Unconditional love. There's an old saying, "A dog is a man's best friend." In this story "A dog is a boy's best friend." Unconditional love.

And so it was in the case of Timmy and Butch. Butch the dog, the 2-year-old, brown with big-and-small white spots, cocker spaniel, wandered onto the Jameson farm property the day the family had buried Ryan. Mr. and Mrs. Jameson paid no attention to the dog that suddenly showed up as they were in grief, shock, or whatever you call the hours after burying their son.

Timmy found the dog wandering around the target-practice area and, without hesitation, it approached him. Timmy and Ryan never had a dog of their own, and Timmy didn't have any friends who had dogs. Their friends had cats, fish, turtles, rabbits, and one friend had a guinea pig – a filthy thing it was, Timmy recalled. To say the least, Timmy was a bit frightened. He had never even petted a dog before – before what was to happen next. The dog came right up to Timmy and started to lick his hand. The dog was wet from the rainy day, and it was cold. It was almost as if the dog knew Timmy. It was almost as if he was already a part of their family and that he had just returned home and was showing his affection after being away. That's what dogs do, no matter what you do to them; they always return to you and show their unconditional love. Just like brothers do. And that's what Butch did from this day on.

Timmy was now his best friend, his master, his brother. Hmmm, his brother. In a sense, or if we tried to make some sense of this moment when they met, it was almost as if Butch, the stray cocker spaniel, was the embodiment of Ryan. He was there to console Timmy and help him through his grief, a different grief than his parents', but a grief onto itself. A grief that cannot be fully shared, or explained, but only lived through experience.

Timmy didn't believe in God. Didn't really know how to believe in God. He listened in church to all the words that Father O'Malley preached to the half-awake congregation each Sunday morning, and it never really connected. But Butch connected. If there was a sign that this was "meant to be," then this was meant to be. Timmy and Butch, from this moment on, were inseparable. That is, after the Jamesons came to understand and believe that this stray dog, this lost dog, this dog with no tags and no apparent connection to anyone, was there for a reason. The dog was there for Timmy. The dog was there to give Timmy the unconditional love that he lost when Ryan died. The dog was there because he was taking the place of Ryan. And Timmy vowed to himself and to Butch that he would never lose him again. Sadly, that only happens in fairy tales, and this story is not a fairy tale.

The first few days of Butch's arrival brought a different feeling and mood to the family. At first, Mr. and Mrs. Jameson wanted no part of the dog, and argued about what to do with the dog. But Butch was paying no attention to them; he was 100-percent Timmy's. The dog slept in the barn the first night. When Sunday morning arrived and the Jamesons prepared to go to church, they couldn't find Timmy in the bedroom that he once shared with Ryan. Although a slight panic set in, Mrs. Jameson, for some reason, went right straight to the barn where they had left the stray dog the night before in an area with some hay, an old blanket, and a bowl of water. There they were, Timmy and the dog, lying together – a child's arm over a sleeping dog, and a dog's paw on a child's arm. There they were. And that was the moment she knew, it, too, was meant to be.

"So, Timmy," Mrs. Jameson asked when they returned from church the day after Ryan's burial, and the day he finally broke his silence with the questions in the car. "So, what are you going to call him? He has to have a name."

Timmy thought for a moment – not a long moment, not a short moment, just a moment. Would it be a name like Lassie, Rin Tin Tin, or Rover?

"Butch. I'll name him Butch," Timmy replied with a boyish smile.

It was just enough of a smile to let his mom know that the dog was bringing him some happiness, some comfort, some emotional and maybe mental stability, and replacing the loss of his dead brother. And, in that moment, the brown cocker spaniel with big-and-small white spots looked up at Timmy and directly into Timmy's eyes. If a dog could smile, he would have. Butch was a fine name.

Although the Jamesons did try to find the dog's original owner, they never did. Nor did they really want to. So Butch, the dog, settled in as a part of the family. Timmy and Butch were inseparable. He followed Timmy to school, which was only a half mile or so down the path in the woods alongside the country road. Butch would sit there patiently all day at the edge of the schoolyard, waiting for Timmy to return to him.

With the dog as his friend, Timmy began to make new friends. Some of his classmates wanted to pet Butch or throw a ball and watch Butch fetch it. Others just watched. Some wanted the dog to do the typical tricks like sit, roll over, and play dead that dogs do. And Butch willingly and playfully followed the instructions. All except for "play dead." Timmy never used those words. Never, ever used those words. And the classmates just stuck with the ball or stick tossing, and they, too, never told Butch to "play dead."

Mr. Jameson, being the cold-blooded military man, didn't warm up to the dog on the outside, but in his inside, if we can define it as that, he knew the meaning of bonding. In his tour of duty, or "tour of death," as he sometimes referred to it, he knew that his squad, his band of brothers, had their best chance of survival with unconditional love. They would die for each other if need be. So, for that reason, and maybe for a few other personal reasons, Mr. Jameson let the dog stay.

Every so often, when Timmy was asleep with the dog cuddled in his bed next to him, Mr. Jameson would open Timmy's door to check on him, and Butch would know he was there, and would look back at him. Almost as if saying, don't worry, I'll take care of him, too, after all we're brothers, and that's what brothers are supposed to do. Even though, in Timmy's dreams, and in the back of his real-life reality, he felt that he failed his brother. So Butch was his second chance. And this time, he would protect Butch no matter what, and he would never let any harm come to him. Until that day.

CHAPTER 16

AND THE BEAT GOES ON.

The Sunny Side Up Retirement Home didn't have its own choir, but it sure had its own golden voice. Each morning at approximately 7:13 a.m., the angelic voice of Domingo Rodriguez was heard coming from the bathroom shower in Apartment 107.

"Do, Re, Mi, Fa, So, La, Ti..."

On cue, on time, every day, with every morning shower. Like a race car driver warming up his engine before the big race, Domingo had to get his voice started. Every day at 7:13 a.m. exactly, the warm-up exercise for his voice was heard echoing in the retirement home hallway, followed by a melodic and cheerful rendition of "Spanish Eyes." So clear, so vibrant, so warm, so wonderful. A voice of an angel, that flowed from the shower, to the adjacent hallway through the half-inch crack under his apartment door.

And the residents loved it. They either opened their doors to their apartments to let his voice in, or they wandered in the hallway in front of his apartment in their wheelchairs, or bumped into each other with their walkers to hear him sing. Domingo Rodriguez, was 85 years old, tall, thin, olive skinned, and with a bit of "*cucaracha*" showbiz flair. Born in Mexico, an illegal immigrant for most of his life, he was the lone, remaining member of the almost famous singing group, the Five Flaming Flamingos. You may or not remember them, but if you do, they were the first "fully gay" Mexican singing band. Almost made it to the big time. They even made it as far as the auditions of *America's Got Talent* TV show, but lost out to a dog act, featuring a 3-legged mutt who jumped through a burning hoop while blindfolded. And here he was, living the great American dream as a resident of the Sunny Side Up Retirement Home. He was now retired and crooned a tune each morning for the listening pleasures of those residents who could still hear, or at least, partially hear.

Domingo was also a very friendly fellow. He always greeted everyone with his own special accented version of hello.

"High-low, Missus Dorothy. High-Low, Missus Gladyis," he would say with a big accompanying smile.

Domingo always stretched his greeting out and finished it with one of those hand gestures of taking a bow without a bow. And when it came to the holidays, no need to have the retirement home spend a few dollars on some local entertaining singing group performing boring traditional Christmas carols. Nope. It was all Domingo, the living legend, one-man gay band.

He was accompanied, in between heart attacks, by a fellow 91-year-old, overweight resident, Bert Futz, on bongos. With his own personal, colorful maracas, Domingo shook and shimmied across the retirement home lounge area, singing his favorite rendition of "Jingle Bells" (which sounded more like Jingle Balls!), and "Rudolph the Red-Nose Reindeer," all in broken English, with Spanish accents on certain notes and a voice that mimicked an older Elvis. What a singer! What a show! What a guy!

"Tank yew berry mucho. Tank yew berry mucho," Domingo said repeatedly at the end of each song with a twist of his hips and a look to the heavens above.

Some oldies, that is, people from nearby, adjacent retirement or nursing homes would come to Sunny Side Up just to hear him sing. Maybe they remembered him and the other four Flaming Flamingos from 50 years ago, or maybe from their failed revival tryout on *America's Got Talent.* Whatever the reason, it was always a packed room when Domingo sang and danced. Some of the lucky ladies even cha-cha-cha'd with him while sitting in their wheelchairs.

His favorites were the fat ladies. He loved the fat ladies, and they loved him.

"Give mee a little sugar, mee special hon-knee," he'd exclaim out loud, while blowing a kiss to some tubby wubby, in between taking deep breaths to recover from overexerting his aging and failing body.

Domingo was so popular, he would have given his fellow retirement home resident, The Great Merlin, a lot of competition in bedding the ladies, except Domingo preferred men.

Whenever he performed, it was definitely an evening to remember. An evening to remember just like tonight, as Timmy found his way into Domingo's apartment. Apartment 107. It was a lot different than most of the other apartments. In those apartments, there were either pictures upon pictures of the resident's children, grandchildren, or great grandchildren, and, almost always a wedding picture, nearly faded from a time long gone by, or some garish landscape pictures, like the ones found and bought in garage sales and now rehung, adorning their walls. Apartment 107 was quite different. It was filled with a lot of differently sized posters of the Five Flaming Flamingos with show dates and places where they performed all across the United States. And then, there were the pictures of their performances – so many pictures – mostly thumbtacked or taped to the walls next to the posters. If you looked at them closely, you could actually see the progressive ages of the five smiling amigos from photo to photo. A "living museum" room full of fading pictures of Domingo and his happy, singing, dancing, and prancing band buddies plastered on every square inch of wall and table space.

You might think Domingo really liked himself. Or they liked him. And he did, and they did. They were more than a singing group, or a band, or an act; they were a family, and they were lovers. They were proud to be the Five Flaming Flamingos. And "flamers" they were. You could see that in their smiles with gold-capped or missing teeth, and their obvious "twinkles" in their beady little eyes. They were fun, and definitely "unique" entertainers.

But, what stuck out the most to Timmy was the life-size plastic mannequin head that held Domingo's aging and fairly worn-out toupee. It sat on a small wooden end table in the center of his living room where he took it off every night before he went to sleep and put it on every morning before he left his apartment. He had worn it most of his life, being prematurely bald at around the age of 20. They say it was caused by his mother's side of the family. They were all "cue balls" or had cue-ball bald heads. It was a bit obvious that he wore a toupee, for sometimes he put it on backwards by mistake, and sometimes when he didn't attach it right, it would slide across the top of his head like it had a life of its own, especially when he did the signature Five Flaming Flamingos' group move where he shook his butt, then his chest, then his head while simultaneously moving his arms up and down like a bird trying to take flight. Yes, he was imitating a flamingo. Bingo, that's why they had the name. The five gay guys danced and pranced like flamingos on fire. (Makes you think why the Fab Four called themselves the Beatles.)

So, it was about 11:30 p.m., way later than most of the Sunny Side Up Retirement Home residents' bedtimes, and Domingo, alone, and clad only in his tighty-whitey underwear and knee-high black socks, was doing some improv dance steps while watching an old Ginger Rogers and Fred Astaire classic movie on his 14-inch TV. It was quite a scene. His bony legs, thick black curly, hairy back (if only it grew on his head), and his heaving-ho, sunken-in chest. He was prancing and dancing to one of his Flaming Flamingo dance routines. It was enough to make you pause, laugh, or maybe throw up in your mouth. It was a sight to see. And, as he swiveled his hips and gyrated his pelvis like Elvis, Timmy stood close by and silently pointed his gun directly at Domingo's head and started to squeeze the trigger. Then he stopped.

"What dah....?" Domingo exclaimed in shock, as he stood nearly naked in his tighty whities, staring at his unknown intruder, Timmy.

Then he saw the gun.

He stared at the gun Timmy held. Domingo stopped his dancing when he was surprised by Timmy's quiet entrance. But a gun pointing at his head? All that moved now were his trembling bony legs. His knees seemed to knock together, like teeth chattering. Whether it was fear in his eyes, or shock, or disbelief, or whatever it was, it was hard to say. Timmy just stood there, standing next to the worn-looking toupee on the mannequin head displayed on the wooden end table. Timmy didn't pull the gun's trigger. His finger loosened on it. Instead, he just continued to point the gun. Pointed it directly at Domingo's bald, wrinkled head.

Without a word, Timmy's one free hand reached for the toupee. He picked it up and held it outwards to Domingo.

"You must be cold. Put it on," Timmy ordered.

"What an odd thing to say, 'You must be cold,'" Domingo thought to himself in between trying to compose himself, or prepare himself, for god knows what comes next. Certainly, he should have been cold, prancing and dancing in only his undies and knee-high black socks. Looked like a scene out of an old amateur, silent, porn film. But the heat in his apartment was nearly 85 degrees. Domingo loved the heat. It reminded him of his childhood days, playing on the hot, sunny beaches of Mexico, building sandcastles, and dreaming of what his life was to become. How little did he know; how far did he come. And now, all of this.

Domingo slowly reached for the toupee. Cautiously, he put it on, as instructed. He didn't want any sudden movement of his to make this unknown kid pull the trigger. Actually, he didn't want *anything* to make this young boy pull the trigger. Nervously, he put his hairpiece on backwards, then realized his mistake, and turned it around the right way. Then he stood there, silently, awkwardly. Waiting for whatever was to happen next. The only sound in the room was from the TV movie and his heart, which seemed to beat so loudly in his head from the fear he was experiencing that he did not hear the TV.

Timmy broke their silence.

"I like the song, 'You Are My Sunshine,'" he said politely, as if making a request to a band.

"You Are My Sunshine?" Domingo's mind raced for the words. *"You Are My Sunshine. Why not 'Moon over Miami,' or 'Row, Row, Row Your Boat?' You Are My Sunshine?"* he thought to himself.

Afraid to question the young boy standing before him, pointing a gun at his head or actually what appeared to be pointing the gun at the toupee on his head, he nodded in agreement to the request.

He said to himself, *"Did he make me put it on only to shoot it off my head? Am I a sitting duck in some amusement park shooting range? What the...?"* but before Domingo could finish his thought, his voice overcame his questions and fear, and he started to sing.

His mind and mouth connected. Domingo started, slowly, off key, but making it right, making it better, with the new pronunciation of each and every word in the song.

"You are my sunshine. My only sunshine," Domingo started to sing.

His voice and the song grew in key and tone with each new lyric.

"You make me happy, when skies are gray. You'll never know, dear, how much I love you. Please don't take my sunshine away."

It was the best singing he had ever done. Whether he was singing for his life, or singing because he was a singer, this is how he sang: with meaning, with feeling, with everything he felt in his heart.

A small, lone tear came from Timmy's eye. It rolled down his boyish cheek. With a slight sniffle he raised the back of his left hand and wiped it away. He didn't say a word. He didn't have to. The lone tear said it all.

Throughout the song, the gun remained pointed at Domingo's head. Although Domingo's knees had stopped shaking, his heart had almost stopped beating in fear. He stood there, glad for what he sang and how it affected the boy, and sad for what the words meant and why it must have affected the boy.

"My mom sang that song to me and my brother." Timmy paused, sniffled one more time and continued, "My brother loved that song. It was his favorite. My mom loved to sing it. She always sang it. My mom loved us."

"You loved the song, too?" Domingo asked, as if they were now friends.

"She doesn't sing it anymore. She doesn't sing anymore," Timmy replied without a trace of any emotion. Just words. No longer sniffling. The one lone tear was long gone.

Without any further explanation, without any further words, Timmy lowered his gun to his side and turned to leave. Domingo stood exactly where he was. Stunned. Shocked. Afraid. Not knowing what he should do or say next. So, he said nothing.

As Timmy reached for the apartment door, he stopped, he turned, he looked back directly at Domingo, who stood trembling in his tighty whiteys and long black socks.

"Thank you," Timmy said without any emotion, without any hesitation.

And he left Apartment 107, as suddenly as he had entered it.

Domingo remained standing, staring at the door. Expressionless, exhausted, confused. No one word or groups of words could describe what was going on in his mind. He was filled with so many fleeting thoughts. It was as if his life was being played out before him. You've heard of that. When someone is about to die, their life is said to be replayed in their mind in a moment of unmeasurable time. But not tonight.

Domingo wasn't going to die. He wasn't going to get a bullet in his head, or have his hastily put on, worn-looking toupee shot off his head. He was left alive. He "dodged the bullet," as the old expression goes. He was alive, and alone. Alone, like most of his life really was. The glamour, the glitz, the singing. It was all a bunch of showbiz hooey. Like a light switch, it could be turned on and then turned off. The Five Flaming Flamingos really were his only family. He never married, never had children, never really had any real friends outside the other four dancing guys. And now they were all dead, they were all gone. And he was left alive. Alive and alone.

In retrospect, nothing had as much meaning or impact as that very moment as he stood in his underwear and his knee-high black socks. For in his loneliness he finally found peace. He was never really alone in his long life. He always had his songs. In the end, you really can't take anything with you, but you can leave your song behind. Whether you like a song, sing a song, or just hum along with one, we're all singing songs in one way or another. We all have one special, one very special, one very meaningful, one very personal song all our own. And, at that very moment, he started to sing his. It was his mother's favorite song also. He recalled fondly how she used to sing it to him when he was lonely and sad as a child. It was all that he had left now, all that he needed.

"You are my sunshine, my only sunshine, you make me happy when skies are gray. You'll never know, dear, how much I love you. Please, don't take my sunshine away."

And then, he started to cry.

CHAPTER 17

A NEVER-ENDING STORY.

Every community has a mayor. Whether a big city, small city, whatever size, each community of people has a mayor. The Sunny Side Up Retirement Home was a community in itself. It was a sprawling 22-acre facility with eight adjoining buildings, each two stories tall, and each looking the same except for the different exterior colors, and of course, a large number on each entrance that identified its address. Timmy's story takes place in Building #7. Unlucky #7, not because of all the horrific killings that were unfolding in this one crazy night, but because it also had a lot of maintenance problems.

For example, the main water supplied to the building took too long to come into the bathroom showers. Poor shivering Domingo, naked in his warm-up song, stood waiting in a cold, empty shower stall every morning. Maybe that's why his voice resonated so well.

Another problem was the hallway carpets. They seemed to buckle with certain seasons, something to do with changes in humidity. As a result, every day in Building #7 there was always a traffic jam of wheelchairs trying to get over the hallway carpet bumps. And, of course, the heating. When it was cold outside, the air conditioning would turn on. When it was warm outside, the heat would go on. There was always *something* in unlucky Building #7. But the eclectic group of aging residents who lived out their lives there, and put up with all the various maintenance problems, had the one best thing no other building had. They had "the Mayor," or so she called herself, or as others sometimes referred to her.

DeeDee Lapinsky, age 89, going on 70, was the most friendly, talkative, bubbly, enjoyable, and yet most unenjoyable person you would ever want to meet. She was the official greeter, the official talker, the official gossip queen, and the official know-it-all about everyone's business. She was non-stop hustle and bustle, involved in everything that had anything to do with the Sunny Side Up Retirement Home. One could say that DeeDee "knew everything about everything, and nothing about nothing." She fit the role perfectly of the unofficial, official "Mayor" of the community of oldies, as she jokingly referred to herself, and them.

As for all those problems that Building #7 had, and even the ones not mentioned because they're too boring to even mention, DeeDee Lapinsky was on top of it – although nothing ever got done. It didn't matter. She was the Building #7 spokesperson in the retirement home yearly management and resident meeting. And when she spoke, the oldies listened until they fell asleep because she never quit talking. Even when she was alone in Apartment 108, right next to Domingo's, she talked to herself. She never considered herself alone, because she had herself to talk to. She was as happy as happy can be, for this was her life, and she embraced it every day, no matter what, even when she was constipated.

If you could turn back the clock of time and look at 5-year-old DeeDee way back in kindergarten, you could tell she was destined for greatness, well, at least "Mayordom," as it eventually turned out. She was always the class leader, and her take-charge attitude continued into, and throughout, all her school years. It was hard to give a nickname to a name like hers, DeeDee. Maybe you could call her Dee, or D? But everyone has a nickname. So she got one, too – "Chatterbox." It was a perfect name that everyone called her, and that never bothered her, because she was too busy being friendly. No need to say more, she said it all, and so did the nickname. Never a dull moment with Chatterbox, that is, DeeDee.

She was not only downright friendly, but downright pretty. She was perhaps the prettiest of all the girls in her school class. Actually, she was the most beautiful. But she never really knew it, because she would never hear the compliments from all the boys who chased after her, since she was always too busy talking, and they could never get a word in.

DeeDee became everyone's friend. She actually had too many friends. She never had a birthday party because her invitation list was too long, and she'd have to invite the whole school. That was a problem. Her parents didn't know what to do, being somewhat poor, so they kept forgetting, on purpose, to celebrate her birthday. It didn't really matter to DeeDee; she was so popular, she was invited to everyone else's birthday party. Her life was basically going to school and then going to a birthday party after school. She even brought home any duplicate gifts that her friends received. She was that popular. She would comment on how amazing the gift was, how wonderful it was, how she wished she had a gift like that, and how gifts like that were so special, so nice...and on, and on, and on, until the person who celebrated their birthday just gave her the duplicate gifts to make her stop talking. And it did, for maybe a moment.

In her high school's Senior Class Last Will and Testament that the students put together to predict the future, hers read, "DeeDee Lapinsky, 'Chatterbox,' blessed with looks, knowledge, and a voice that never pauses. Destined to be a beauty queen or politician, and definitely a Mayor of some community." How appropriate! They got it right. In both cases.

Regarding her "beauty," at age 21, she almost won the Miss Wisconsin Beauty Pageant with her shapely figure and stunning looks. Came in a close

2nd, but she should have been 1st. It was all about the question-and-answer segment for the final judges' points. DeeDee, like all the other remaining contestants had 30 seconds to respond to some silly question about how they would save the planet in some sort of meaningful manner. And she knew the answer. She was very intelligent and knew how to actually save the planet. Unfortunately, she took four minutes, and counting, to answer when they finally cut her off. "Chatterbox." Loved to talk. And in retrospect, and as to where we are right now at this very moment in this story, that is important, very important, especially on this night when Timmy entered her apartment with a gun full of bullets, and found DeeDee talking to herself.

"Oh, a guest! How nice! You must be thirsty, or maybe hungry. Why don't you come over and sit down," DeeDee casually remarked upon Timmy's sudden entrance into her apartment.

No sense of shock. No sign of fear. For her, just the start of a new conversation.

"Usually there are some cookies in the front lobby, but maybe they're all gone. I especially like the chocolate chip cookies, don't you?" she quickly added.

You might say this is not the kind of greeting you would expect between an 89-year-old woman, and a 10-year-old unknown intruder, but there is one more thing you need to know about DeeDee Lapinsky, aka Chatterbox, and aka the Sunny Side Up Retirement Home "elected-in-her-own-mind," the Mayor. DeeDee was a bit touched. In other words, she wasn't all there upstairs. It seemed there was an empty space between her left ear and her right ear. She would repeat herself, she would forget, and she would repeat herself again. Maybe it was the dementia she was struggling with each day, or maybe she talked so much in all her years that she had emptied her brain with the many, many, words she had used. Or, maybe, things just weren't "right" with her.

Other than that, she was perfectly normal and capable at her age to live a full and happy life. Dressed to a "T" even now at 11:40 p.m. in the evening: Nice stylish dress with a cute flower pattern, with a little frill here and there. Even a hint of a red ribbon woven along the neck line. A very nice silver necklace on her wrinkled, but not-that-wrinkled neck. Must have been all the lotions and potions she used to keep her youthful look. Average height, good posture and a full set of her real teeth. And there, on her thin and bony left hand, she wore a very large and expensive four-carat diamond wedding ring. The ring was so big and so shiny that it sparkled like a lighthouse beacon when she waved her hand with warm and friendly gestures. It was such a big diamond that it reflected all the lights from throughout the room. This giant-sized jewel must have cost someone a lot of money – someone who must have really loved her and wanted her to have such a big rock as this. "Diamonds are a girl's best friend," and this certainly was the "bestest of friends" she could possibly want. Whenever the chance arose, she would show it off as she was inclined to do, as she did right now. With every sentence she spoke, DeeDee waved her hand with the ring like an orchestra conductor to punctuate her words. But it didn't matter to Timmy. For all he knew, it could have been cheap costume jewelry. And, maybe it was.

When DeeDee spoke her long, run-on sentences, she moved her slim body like an elegant model on one of those TV shows like *The Price is Right* or *Wheel of Fortune.* Her combined hand gestures and body movements were perfect, mesmerizing. And, like icing on top of a cake, she still had all the looks, poise, and glamour that made all the resident men there turn their heads like spinning tops when they saw her. DeeDee probably would be crowned a beauty queen if they held a contest here at the Sunny Side Up Retirement Home right now, this night.

DeeDee Lapinsky, "the Mayor." She had everything any woman her age would want, or might be jealous enough to want. She was perfect, or almost perfect. It's just that, with all her constant talking, and there was a lot of it, she was going a "little bit crazy," as some of the other oldies said about her. And they should talk, as they were all starting to lose it as well. They were all a bit crazy, some more than others. After all, it comes with age, doesn't it?

"No thank you. I don't eat cookies," Timmy lied.

"Don't eat cookies! My, my, my. I never a met anyone in my life who didn't eat cookies. Especially chocolate chip cookies. They're my favorite cookies. They were my first husband Louie's favorite, too. Why, I would bake us, mostly him, a batch of chocolate chip cookies every night just before we sat down and watched TV. Got them in one of those frozen packages in the supermarket. Usually bought four or five packs at a time. And he'd eat the whole bunch of them, once I baked them up. But he liked pizza, too – pizza and cookies. Do you want me to make you a pizza?" she asked in a sweet, sing-songy voice, while never missing a beat.

"No thank you. My mom says I shouldn't eat pizza. It's not good for you," Timmy answered, again in that matter-of-fact, conversational tone, as if they were best of friends.

"Not good for you! Well, she might be on to something there. I mean pizza is a favorite snack, or meal, of a lot of people these days, and it does come in many different varieties with a whole lot of different things to put on top of it. I heard they even put little pieces of fish on it. Can't imagine who would want little pieces of fish on a pizza, but I just guess you can have fish on a pizza if that's what you want. Why, my first husband Louie, he loved pizza. He also liked chocolate chip cookies, too, but like your momma said, pizza isn't good for you. Now that you mention it, it wasn't good for Louie either. Dear, dear, Louie. He would love to eat his pizza especially on a Sunday afternoon when watching them sports on TV. He always sat and watched them, and always had a beer in one hand, and a piece of pizza in the other. And when he got angry, he would shout and wave that piece of pizza around in his hand, and it's a good thing there were no little pieces of fish on it or they would have flown right off. He especially got so mad at one sporting thing they call football. Now mind you, I didn't watch them sports things with him; never could figure them out. A lot of shoving, pushing, and hurting each other. Especially football, I think it was called that. But I remember the one time I watched a few minutes of it and they were throwing the ball, running with the ball, and also kicking the ball. Football? I didn't understand why they just called it that one thing. It should have been 'Running, Tossing, and Kicking Ball.' Do you like football?" DeeDee finally concluded, without taking a single pause, or extra breath, in between any of that.

"My dad didn't like watching sports," Timmy replied in what was certainly a one-sided, yet somewhat interesting, conversation.

"Well, your dad is real smart, like your momma too. If only Louie would have been smart like them, he'd be here with me today. But no, he watched his sports stuff and ate his pizza stuff and got all excited and, well, it just happened. Just sort of happened. Hard to explain how it happened. I mean, yes, I was there when it happened, but I wasn't really there when it happened, because I didn't like that sporty stuff, so I was in the upstairs bedroom, nice and quiet up there when he was down there in the living room, yelling at the TV. He yelled so loud I heard him all the way upstairs and I had to stomp my foot on the floor to let him know I could hear him. I was just watching my favorite TV movie, it was around Christmas time, yes, it was exactly five days before Christmas and Louie really spoiled Christmas that year, long time ago. I was 41, 42, he was a few years older 45, 46. Anyways, what happened, or must have happened from what they told me, was that he put a big bite of pizza into his mouth, but no little pieces of fish on it, maybe some pepperoni, he did like his pepperoni, and as he went to swallow it, he got mad and yelled at the TV sports stuff going on and it just got stuck in his throat. Just like that, stuck in his throat. He must have tried to get it out from the nail marks on his face and neck, nasty looking marks, but he didn't make any sound, or at least I didn't hear any sound, as I must have had the volume on the TV movie up too high because of his yelling. They always had a lot of loud piano music in the movie, real romantic movies, I really enjoyed them even if I had seen them before, I always watched them again. You could always see something you may not have seen the first go-round. Anyways, he must have struggled, poor thing, 'cause they said from the mess he made, he had to have been rolling all over the floor. Must have been kicking his legs a lot. Even left some shoe scoff marks on the one wall next to the couch, which was turned over. Maybe he was angry or maybe it was a way to get the stuck pizza out of his mouth, but he knocked his beer over, too, stained the carpet – a real nasty and smelly stain. Beer has a strange smell. I don't like beer, but Louie sure did. I remember how hard it was to get the smell out of the carpet after they moved his body. I told him not to drink beer in the TV room! I told him to drink milk, milk doesn't stain, but he never listened. He even knocked over the plate of chocolate chip cookies I had baked him, and somehow one of his shoes came off. Well, when my movie was over, I came downstairs to see if he wanted any more cookies or pizza, and there he was, all dead on the floor. Dead, but somehow sitting on the floor with his arms and hands slumped by his side. His face was blue and a some of the pizza was still sticking out of his mouth. A real mess. A real mess. He didn't even finish the cookies I baked him. So, I guess you're right, pizza really isn't good for you," DeeDee finally concluded, almost sadly.

Timmy didn't reply. He stood looking at some variously sized, faded, framed photos that were displayed on a nearby table. Lots of framed photos of what must have been her family. Her kids, her grandkids, and even one of a fat cat that looked like it only had one eye. There were lots of framed photos, all neatly placed. Not a space left for another photo. Timmy picked up the one of a smiling man and a smiling woman celebrating some sort of a major family event at a picnic. The man was holding a large plate of food. Next to the man in the photo was a younger version of the woman who stood in front of Timmy, probably in her mid-30s. She was pretty then, and was still pretty now. The man was about fortyish, nice looking, but a bit overweight. It must have been her dead husband Louie holding the food. On the plate he held in the photo were several slices of pizza and a few chocolate chip cookies.

There was an awkward moment of silence between Timmy and DeeDee. Maybe she was catching her breath before she began again, or maybe she was thinking of Louie on the floor with that piece of cold pizza still stuck in his mouth, or maybe she was thinking of something else. It definitely was something else.

"Oh, I'm sorry. Excuse me," DeeDee suddenly broke the silence. She did a sort of girlish giggle, or a forced, but somewhat cute, embarrassed laugh.

From the table stand next to her, she quickly grabbed a pack of matches, lit a match, and waved it around in front of her. She was trying to clear the air.

"Constipation. I've been constipated for days. Must have been something I ate. Are you sure you're not hungry? I can make you some cookies. Chocolate chip cookies are my favorite. Do you like chocolate chip cookies?"

She smiled, with the air now clean, at least for the moment.

"Oh my," she paused, as she shifted her weight and let out an unexpected, small, hardly noticeable, but definite long-sounding fart. "I must be constipated. I hate being constipated."

She sniffed at the air paying no attention to him, deciding whether she needed another match.

"May I use your bathroom?" Timmy politely asked.

"Why, of course. My bathroom is right there in the hallway. There are clean towels on the sink. I do my wash twice a week, and I just had the towels washed the other day. They're all nice and clean and really fluffy. I just love fluffy, clean towels, don't you? Feels so nice and soft on the face," DeeDee concluded, while mimicking wiping her face with an imaginary towel.

Without replying, Timmy went into the bathroom. It was just about the right size for a person who lived by herself, small but suitable. It was very clean and neat. There was only one picture hanging on the wall adjacent to the mirror – a picture of a horse in a field at sunset. It was a very nice photo and it was nicely framed. Timmy noticed that it was signed on the lower corner with just a single written initial, "A." Maybe a family member, maybe a famous photographer, maybe a garage-sale, framed replica photograph, as was pretty much the norm in most of the other oldies' apartments. It didn't really matter. Whatever the reason, to Timmy it was just a moment in time, hanging on a wall. But it was a very nice picture.

Timmy washed his hands in the sink, and then turned his attention to the fluffy towel on the sink counter. He gently touched it. The towel was light tan colored and looked exactly like any bathroom hand towel you would expect to find on a sink counter. He picked it up and held it in his hands and looked at it. It was soft, just like DeeDee said. He turned it over and looked at the other side. He ran his hands back and forth over one side and then the other. Both sides were equally soft and fluffy. He brought the towel to his nose and smelled it. Yes, it was clean. It reminded him of when his mom did the Saturday wash and there were clean and nice-smelling fresh clothes to wear, and for him and his brother to get dirty all over again. He placed the towel back on the sink. He didn't thoroughly dry his wet hands because he didn't want to get the towel dirty from the small traces of blood that remained on his hands. He knew the towel might never be washed again. Instead, he wiped his hands on his pants.

Timmy turned to leave, then abruptly stopped. He stood there seemingly lost in thought, and then slowly turned to look at himself in the mirror hanging on the wall. He hadn't looked in the mirror when he first came into the bathroom. Most people do. Funny thing about mirrors. People always seem to look in them, even though they know what they look like. They always look at themselves. Just habit, just a personality trait, just curious, just egotistical, whatever the reason, people always look in the mirror to see what they look like. Good, bad, or indifferent, they want to know what they look like, even though they know what they look like.

Timmy had not. He paid no attention to the mirror. He looked at everything else in the room. Maybe because he knew what he looked like. Or maybe because he didn't want to know what he really looked like. He only looked in the mirror if he had to. Like when he wanted to see if he needed to comb his hair which sometimes hung in his face and indicated he needed his mom or dad to get the scissors out and cut it.

But now, for some reason, some reason that only he knew, he turned his face to the mirror and looked at himself for the first time in a long time. And his image looked back at him, for the first time in a long time. He looked directly into his eyes, and they looked directly back into him. There really wasn't much to see. There really was no expression on his face. There was no trace, no indication, no sense of confusion, no happiness, no sadness. And there was certainly no look of evil in what he was looking at, or what was looking back at him. There was nothing other than the face of a 10-year-old boy. He didn't even look tired. If he did, it didn't show. Maybe he just felt it. Even though it was past his bedtime, the face in the mirror knew it was. The face in the mirror always knows, because there are two people in every mirror. There's the one that you can see, and there's the other one, the one you don't want to see. In that reflection are things that we hide from the world and pretend we don't know; it's what only we see. But it knows everything we've done, and everything we are. The image in the mirror saw his soul as clearly as it saw his body. And when it looked back at Timmy, it showed him what he really was. And in that secret revealed, it made Timmy smile. In the mirror was both a boy and a monster. And what he saw, and what looked at him, both knew that he still had a few more people to kill.

DeeDee was standing next to the table of framed photos when Timmy came out of the bathroom. She didn't ask him about the fluffy towels, or if he had wiped his hands on them. She seemed to be lost in some thought of a time long gone by and was brought back to life by what she now held in her hands. And so she continued speaking, as if he had never left the room.

"My second husband, Andrew, that's him in this picture, was quite an adventurous man. Before I met him, he was a well-known photographer, traveled the world, had countless pictures published in magazines and books," DeeDee said proudly.

And for a moment, Timmy thought of the picture of the horse in the bathroom with the letter "A" on it. Perhaps his initial? Or, perhaps, just a coincidence. Didn't really matter.

"When we first met, I was in a park, not far from here. I don't think it was that far from here. It was summer. It was a warm day. Not too hot, just a nice warm summer day, and I was wearing a nice pair of shorts. I remember I had just gotten them at the nearby store, it was a new shopping center, lots of stores to shop in and it wasn't far from the park, and I had on a blue halter top, not too low cut, but enough so you could see my nice figure. Andrew always said I had nice figure. Louie never did – never gave me many compliments. It's a shame, a woman always likes compliments, no matter what age. Louie just liked to eat and watch them sports stuff on TV. So, Andrew must have been taking some pictures for some assignment, and he just came right up to me, and I remember his smile, it was a sweet smile, and he was also handsome looking, he had a very nice build for a man in his early 50s. It was apparent that he liked to take care of himself, ate mostly good food, not the chocolate chip cookies and pizza that Louie ate, but he did eat some. Sorta snuck them every once in a while. Guess we all have a sweet tooth don't we? Are you sure you don't want any cookies? I can bake you some. My husband Louie liked chocolate chip cookies."

This time there was no response from Timmy. He just smiled and waited for her to continue.

DeeDee sat down on her couch. It was from a generation or so ago, still nicely kept. A design of big green palm trees, or at least what looked like big green palm trees, flowed across it. The cushions were soft, not worn, probably from not having much company visiting her these days, but you might assume differently because of all the family pictures. Timmy sat next to her, close, but with a distance between. She was still holding the picture.

"Through his picture-taking, Andrew introduced me to a whole new life. He took me most everywhere with him, wherever he travelled. A lot of travel magazines wanted him to take pictures for them. He had 'a good eye,' they would say. He saw things differently. He always used me to model in a lot of the pictures. He always told me I was perfect for the picture. He was so full of compliments. I remember once, I was standing at the edge of the Grand Canyon, really an amazing place, and he called it a 'big hole in the ground.' He had a funny, you know, funny sort of humor; not everyone got it, I did, though. And it really was a big hole in the ground!"

DeeDee laughed out loud at what she said, while waving her ring finger and hand in a big circle of air before her.

"That's probably why they named it the Grand Canyon. Anyways, he had me stand on the edge of some cliff looking over the valley and point. Don't remember what I was pointing at. But I was pointing, and I stepped a bit backwards and stumbled on some loose rocks and almost fell in. Almost fell into that big hole in the ground."

DeeDee broke into a nice warm smile with the memory.

"He caught me. Almost lost his camera, almost tumbled backwards with me. We might have both fallen in that big hole in the ground, but we didn't. Good thing, too, or I wouldn't be here to tell you about it. We just fell together onto the ground, his arms around me, and my arms around him. He really liked to hold me. I remember him holding me, like it was yesterday."

She paused, reflecting on that romantic moment, while unknowingly moving her hands gently up and down the front of her arms, as if someone else were holding her.

"We sat on the ground and both broke out laughing. It was quite funny at the time. I mean we almost fell in. But no matter what the danger, we always found a way to laugh about it. We laughed a lot in our life. He always found a way to make me laugh, even in a moment like that where I almost fell, or we almost fell. I remember it like it was yesterday. It was a special moment, because when were done laughing, he kissed me. Right there in front of everybody, on the edge of that big hole in the ground. The sun was going down. I remember it was a long sweet kiss. A gentle kiss. A real nice kiss. He really loved me. I know it. And I loved him, too," DeeDee said fondly, pausing again in reflection, this time with a small tear forming in her eye.

And then she abruptly got off the couch and hurried over to the counter where she picked up the packet of matches. There were only a few left. She hurriedly lit one, and waved it around in the air, just like before, just like she always did at moments like this.

"Constipation. I've been constipated for days. Must have been something I ate. Are you sure you're not hungry? I can make you some cookies. Chocolate chip cookies are my favorite. Do you like chocolate chip cookies?" She smiled, with the air once again clean, at least for the moment.

"No thank you," Timmy replied politely.

He picked up the picture from the couch where she had suddenly dropped it. Timmy silently got off the couch and put the framed photo back on the table with all of the others. He then started to reach into his coat pocket, as she continued, as if nothing had happened.

"But then things changed. His photography jobs began to get fewer and fewer. Seems everyone now can take pictures with their phones. Imagine that, taking pictures with phones! Not real pictures like you take with a camera, but something called digital, whatever that is. In my day the phone was attached to a cord that went into a wall. Now there are no cords, no holes in the wall, and you can take pictures with them. Now everyone who travels anywhere can take pictures. So, all his years of schooling and learning everything about how to take a picture, a really great picture, was all changed now. All you needed was a phone. How silly is that?" DeeDee added, as if asking herself.

Timmy's hand was now in his coat pocket. His hand had reached his gun.

"Andrew became depressed. He couldn't figure it out; maybe didn't want to. But an assignment came out of the blue – that's a funny expression, isn't it, 'out of the blue'? And it was a really different assignment from what he was used to, like landscapes and waterfalls, and lots of pictures of horse shows. Our granddaughter rode horses. Big animal for a little girl. Did you ever ride a horse? They like apples and carrots."

DeeDee took a short breath with the question and answer she gave.

Timmy nodded. Now he knew that the letter "A" on the picture in the bathroom of the horse at sunset was her husband's initial, and it was a picture he had taken.

"Anyways, a scientific research company that Andrew once did some work with contacted him and had a secret-type assignment for him. He didn't, or maybe he did, want to share it with me, but he didn't even if he could, 'cause it was a secret project and it had to remain a secret. But he told me anyways. Seems there was some activity, or something going on in a desert military base, Area... Area... Area 57, I think, sort of like the number on the Heinz 57 ketchup bottle. Maybe the military was secretly making ketchup. Wouldn't that be something, secretly making ketchup?" she added to her last comment.

Timmy didn't comment on her comment, or say any words, or give any response. He didn't even nod in reciprocation of understanding what she said, or not understanding what she said. He just stood there. His hand remained in his coat pocket with his fingers wrapped around the gun.

Without missing a beat, DeeDee continued her one-sided conversation.

"That's how I remembered it. Something to do with UFOs – you know, them flying saucer things that they show in the movies. And he had to go there to the military factory where maybe they made ketchup and take some pictures of a captured UFO, which was supposed to be a secret, like the other ones that were supposed to be a secret, too. Must have had something to do with ketchup. So, he kissed me goodbye, right here on my right cheek."

DeeDee pointed to her cheek.

"Andrew always kissed me goodbye on the exact same place on the cheek whenever he left the house to go anywhere. Just his way of letting me know he loved me, and he smiled at me, and said he'd be back in a few days."

DeeDee paused. It seemed like a longer pause than even she expected. She seemed to be trying to remember something, but, couldn't quite put the right words together.

Timmy's hand remained in his coat, fingers wrapped tighter around the handle and trigger of the gun.

"He never came back. It's been 15 years. 15 years, 2 months, and 8 days. He never came back. I never heard anything from him. Not a word, not a peep. Nothing. And when I tried to contact the people I thought were the ones he said he was going to photograph the secret project for, I couldn't remember their names. So, I contacted the police, and they finally contacted the people who I couldn't remember their names. The police said no one they talked to knew him, nor knew of any photography project, especially a secret UFO project! The police said UFOs only exist in movies. That's what I thought, too, but I might have seen a UFO once when I was a child, it was while we were on vacation in Ohio visiting my Aunt Edna. I remember my Aunt Edna said she saw one, too. She was such a nice aunt. Big and jolly. I really liked my Aunt Edna. She even looked like Santa Claus without the beard. She even played Santa sometimes at Christmas. Oddly, she even died on Christmas Day some years back. Was allergic to ketchup, and accidentally had some, and she just dropped dead, right on Christmas Day. So, there must be UFOs; they're just secret. That's why it was a secret project. Have you seen any UFOs?" she asked in a curious sort of tone, almost as if she thought this young boy might have the answer to her unanswered questions.

But Timmy didn't answer her. Instead he quickly pulled his hand from his coat pocket. His hand was empty. There was no gun in it.

He looked at her for a long moment, or maybe a short moment. Time didn't seem matter to DeeDee anymore, except for the exact time she somehow remembered the day Andrew left on his secret photo project.

Timmy turned to leave. Didn't say a word. Didn't answer her question about the UFOs. Didn't say anything. Just started to walk towards the apartment door that he came in from. As quickly as he started to leave, he quickly stopped, and turned back to the woman who was still standing there. Standing, waiting for an answer. Standing, lost in thought about her lost husband. Or, just standing there, without anything else to say. Imagine that, nothing else to say. DeeDee Lapinsky, the "Mayor" of the Sunny Side Up Retirement Home without anything else to say.

So, Timmy spoke first.

"I'll have a cookie. A chocolate chip cookie," he said without expression, or maybe with just a tiny smile. Hard to sometimes tell on the face of a 10-year-old child, especially the face of a Killer.

DeeDee smiled back. She was always full of smiles. That's how she always greeted people. To make them feel wanted, to make them feel comfortable. After all, she was the official, unofficial "Mayor" of the Sunny Side Up Retirement Home, and she really wanted to make this young visitor feel welcome. And with her smile, she nodded her head also, as if that was the right thing for Timmy to have, a chocolate chip cookie. Or, maybe two or three cookies, like her dead husband Louie used to have.

"My husband Louie liked chocolate chip cookies. He also liked pizza," she replied.

And then he shot her!

One bullet, right through her forehead. It happened so fast. There was no warning. There was no time to change her smile into a frown, or a scared look, or whatever the look is when you're shot in the head, just like she was. She staggered backwards, almost in slow motion. Then teetered sideways, left, then right, then fell back onto the table with all the family pictures.

8x10s, 5x7s, a couple more in smaller frames. They all tumbled off the table and on top of her dead body and across the blood-splattered carpeted floor. She just lay there. Peaceful. Covered in framed family photos. Maybe a family reunion. Maybe just a coincidence.

Timmy stood there looking at the blood coming from the hole in her head and flowing onto the pictures. He adjusted the silencer on the front of the gun barrel and put the handgun back into his pocket. Without hesitation he walked over to the counter where the pack of matches were placed after the last time she used them. He picked them up, and looked at them slowly, with the curiosity of a child who maybe was warned and forbidden to play with matches. Maybe it was something he had done in his earlier years, or maybe it was something his dead brother Ryan had done once. But it was pretty obvious from the way he looked at the pack of matches that he had to be real careful. He opened the flap, tore out a match and struck it on the side of the match cover, immediately lighting it. He held it close to his face and looked at the flame. He watched it burn down on the small cardboard handle he held. He didn't wave it around in the air like DeeDee had done when she was alive. There was no bad smell in the air he needed to erase with the magic burning match. There was nothing here but silence, and maybe, just maybe, the sweet smell of death.

Timmy blew the match out. Holding it between his two fingers, he turned it back and forth. He placed it neatly on the counter in the same glass bowl DeeDee had placed all the other burnt matches she had used that day. There were a lot of them. A lot of burnt matches.

Timmy put the packet of matches in his pocket. Without another glance at DeeDee Lapinsky, the friendly and talkative woman with the hole in her head, and covered with bloody family pictures, he left. He closed the door behind him as the fresh hole in DeeDee's head still trickled some blood down her wrinkled, but still attractive face.

If he had paused and looked back at her one more time, he would have seen DeeDee's mouth still moving. No actual words, no cry for help, no actual sounds, just a strange silence as her mouth continued moving in the last gasps of air between just being shot and being really dead. Slower, and slower, and slower, her mouth moved, opening and closing. Moving like a puppet's mouth being moved by someone else holding the strings. Slower, and slower, and slower.

Her mouth finally stopped moving.

And then her dead body let out a small fart. Small, but stinky.

If only there were matches. Even in death, she was still constipated.

CHAPTER 18

QUACK, QUACK.

A duck walks into a bar and climbs up onto a bar stool. The bartender comes over and says, "What do you want?"

The duck says, "I'll have a beer."

The bartender says, "We don't serve beer to ducks. Now get out."

The duck leaves the bar, stands outside for moment, then goes back into the bar. The duck climbs back up onto the barstool. The bartender comes back over and says, "Now what do you want?"

The duck says, "I'll have a beer." The bartender is furious. He says, "We don't serve beer to ducks. Now get out. And if you ever come back, I'll NAIL your feet to the bar."

The duck leaves the bar, and stands outside thinking about what the bartender said, then goes back into the bar. The duck climbs back on top of the barstool. The bartender angrily comes over. "Now what do you want?"

The duck replies, "Nails."

The bartender replies, "We don't have any nails!"

The duck says, "Okay, then I'll have a beer."

There's an old saying, "In life, you don't always get what you want." There's another saying, "If you don't always get what you ask for, ask again."

Milton Schwartz was a funny man. Actually, he was a funny-looking man. Overweight and under height, expected height, that is, as the doctor told his parents that Milton would be a tall man when he was fully grown. Unfortunately, he ended up on the short end of the yardstick, about 5 foot, 4 inches on a good day. And now, maybe an inch or so less because he was shrinking with age. Whatever. He also had a fat face, big jowls, and a thin, pointy nose. He was Jewish. But what really made him funny looking was his Dumbo-size ears. (Dumbo is a Disney® cartoon elephant, if you didn't know.) And on top of all that, Milton Schwartz was also bow legged. So, he waddled, sort of like a duck. And when he told his famous duck joke, he would waddle back and forth like the duck in the joke, which made it all the more funny.

Milton Schwartz was not just a funny man, he was a comedian. He really was funny. Funny looking and funny. Now approaching 86, and a decade or so into his retirement years, he had recently been relocated to the Sunny Side Up Retirement Home after his first of many mini strokes. He survived them all, and even used the line, "Here comes another one!" in his comic routine. Especially when he felt one coming on and his body would start to shake and then he would suddenly go numb and start to drool. Not a good picture, but from a distance it looked like an old guy trying to dance by himself, or maybe being stung by a bunch of bees. It was a funny routine.

Through all his medical ills, Milton was still a comedian at heart. No matter what time of day, no matter how many people were around, or near him, Milton would always tell jokes. He not only joked about his mini strokes, but he would tell everyone how he was still waiting for the "really big one," so that he could finally shake the wax out of his ears. The punchline was how Milton made the gesture of a fat balloon being popped while waddling back and forth. I guess you had to see this in person to really see how funny it was.

Milton Schwartz was the Sunny Side Up resident funny guy. There was never a dull moment with Milton around. He would always find a way to get into every conversation. No matter what the topic was, he would find a way to leave his listeners laughing. For example, when Dorothy Paine came to the dining hall breakfast buffet without her teeth, he always said to her, "Must be that new toothpaste you're using. It makes your teeth so white, they seem to disappear!" Dorothy always laughed at that. She'd belly laugh out loud for two reasons: one, because she forgot her teeth so much, and two, because he repeated the same lines so much. She even called it the "disappearing teeth joke." But the real joke was on her, as she tried to eat her breakfast pancakes without her teeth. She just gummed them into little pieces. Now that was funny. That was the real joke. I guess you had to see this in person, too, to really see how funny it was.

Each night, it was only natural that Milton stayed up late to watch TV. He had just put on his bedtime pajamas with the built-in "poop shoot" in the back and was settling in for some late-night television comedy he could steal. He even heard a joke recently about the poop shoot. "Hey, at that age, when you gotta go, you gotta go." Milton loved the feel of his plaid pajamas and he loved poop jokes. Who doesn't? Especially when you throw in the sound effect of a fart or two. So here he was in his poop-shoot plaid pajamas, watching the late-night TV shows, changing channels, and still looking for Johnny Carson. Milton didn't find the new late-night talk show hosts funny. Too much politics. Boring. "Poop" jokes were a lot funnier. He just kept looking for the Johnny Carson show, even though it had ended years ago. Too many channels! He would make a joke about that, too. He always had the comic's timing of making a joke about anything and everything. But tonight, the joke was going to be on him. There was no Johnny Carson show to watch, there was only a 10-year-old boy standing behind him with a gun pointed directly at his head.

Surprise! As he would sometimes exclaim after a joke. Or, sometimes add a funny gesture to a joke that needed some funny hand gestures, or face gestures, or whatever, to make it funnier. Surprise! This was not exactly a funny moment for Milton. But it was about to become one.

"I hope that's a prop gun kid, and I hope it shoots out a flag that says, 'BANG.' You don't want to wake up the living around here; they're mostly dead anyways," Milton blurted out, almost as if trying to be funny at a moment like this.

Always the consummate comedian. Always making fun of anything and everything.

There was no reply from Timmy. He stood there unwavering, pointing the gun directly at Milton.

Finally, Milton broke the silence.

"If you're looking for money, take my wallet. If my wife were alive, take her, too," Milton added half serious, half joking.

He did have a wife once. A pretty young thing. A foot taller than him. Sort of an odd-looking couple they were. But he always liked taller woman. He enjoyed slow dancing with them.

"She even had a matching set of big pillows for me to rest my head on," so he would joke.

"They were so fluffy, yet firm, that they lulled me to sleep, or at least my feet to sleep."

When he would use that in his comedy routine, he would walk, that is, waddle, bow legged, as if his legs were really asleep. Again, you had to see it, to see how funny it was.

But after 20 some years of a mostly unhappy marriage, she left him for an old high school boyfriend she found on the internet. Just packed up and left on a night while Milton was performing in some nickel-and-dime bar full of drunk patrons who loved his poop jokes. But her leaving was no laughing matter. He cried for days, had his first mini stroke, of many to come, and never used the internet, or a computer again the rest of his life. Not that he knew how anyway.

So, it was around midnight when Milton Schwartz found himself standing in his apartment in his plaid pajamas with a poop shoot, looking at a gun pointed at his head by a young boy he had never seen before. Or had he?

"Hey...I recognize you. You're that..." Milton slowly said out loud, as he had some trouble remembering exact details since his last stroke.

"You're that kid. Yeah. The one with the dog. Yeah, you're that kid. But what are you doing here? And how did you get in here? And why are you pointing a gun at me?"

There was no immediate response from Timmy. Milton just stood there and thought about the situation for a moment and decided that maybe he could take the gun away from the kid. After all, he was the adult, and this was a young kid, although you could hardly tell the difference because they were both about the same size. But still he was the adult, and this was just a kid. And maybe the gun wasn't a real gun, or if it was, maybe it wasn't loaded, or maybe he was afraid to really use it, after all he was just a kid, and he was the adult. A lot of maybes. Maybe right. Maybe wrong. So, Milton sprang into action and started to waddle toward him.

Timmy held the gun firmly and started to squeeze the trigger.

BANG-BANG – YOU'RE DEAD

CHAPTER 19

"THE WHEELS ON THE BUS GO ROUND AND ROUND" – ALL LIFE LONG.

Charley Harris was a crazy person. He really was crazy. Not bad crazy, but crazy crazy. At least that's what the other Sunny Side Up Retirement Home residents said about him, or whispered behind his back. They called him crazy because he was different from them. He made it clear to everyone that he didn't like living in the Sunny Side Up Retirement Home. He didn't like going to the little in-house breakfast café every morning where they would congregate as the sun came up. He didn't want to socialize with them about trivial matters they mumbled or grumbled about, or to reassure them, or count those who made it through the night, or who may not have.

Charley never sat in the grand entranceway at night with the other residents near the big piano next to the winding staircase to the 2nd floor. He didn't even know about the legendary Franklin Dixon who attempted the climb the stairs but ended up in a body bag instead. Nor did he care. He didn't watch TV, or read, or paint, or do puzzles, or do anything. And most of all, he didn't like women wearing any jewelry or big colorful tattoos, for whatever that's worth.

Charley Harris was a loner. He didn't go to any of the many activities the Sunny Side Up Retirement Home offered. He stayed to himself, and by himself. What made him most crazy to all the other crazies, who didn't admit they were crazy, too, was that he talked to himself. Not in a normal tone, but in a whispery tone. And this was very disturbing to many of the residents who mostly were deaf or going deaf, and it looked like his mouth was moving and nothing was coming out. But in a place like this, maybe that wasn't crazy. Maybe more like the norm, if there was such a thing here. There was a reason why, but to understand "that why" you first have to understand that it wasn't always this way. Charley actually came into this world with a baby cry that was so loud it woke up all the other babies in the hospital, and even scared the attending doctors and nurses. And as he grew and began to speak his first words, they were "loud." Like very loud. Now that's pretty crazy. Charley Harris was born with, and always had Vocal

Immodulation Syndrome, VIS. In other words, he talked loudly. He couldn't help it. He just did. It was a diagnosed illness. Not a well-known illness like cancer, god forbid, but one out of every "so many millions of people" have some sort of VIS. And when you have the Vocal Immodulation Syndrome, you talk loudly. And when he did, everyone nearby, or far away, could hear him. Everyone heard him. And if you didn't know his medical condition, if you can call it that, or even if you did know it, if you admitted that, Charley was still crazy. Just a "crazy old guy."

You can probably imagine how challenging it was growing up for Charley. Some kids shunned him, some kids loved him. Some thought he was cool. Some thought he was a fool. Didn't matter what everyone thought. It was what it was. In school, the teachers would refuse to call on him because his voiced answers were too loud and disrupted class. After school, he tried out for a variety of team sports, but mostly scared the other players and coaches with his excited voice, which was even louder. And, when it came to dating, the few women he did bed were shocked beyond their own orgasm with his loud moaning and sexual groaning. Remember the word loud. He was so loud during sex that it frightened his partner so much, they even orgasmed again. Not that that's a bad thing.

But no matter how he scared or turned off other people, Charley did eventually find love. She was a cute Mexican girl named Rosita, who came to America illegally, and worked in a local bowling alley giving out bowling shoes. Even though when he met her he was bowling by himself, and even though the noise of bowling balls smashing pins filled the air, and even though his loud voice giving her his shoe size was deafening to everyone near and far, it didn't matter to her. It was love at first sight. She was deaf. But she could read lips. On the night he held her in his arms and kissed her for the first time, he shouted out to the world that he really loved her, while she lip-read his words. He truly loved her for the 40 years they were married. Charley and Rosita made a perfect odd couple. What struck most people about them was that, when they argued, it was the strangest of sights. His angry voice raised the roof, and her angry fingers, doing her silent screaming back, went a mile a minute. But they always kissed and made up. They were happy, in love, and he was far from crazy.

Unfortunately, their fairy tale love story had a sad ending. It happened on a foggy and rainy night, when her 11-year-old, tan-colored, Volkswagen Beetle car, with an aging and somewhat wet car battery, stalled on the one and only town railroad crossing. What are the odds of something like that happening? Can't imagine. She never even heard the train coming, not that she could. Probably a good thing. She was most likely trying to restart that damn stalled engine when the train hit her broadside at a full 80 miles an hour. Wasn't a pretty sight, but it was a pretty quick death, so Charley hoped. And then he moped, and then he started drinking, even though he never really had much to drink before that night – that foggy, rainy night, seven blocks from the bowling alley where she worked, and another seven blocks from their home where they lived so happily. Lucky number 7.

So, the drinking began. He never quit, until his liver gave way, and the blood came out of his nose, ears, and pee-pee. Odd word, pee-pee, but his little lovely Mexican Rosita loved to call it that in her sign language, with her hand moving up and down like, well, you know what I mean.

So, once the liver went, the kidneys followed, and something happened with the rest of his internal body plumbing, and he ballooned up in just over a week or two, or maybe three (who's counting?) from a 70-year-old, 5-foot, 9-inch man weighing 165 pounds, to a 5-foot, 9-inch man weighing 365 pounds. Weirdest thing to see him then, and now. And as suddenly as all that happened, he just stopped talking. For five years. Not a single word. Nothing. From years of a deafening voice, to five years of saddening silence. He only nodded, or made a few futile hand gestures, as he never really understood the whole sign language thing.

Charley and Rosita were never blessed with any children. Could have been the homemade Mexican hot sauce (who knows for sure?), and now being alone, he had a whole lotta trouble taking care of himself. Fortunately, his one childhood friend, who had always remained a friend throughout his entire life, Bobby Toast, got him an apartment at the Sunny Side Up Retirement Home. And none too soon, as a week, or maybe two, or maybe three weeks after Charley moved in (no one was counting), Bobby didn't wake up one morning. Died in his sleep. And as fat and silent and sad Charley waited for him to come for his daily planned visit, he never did that day, or ever again. It was a very emotional time for

Charley. He was in no physical or emotional shape to attend his departed friend's small funeral, so all he could do was stay in his apartment and cry. Cry silently, at first. But then, after a whole lot of tears, and an open mouth of wailing nothing, Charley started to make sounds again, but this time, only in a whispering voice. Seems that everything he had experienced over the years, all the roller-coaster rides of happy and unhappy times throughout his life, just suddenly cured him of his Vocal Immodulation Syndrome. And at the same time, in a week, or maybe two, or most likely three, he lost all of his weight, and became a normal-looking 5-foot, 8-inch man. He did somehow lose an inch, don't know why, but he was right back at weighing 165 lbs. once again. Medically, there was no answer. Maybe a miracle. Crazy stuff, all of this. Didn't matter how, or why. It just happened, just like that. But it all made sense to everyone around him. All the residents just thought he "really was crazy." Especially with everything he had gone through. Especially because, with his low, whispering voice, he seemed to be talking to himself, which he was.

Being a loner, and having everyone think, or know, or believe he was crazy, Charley hated to go outside of the retirement home. Except this one time, earlier today, when he just got up and went on the weekly Wednesday afternoon retirement home planned bus trip to the nearby local mall. He sat by himself and stared out the window the whole trip. When the bus arrived at the mall, he stayed on the bus. And, when the driver came back to him and asked if he was going to leave the bus with everyone else, he didn't answer, or maybe he did, but it was just a whisper. He just sat there in his seat staring out the window. Charley sat and watched the eleven other retirement home residents being helped off the bus, and into their wheelchairs, or guided to their trustee walkers.

They slowly, but surely, in a strange single-file snake-like formation, left him behind to stare at them. There had to be something wrong with him. He just sat there, staring out the window, whispering to himself. He wouldn't leave the bus. He was crazy. Had to be crazy. He left his apartment, rode all the way to the mall, and now he wasn't leaving the bus. Yes, surely, they must have thought, he was crazy. But maybe, just maybe, he wasn't the crazy one. Maybe, just maybe, they were the crazy ones. Maybe he saw something, or knew something, but for some reason, whatever reason, he wasn't getting off the bus. It was that bus ride that changed everything for him, as it would for everyone else on that bus, that day.

CHAPTER 20

THE STRIPPER.

When one is born in a small town, grows up in a small town, works in a small town, never leaves the small town, lives their whole life in a small town, and grows old in the small town, the expectation is that they'll die in the small town. And that's exactly the story of Susan Deerwish, 88 years young, as she would say, dyed platinum blonde hair, as she hated gray (it made her look old), and a stunning beauty at this age, or any of the ages she had lived. Susan Deerwish was the one who made all of the men's heads turn, as slow, or as fast as they could at their age, especially now in the Sunny Side Up Retirement Home where she lived.

Susan had a lot of male friends here; every guy wanted to be her friend. Why not? She wasn't just hot to look at, she was hot through and through. And because of that, she also didn't have any female friends here.

Susan was a legend in the small town where she was born, and soon to be a legend in the small town she was destined to die. She really was a legend. Who, after all, could forget her from her working days as "Sexy Susie," the strip-tease queen, the stripper, with the big, really big, size 44 double D, plastic boobs? Yes, that was her. And now, in her golden years, with dyed platinum blonde hair, she was a legend in the fading memories of the men who lived in the Sunny Side Up Retirement Home. She was also a legend in her own mind, now living her remaining days unable to dance or prance, let alone walk, with severe arthritis, and confined to a wheelchair with a motorized battery. No more jiggle in her wiggle.

When Susan motored down the hallways of the Sunny Side Up Retirement Home, it wasn't the headlights on her wheelchair that caught everyone's attention, it was her other set of headlights. It was her large breasts. Her "cupcakes," as the old geezers, who still had somewhat of a stirring of desire somewhere in their loose undies, would refer to them as. Her cupcakes. In her younger days of bump and grind, actually she worked at night at "Winnie's Dollhouse" right off the expressway next to Route 69 (how appropriate). She was the one the guys from all over town and from the surrounding towns would come and see. Susan Deerwish, aka Sexy Susie, aka "Cupcakes," had the body of a burlesque queen goddess, long legs that led the eye up and down her curvaceous five-foot-ten figure, leaving the male onlookers dizzy from their imagined lusting.

Her "Hootchie-Koo" dance to the rock-and-roll song "Devil with a Blue Dress On" made the few or many men who attended her nightly shows whistling, shouting, and clapping for more. And it was a sight to behold when they placed dollar bills between her two cupcakes. During any given performance, she had so many dollars held tightly between those two stacks of plastic flesh, that she could even make change if the nightclub owner asked.

"Sexy Susie" – she'd take your breath away. That was then; alas, this is now. How sad life betrays us. The town's once "sexy goddess" was now confined to a dented and fairly worn wheelchair. Her once tight, beautiful, perfectly tanned skin that made men fools with their drool, now was like a changing seascape of sagging flesh. Gravity rules. Except for the two big-as-ever implants that still looked, and probably felt the same. Always invest in plastic; can't go wrong. She must have paid a lot of money for the amazing work that made them so picture perfect. Must have had an amazing warranty that came with them. So, here was "Sexy Susie" sitting alone in her wheelchair in her apartment, filled with so many glamour pictures of her in the bygone days of taking it all off, jiggling and wiggling, when Timmy silently entered.

CHAPTER 21

THE DANCE OF DEATH.

It must have been the waddling that made the bullet miss its intended mark. Timmy was a marksman, make that "marksboy," but he was only 10 years old, and he never shot at a waddling, charging comedian before, just stationary targets. The bullet did graze Milton's head and left a stinging cut across his cheek and through his right ear. It even took part of his ear off. The bullet then hit the poster on the wall behind them. It was an advertising poster for one of Milton's long-ago nightclub comedy shows. Even had his smiling face on it, as he held a prop gun in his hand pointing at his head. What made it funny was that a white flag had come out of the gun with the word "BANG" on it. It was a funny picture, on a funny-looking poster. To make all of this even funnier, the live bullet that grazed Milton's real head, actually lodged itself into Milton's pictured head on the poster. Bullseye!

Whether it was the unexpected charging of the old, waddling man before him, or the fact that maybe, just maybe, Timmy really was going to shoot Milton again, the scene played out in a comical manner. Sort of.

Charging straight at Timmy, Milton tripped over his own waddling feet, and fell forward as Timmy pulled the trigger a second time. This time the bullet actually parted Milton's few remaining hairs on the top of his balding head. However, the intended second shot did find another target, striking the Milton poster again, right between the eyes. Bullseye again!

As Milton fell, his outstretched hands struck Timmy's hand, knocking the gun from it. Milton proceeded to fall onto Timmy's legs, and this resulted in Timmy falling backwards onto the floor as well. So there they both were, sprawled inches apart on the floor, dazed and somewhat comically confused, looking at each other. The unexpected then became more unexpected, as Milton struggled to get up, and again fell forward right on top of Timmy. Milton seemed to have a momentary advantage, as he was atop the younger boy, but only momentarily. Timmy, having more of a youthful quickness to him, pulled one of his hands away from Milton's grasp, and quickly punched the older man in the face where the first bullet had grazed and cut him.

"Owww! Shit," Milton responded, as he struggled to get the kid's hand back down on the ground using the advantage of his weight.

Even though Milton weighed more than the young boy beneath him, he had lost a lot of strength as good ol' Father Time took it from him over the passing years. Timmy pushed Milton's hands upwards, trying to break Milton's grip. Both the boy's hands and the older man's hands were locked together, pushing up, pushing down. Suddenly, one of Milton's wrists snapped. It was a sickening sound, accompanied by another sound.

"Oh, shit!" Milton screamed, as he let Timmy's hand loose from his now broken wrist.

With this sudden turn of events, Timmy used his weight and free hand to turn Milton over onto his back as he rolled atop the older man. But Milton's arms were longer than Timmy's, and his one free hand grasped Timmy's neck. Timmy reacted quickly and tried to punch Milton again. He couldn't reach Milton's face, but he could punch him in the one arm holding his neck. Milton used all his strength to tighten his fingers around Timmy's throat. Timmy stopped his futile punching and put both hands on Milton's arm to dislodge his stranglehold. As Timmy straddled Milton and started to take the old man's hand off his throat, Milton bucked his knees upwards, hitting Timmy fully, and painfully, in his back.

Timmy lost his grip on Milton's one hand.

Milton resumed the squeezing of his fingers into Timmy's neck. Timmy pulled his head backwards to try to loosen Milton's hand, but the older man's grip only grew tighter. Timmy began to experience a loss of breath, and his eyes began to swell with water, and perhaps fear. Fear for the first time, in a long time. Again, Timmy swung at Milton's one arm and hit it as hard as hard can be.

"Owww!" Milton cried out, but continued his death-like vise grip on Timmy's throat.

The struggle between young and old was turning into a struggle between survival and death. Milton's fingers dug deeper into the young boy's throat, and trickles of blood came from within his skin.

Timmy tried to force his head downward in another attempt to break the old man's grip but couldn't. He was losing his breath, he was losing the struggle, and his hands were losing their power and grip on Milton's one arm, and one hand was tiring. Milton closed his eyes, drew all his remaining strength, and forced it upwards, tighter into his chokehold. It wouldn't be much longer, he could feel the boy's struggle to fight back weakening. With no air to breath, the boy would surely collapse unconscious, or even die within another moment or two. But a moment or two was too long for what happened next.

Timmy shifted his weight atop Milton on the floor, shifted it just enough to bring his one knee up, and then quickly downward into Milton's unprotected groin. The pain was horrific as his testicles were smashed into the floor from the boy's knee, which continued to crush them further with all his weight.

Milton lost his grip on the boy's throat. He let out a yell that sounded like it came from the bowels of hell itself.

"Ahhhhhhhh!" he yelled in a pain-filled, distorted voice.

But the scream was short lived as Timmy slammed his forehead straight down into Milton's face. "Crack!" Timmy heard the sound of bones breaking, as Milton's nose took the full force of Timmy's forehead. Blood shot out of both Milton's nose, or what was once a nose, and from his mouth, which also sustained some broken teeth from the sudden impact. Timmy shifted weight off of the old man's broken balls, and lifted his right arm to throw another punch into the screaming man's bleeding face.

But Milton wasn't done yet. Or maybe he was, but his body wasn't. Somehow the remaining strength, courage, will, or whatever you want to call it, was summoned throughout his bleeding and battered body and Milton turned his body suddenly to the left. Just enough to have Timmy fall off him, tumbling onto the blood-splattered rug.

The gun.

Milton eyed the gun.

The gun.

Timmy eyed the gun.

They both reached for it. They both wanted it. They both needed it. The gun would end the struggle. The gun would kill one of them. The gun was the only way to finish this seemingly dance of death between an old comedian and a young killer.

The gun.

They both grasped it together. The young hand first; the old hand second. But the old hand was atop the young hand, and another struggle began. Their bodies pulled closed together. They were both on their knees. Timmy used his other hand to reach atop the old man's hand. It was like the game of putting your hands on a baseball bat from the bottom up to reach the top. Milton was losing his strength now. He was the older warrior, but the more exhausted warrior. The younger warrior was winning and would soon control the gun. And the old, bleeding warrior would soon lose. He would lose his grip. He would lose the fight, and he would be shot. And he would die.

But there was one last chance to win. One possible chance. He spit a mouthful of blood directly at Timmy's face, surprising the young boy enough so that he didn't see Milton swing his arm with the broken wrist. It hit him full in the side of his face. Timmy lost his grip, let go of the gun, and stared at the distorted, bruised, and bleeding face of a badly beaten man who now held the gun.

There was a pause.

An awkward pause.

A seemingly endless pause.

They both stood up and silently stared at each other, breathless, and waiting.

The gun was held tightly in Milton's bloody and shaking hand, pointing directly at Timmy.

Milton the comedian, Uncle Miltie, as the other residents would playfully call him, spit out a broken tooth and smiled.

"Looks like I get the last laugh, kid," Milton stared directly at 10-year-old Timmy and slowly squeezed the trigger.

The bullet missed.

What? The bullet missed Timmy? Timmy, who was no more than four feet away from the pointed gun. Timmy, who had just stood there, not bobbing and weaving like a boxer, slipping punches from his opponent, just stood there like a practice target in a shooting range.

The bullet had missed.

Are you kidding? No, this wasn't a joke, or even a funny moment. Maybe a tragic moment, as things still had to play out.

The bullet had missed Timmy at close range.

How could this possibly happen? It just did. Think about it. An 87-year-old man is holding a real gun for the first time in his life. He is not at all familiar with the gun, nor has ever fired one in his entire life. Maybe, as a young boy, he played cops and robbers, or maybe cowboys and Indians. But those were either toy guns, or just fingers on a child's small fist making the shape of a gun and shooting pretend bullets. Milton did hold a prop gun once in a promo picture for his nightclub act. He pointed the gun at himself making a goofy face as the prop gun and a white flag stuck out the barrel with a word on a white flag that said, "BANG." He had made such a funny face, and the whole picture was so funny, that it became a popular poster to steal from the clubs where he performed.

Milton was never in the armed services, never went to carnivals or state fairs, or amusement parks, and never shot BB rifles at moving metal ducks to win a prize. He did tell duck jokes. No, he never had held or fired a real gun in his life. Until now. Let's add to all of this that he was an exhausted, bloody, and beaten old man, who may have sustained a concussion or even brain damage from the hits he took to the head. And let's add "to this, and to this," that his vision at this age wasn't a perfect 20-20 anymore. He wasn't sure what his vision was, as he hadn't been to the eye doctor in years. He could still see the shape of a pretty girl, and he would always make up a joke about his waning vision to others, while thinking about his bygone youth to himself.

And, yes, of course, he did have a broken wrist on one hand, but the gun was held in the other hand. However, he was at the height of an emotional situation, and his nerves, let alone his blood pressure, must have been going in overdrive, if ever there was such a human-based explanation of a moment like this. And, of course, the hand that held the gun was shaking from all the excitement of the life-and-death struggle that he had just gone through.

Finally, of course, he didn't look down the sights of the gun and take aim. No, add it all up, and of course, the odds of hitting the young boy, who stood a mere four feet away from him weren't exactly the best betting odds one would wager on. So, he missed.

But he did hit the target – his poster on the wall behind Timmy, the poster of him holding the prop gun pointed at his head with the white flag with the word, "BANG," and a very funny expression on his face. The poster that already had a bullet or two in it from the early moments of the struggle between them. Now this was funny. A comedian shoots himself. Shoots his picture on a poster of him shooting himself with a prop gun with the word,

"BANG." Think about it, this was really funny. Especially since the bullet meant for Timmy went right smack dab into the face of the funny face Milton made on the poster. If there was a time to just have a beer and step back and think about it, Milton probably would have laughed at this. But even though he was a comedian, and he really was a funny man, this was not a joking matter. It was only a matter of time before someone would really die. And the odds now shifted back to Milton.

His body trembling, Milton lowered the gun to his side. You would think, with all the noise they had made from their fight and the gunshots fired, that the neighbors in the adjoining apartments would have heard this commotion. But they didn't. Most of them had shut down their hearing devices long ago after a nightly routine of eating an early supper in the Sunny Side Up Retirement Home dining room. Most were in a deep sleep somewhere between the remaining life they had in them, and the impending death that would catch up to them one way or another. If not tonight, then another day. In other words, they couldn't, or wouldn't be bothered by any noise. Especially muffled gun shots and strange yelling.

Milton remained there in a state of shock, bewilderment, and not knowing what to do next. In his mixed-up mind, the only thought he had was, *"Don't tell a joke, Milton."*

While Milton stood swaying on his legs, exhausted, trying to catch his breath, trying to make sense of all of this which made no sense to him, Timmy reached behind his back and underneath his jacket. It was still there, in the leather sheath that he used to carry it in when he went hunting with his dad. Yes, there still was some blood on it from having been used earlier. But now, there was about to be even more blood on it.

In one swooping move (ahh, to be young and fast again), Timmy pulled out the 7-inch, shiny, and very sharp hunting knife that he had stabbed Miles with earlier. Timmy stepped quickly towards the still-shaking Milton and lunged the knife suddenly and deeply into Milton's panting stomach. In and out, as quickly and silently and deadly as that.

And when the knife was pulled out of his belly, Milton stopped shaking, just for a moment. He looked down at his stomach, which had just experienced a sharp and painful knife going in and out of it, and stared in shock at the gaping hole in his belly.

How much more shock, pain, and hurt can this old guy take? Timmy wondered. Or maybe he didn't wonder at all. Or maybe Milton wondered, or maybe he didn't wonder at all. Who knows what a killer really wonders, or thinks about at the exact moment he, or she, plunges a sharp 7-inch steel knife into some old geezer's gut?

"Ohhh, shit," Milton said matter of factly, as he clutched his stomach wound with one good hand and with the bad hand with a broken wrist.

"Ohhh, shit," he said again, as his eyes widened even wider, in the terror and horror of this tragic moment.

And then his blood squirted. It really did, straight out of his belly and onto the carpet below. Here we go again. Another newly installed carpet in the Sunny Side Up Retirement Home ruined by a lot, and I mean a lot, of blood. Amazing how much blood old people still have in them!

Timmy stood silently watching Milton bleed. He showed no expression, no compassion, no nothing, to the confused, badly beaten, now badly cut, and soon-to-be-dead comedian.

But there's more to this situation than you would think. There was still some "fight" left in this old warrior. You never know how much fight one still has until one actually fights for his life.

Unexpectedly, Milton waddled forward towards Timmy. Not that he would be able to do much harm to the boy as he was bleeding more and more with each waddle. Milton moved towards him maybe out of a final reaction of anger, fear, or just out of a lack of anything else his dying body could do.

Milton reached out with his good hand to maybe strike the boy, or hold the boy, or maybe hug the boy. It didn't matter. As Milton came as close as close can be to Timmy, the young boy quickly thrust his hunting knife directly into Milton's balls. His smashed, scrambled, squished balls from the knee, or knees, he took earlier in the fight. And the knife cut into them, and cut them, into smaller balls. Not that they were that big to begin with.

"Ohhhh, fuck!" he exclaimed, as Timmy held the knife deep into Milton's shredded testicles, and twisted it back and forth, like turning a screw with a screwdriver.

"Ohhh, FUCK!" Milton shouted, with blood spitting out of his mouth from the broken teeth that remained, combined with the blood from the broken nose that still dribbled down his chin.

Timmy finally and mercifully pulled the sharp knife out of Milton's testicles.

Milton's legs gave way, and he sank to the floor, landing upright on his bony bloody knees. A few of his knee bones were heard breaking and snapping. But he was still upright, clutching his stomach and groin.

He stared at the young boy who still held the knife in his hand. His blood dripped off the not so shiny blade.

"Why?" he asked, trying to overcome the pain, the ungodly amount of pain, with some sort of realization of what the fuck was going on.

"Whyyyy?" he repeated, in a pleading, dying moan.

And then, with all the pain, all the shock, all the drama, all the horror of this horrific predicament he was in, he suddenly knew why.

"It's all about the…"

And before Milton could finish his sentence – before Milton could come to terms with the reason of why, and answer his own question, Timmy slashed the knife across the comedian's throat, leaving a perfect cut from right to left. And the blood quickly came out, in gasping spurts. Milton could no longer speak, let alone finish his sentence, let alone answer his own question. Didn't need an answer from this young boy with the bloody knife. Nope. He knew. His eyes knew. His beaten, bleeding body knew. They both knew. And then he fell dead, his exhausted, battered, old, and worn body slumping sideways and rolling onto his back.

Milton's dead eyes and bloody face looked upward, as if to get one more laugh from an audience of angels staring down at him. Or at least a ripple of applause. This had been truly, without a doubt, one of his most remarkable, almost comic, performances ever. But this ending wasn't funny. Nor meant to be funny. Although it was sort of a sick funny, the way everything had played out.

Uncle Miltie, the resident funny man of the Sunny Side Up Retirement Home was dead. But if there was any humor in this, it was the way he lay in his own pool of blood, all twisted up, pretzel-like, as the eventual rigor mortis set in.

With fish-like open eyes staring upwards, but not at the pearly gates above, maybe he would have liked to imagine that he was staring at a final adoring audience in a nightclub called "life," where he had just performed his final act. But there was no audience staring back, there was something else dead Milton was staring at, and it was staring back at him – the poster on the wall. The poster of him with the prop gun and the white flag with the word, "BANG," making a funny face, and now with three bullet holes in it. Bullseye.

The final curtain should have come down on the scene right here and then, but no, there was more to it. As if taking an extra bow if he could have, his dead body twitched. "Once, twice, three times a lady," as the expression goes. Timmy watched this. Not in amusement, or in some form of curiosity. He had killed several people already, so this was nothing new. It just sort of happened. And with the last twitch, Timmy did something different. Something he had not done to any of the others he had killed that night. Timmy got down on his knees next to Milton's dead body, and for a moment, it looked like he was going to pray, as he put his two hands together, in front of him. But it wasn't going to be a prayer. The young boy's hands still held the sharp, bloody, hunting knife, which he lifted high above his own head, and then plunged deeply into the dead man's chest. Not once, not twice, not "three times a lady," as the expression goes, but eight, nine, ten times. And then another ten, and then another ten. Fifty, sixty times. In out, in out, in out. And like a garden hose with a lot of little cuts in it, Milton's body sprung a whole bunch of tiny leaks with little squirts of the last remaining blood he had left in him.

As suddenly as he started the stabbing, Timmy stopped.

There was no more blood pouring from any of the many stab wounds. To say the least, this was "not a pretty picture" like the pretty landscapes that adorned dearly departed Dorothy Paine's blood-stained apartment. No, this was not a pretty picture like the photo of the Grand Canyon in now 25-minutes-and-counting dead DeeDee's apartment next door. In reality, if there was such a thing for Timmy, in his reality, you could say there was never any intent that Timmy's killing would be a pretty picture. Unless you wanted to say, he had just painted in blood what "Hell" actually looks like!

With knife in hand, Timmy remained kneeling over the body of Milton. Even a 10-year-old youthful boy can become exhausted when playing too much, or killing too much. Timmy's heavy breathing from all the stabbing he just done on the old man's dead and mutilated body slowed and became more normal. He stared at what was left of Milton. It wasn't much.

Without any indication of what was going on in his mind, Timmy started to cry. Really cry. The tears flowed heavily down his blood-splattered face. He gasped for air with the breaths he tried to take. The crying sound he made was just like the sound you would expect to hear from a 10-year-old child, a 10-year-old boy, a 10-year-old killer, who had fought for his life against an adult eight times his age – combined emotional sounds of rage, remorse, pity, confusion, and maybe sprinkled with a little bit of happiness somewhere in between. A quirky type of happiness to have done what he did, because he had to do what needed to be done. Another piece of the puzzle completed? Perhaps. Or perhaps, this most unusual, and maybe unexpected, horrific night of "a life-and-death game" was nearing an end.

Certainly, the end for his dead victim covered in blood before him, and most certainly for all the previous victims he had left behind throughout his killings that night. A lot of killings. Yet, the night was far from over, especially for the "soon to be dead" victims that were still to come.

As he knelt over Milton, he thought of his dead brother, who was his first killing. His first victim. His playmate, his best friend, his brother. Timmy's tears flowed even more. The crying turned into mumbled sounds, then identifiable words. And the words became a song. Timmy started to sing to himself, and to the dead man who lay before him. Words mixed with tears, sniffles, and gasps for air. *"You are my sunshine, my only sunshine. You make me happy, when skies are gray."*

The song his mother used to sing to him. The song that Domingo sang to him.

"You'll never know, dear, how much I love you."

And then, Timmy started to stab the dead body of Milton again. And again, and again, and again. "Once, twice, three times a lady" as the old expression goes. You know it by now. Twenty, thirty more times, if not more.

"Please don't take my sunshine away."

Timmy's singing and crying, and every emotion he showed, or still had hidden within him, abruptly stopped. And so did the merciless stabbing and butchering he so casually and intensely performed.

If you were a casual observer to all of this, you might begin to question the sanity, or logic of what just played out. You might ask yourself, *"What form of madness dwells within our souls? What limits can one endure during an emotional and traumatic breakdown? What is the fine line that separates good from evil? Or are they both one and the same? What makes our mind tick and drives our body to snap?"* Every breath we take is like a grain of sand disappearing in an hour glass. Each moment we live exists only in the time we use. We have so much time; so little time. What is time? It is measured by the hands on a clock ticking away the moments of one's life. We can't stop the moment. We can't stop time. All we can do is stand and watch it, try to embrace it, try to hold it from passing us by. Time leaves memories of happiness and sadness, with a lot of unknowns in between. Time never stops ticking; it continues until there is no more left. Time is the underlying madness, which makes one kill.

In the dim lighting surrounding the silence of the room, there was no resemblance left of Milton in the totally disfigured dead body on the apartment floor, just bloody slabs of swollen and mutilated flesh in a pair of red-stained plaid pajamas with a poop shoot.

Timmy stood up and stared at his work of killing art. He wiped his blood-dripping knife on his pant leg, and then put it back into the sheath strapped to the back of his belt. He paused for a moment, another moment of time that would be gone forever. He reached into his pocket and pulled out a folded piece of paper. Opening it, he scanned down a list of names. Milton Schwartz's name was on it, beneath the names of several residents that Timmy met and killed earlier. He took out a small pencil that looked like it had seen better days. It even had a few teeth marks on it. He drew a line through Milton's name and refolded the piece of paper, putting it back into his pocket, along with the pencil.

Timmy scanned the room, looking for something, and found what he was looking for. The advertising poster of Milton on the wall with the three bullet holes in it. He stepped over Milton's body, and walked to where it was hung. Timmy looked at it. Studied it. Thought about it. He then ripped it off the wall, holding it in his hand. Timmy immediately walked back over to where Milton lay. He bent over the dead man, and placed the poster on his chest, gently, almost like someone placing a beautiful rose on a coffin. Except this was not a rose, and there was no coffin for the mound of chopped human meat that the picture was placed on. And if this whole living nightmare of unimaginable death had another part to be added, it did. Timmy unzipped his pants, pulled out his "manhood," (let's call it "boyhood," after all, he was a 10-year-old boy) and started to pee. Maybe he didn't have the time to make it to the bathroom. Maybe it was just a urinary problem that surfaced itself unexpectedly. Or maybe it was what he wanted to do, what he needed to do, to put an exclamation to this craziness. Just like some bad-ass gangsters once peed on the broken body of Casper Cosmo Merlinski. Isn't this what bad-ass killers are supposed to do? An exclamation "point" to their craziness.

Timmy peed all over Milton, and all over the torn and now bloodied poster of Milton. He stood there and peed till he was finished. It was a long pee. With two shakes, and a quick tuck, Timmy zipped up, and started to walk away.

He picked up his gun on the floor, emptied the magazine in the handle, and reloaded another full magazine in it. He then looked back at what was left of his killing art.

He pointed his gun, pulled the trigger, and fired another shot into Milton's unrecognizable head. Bullseye.

CHAPTER 22

MAKE YOURSELF COMFORTABLE.

When Timmy entered Susan Deerwish's apartment with the same security key he had been using all night, he was covered in a lot of blood from the scene that had just played out in Uncle Miltie's apartment next door. To the casual observer, one might be startled by the blood, but unfortunately, or fortunately, for Susan, besides losing her beauty battle to Father Time, she was also losing her sight. For the past few years she had been experiencing debilitating macular degeneration. In layman's terms, she was going blind. In one sense, it was a blessing, as she didn't have to watch her skin sag further every day; but as a curse, it had left her bumping into walls as she wandered her apartment, or into the walls throughout the Sunny Side Up Retirement Home hallway on the way to breakfast, lunch, or dinner. Thank god for her big breasts. They cushioned the blows. But now in a wheelchair, Susan no longer had bruised breasts, she had bruised shins.

Timmy closed her apartment door. He stood quietly looking at her. She stared back, as if almost expecting a visitor at this late hour.

"Miles, is that you?" she asked in a sweet voice – an almost sexy voice, hoping it was, of course, him and hoping for another what she would refer to as "an erotic midnight ride in the wheelchair."

Yes, 88-year-old Susan Deerwish was still sexually active in her golden years. She had always loved sex, from the first time she experienced it with Billy Keegan, the neighboring 14-year-old boy whose bedroom window looked directly into hers. She was coming of age as she turned 13 and had already lost interest in playing with dolls. Her young mind was fantasizing about playing with other things. Because the houses were so close to each other, she could sneak a peek into Billy's bedroom window and watch him undress at night before bedtime. And, of course, watch him touch his "thingy," as most young girls first call it. She would watch him use his fingers and hand almost as if playing a musical instrument while he looked at some "girly magazines" he must have borrowed from underneath his daddy's bed, which is where most fathers keep those type of magazines. As she watched him, it was only natural that a curious young girl like herself would explore her own budding body as most teenagers do. Since girls were known to mature sooner than boys, she was already on the "fast track" with an abundance of overdeveloping youthful sexual energy. Adding to her overdevelopment, her boobies, as most young girls referred to them, were much larger than any of her girlfriends' smaller-sized boobies. They were already "more than a mouthful." Watching Billy "beat his meat," Susan "squeezed her melons."

Being masturbating neighbors, it was only a matter of time before they eventually got together, and the beating and squeezing led to moaning and groaning, huffing and puffing, sweating and squirting. And...almost a baby.

Her period came late.

They learned their lesson, and after a short "we-almost-had-a-baby" break in the playing doctor scenario, they resumed their youthful, sexual, playful passions. Until they finally got caught.

All kids do naughty things. It is expected as a part of growing up. Some steal candy from the corner convenience store. Some steal money from their mother's purse. Some take a little swig of whatever it is in their parents' unlocked liquor cabinet. Some even look at their daddy's dirty magazines hidden in plain sight under daddy's bed. *Doesn't mom know?*

But what they did was really naughty, considering she had just turned 14, and he was just 15. Ahh, to be young and stupid again. They got caught, buck naked, in the back of Mr. Keegan's car, parked in his garage on a warm summer night. Two young, wrinkle-free bodies, shifting their own sexual gears as their speeding sex-driven climax approached. Susan's bare feet pointed upwards, touching the interior roof of the car, leaving an outline of her footprints above, while her sweaty, big, bouncing buttocks slid all over the plastic seat beneath her, while Billy drove "it" home. You'd think he was a race car driver with all his moves. And just as the two young bodies were about to cross the orgasm finish line, the swaying car called attention to itself when Mrs. Keegan went in the garage unexpectedly to take out the garbage. What an eyeful and earful she saw and heard. Naughty, naughty.

As one would expect, the repercussions of that "night to remember" was that Susan and Billy were forbidden to see each other again.

As for the exiled Susie, her unabashed and over-awakened sexuality was put on hold. Susan was sent to live with her overweight, undersexed, Bible-reading-and-thumping Aunt Florence in another city downstate. To make it even worse, Susan was enrolled in an all-girls Catholic school. No boys there for her insatiable sexual appetite.

As for bad boy Billy, he was put in nightly lockdown under his mother's strict house rules and couldn't leave his home other than to go to and from school. But Billy did become, and still is, the town's urban sexual-legend hero. All his pre-adolescent guy friends idolized him and fantasized about Billy's "hands-on and thingy-in" experiences with naughty, naughty Susan Deerwish. Oh, and if you wonder how a horny boy like Billy got over Susan's departure, thank goodness for his dad's under-the-bed girly magazines.

Susan eventually graduated from the all-girls Catholic school. She was voted the dubious Catholic label of "most likely to keep her legs closed." Susan moved back to her home town and at the ripe young age of 18 became a stripper in the only adult strip joint in town. Makes sense, doesn't it?

Billy flunked out of school, joined the army, was sent to Nam and had his legs blown off in a rice field turned mine field. Both legs completely gone, but his thingy was intact. Such a miracle! Got a hero's welcome when he came home. God Bless America! Unfortunately, there wasn't a whole lot of prosthetics back then. In the 4th of July Parade down the middle of Main Street, he sat in a little wooden cart on a red, white, and blue fluffy pillow, waving a miniature American flag while being pulled haphazardly by two local, bored, pimply-faced boy scouts.

Expectedly, Billy and Susan's paths were destined to cross again – not at the parade, but after the parade, when some of Billy's friends brought his remaining upper torso, with his still-attached thingy, into the nightclub where Susan, now named "Sexy Susie" was performing her nightly bump-and-grind show. There she was, all grown up; a stunning 22-year-old big-boobed blonde-bombshell stripper with a handful of customer dollar bills tucked between those even bigger bodacious, ripe-looking melons.

After her set (and what a set she had!), she came down from the neon-lit wooden dance stage and gave Billy a big hug filled with fond memories of the amorous adventures they once shared. Sexy Susie, with a little bit too much alcohol or drugs in her system, unfortunately failed to notice there was only half a Billy there that night. After a quick jiggle and wiggle, she attempted to climb atop him to do her trademarked exotic lap dance. With a wink and a tongue-licking smile, Susie put one of her long naked legs over his head and tried to climb aboard. Sadly, it was an awkward moment that the surrounding drunk patrons never forgot, nor did Susie or Billy. There wasn't much of a lap left to wiggle and giggle on, so she quickly slid off and onto the floor where she promptly hit her head and knocked herself completely out. Not knowing what to do, and thinking maybe she was dead, Billy's friends picked him up and carried him out after stuffing a few dollar bills between her exposed big and beautiful breasts. Even sprawled unconscious on the drink-spilled strip-club floor, it was still a good night for her with the extra "tittie tips."

They never saw each other again. Rumor has it that Billy joined a circus sideshow and changed his name to Matt. Sexy Susie kept on bumping and grinding for the next ten years until she threw her hips out and needed surgery. Her parents passed, and she moved back downstate to live with Aunt Florence, who now claimed to have a direct religious line to Jesus. Susie became a Jehovah Witness and sang in the choir. With her still glowing looks, she was trained to perform her spiritual duty and go door-to-door, giving out religious pamphlets. What guy wouldn't open his front door to get an eyeful or earful of her? But she missed the sex, and eventually took the holier-than-thou pamphlets into many a man's inviting bedroom. Here she would discuss the evils in the surrounding world, while offering up her continually getting bigger melons as an example of her new-found religious goodness.

So it was that, one night, while Susie was out late on pamphlet delivery, Aunt Florence fell asleep in bed while reading the Bible, talking to Jesus, and smoking a cigarette. She set her flannel nightgown on fire, ran screaming from her bedroom into the darkened hallway, tumbled down the unlit stairs, breaking most every bone in her overweight body, and landed sitting on her large and flabby rump against the front door to the house. Burned to death, rump roast and all. Also burnt the house totally down. Having mistaken this, or taken this as a sign from Jehovah, Jesus, or the Big Guy upstairs, and with no place to go, Sexy Susie made a triumphant return to her hometown. She lived at the local YWCA and resumed her former dancing career. Susie still looked good for a 50-year-old woman, but gravity was beginning to take its toll on her at this age, and also on her now over-ripened melons. Rumor has it that she did some porn, wrote children's books under an alias name, and eventually married a used-car salesman, Big Jim Blowonsky, who only had sex with her while in the backseat of one of his demo cars parked in their single-car garage. Kind of kinky, or, maybe, just maybe, what goes around, comes around.

With a lot of mileage on his aging body, one warm afternoon, Big Jim unexpectedly died of a heart attack in the back seat of a 2001 demo Ford Taurus, fully loaded and with only 69,000 miles on it. Strangely, it had nothing to do with his kinky sexual appetite. It happened while at work, showing the car to a young couple during a test ride. Good and bad news for Jim – he did make the sale, but never saw the commission.

Years continued to pass. Susie got old and the few remaining dollars Big Jim had left behind were spent on all sorts of useless and expensive lotions and potions trying to save her sagging skin. Without any family to take care of her and with losing her mobility and capabilities to take care of her now lonely home, there was only one place to go with the rest of her few dollars. She came to be a resident of the Sunny Side Up Retirement Home.

Susie, or Susan, as she now referred to herself in this final act in her life, made a few friends, and kept mostly to herself. But she did make one special friend and looked forward to his once-a-week nightly visit. And it was just about the time tonight when that weekly visit was scheduled on her wall calendar that hung crooked, held up by the small, purple-colored magnets on her fridge. A calendar that her failing eyesight could no longer read, but hung there just in case her eyesight ever came back.

Here she was, decked out in her sexiest red bra and panties, with a few remaining fake rhinestones glued on it. It was the same outfit she wore on many a night in the local, now long-gone and closed strip club she performed in. Standing statuesque in her high red heels, she had her overly dyed blonde hair teased just like she had worn the day she first watched Billy, her next-door neighbor, through her bedroom window. A long, long, time ago. Now here she was, at age 88, nearly blind as a bat, and with big, but still bodacious, plastic breasts overflowing the faded and old, red bra. She was warming up her engines and getting ready and willing to perform her private one-woman, once-a-week striptease to that handsome security guard with the one eye patch and the one big thingy. Miles Patchwork. After all, chocolate was her favorite ice cream.

When the apartment door opened, and Miles was expected (although he was already deader than a doornail), instead stood a young boy, splattered in a mixture of other Sunny Side Up Retirement Home residents' blood. Mixed with the dim lighting of the candle-lit living room, he stood silently holding his gun, and looking curiously at Susan Deerwish as she moved her surgically repaired hips to and fro. From where she swayed, all she saw was a shadowy figure in her apartment doorway that she presumed was Miles.

"Sooooo...what are you waiting for, big boy? Let the party begin," she moaned in her Sexy Susie stage voice that had once turned on so many, many men.

But tonight's performance was to be cut short. The party began and ended quickly. Timmy lifted his gun, pointed, and shot her in the head. Just like so many of the others he had killed before.

CHAPTER 23

ALL THE PIECES OF THE PUZZLE.

Typically, it takes twenty-two minutes via shuttle bus to drive from the Sunny Side Up Retirement Home to the Twin Oaks Mall. It's an easy drive with half of the twenty-two minutes on the Glen Eden Parkway, which exits right there at the center entrance of the two-story brick-and-mortar sprawling mall. The first part of the trip is simple – as the shuttle bus leaves the retirement home main entranceway, it turns left onto Cooper Road, goes two stop lights to the main intersection of Long Pond Road and Greenleaf where King Burger is on one side and a 24-hour convenience store is on the other side. There the bus turns right, going past the Capone Bakery, where it sometimes stops for freshly made jumbo whopper cinnamon-glazed-with-sprinkles donuts. The residents love them. Then the bus takes the left fork in the road at Clinton Avenue and continues straight ahead till the Glen Eden Parkway North. Twenty-two minutes, plus the donut stop if need be. Or, on a rainy day, maybe twenty-four minutes, and on a snowy day maybe thirty minutes. It all depended on the weather. But today it depended on the accident. The first of two.

As the Sunny Side Up Shuttle prepared to leave the mall for its return trip back, Marvin Fox, the part-time, not-on-staff bus driver checked the passenger list. Eleven came back, some slower than others (*"Damn walker and wheelchair parade."*) plus one who never left the bus. They had to be back at the retirement home by 4 p.m. as mealtime was always on schedule from 4:30 to 6 p.m. The residents on this trip had a hungry appetite and didn't want to be late and maybe miss out on the limited special dessert, which was only available until it ran out. And today, they all wanted that dessert, 'cause Capone's Bakery with those jumbo whopper cinnamon-glazed-with-sprinkles donuts was closed for remodeling.

"How could they!" grumbled some of the passengers, while others gave a look of disdain as they passed by it earlier.

But of course, they did, and, of course, it was.

So, as Marvin Fox prepared to check off the passenger names, he did he his famous dance, his "come-on, let's-get-going dance." Marvin was an impatient man. He didn't like this part-time, bus-driving oldies gig, but he did it because it helped pay for his nasty habit. He was a "coke head." And yes, he also drank Coca-Cola®. At age 59, he had gotten hooked on some pain killers after an accident that might have been avoided if he had paid attention when returning from an airport drop-off. He forgot there was a curb, stepped into mid-air, and went "wham-bam, thank you, ma'am," landing flat on his face on the warm summer-baked concrete. It left quite an impression in his face. Also broke his nose. Needed 23 stitches on his balding forehead. After a botched stitching job by the local town surgeon, who must have been drinking that night when he was called into the hospital for this emergency, poor Marvin's newly remodeled features resembled the stitched-up face of the famous monster Frankenstein. Really did.

Marvin took the usual after-surgery pain killers but took one too many pills one night while greeting trick-or-treaters at his front door. They thought he had a mask on. Some kids pointed and giggled, and some were downright scared and screamed. It was just his "Frankenstein-like" stitched face. Higher than a kite, he looked in the mirror later that night and almost screamed himself at what he saw staring back at him. It was only natural that he took the rest of the pain killers. Marvin was found buck naked the following morning on his front lawn with a hand full of candy in his clenched fist and was hospitalized for an overdose. As luck would have it, when he was finally detoxed enough and cleared to go home, he tripped over a plastic bed pan that had fallen off his bed, fell face forward and...12 more stitches were added on his already over-stitched face. And of course, more pain killers. He had lots of time off from work, and even took a few sips from his nearly empty bourbon bottle that he kept on his kitchen table next to all his meds. Good thing he had the President's signature health insurance.

Marvin was recently employed by the city school district as a bus driver. It was all he could get, after being found guilty of embezzlement in the financial firm he had worked in for over 20 years. After a not-so-nice vacation of two years in a nearby prison, he was released back into the real world. He only knew how to do illegal financial transactions, and how to make license plates. It was only natural that he became a city school bus driver.

The school district didn't have the manpower, or smarts to do a background check. At the end of his first work day, Marvin hated the school kids and his job. The school district doctors helped him as best as they could to cope with driving screaming kids by putting him on prescribed medical marijuana. But it wasn't enough to help keep him off the pain killers. Of course, do one drug, do another. It was only a matter of time before Marvin graduated to cocaine. His dealer was one of the high school students on his bus.

As the Sunny Side Up Retirement Home residents stood in line to re-board the bus for the ride back, here he was doing his "all-coked-up-on-coke" anxiety dance. He couldn't wait to get these old coots back on the bus and get them back to what he referred to as "their-last-stop-before-the-cemetery" home. The residents just thought he was cranky. Even though they, too, were mostly medicated, they had no clue he was even more medicated. They even gave him a nickname behind his back, "Cranky Pants." Just thought he was a cranky man. One of the residents even called him, "Cranky Franky-Stein." Didn't matter; Marvin was too drug-numbed to even contemplate what that meant.

With clipboard and pencil in hand, he checked them in, one by one.

One. Dorothy Paine, slow as molasses.

Two and three. The MaGoo sisters, never can tell which one is which.

Four. Father Novak, "Hey, say a prayer for me," Marvin muttered under his breath.

Five. Johnathon Stone, a would-be psychic. Thinks he knows the future. "So, who do I bet on tonight?"

Six. Clive Rinaudo, always asks if he can look at my change. Weird.

Seven. Casper Merlinski, always pulls a coin from behind my ear. How does he do it?

Eight. Domingo Rodriguez, definitely a flamer.

Nine. DeeDee Lapinsky, don't say anything to her or she'll talk your ears off.

Ten. Milton Schwartz, same old duck joke, every time.

Eleven. Susan Deerwish, what a rack!

And, of course, Miss McDermott, the accompanying nurse, quite a looker for being a bit chubby.

And Mr. Scott, the twenty-something flunked-out-of-college group bus leader. Spends most of the time on the bus checking e-mails on his phone. Marvin hated those devices – a waste of time, unless there was some free porn to find.

They followed behind making sure everyone was accounted for. Mr. Scott also carried some of the items the residents bought at the mall. Mostly trinkets and useless things. At this age and stage of their winding-down life, what else would they need to leave behind after they died? Just more clutter to toss out, or sell, when their apartments were cleaned out.

One last check mark: Twelve. Charley Harris, the resident odd ball, never left the bus. Strange old fart.

Once they were all aboard. Cranky, that is, Marvin, turned the key in the shuttle-bus ignition, gunned the gas, slipped into first gear, and started to pull away from the mall. He didn't even wait till they were safely buckled in. A few of the slow-poke oldies slid across their plastic-covered seats, bumping into one another.

"Whee!" came a sort of happy cry from some unidentified resident at the back of the bus.

"Maybe they enjoy the thrill of the ride," Marvin thought to himself. It didn't matter. He was on the clock, didn't get overtime, and wanted to get out of the mall area before the rush-hour traffic got worse. Driving erratically through the winding parking lot, the Sunny Side Up Retirement Home shuttle bus nearly hit a few mall customers who scampered out of the way, cursing. Marvin beeped the bus horn as much as it pleased him. He loved the horn; it made him feel important, in control, just like the last snort of coke he sneaked before they all boarded.

And off they went. Twenty-two minutes to get

there. Usually twenty-three minutes to get back by beating the traffic, but not today. Today would be different, much different. Today would be the day the pieces of their life puzzle would all be jumbled around, only to be put back together, after they were all dead.

CHAPTER 24

TOGETHER AGAIN.

Faces. We all have different faces. Changing faces, as we journey through our years.

The innocent face of a new born baby. The inquisitive face of a growing child. The carefree face of a maturing teenager. The grown face of a young adult. The mature face of middle age. The wrinkled face of so many passing years. And the aged face of a person whose life is finally coming to an end.

Lots of different faces. Faces that define who we are at different points in our life, and faces of where we are at that exact point in our life. But of all the faces we wear, the most important face of all is the one that can be seen and felt by everyone, and especially the one who wears it. A smiling face.

And tonight, while all the horror and death was happening throughout the Sunny Side Up Retirement Home, there was one person who couldn't care less about the faces of everyone else. For Charley Harris, the only face he cared about was the face of his dearly departed love of his life, his Rosita. And as he thought about her face, the one that had sparkling eyes and a love shown bright from her heart and touched his life forever, he smiled.

Perhaps that is why he was such a loner here. He had only thoughts for her, day in and day out, ever since she died so suddenly, so unexpectedly, that night so long ago. Ever since then, he became withdrawn. He didn't care to meet anybody, talk to anybody, do anything with anybody. He just thought of her and waited. Waited for "his time."

And each night as he knelt before his bed, he prayed for the one thing he wanted most in his life, to be with her again. To hold her again, to love her again, to smile with her again. Together, forever, in death. And that made him smile even more as he prayed. Because Charley had no fear of dying. He wanted to die. The sooner the better.

His aging, tired body was wearing down more every day. The aches and pains never went away; they just reminded him of what it meant to be old. It didn't matter that his face had changed so much through the years; his heart remained the same with his love for her. But what worried him the most, and especially of recent, was that his memory was fading. He was concerned that he would soon lose her altogether somewhere in time – the time they shared, the time he still hung on to, the time that slipped through his fingers, and now his disappearing mind.

Since the bus ride today to the mall and back, to the accident he was part of, and the moment he now lived, he knew that his time would soon end. He had that premonition for days, and especially today on the bus, and that's why he never left the bus. Charley wanted to be sure to be on it so that he could return here, for tonight. He believed his prayers would come true and tonight he would finally find his peace, and he would finally be with her. And tonight, he was right, as his prayers would be answered – in a twisted sort of way.

Timmy silently entered Charley's apartment and stared quietly at the bedroom doorway ahead, where he could see him kneeling. Timmy touched the gun in his pocket and walked towards Charley's bedroom.

Charley remained kneeling and never heard Timmy approach. His hearing, along with his memory, was also deteriorating. He should have gotten hearing aids like most of the other oldies here, but he really didn't care to hear anymore. Rosita was born deaf, and he just wanted to be part of what it was like in her world.

Timmy stopped a few feet from behind him. The bedroom was sparse, no garish landscaped paintings on the wall, or pictures of lots of silly-looking children and grandchildren in silly-looking poses. Just a single framed picture on the brown wooden nightstand next to his bed. It was of a woman, an attractive middle-aged woman with long curly black hair and bright happy eyes. She was smiling. It was a nice picture, nothing more, nothing less. Important to the kneeling man, meaningless to the young boy who could be, and probably would be, his executioner tonight.

It could be as simple as a single shot in to the back of this man's head, or maybe Timmy would take a few moments and talk to him, learn about him, and maybe even let him live. But probably not. Why should he? This man was part of the madness that made Timmy the killing machine he had become.

And then the silence was broken.

"Why do you pray?" Timmy asked in a reserved, non-threatening voice.

And then the silence continued.

"I said, why do you pray?" Timmy asked again, raising his voice just a little, but just enough.

Again, no answer.

The old man remained kneeling, hands in prayer, leaning on the bed, not even acknowledging the intruder. Not even caring.

"Do you know why I'm here?" the young boy asked.

But the old man still didn't answer. And in not doing so, that was beginning to frustrate Timmy.

The young boy slowly looked around the room. Maybe looking for an answer to why this man didn't answer. But the room revealed nothing. Just shadows on the walls in the dim lighting from the one lone lamp that stood on the end table next to the woman's picture.

Timmy stepped forward, taking his gun from his coat pocket and pointed it directly at the back of the praying man's head.

"Do you want to die?" Timmy asked him sternly.

Again, no answer.

"*Why didn't he answer?*" Timmy thought to himself as his finger began to tighten on the gun's trigger while slowly moving the gun closer to the old man's head, stopping an inch away from it.

Timmy stood there pointing the gun. Pointing the gun for what seemed a long, long time, waiting for an answer, waiting for the old man to turn around, waiting to understand why he just remained there praying, not showing any concern, not showing any fear.

And then he waited no longer.

Timmy shot the old man directly into the back of his head. And the bullet went straight through it and lodged itself somewhere into the mattress of the bed he was leaning and praying on.

Blood, bone and whatever else would be a part of blown-apart brain matter sprayed outwards.

Without a sound, the old man was dead.

Without a sound, Timmy turned and left the room.

Without a sound, the old man's body slumped slightly forward, but remained in a kneeling, praying position.

For Charley Harris, his prayers had finally come true. He was now, after all those long years since last being with her, finally, reunited with her. Finally.

But no thanks to Timmy.

Charley had actually died before Timmy came into his bedroom. Before Timmy entered his small, lonely apartment. Before Timmy had killed any of the other residents there tonight. Charley Harris died earlier that night of a broken heart. A heart attack while praying. Praying to die, and to be with his Rosita.

And on his face, as the bullet entered and exited his head, a smile remained.

CHAPTER 25

NO ONE REALLY KNOWS THE FUTURE, DO THEY?

Seventy years ago, to this day, five-year old Jennifer Hammond disappeared from her parents' home. She was an only child. A happy child. A pretty child. She had lots of friends in kindergarten and was always kind and friendly to everyone she talked with. Probably due to her upbringing, as both parents, Tony and Sharon Hammond, were pillars of the community. Both were involved in a variety of goodwill community projects. Friends to so many families, especially so many of the homeless, who they helped in the Open-Door Mission they owned and ran. Lots of needy people.

Lots of seedy-looking people. But all "good people" as the Hammonds would refer to them as. Just people like you and me, who needed help.

When their daughter wasn't in her stuffed-animal-filled bedroom that fateful morning, nor to be found anywhere else in their sprawling two-story brick house, it was only natural that the police would look first at the different types of "characters," as the police called them, "who frequented the Mission." But no clues came from all the investigations. Just a lot of real homeless people who needed a real roof over their head and a real meal in their belly. No real kidnapper here. The clues dried up, and the case eventually went from "hot to cold." It was widely believed that she was dead, even though no body was found. The Hammonds, distraught and fatigued from the stress-filled investigation, closed their homeless shelter, blamed each other for the kidnapping, and talked divorce. It didn't look like a happy ending was coming; it certainly didn't end that way for them. But for their missing five-year-old daughter Jennifer, it all changed by chance, as if it was meant to be.

Jonathon Stone was a world-renown psychic. A mind reader, a fortune teller, a clairvoyant, a medium, a man of mystery. At least that was what his press clippings said, as he travelled from city to city to help solve mysteries that no one else could. Tall, dark, and handsome. Shoulder length, jet black hair. Walked with a cane, and exuded a sense of confidence. When you looked at him, there was always a feeling of something strange, something different, something unique. He was all of that, and more.

His past was hidden from public scrutiny, and his present was ever changing. In one word, if there was only one word you could use to define him, he was "mysterious." Two words: "Really mysterious." Truly a man of mystery. You just couldn't figure him out. Was he for real, or was he not? At age 40 or maybe 50 (no one knew his real age for sure, perhaps not even himself), he was at the height of his fame. Everyone tried to contact him, to ask him questions, to search for answers. He was known worldwide. One day he would solve a case in Paris; the next day he would be seen in Ohio. Like a person hiding in shadows, he would come and go, be seen, and disappear. Some didn't believe he really existed; some believed he was a messiah. Although many believed in him, many also doubted him. But for those who would listen, he would always tell them, "It's not what you always believe it to be; it's knowing the truth that holds the real answers."

Profound. Righteous. Phony. Real. In Jonathon's case, perhaps all of these, and more.

They say that if you look into one's eyes, they are the pathway to the very soul. Not so, in Jonathon's case. If you did look directly into his eyes, they most likely scared the daylights out of you. Two deep and dark sockets. Born that way. No eyes. Just two big holes where eyes should have been. Empty eye sockets that seemed to hold secrets, or empty eye sockets that actually found secrets. A freak of nature, or a gift from God. Perhaps a little bit of both. Truth is, no one really knew, and if he did, he wouldn't tell you.

Ever since he started to talk, there was something unusual, something different, something really unnerving about him and what he said. He could predict the future.

In his early childhood, he would say things to his parents, who in turn would listen in wonder, or plain bewilderment. But then as he became older, he would say things that made them all the more wary and protective of him. Whatever he said always came true. Always.

For example, young Jonathon would tell you what type of weather there would be tomorrow. It wasn't like someone asked him. After all, who would ask a seven-year-old child what the weather would be tomorrow? You didn't need to ask, he just told you. Jonathon would tell you lots of things. He would tell you that the phone would ring, before it rang. Or that someone would be at their front door, before they knocked. At first, his parents thought and said it was just coincidence. What else would a parent think or even say? But coincidence soon became a frightening reality. Especially the day young Jonathon told his family doctor, in front of his parents, that he knew the doctor was sick and was going to die. What 9-year-old Jonathon said gave everyone in the room a startling pause. You could hear a pin drop. For that very day, Doctor Adams had been diagnosed, and only he knew, that he had terminal cancer.

As Jonathon began to make more predictions, which all came true, his parents realized that they had to keep him out of the public eye. They feared he would be sought out and bothered by everyone and anyone who knew of the young blind boy's fortune-telling gift. Jonathon was home schooled, never had much outside contact with the world that he could never see, but could always predict. When he did go outside, he always wore dark sunglasses to cover up his missing eyes. Long black hair, confident in his posture, he was a handsome boy, but a mysterious boy. Other kids in the nearby school and in the surrounding neighborhood always wondered about him and what his "story was" because he was always confined to his home. It was only natural they gossiped about this "strange boy." How little did they know! And how much did he know?

When he turned 16, a young girl, Veronica Summers, an attractive and very inquisitive girl, snuck into Jonathon's parent's fenced-in backyard that was doubly protected with overgrown thick and tall bushes. She found him sitting by himself, neatly dressed, wearing sunglasses, and staring upwards at the midday summer sun. When she approached him cautiously and quietly, he was the first to speak.

"Hello, Veronica," he said, as if he knew her all his life, or at least knew that she was coming to visit that day.

Surprised by his calling out her name, Veronica stopped in her tracks. She certainly wasn't expecting to be called by name. Actually, she didn't know what to expect.

"It's okay," he continued. "I knew you were coming to see me."

Stunned, surprised, amazed, and even shocked, Veronica kept her composure and quickly replied.

"You know who I am? You can see me? Everyone says you're blind."

"Blind," he sighed, and smiled in response.

"You don't need sight to really see someone to know they are really there. Some people only see what they want to see." He continued matter of factly, "You just need to know."

The young girl stood there frozen, taking it all in, with the warm summer breeze caressing her long and wispy blonde hair. She was dressed nicely, in a seasonal halter top, with a pair of shorts that extended below her knees. He was also dressed nicely – clean pullover, light blue, short-sleeved shirt, and a pair of dark pants. She studied him, wondering why she took the dare to come here and meet him, to find out what he really was, and if what all the kids said was really true. Or, maybe, maybe it was because there was something else she needed to know. Something that only she wanted to know.

"I don't understand. If you can't see, how do you know?" she questioned his words.

"Knowing is a gift. Knowing is everything. Knowing is all one needs to really see," he mused.

"How did you know my name if you can't see me? How did you know I was coming here?" Again, she questioned his answer as if playing a game of checkers. Your answer; my question. Next move.

Intrigued by his good looks and his soft, polite voice she decided to step closer, but kept a short distance, still far enough apart, so she could turn and run away if she needed to.

There was an awkward pause between the two of them as a gust of wind came through the overhanging backyard trees. The gentle and warm wind made her hair move as if someone were running their invisible fingers through it. She brushed her hair back with her fingers, but she had felt something, or was it her imagination?

"Your name is Veronica Summers. Today is June 21st, remarkedly the first day of what we call summer. Perhaps a coincidence with your name. But I knew you were coming. I know what you want. It's okay. You needn't worry. I won't hurt you." Jonathon paused. "I will only tell you what you came for."

Now there was a long, silent moment between the two of them. Only the warm summer wind could be heard in the trees surrounding them. Only the warm summer temperature could touch them as they stood inches apart from each other. She felt more at ease to be this close to him with each passing second. She turned her head slowly to the left, then to right looking at him, fascinated by his demeanor, his good looks and his mysteriousness.

Was she thinking of another question, or was she trying to sort out what he already said?

She was ready to speak again, but he spoke first.

"Take my hand, Veronica. Don't be afraid. Take my hand and ask me," he stated, commanded, or just said in a calming voice of someone in control.

Another awkward pause, and then her hand slowly reached out the few remaining inches between them and touched his hand. Her hand took his hand, and she held it tight. It was smooth, it was gentle, it was warm. It was comfortable. And she felt relaxed enough to finally ask.

"Am I dead?"

Jonathon smiled gently. He carefully put his other hand on top of hers.

"Yes."

It was like all the breath had been taken from her. She had prepared herself for this moment, for this answer. She took the dare to come here, not only because it was a dare, but because she felt that he may know the truth to what haunted her the most. And with his words, she knew what to expect. And yet, she didn't know what to expect next.

"You are believed to be dead." Jonathon continued, "You have been mourned. You have been forgotten by most. But you will always be remembered by those who hang on to your memory. You are only dead to those who believe you are dead, but you are alive to those who want you to be alive, and to those who know."

There were no more pauses. No more wind between them. Only a deafening silence. It was as if time and everything around them had stopped, just leaving the two of them alone in this world. Alone in this moment. Not knowing if it was a dream or a reality. Without hesitation, she moved the remaining step, closing any gap between them. With a tear in her eye, and a deeper touch of his hand on hers, she softly spoke, "I know. My dreams tell me who I am. But I was afraid to believe." Veronica answered both to him, and to herself.

"Yes, you know. You know in your heart. You know in your dreams, and now in your mind. You are alive. You have always been alive. Do not be afraid to believe. And it is up to you to tell the world that you are alive. If, you want the world to know," Jonathon added softly.

Her next words came in a slow, soft voice. Not a voice that was afraid to say what she had to say, but a voice that had to say for the first time what she had always wanted to say.

"I was kidnapped."

"Yes."

"I was presumed dead."

"Yes."

"My new parents were the ones."

"Yes."

"They took me."

"Yes."

"Why?"

Again, the soft wind. Again, a slight pause. Not awkward, not concerning, maybe just catching one's breath, forming one's thoughts, preparing the next answer, revealing more of the truth.

"Because your real parents were destined to die in an accident, which they did, and you would have died if you were with them," Jonathon again stated matter of factly, answering in a tone of both comfort and understanding.

"They kidnapped me, so I would live? They took me away from my real parents who then suffered and believed I was dead, so I could be alive? Is that why?" Her response was mixed with anger and understanding.

"Yes," Jonathon answered.

A direct ray of sunshine broke through the overhead tree leaves and touched both their faces at the same time. And with that, a tear finally rolled down from her eye to her now-quivering lips. Shock. Denial. Sadness. Happiness. Truth. Relief. Knowing.

A tear rolled down from beneath his sunglasses, as well.

Jonathon gently reached out his one hand and touched her tear, then wiped it away. His warm hand remained on her cheek, as if giving her the strength to remain calm in the revelations just shared, and that yet to come.

"There is no shame in knowing the truth. There should be no sadness for what once was. There should only be a sense of happiness for what will be. Your destiny lies in your future. Your future holds an important cure. You will grow to be a woman, a mother who will have a child, a child who will become a man, a man who will save many innocent people. Your destiny was to be as it is. That is all I know. That's all I can tell you."

And with those words, she let go of his hands, and started to slowly back away. Confused, relieved, and frightened by everything he just told her about her past, and everything that he foretold her about her future.

She stopped. Turned. Hesitated, and had to ask one last question. A question to which she needed an answer. A question that would remain with him all his life. A question that would constantly haunt him through all his years ahead, right up to that fateful day as a resident at the Sunny Side Up Retirement Home. A question that he already had an answer for, because he already knew. After all, Jonathan Stone really was a psychic, a mind reader, a medium, a clairvoyant. Jonathon Stone was really gifted, or maybe really cursed. He didn't need any sight to really know his own true destiny.

"Are you the devil?"

"No." He paused, and the next words he said had no accompanying emotion. "But, one day, I will meet him."

CHAPTER 26

AN APPLE, A STRAWBERRY, A PLACE TO DIE.

Fat Frankie Fantozzio's Fresh Fruit Farm had been around for about a hundred years. It was a family-owned business, passed on through several generations. During the Great Depression, migrant workers not only picked fruit for sale, but lived there in tents among the 150-acre, sprawling orchards.

Located on Route 1, just south of the city, the farm provided produce for both local and statewide grocery stores and markets. There was something extra sweet and special about the fruit's taste. Different from so many similar fruits in the neighboring farms and counties. Something "very sweet – and very special." People from all over the state drove there to sample the fruit and take a leisurely stroll through the orchards. Fat Frankie Fantozzio's fresh fruit even set a record by winning all the blue ribbons in every year's State Fair beginning in 1930 and continuing till the day the farm was finally sold. All the different varieties of Fat Frankie's fruit had a distinct flavor that was both juicy and tangy, which seemed to stay in the mouth long after it was eaten. It was so tasty, you'd always want to take another bite.

Other nearby farmers thought it was a secret fruit spray they used each spring, or maybe a special home-grown fertilizer that filled the fields, or maybe the way the fruit was washed in some mineral-free purifying water. No one knew the real secret except for Old Man Frankie himself. And it was secretly passed on through the generations to follow from his son, to his son, to his son. There certainly was a really unique and real secret ingredient that made the fruit extra sweet and special. Yes indeed. Very special. Dead bodies.

Fat Frankie Fantozzio was the nephew of Carlos "Gumby" Gambino who was the righthand man of "the" Al Capone. The legendary Al Capone. Big Al. Mobster, Bootlegger, Gun Runner, Womanizer and Killer. Al Capone, Head of the Chicago Crime Syndicate. His resume would read, he was all of the above, and was especially good at "offing," that is, killing, people. In the beginning of his crime empire, the dead people, or alive people but soon-to-be-dead people, were put in cement and thrown into the

Chicago River or Lake Michigan to disappear forever from the public. But some of the mobsters' wives who knew about this didn't want their young children swimming with those who were unlucky enough to "sleep with the fishes." A gangster expression for dead bodies. So, Carlos, aka "Gumby," was given the task of finding another resting place for the dearly departed, as Big Al would refer to them. And what better place than the sprawling 150 acres of Fat Frankie Fantozzio's Fresh Fruit Farm just across state lines. And, think of the money saved on the cement boots used to hold the bodies down in the water!

Week after week, month after month, year after year, the dead and departed were driven to their eternal resting place underneath Fat Frankie's apple trees, or next to Fat Frankie's strawberry bushes. And the delivery service, a couple of good goombahs – mobsters on the payroll – always brought back a basket or two of Fat Frankie's fresh fruit. Big Al loved fresh fruit. A win-win for everyone involved, including the dead.

As the mobsters would look for ways to cut their business costs and save money – yes, even gangsters had to find ways to reduce costs – the "special burial disposal" of the dead bodies held the answer. These bullet-ridden bodies wouldn't have the luxury of a nice, neat-looking casket, or an ornate wooden coffin, just a bloody, soiled hotel sheet hurriedly wrapped around their stiffening lead-filled remains. Another "win-win" for the mob.

Seasons changed. The bodies decomposed, helping fertilize the soil and add to the nurturing of the plant roots, which grew into the yearly sweet-tasting fresh fruit that Fat Frankie would sell and ultimately win blue ribbons. As the taste for the fruit grew, so did the number of bodies. Lots of bodies. Year after year, even after Capone was replaced by another mobster, who was replaced by another mobster, one thing remained the same: Fat Frankie Fantozzio's Fresh Fruit Farm was the place to be. That is, the place to be buried in. The count of the dead, buried bodies grew to a point of who's counting anymore? One could say people were dying to get in there – a mobster joke. In other words, there were a lot of dead people helping to increase the sales of Frankie Fantozzio's fresh fruit.

Again, seasons changed. And so did the mob. With gambling, prostitution, and some drugs legalized (no longer outlawed by the cops), the mob's business motto, or if you want to call it a "mission statement," changed. The disrespected gangsters became the respected, got chummy with government officials and celebrity singers, and started investing their illegal dough in Nevada real estate. What better way to launder and hide the money from all the other illegal activities going on behind the scenes, which we won't talk about! Vegas hotels and casinos, shopping malls, housing tracts, race tracks, and even retirement homes. And, of course, this business strategy went from state to state. As the good ol' USA grew, the cities sprawled into the suburbs. It was only a matter of time before the last remaining member of the Fantozzio family, Freddy "the Fairy," a gay and eccentric mobster, who enjoyed cross-dressing like the famous FBI guy J. Edgar, broke ground with a group of government officials to build what was touted as a "state-of-the-art" retirement home on the Fresh Fruit Farm. First to have Wi-fi in every bathroom. Just what the oldies wanted. They didn't even know what it meant. One retired resident who moved in on day one even thought it had something to do with waffles. Sort of makes sense. Sort of.

With the first shovel in ground, you would expect that a lot of human bones would be found. And they were. Lots and lots of human bones. But this was a crew of union construction workers, controlled by the descendants of the long-gone Big Al and his syndicate. So, rather than doing a lot of digging and removing, and to cut, hide, and illegally pocket costs, more dirt was brought in to build a hill over the dead. This also kept the ground nice and fertilized for the few remaining apple trees that were to surround the newly landscaped retirement home buildings.

Freddy the Fairy also raised chickens on the surrounding farm grounds, so it was only natural that he came up with the name "Sunny Side Up" for the new retirement home. Chickens lay eggs, eggs can be scrambled, hard boiled, cooked or flipped over with the yellow color facing upwards, thus the name "Sunny Side Up." Again, sort of makes sense. Sort of.

Unfortunately for Freddy, as luck would have it, he never saw the completion of the retirement home project. The FBI was always looking for a way to collar him and he was arrested for raising chickens without a poultry license. After plea bargaining and trading a year's supply of his former farm's fresh fruit to the sentencing judge, Freddy was sent to a "state-of-the-art slammer," where he was seen performing in the prison play, *The Book of Mormon.* A Wop playing a Mormon. Even got good reviews. How about them apples!

The retirement home was built on schedule, and, of course, over budget with additional subsidized government funds going under the table to the unions and to some of the government officials who were friends of the unions. When completed, it was an amazing facility. Eight two-story, elongated buildings that were all attached via hallways to a center circular core. There were restaurants, hair salons, a mini grocery store, a mini movie theater, a library filled with used books, a bingo parlor, a bowling alley with plastic balls and pins, and a never used "state-of-the-art" workout and fitness center with thousands of pounds of weights to lift. Thousands of pounds. At least it looked nice.

Each two-story building had 16 similar-looking apartments on both the first and second floor, eight to a side. Each apartment had the same layout: a modest-sized living room, a small den, a bedroom or two, a nice bathroom with walk-in bathtubs, and a small stand-up kitchen with a single-person fridge, stove, microwave and four-slice toaster. Toast was popular, and easy to chew when you didn't have many teeth left in an aging mouth. There were also identically sized closets scattered in between their rooms, where the residents would put their outdated clothing and well-worn shoes, and other stuff they still kept for who knows what reason. Sometimes it's hard to part with stuff, especially when you're old and your mind parts ways with you first. Each building also had a storage area. At the end of each main hallway, every apartment had its own 8×10-foot, chicken-wired, padlocked, storage space for the rest of their junk that couldn't fit into their apartments. Most residents forgot or couldn't even remember that they had such a space, so they remained mostly empty.

The entrance way to each building had a large lobby with a grand staircase leading to each building's second floor. An elevator was tucked neatly behind it, and was the way not most, but all residents went up and down. In each lobby there was an identical front-desk area where residents and or visitors were checked in and out. A small business office was behind each front lobby desk, along with a small, adjacent security office and part-time maintenance office. To save even more money budgeted to run the facility, a single security guard walked from building to building, making the nightly rounds. When the Sunny Side Up Retirement Home first opened, separate security guards were assigned to each building. But after a few months, and with most of the oldies asleep by ten o'clock, corporate decided that one guard could manage the entire place each night. Why spend all that money on unnecessary security, when it could be put to better use being "pocketed" by the owners instead? After all, who would want to come here and harm old people?

Each building had been designed and built with the exact same layout. It was cookie cutter made, and cost effective budgeted, of course. Most of the building materials, although advertised as the best money could buy, were actually the worst and cheapest that could be used. Once again, the business model was that money could be diverted elsewhere, especially to the owners' deep and hidden pockets. It was a great business plan for the mob, which now was run by gangsters with college degrees. Throughout each building, the paint colors were bright and comforting, the daily piped-in taped muzak was soothing and relaxing, and for most of the oldies, especially those going blind, losing their hearing, or in the early stages of dementia, it really didn't matter what it all looked like. This was their "home."

The marketing for the Sunny Side Up Retirement Home was uniquely targeted for a single person, average age 80 and up, who may have lost a loved one, or never found a loved one in their fleeting, gone-so-fast lives. It was financially affordable and had all its living expenses, such as food, electricity, and maintenance capped, so as not to leave any resident, who might run out of money, homeless.

Being run by a conglomerate that was a generation of gangsters, each apartment came with an iron-clad contract that had so much mumble-jumble legal jargon that it was hardly ever read, yet alone understood. You needed a lawyer to figure it out, and most of the lawyers hired were all connected. Basically, each lease stipulated that the building ownership would acquire all of the resident's belongings including jewelry and shoes upon their deaths. The jewelry was fenced and was another profitable way to add to the already overflowing deep pockets of the owners. And, interesting enough, everyone needs shoes. The second-hand resale of used shoes was a big market in foreign countries, also operated by the mob. Sort of an "add-on, wait-until-death, non-refundable security deposit." But contract and living stipulations aside, it really didn't matter to the residents, as there was a definite positive plus that all the residents agreed on that was an important factor in their choosing this place to live – "the fresh, home-grown fruit." The few remaining vestiges of Fat Frankie Fantozzio's Fresh Fruit Farm were scattered throughout the grounds and the adjoining buildings. The small, but still productive fruit bushes and trees were still "specially" nurtured, home grown and secretly tended to, and added to. It was all part of the landscaping plans for future buildings yet to be placed, so not to disturb, destroy, or reveal the hidden secrets in the earth below.

A bowl of fresh fruit was available daily in the lobby of each of the buildings, next to each building's grand staircase, next to each building's unused stairs to the second floor. All the residents loved the fresh fruit, which was mostly all gone, all gobbled up before 9 a.m. each morning. Some even said the sweet lip-smacking taste was like something they never experienced before and couldn't wait to have more the next day. If only they knew.

Yes. Without a doubt. The Sunny Side Up Retirement Home was the perfect "place to be." The perfect place to live. The perfect place to make friends. The perfect place to laugh. The perfect place to enjoy the remaining days in life, before their next stop and final destination, death. Although most of the residents there were in the upper 80-plus years of age, death seemed distant from their minds. Too many good memories to think about and dwell on; no time for death. Especially today. Good memories for all the neighbors of Building #7 – Lucky #7, as they referred to it, because it was such a nice building with never, ever any trouble or problems with the residents. They were like a family, or at least good neighbors, or maybe just good friends, with a few oddballs sprinkled in between. Even with what happened today on the way back from their weekly fun and planned bus trip to the mall, it really didn't spoil their day. After all, they still had just enough time for their dinner and dessert, had enough time to fall asleep on the front parlor couches with the plastic covers, enough time to wander to their apartments to watch their favorite shows on the Hi-Def TVs they never could figure out how to use, and, finally, enough time to prepare themselves for another night of restful sleep. Restful, undisturbed, planned sleep. At their age, time was all they had. Even with the unplanned accident that they were all involved in, and that most of them had already forgotten, they still had enough time to do everything they had planned to do.

It was another perfect day in the perfect "place to be."

Yes, the perfect place to be. Except for tonight. When time would finally run out. When all would die. And it would be the perfect "place to die."

CHAPTER 27

AS TIME GOES BY.

Months passed quickly since the tragic death of the young Jameson boy. Timmy sat in his usual chair at his usual desk in class and listened on and off to his teacher giving the usual uninteresting facts about rocks and minerals, stones and dirt, and whatever else he blabbed on and on about. Timmy went to school that day just like all the other recent previous days with his dog Butch following along. Before going into the school, Timmy petted and hugged him goodbye, telling him he was a "good boy," and left him on the school's front lawn near the flagpole.

At first, some of the teaching staff complained about this strange dog sitting all day, day in and out, while Timmy was in class. But it was Ms. Judy Griswold, in her role as school psychologist and grief counselor, who came to Timmy's defense and basically convinced the school administration that it was a "therapy" dog, even though it really wasn't.

Not really understanding any of this "back and forth" behind-the-scenes stuff about the dog, Timmy was just happy the school let his dog stay. Of course, Butch had to be put on a leash, tied to the outside flagpole, and had to have all the necessary animal vaccinations, as deemed by the law and insisted upon by the school principal.

When Butch first came into his life out of nowhere, and after a somewhat futile search for the original owner was made by Mrs. Jameson, the dog quickly became a part of the family. It even got a leather dog collar with fake jewels on it and a shiny silver dog tag with its own name on it. Or, at least, the name of Butch on it.

Since it was late fall, and winter was expected soon, the weather began to change with each passing day with the first traces of brief flurries in the air. The school administrators, especially Ms. Griswold, began to ponder what to do with the dog in the winter. It certainly couldn't sit outside in the cold and snow all day, and it certainly wouldn't be allowed to come inside. But all that pre-planning and thinking really didn't matter. Winter would never come for Butch.

As the calendar days were crossed off, and with a frosty chill in the air, something was beginning to happen, and the dog wasn't acting normally. Butch's playful and patient demeanor began to change. Instead of just sitting, or lying down, and staring at the school entrance waiting for his master, his best friend, his brother, Timmy, to return, as he did each and every previous day, Butch started pacing nervously around the flag pole. His leash didn't allow him to do more than two rotations before it wound tight, so he went back the other way until the leash was extended as far as it would go. Then Butch started all over again. Somehow, this caught Timmy's attention from where he sat in class, as he could look out the classroom window. Back and forth his dog went, back and forth, until finally, it happened. The leash came undone, as simple as that. But the dog didn't run away or continue to pace anymore. Butch stood staring directly at the classroom window, waiting for Timmy to see him. It was almost as if he were trying to communicate with Timmy through the special bond they had created since his unexpected arrival at the Jameson farm a few months ago. It was almost as if he had something important to tell Timmy, or show Timmy, or for Timmy to see. The dog just sat staring, trancelike, at the window.

A sudden cool breeze came out of the trees and seemed to caress and brush the dog's long brown and white coat. Waiting. Staring. Seeing something no one else could possibly see or want to see, Butch slowly started to growl. A low, rumbling growl, which turned into a loud, very loud, dog bark.

Butch barked loudly, not that it could be heard through the closed school window, but he barked for Timmy. Finally, their eyes met. Whether it was a call for help, or a call for something else, it didn't matter, it was a bark, followed by a circle or two, another bark, and off Butch went away from the school yard.

Timmy saw this play out and understood. Any boy who had a dog who bonded like a brother would understand. Butch was barking for Timmy to follow him. He needed "his master" to follow him. And he did.

Abruptly getting up from his school desk, the young Jameson boy rushed out of the classroom door, grabbing his jacket. Mr. Bostick, a middle-aged, plump and jolly science teacher, stopped his "blah blah blah" and yelled out after Timmy, "Hey, you can't leave class! Get back here!"

The entire classroom and befuddled teacher all turned and watched their classmate hurriedly disappear out the door.

The lone security guard, who was dozing off, as usual, right about this time of day, was startled awake as Timmy ran by him and out the school's front door.

"Hey, kid, where you going? You didn't sign out," the guard shouted after him.

Following school protocol, this was as far as it went. The security guard's job description did not include chasing after some mixed-up 10-year-old kid who just left without permission. Besides, the sudden awakening from his drifting slumber made him want to pee. He most certainly had to do that before attempting to run after this kid.

Butch was circling and waiting about 30 feet ahead at the edge of the school grounds. His tail was wagging furiously as if something special was about to happen, and it was.

When Timmy came charging out the door and across the school's front lawn, Butch barked his acknowledgement to him, and quickly turned and ran towards the woods adjacent to the school property. With late fall in the air, there were a lot of leaves already off the trees, and the woods looked both like a landscaped autumn painting and also a foreboding image from a horror movie. As Timmy and Butch ran along a leaf-covered path behind the new tract of homes that had been going up for the past two years, his classmates and teacher stood at the classroom windows watching the boy and dog disappear into the shadow-filled woods.

There were several paths, or trails, throughout the woods that led in different directions. Butch led Timmy down one of the most well-worn dirt paths that a lot of kids, daytime joggers, or strolling evening lovers sometimes followed that led to, and along the Waukegan Creek. It was a creek named after some of the American Indian tribes who used to own, live, and farm the adjoining lands. But that was a long time ago. A long, long, time ago. The creek had a snake-like appearance as it meandered for several miles through the top part of the county. From the Jameson home, which was about three miles to the west, you could see it close to their property line when all the fall foliage disappeared, allowing one to see deeper into the woods. The creek flowed strongly in the spring, less in the summer, and at this time of year it was fairly low with any remaining water. A rainstorm was predicted for later that day.

Sometimes the forecasters had difficulty with their predictions because of the way the northern Canadian winds would come down along the Great Lakes bordering the state. And if the temperature dropped, the rain could turn into some snow showers.

As they ran, some of the distant darker clouds indicated a storm was gathering, and surely it was. A big storm, that had many consequences to come.

Butch continued leading the way, as Timmy ran swiftly behind, closing the gap, but never quite catching up. At first, Timmy had no idea where they were going, but it slowly became clearer to him as Butch veered off the trail and ran through a clearing at the top of the ridge. School was far enough behind them. Timmy's home was far enough in front of them. What remained in between was where they were going. Timmy knew. Timmy understood.

The dog disappeared over the ridge and Timmy finally came up to the top. There he paused, catching his breath, watching Butch go through the rusty gates, which were one of three entrances. Wood View Cemetery. It was built over two hundred years ago by some of the early settlers who lived and died in the region, and sprawled across the few hills, small valleys, and up to, and ending at the Waukegan Creek.

Old tombstones gave way to modern-day grave markers. A mixture of everything old and spooky from the cemetery's past blended into today's newer and more friendly "resting places." A good area for the backdrop of a murder mystery novel, or a tranquil place to come and pay respect to the loved ones who passed. A final and peaceful resting place. Six feet under, years and years of the long-gone dead, and now the newly, and recent dead. Six feet under. A "city of the dead." Ryan's home.

Timmy continued to run after his dog. He knew exactly where to go: In between and around some 6-foot-tall stone monuments. Lots of crosses and large-lettered names. Pointed pillars, small, boxy-looking, carved stonework, and a few half-story tombs now covered in the ever creeping, ever growing patchwork of thickets and tall, uncut grass. Over one hill. Down another. Under a few large, very large, gnarly-looking trees with hardly any leaves left. Empty limbs reaching out as if pointing the way. Through countless piles of dead leaves, which collected in the fall winds and were cut in half by the jagged, crumbling, stone monuments that worshipped the ghosts, who legend said, still lived and haunted there.

The sun was beginning to set, the shadows were becoming longer, and the wind was beginning to whisper a mixture of sounds from the souls below.

Timmy finally came to the new section. And there stood Butch, directly on top of his brother's grave.

The dog was sniffing the ground, never looking back to see if Timmy was there. The dog knew he was there. The dog knew Timmy's brother was there. The dog knew they were all there together.

Timmy was hesitant to come closer. He had only been there once since the burial, a few months ago, the day of his brother's birthday. Ryan would have been ten. It was just his mom, dad, and himself. Mrs. Jameson brought a simple rose that she placed on the grave marker's name. He remembered that she made the sign of the cross and silently said some sort of prayer. That's what people did in the church services, and what people do when they seek solace or guidance from their Lord. He remembered that because, as she prayed, tears rolled down her cheeks. Soft-looking tears that didn't disturb her make-up, not that she wore much, but the type of tears that one would see in a close-up of some romantic, or sad scene in a movie.

As for his dad, he remembered he just stood there. He didn't make the sign of the cross. He didn't bring his hands together in prayer. He just stood there. Silently. Strangely, if that word can define the moment. At least that is how it appeared to a 10-year-old mind, which was still trying to sort out all the whys of "why this happened." Timmy remembered his own feelings. He was confused, saddened, and angry. He had no emotion, he had just stood there, and he remembered how he began to rock back and forth on his feet as he remained there waiting to leave. It was just the three of them. It weighed heavily in his mind. And it would always remain a part of his mind.

And now at this moment, as he stood staring at his brother's grave again, he remembered the last time he was alone with him, laughing, playing, enjoying the mid-summer days. He remembered pointing his finger gun and shooting his brother in a pretend game that came to life unexpectedly and tragically. He remembered holding his dead brother's body in his arms as it changed from warm to cold, alive to dead. And he remembered how alone he felt, and how that loneliness changed his life forever.

That was the last time he was alone. That night, after they returned from the burial, Butch wandered into his life. And when he returned to the cemetery with his parents to pay respect to what would have been his brother's birthday, he had left Butch at home. His parents felt it should be just the three of them.

But now, Butch led him here. Why?

A distant roll of thunder brought Timmy's attention back to the here and now. A storm was approaching, not that it mattered. Nothing really mattered at this moment except what Butch was about to do. He started to dig.

A few swipes of his paws moved some of the grass off the top of the dirt on the grave below. He then started to dig faster. His paws seemed to work in overtime. He broke through the top inch or two and started to dig a hole into the ground. Timmy wasn't sure if the hole would lead to heaven or hell, but he knew it would lead to his brother's coffin.

"No!" he screamed at the top of his lungs. "No!"

The dog stopped his digging, his paws dirty and wet from the light rain which had just begun to fall.

"No, Butch, no." Timmy softly spoke, as he slowly approached his dog.

He was about a foot or two away when he stopped. Butch turned to look at him and started to growl. A low, rumbling growl. A sound Timmy never heard from his dog before. It made him stop right where he was. A sound which seemed to be more than a growl; a sound that seemed to be more like a distant voice calling to him. A distant voice of a scared young boy who was calling out for help. A voice which seemed to, and became, the voice of his dead brother. A voice that echoed into his mind and resonated deep into his troubled soul.

"Help me, Timmy... Help me."

Butch stopped growling. Then, he started to whimper. Then he stopped altogether and remained quietly transfixed on Timmy. The only sound that remained was the whistling wind between the grave stones. The storm was getting closer. A flash of lightning in the near distance revealed the dog's face. It wasn't the face of an angry animal. It wasn't the face of an animal at all. From within his two brown, sad-looking eyes, tears began to flow gently down his fur-covered face. Tears that were shaped like the tears Timmy remembered his mother cried. Tears he would never forget from the day they visited Ryan's grave together. Tears that tried to wash away the pain from within, and, pain from below.

Kneeling in the muddied dirt and wet grass next to the small, freshly dug hole in the ground, Timmy lovingly hugged Butch. He hugged him tight. Hugged him like he once held his dead brother. Timmy hugged him like he would never let go. And Timmy started to cry.

CHAPTER 28

HAPPENSTANCE.

It was starting to rain as the Sunny Side Up Retirement Home shuttle bus was leaving the Twin Oaks Mall. Not a heavy rain, but one of those light, dreary rains as dusk was approaching. And, just as luck would have it that day, flashing police-car lights on the main roadway up ahead slowed traffic down. This unexpected delay did not make any of the passengers aboard the bus happy, or give cheer to the already overdosed, over anxious, over coked-up bus driver, Marvin Fox.

The bus crawled to a stop.

Marvin rolled down his driver's window and an overweight cop, with a bright red, burning flare in one hand and a half-eaten donut in the other, shouted out directions.

"Big accident on the Parkway. You'll have to find an alternate route."

"Uh huh," Marvin replied, not wanting to draw suspicion to his euphoric, out-of-mind state.

Marvin closed his window and shouted back to his passengers, "Gotta detour. Some morons crashed on the Parkway."

"Will we be home for the early-bird specials?" yelled out Dorothy Paine in a weak but audible voice from the middle of the bus.

"I don't want to miss the weather report on TV. I gotta know the weather. You always gotta know the weather, I mean how can you make plans if you don't know the weather. What kind of weather can affect what kind of plans..," a seemingly distraught DeeDee Lapinsky chimed in right after Dorothy, and continued talking to anyone and everyone including herself.

"Morons and idiots," Marvin thought to himself. *"I live in a world of morons and idiots! Gotta eat the early bird! Gotta eat a donut!"* His mind repeated his thoughts, mingled in with their words, and the cop's directions. If he would have taken a moment to look at himself in the driver's mirror, he would have seen his eyes rolling around in his head like ping-pong balls.

"Yeah, yeah, everyone keep your shorts on. We'll get there," Marvin bellowed back in anger, while drumming his thin, boney fingers on the worn black-plastic bus steering wheel.

"Right, get there, hmm." He tried to put some coherent thoughts together as he mumbled out loud to himself, "Do I take Route 14 to Clifton? No, Lake Street to the Northside Bridge and over to the..."

Cars behind him started to honk as his bus was standing still. Marvin suddenly snapped out of his confused and personal moment and realized the cop with the now almost fully eaten donut was outside his driver's window staring at him.

"Fuck it," he half shouted to himself, as he gunned the gas, and the bus zoomed ahead, making the first turn on the right that he could see.

As the rain continued to intensify, the windshield wipers on the bus started to give off one of those irritating, low-pitched, squeaking sounds. Worn out rubber on a wet window.

Screech, screech, screech, with the beat of each wiper on half-wet glass.

Didn't matter to Marvin, as he was trying to figure out where he was, and why he had turned right instead of left. Or maybe he should have turned left instead of right.

"Shit," he muttered to himself, tapping his fingers even faster on the steering wheel that he held tighter and tighter with each screech of the windshield blade.

Marvin was too coked up to know the difference from left to right, or right to left, or let alone know how to get back to the retirement home.

He peered out the window into the darkness. It was as if the sprawling black roadway, mixed with the rhythmic beating of wiper blades and pouring rain on the windshield, was hypnotizing him into a trance. Without caring if any of the oldies on the bus could see him, Marvin put his left index finger under his nostril and took a long deep snort, hoping to bring further down into his nose the last bit of cocaine still there. With glossed-over, bloodshot eyes staring straight ahead, his drug-filled mind wandered to a childhood song his mother would sing to him when he was confused, scared, and about to cry.

"The wheels on the bus go round and round, round and round, round and round. The wheels on the..."

With his disappearing reality becoming more distorted by the moment, tears started to well up in his eyes. The rain on the front bus window changed to the tears of his mother the day her husband, his father, died suddenly of a drug overdose. Marvin saw himself as a young boy staring at his dad's dead body, slumped over their cheap metal and cardboard-topped kitchen table with a needle in his arm. Dried vomit and a small pool of red chunky blood was still hanging from his blue lips and half-opened, frozen-looking mouth.

"Hey, I gotta pee," someone shouted from the back of the bus, waking Marvin from his dream, his nightmare, his haunted memory, and bringing him quickly back to some sense of here-and-now reality.

"Hey, bus driver, you're on the other side of the road!" another voice came from behind him.

Startled back to some semblance of the moment, Marvin shook his head, let his memories go, and quickly refocused on the drive.

"Yeah, I have to pee, too, and yeah, yeah, I was on the other side of the road," Marvin yelled back to no one in particular but to anyone and everyone who would listen or could hear.

"Morons and idiots. And fuck, I wish I had a donut!" He kept his thoughts to himself as he shook his head again, trying to shake any remaining cobwebs out of it, and return to some form of normal, while sniffing his nostrils deep and hard.

Changing lanes, Marvin seemed to recognize a road with a gas station on the right.

"Right is right, left is wrong," he laughed to himself. It was an old inside joke he once heard from a young high school friend of his who referred how the direction a guy's pecker hung, indicated a choice of right from wrong.

"So, right is right," he smiled to himself for his choice as he turned down a road, Mill Lane Road, that was really "not right" but was really so wrong. The way he was going was so very wrong.

Marvin was lost, and now on some lonely, unlit road, where darkness was all around him. He was clueless to where he was, or how he got there. If only he had some more of that wonderful white powder, everything would be alright. But there was no more to snort. He had snorted way too much already, and things were going from bad to worse by the moment. *"Is this the way back? Or is this the way to someplace else?"* His thoughts scrambled together like raw eggs being stirred up in a bowl with a spoon. He was certainly headed someplace. Someplace that would make everything right, or someplace that, maybe, would make everything worse?

"*Where the hell am I?*" his confused and disoriented mind screamed at him. Maybe for not asking himself any road directions, but maybe trying to admit his failure in the missed signs of his life directions. For sure, Marvin was lost in more ways than one. And, for sure, this road was going somewhere. *"Somewhere where? Somewhere good, or somewhere bad? Somewhere there...somewhere ahead. The wheels on the bus go round and round, round and round, round and..."* Amazing what drugs can do to a fragile mind, and Marvin's mind was cracking open even more by the moment.

"Happenstance." Not a word a lot of people use in their daily vocabulary, but an interesting word. Webster's definition, happenstance is defined as "a chance, or accidental happening." An appropriate word which would sum up what was currently happening, and what was about to happen next to Marvin and all the passengers on his bus. No, this wasn't the road that led back to the Sunny Side Up Retirement Home. Nor was this the road that led back to the mall from which they had just come. No, this road was the road that would lead them all – directly to Hell.

"The wheels on the bus go round and round..."

CHAPTER 29

RAIN, TEARS, AND TRAGEDY.

As the rain started to come down harder, Mill Lane Road, an unlit, old farmer's road between Highway 14 to the north and the mall far behind, was dotted with intermittent lighting from the nearby adjoining farm houses. Timmy was returning from a visit to his brother's gravesite at the cemetery with his dog Butch, and the light, wet rain was refreshing, as so many of the previous days had been dry and hot. Unpredictable Wisconsin weather. The weather reports hardly ever got it right. The few remaining farms in the area badly needed the water for their last remaining crops before fall ended and winter started to set in.

It had been one of those long "hot-as-hell" summers, followed by an on-and-off rainy autumn, "mostly off" as Timmy's father would bemoan. They always joked about moving south, maybe to Florida, but that was as far as that conversation got, just a laugh and maybe a silent wish.

The rain that started as a light drizzle, and now was becoming a bit more, brought a smile to Timmy's boyish looking face, and a few barks from his happy dog who ran beside him. Timmy enjoyed running with Butch. Timmy used to enjoy running with his younger brother Ryan. But since his death, Butch was the "one" most important thing that brought some joy to his broken heart. As a result of Ryan's tragic and untimely death, which still haunted him, Butch had become his new best friend. Butch had helped Timmy put his fragile mind back together and literally was "the glue that held him together." They were inseparable. They truly loved being together. Nothing could ever keep them apart. Timmy would never ever let anything, or anyone, do that to them. His mom and dad realized their special bond. Butch seemed to get Timmy back on track and out of his self-made shell over the past year. And without any real friends from school or the neighboring houses, Timmy's whole world revolved around Butch, and Butch's whole world revolved around Timmy. A boy and his dog. Unconditional love.

It was only natural that, as it started to rain harder, Timmy and Butch ran faster. Home was just around the next bend, over the slight grassy hill of the adjoining farmer's field, and up the long (but not so long), worn, and cracked asphalt driveway that needed repair. It was just a matter of time before they would be dry and warm and spend the rest of the night in Timmy's bedroom, when they would both crawl under the covers and go to sleep. Timmy's dreams improved since Butch came into his life. Good dreams chased away the nightmares that haunted him so much since his brother's death. Butch protected him from the bad dreams. And Timmy loved him all the more for that. Timmy believed that when Butch slept next to him, his dog's dreams were probably good, too. That was how it should be, and always would be, in Timmy's young world. A boy and his dog. Best friends. Unconditional love.

From around the bend, as Timmy and Butch got there together, the headlights came first. The speeding, out-of-control retirement home shuttle bus came next. It happened so quick. It was like blinking one's eyes. Before and After.

Marvin was too stoned to react, and even if he could, it was too late. The shuttle bus was skidding off the road, swerving right, left, right, left, and right into them. Or, as it was, into one of them. Somehow Butch knew. Somehow Butch reacted. Somehow Butch jumped up and knocked Timmy aside, as the bus went full speed into the dog's body where Timmy, moments ago, had stood. The impact of the speeding bus snapped Butch's back in half, sending the dog airborne, landing a few feet from Timmy.

Timmy. His master, his best friend, this human boy that he belonged to, and would always be part of. Butch and Timmy. Inseparable. Unconditional love. Butch gave his life to save Timmy's. Butch was more than just a dog. He was a hero. He was a guardian angel. He was Timmy's brother incarnate, who had returned here to protect him.

The skidding bus slowed to a stop yards ahead of the accident. Timmy crawled across the wet ground, and through the rain and ground puddles to the still-breathing, but badly bleeding body of Butch. With dirt and mud across his clothing, he reached out his shaking hands for his dog. The rain seemed to change to tears as Timmy held his dog's head carefully, gently, lovingly in his arms. Butch slowly, painfully, looked up at him and licked at Timmy's hands. It was just a matter of moments. A few moments. They both knew it. They both felt it, though neither of them understood it.

The dog's licking stopped. Butch's eyes closed, and he died. Just like that. Before and After. Before, he was alive. After, he was dead. Timmy held the dog's dead body tighter and started to rock back and forth the way he once held the dead body of his brother. Back and forth, before and after. Back and forth.

A mixture of shouts rose up, approaching him in the rain.

"Jesus Christ, that dog almost killed us!" shouted Marvin, not caring or believing that he was the one at fault, that the dog was just doing what it had to do to protect his master. Doing what Timmy had failed to do, to protect his dog.

Marvin's words resonated in Timmy's mind, *"...'that' dog almost killed us." "...that dog almost killed US!"*

"Next time, keep your mutt on a leash. There's a goddamn leash law. You probably damaged my bus," Marvin yelled at Timmy, as the rain continued to fall even harder.

"Come on, Marvin, we gotta go. I'm gonna miss the weather report." The voice of Susan Deerwish came from an open bus window, mimicking what her friend DeeDee said earlier.

Timmy didn't hear her voice, or any of the others. In a kneeling position on the muddy side of the road, he held his lifeless dog in his arms and continued to rock back and forth. He was too numb to say anything. He was too angry to find the right words to reply. He was in a state of shock. A very bad state of shock.

The twelve residents left the bus now and came slowly upon the scene. With their walkers stowed away in the bus lower compartments, they held on to one another for support. A few had their canes. A few held their arms outwards, balancing themselves as if walking a tightrope. They swayed back and forth, unsteady, almost mimicking Timmy's movements while appearing ready to fall over at any moment. They shuffled through the puddles as the rain continued. It was like a "march of the penguins," or a "march of the future walking dead." They slowly gathered in a semi-circle around Timmy and his dog. In the midst of the headlights from the parked bus, a nearby rusty light on a telephone pole, and a flashlight held by one of the residents, it was a very eerie scene to behold, or be a part of. It became very, very quiet. The only sound was the splashing rain drops on the asphalt roadway they stood on, while staring at Timmy and the dog in his arms.

"Well, if you had an elephant instead of a dog, this would never have happened," Casper Merlinski broke the silence.

And then they all started to talk. One by one, some on top of each other's comments.

"This weather reminds me about a story about a duck who went into a bar." Milton Schwartz laughed out loud at his own joke.

"You and your jokes. This isn't funny; the kid's dog is dead," a somber Casper calmly stated.

"I'm getting wet. Can't help him now. It looks like the dog is dead," Clive Rinaudo followed Casper's comment with a similar assessment of the situation. Then his attention went to a shiny object in the dirt. "Well, look at that! A penny!" He quickly pocketed his prize.

"All da-da-dogs go to heaven. This da-da-dog is now-now beside da-the Lord," Father Novak stuttered to everyone in a sermon-like voice.

"We'll miss the early-bird specials. Today's clam chowder soup. I love clam chowder soup. And chocolate chip cookies, I even like to bake them. My first husband loved my chocolate chip cookies," DeeDee Lapinsky explained to the entire group that didn't pay any attention to her.

"DeeDee's right. Unless we leave now, we're going to miss supper. The restaurant is only open till 6:30, and they don't serve a minute after that," Mr. Scott, the twenty-something chaperone added while looking at his watch, obviously more concerned with getting back to the retirement home so he could go out with his friends later that night.

"It's exactly 5:44. We'll be there 7 minutes before the restaurant closes," Jonathon Stone predicted, knowing what time it was without looking at a watch, which he didn't wear anyway.

"Hey, is that a dog? It looks like a nice dog. I had a dog once, used to bark all the time. Real noisy dog. Cats are quiet; they don't bark, but this dog is real quiet. Maybe it's a cat," DeeDee chimed sweetly back into the conversation.

"My grandkids are coming to visit. I don't want to miss them," Dorothy Paine moaned out loud, mostly to herself.

"I think it's raining. I'm getting wet. It must be raining. I can't get my makeup wet." Susan Deerwish held one hand over her head as if to protect herself from the rain.

"I'm catching laryngitis out here," complained Charley Harris quietly to anyone else who was listening, but wouldn't hear him anyways.

"My walker is gonna rust!" Bette MaGoo exclaimed with a sense of urgency.

"You don't have a walker. You hung on to my arm," her sister Joan quickly tried to remind her.

"I want my walker. Your arm is wet," Bette shouted back at her sister, as if she were deaf.

"Oh, stop it! You're an old coot," Joan quickly shouted back at Bette.

"I am not. You're an old coot," they both shouted out loud at each other at the exact time.

"You're an older coot," Bette mumbled after a moment of silence under her breath, as she turned away to look for some vocal support from anyone else in the group.

No one responded, because no one cared, or even listened. Most of the residents had just come out of the bus into the rain from curiosity, not any real concern for what just happened. Their only real concern was for themselves.

Bette turned back to her sister and reached out to hold her arm, forgetting what they both had just said.

"Oh my. My makeup is ruined from the rain, too. Why aren't there umbrellas? I need an umbrella. I once had a nice red umbrella; always could find it because it was a bright red umbrella. All umbrellas should be bright red cause then you can find them easier because they are bright red just like firetrucks are bright red," DeeDee Lapinsky concluded, even though no one listened or even cared.

Between the rain and accident, Marvin's coked-up, mixed-up mind state was diminishing. Some sort of normal, if you could call it that, was returning to him. And in that normal, his first thought was, *"I gotta get more coke."*

"Enough. Enough. Jeezuz. The show's over. Alright. That's enough. Everyone back to the bus," Marvin barked to the surrounding group of geezer onlookers.

"Okay, group, let's go back to the bus," the two retirement home chaperones Miss McDermott and Mr. Scott shouted above the falling rain and the residents' continued mumblings.

Slowly and methodically they started to gather them together as if they were two sheep dogs, herding their wandering flock in the direction they needed to go.

They collectively all turned, as if they were trained to follow instructions. They held onto each other's hands, arms, shoulders, canes, or waved their hands in the air as if holding an imaginary friend. Shuffling, wobbling and staggering through the rain, they returned to the bus. Without any further comments or heartfelt compassion, they left the still sobbing Timmy in the mud and grass beside the road holding his dead dog.

They all walked away, all but one. Domingo Rodriguez.

"Mucho sorry, ked. Damn shame your dog's dead. Damn shame," Domingo said sadly, and softly, to the grieving young boy kneeling before him.

Without another word, Domingo turned, and slowly walked away. He was the last to board the bus. And just before he climbed into the open bus door, he stopped and looked back. Shaking his head, he repeated to himself the same thing he said to the boy, "Damn shame."

As the bus engine cranked over, it let out a loud backfire noise from the rusting muffler. From inside the bus you could hear a couple giggles, laughs, and shocked "Oh my's." Just like a bunch of school kids; not something you would expect a bunch of 80- and 90-year-olds to do.

The muffler's noise made most of them forget the weird spectacle they were just part of. Even though they were wet and tired, whatever was left of their fading minds and forgetful memories, all reverted back to one single thought, *"Gotta get back before the restaurant closes."*

As the bus pulled away, it startled Timmy enough to bring him out of his shock. Kneeling on the ground next to the roadway holding the dead dog, he could see the fresh dent on the front of the bus where it had hit Butch. There was a streak of red blood from the impact dripping off the dent and mixing in with the falling rain. Timmy watched the bus pass him, leaving him alone. His eyes saw the bus tail lights illuminate the imprinted words, "Sunny Side Up Retirement Home."

"Friendly. Happy. The Place to Be."

"Enjoy Your Life. Safe and Carefree!"

The bus tail lights became smaller and smaller as it traveled away into the darkness and steady rain, leaving Timmy alone, still holding Butch. His rocking back and forth on the ground slowed as he watched the bus leave. But now, left all alone, with nothing but a broken heart, he started to rock faster again. Real fast. He began to whisper to himself, then to the empty world that surrounded him. Then to the heaven above, and to the hell below.

"They killed Butch. They killed Butch. They killed Butch. They killed Ryan. They killed Ryan. They killed..."

There on the ground in the mud not far from Timmy and the broken and bleeding body of Butch was an identification badge. It had belonged to one of the old people who had stood around him. One of the old people who didn't care about him, or his dog, or his brother. They only cared about their interrupted time, the troublesome rain, and missing the comforts of their "place to be."

As suddenly as he started the rocking, he stopped. As tightly as he held the body of Butch, he opened his arms and let it fall to the rain-soaked ground. Timmy crawled across the mud, and through the puddles, to where the ID lay on the roadway. He picked it up and looked at it. It had a smiling picture of Dorothy Paine, Building #7, Apartment 101, and the street address of the Sunny Side Up Retirement Home.

He looked at it long and hard. Then he tucked it into his jacket pocket and stared in the direction the bus had gone.

Before and After. Everything in Timmy's life had just changed. Just like that.

The bus lights disappeared into the foreboding darkness. As did Timmy's fragile mind.

CHAPTER 30

WHEN RAIN TURNS TO TEARS.

The rain had finally stopped when Timmy approached the front wooden porch steps to his house. He could see his mother and father arguing through the living room window. The closed window prevented him from hearing anything. Watching his parents moving back and forth in the room and shouting at each other was like watching a silent movie in his mind. They had been arguing a lot since his brother's death. It bothered him, but he didn't understand all the reasons why. It was hard for a 10-year-old child to understand all the "whys" of what parents do, or don't do. There are so many of them as one grows up.

Adding to all those whys, here he was at this moment with another one. Why did his best friend, his dog, who he imagined to be the reincarnation of his brother Ryan, have to die? Why?

Carrying the limp, dead body of Butch in both of his outstretched and blood-covered arms, Timmy climbed the three wooden steps to the porch landing. They were well worn, definitely needing paint. Under normal circumstances, he would put that on a bucket list of things to do. Other than the pitter patter of the falling rain around him, and a distant roll of thunder, he and Butch were both rain soaked and shrouded in an eerie silence. At the top of the stairs, Timmy stopped, stood still, and faced the front door. Now the silent movie became a real movie as the sounds of his yelling parents could finally be heard through the thin glass windows.

"Maybe if you spent more time with him as your son instead of as a soldier, he'd be acting normal," Mrs. Jameson shouted at her husband.

"There is no such thing as normal. The whole world is messed up. We have to protect ourselves. If we don't, no one else will," he replied in an angry, but professional, military tone.

"You're not in the army anymore. Become a parent, stop playing drill sergeant." Mrs. Jameson's words shot back at him, cutting into his heart and soul.

And with that, he slapped her. Right across the right cheek, really hard, turning her head violently, and forcing her to take a step backwards.

Without a rebuttal to his shocking act of violence, she touched her face and could feel the burning sensation under the red flushed skin. Their eyes met in a long, drawn-out silence. She put her hand down, straightened her neck, and slowly, without hesitation, stepped forward.

She spit on him.

He stood there silently as the spit rolled down his face. There seemed to be a long pause. A pause that turned into a long moment that lasted forever. Then she spit on him again.

Timmy saw all of this unfold as he stood outside the window with Butch in his arms. A distant roll of thunder broke both the outside silence and the silence in his mind. He wanted to scream but didn't know how. But that didn't matter, the scream or screams wouldn't have helped. Nothing could help him. He was already teetering on the edge of insanity.

The rain was starting again, though not as hard as before. It was coming down faster and was the only sound to be heard. It splashed on the wooden front porch floor, combining with the additional water falling from the leaky gutters above. Another project that had to be done. Always another "something to do." Maybe that's why his mom would chide his dad with her "honey-do list;" "honey do this, honey do that." Loving parents would have those type of lists to laugh at. But this was no laughing matter. The scene he witnessed was not part of the honey-do list. There was no evidence of family love tonight, just another disturbing "something" to clutter Timmy's already confused mind.

Another sound of thunder. Timmy turned away from the house. He decided he wanted no further part of this argument, this situation, this moment. With stinging rain falling off his face, he proceeded back down the porch steps carrying the limp dog, towards the backyard barn.

A sudden bolt of lightning illuminated his walk through the muddy and grassy ground. The lightning was accompanied by a booming sound of thunder, loud enough to wake the dead. Not yet. Death was to come, but it had to wait for Timmy. But it wouldn't be long. The flash of lightning showed an expressionless face. There were no more tears flowing from his bloodshot eyes. There was only a deep, deep sadness in his eyes. Eyes that led to a very empty soul. Eyes that became filled with more and more hatred with each step, as his anger and pain overcame his body.

Inside the barn, he gently placed the dog in a dry area. He stood looking at it. Butch looked so peaceful in death that one might think it brought some peace to Timmy in life. But it didn't. He turned and went exactly to where he knew it would be – his father's shovel.

Returning to where he had placed him, Timmy picked up Butch, and carried both the dog and the shovel out into the rain. Following the well-worn path through the overgrown goldenrod surrounding the barn, Timmy moved in and out of the shadows away from the house. He went past the small family vegetable garden, which bore little results this year from a long, dry summer, but certainly not today, and towards the top of the hill which overlooked the entire family grounds.

Timmy went directly to the area where he once played with his brother Ryan. To the same area where they had played cops and robbers, cowboys and Indians, and "Bang-Bang. You're Dead." He stopped at the exact spot so etched in his memory of where he once held his dead brother.

Timmy dropped the shovel first, and then placed Butch gently on the wet ground. The rain was now a steady drizzle with the thunder and fewer flashes of lightning in the distance behind him.

Picking up his dad's shovel, Timmy began to dig into the wet ground. It was a good shovel, strong handle, well-placed foot rest, and a sharp, triangular blade. The digging went easy, not saying it was fun, but it went easy as the ground was soft from all the heavy rain, and it didn't take long for just the right type of grave to be dug to place Butch in. Probably two feet deep by four feet wide. Timmy didn't know any better about burial specifics, not that it mattered. But he did know that dead people, and now his dead dog, needed a final resting place. His mom had told him that after Ryan's death. Everyone needed a final resting place. And what better place than this?

Taking off his brown-colored jacket, Timmy held it at arms-length, looking at it. The jacket was a favorite of his; it even had a Cleveland Indians baseball patch that his mother had sewn on earlier this summer. Timmy didn't like sports much, but he did like the Cleveland Indians patch. It had a smiling Indian face. Sort of reminded him of all the times he would play the game of cowboys and Indians with his brother. And when Butch came into his life, it reminded him of all the times he would throw a ball and have Butch run after it in a game of fetch. Butch liked that game a lot.

Checking his pocket to make sure it was still there, and it was, Timmy pulled out a well-chewed baseball that Butch loved to gnaw on. He rolled it back and forth in his wet hand, looking at it fondly, maybe remembering some special moments shared playing with his dog and with his brother. Memories that were beginning to fade, as was his mind.

Returning the ball to the jacket pocket, Timmy placed his jacket into the freshly dug hole. There were a few puddles of water forming in it from the still-drizzling rain. Timmy watched the water splashing in the dirt and it made him smile. It wasn't rain water in the grave, it was the tears of the angels above watching over him. Maybe even the tears of Ryan.

Timmy went back to Butch who lay restful, almost like he was sleeping, in the rain-soaked grass a few feet from the grave. Kneeling beside him, Timmy gently petted him a few last times. Butch's curly brown-and-white coat was matted with mud and remnants of dried blood. His hand felt the dog's still body and his smile disappeared. He thought of how warm it used to be, when his dog would snuggle up with him in his bed, bringing him a comfort that made him sleep peacefully through the night. Now Butch, in his new bed in the earth, would sleep through all the nights. Through eternity, if there really was such a thing.

Sliding his hands and arms under the dog, Timmy stood up, carefully holding him. A closer flash of lightning illuminated the strange and sad scene. There was no emotion on Timmy's face, and certainly none on Butch's. Nothing. Just an eerie emptiness.

Gently carrying his dog to the freshly dug and open grave, Timmy stood quietly holding him for one last time. One long, last time.

Another flash of lightning illuminated the lone tear that came down Timmy's face, falling onto the face of Butch. Maybe it wasn't a tear, maybe it was the rain. Didn't matter.

Slowly kneeling into the muddy ground, Timmy placed Butch on top of his jacket in the open grave. He took the jacket arms and folded them over the dog, covering Butch as much as he could. Butch looked so peaceful. If he were alive, or a part of this strange spectacle, he might have been pleased, if that were possible.

Standing back up, Timmy turned and reached for the shovel which he had placed upright into the wet ground next to the grave. He started to shovel the dirt back in. It didn't take long. When completed, there was a slight mound to the filled hole. That was good, Timmy thought to himself. It looked like a grave. In another flash of fading lightning, Timmy saw two small wooden limbs that had fallen from a nearby tree. Picking them up, he snapped each one over his wet and bloody pants that covered his knee and knelt next to the grave. He laid the sticks across each other in the sign of a cross. It would have to do until he could come back with a real wooden cross that he planned to make.

Making the sign of the cross on his forehead, he bowed his head, and folded his hands in prayer. It didn't matter what he said. It was probably just some mumbo-jumbo words he had learned when he went to some Sunday Mass with his parents. He remembered the words but didn't know the meaning. After all, he was only 10 years old. To really understand the meaning of prayer took a lot of studying and believing. Timmy didn't care for either. He went to Mass because his parents took him to Mass. He didn't believe, because he didn't care to believe. Maybe that was a good thing in a moment like this; maybe it was a bad thing. Whatever it was, it was a personal thing. Timmy's mind was cluttered enough in distorted emotions without trying to sort it all out and make some sense of it.

From a distance behind him he heard a sudden howl of the wind, or at least he thought it was the wind. It was almost an ungodly, unholy sound. It almost sounded like someone crying, or a lot of someones crying. Perhaps the angels, perhaps... As quickly as he heard it, it ended. It had briefly startled him and brought him back to some sort of reality, albeit a reality, twisted as it was.

The rain started to increase again. The storm was still there; it had taken just a short break. Maybe God wanted it that way, so Timmy could do his burial properly. Didn't matter. Rain or no rain. Tears, or no tears. Timmy had buried his dog, and now he had to make things right. No, not in his mind. His mind would never be right again. Timmy had to make things right in the only way he felt things could be right. He had some killing to do. A lot of killing.

CHAPTER 31

WHAT ONLY A MIRROR SEES.

Inside the Jameson house, Mrs. Jameson stood alone in the small, upstairs bathroom in between the only two bedrooms – the one for her and her husband, and the other that the two boys used to share. She looked in the bathroom mirror where her face had been slapped moments ago. It was starting to swell up. She was thin skinned to begin with, so it didn't take much to leave a bruise, a lump, or some sort of swelling. Her shaking thin hand pulled the knob on the mirrored door and opened the wall medicine cabinet. There were a lot of pill bottles there, mostly labeled with Mr. Jameson's name for his post-war depression, his anger, his anxieties, his mood swings, his sexual dysfunction, his high blood pressure, etc.

There were only two prescriptions for her. One was for Valium, to relax her after the burial of her son, and the other to help her sleep. Opening both prescription bottles, she took one pill out of each, and then put the plastic caps back on. She was ready to replace both prescriptions in the cabinet, but instead stopped and held them in her hand. Slowly, she put each on the small wood-chipped sink countertop and closed the mirrored cabinet door.

Looking at herself again in the mirror, her face was even more swollen. Her old-for-her-age fingers touched her warm face where the slap had occurred. Moving them slowly up and down the swelling, she could almost feel the slap again and again. It had hurt her more than just as a slap. It cut deeper, into her loss of feelings for her husband. A loss which grew more each day since the loss of their son. She blamed both herself and him. The slap was just another proverbial "nail in the coffin," as the old saying goes.

Moving her fingers away from her face, her hand reached forward and touched her image in the mirror. Her fingers moved up and down her mirror image, as if they were connected, as if the person in the mirror was real and she was just a reflection. She looked long and hard at her mirrored image, and then into her heart and soul. A single tear rolled down her face and the face she looked at. Her fingers touched the tear in the mirror.

A flash of lightning appeared in the small bathroom window next to her. It was followed by a clap of thunder. Without any expression, she picked up each prescription bottle, took the tops back off, and poured a handful of pills into her hand.

There were a lot of pills. Enough to make all her pain go away, for both herself and her image in the mirror. Enough pills to make her sleep for a long, long time. And make the woman in the mirror disappear forever.

Downstairs, Mr. Jameson sat alone at the kitchen table drinking a beer. There were already two empty bottles next to the half-empty one that was still on the table in front of him. One of the empty bottles was on its side, spilling a few drops out onto the table. Tentatively, Mr. Jameson looked at it, as if trying to make a decision. A decision that weighed heavily on his mind, or what was left of it. A decision that he tried to find a focus on but couldn't. Not yet, but soon.

Reaching his hand out, he touched the bottle that lay on its side in the center of the table. His strong and large fingers tapped on the bottle, once, twice, repeatedly. And then he stopped the tapping as suddenly as he had begun. He spun the bottle on the table. It went around and around. As it finally came to a stop, he looked at it for a brief moment and spun it again. Sort of like the "spin the bottle" kissing game he must have played as a teenager. Except now, at this very moment, there was no one else in the room to play the game with. No one to kiss. Maybe someone to curse. Only he knew. He was playing it all by himself.

The spinning bottle slowed and finally came to a stop. It pointed directly at him. He stared at it, long and hard. In the curved-shaped glass, he saw a reflection of himself, as if he were looking into a mirror. A distorted reflection. A disturbing reflection.

His hand quickly touched the bottle again, and with a twist of his wrist, it spun again, and again, and again. Each time harder and harder. Faster and faster. With each spin, his anger seemed to grow more and more, until the bottle finally spun itself out of control and went careening off the table and onto the worn linoleum kitchen floor. Crashing, it shattered into a million, or maybe two million pieces. So, did his mind.

A flash of lightning came through the adjacent kitchen window, and a roll of thunder hid the sound of the smashing glass. The storm was far from over. It was just about to begin.

Picking up a sharp, broken shard of the glass bottle from the floor, he looked at it curiously, seemingly to examine it, thinking about it, deciding what to do with it. As he did this, he held it in his hand, almost too tightly, and then even tighter, as a few drops of blood came from inside his palm, spreading across his clenched hand like red spiderwebs. Still holding the broken piece of glass, his decision was finally made.

Without hesitation, he left the kitchen, and quietly went up the stairs leading to their bedroom.

CHAPTER 32

WHEN NIGHTMARES BECOME REALITY.

Jonathon Stone sat quietly in his favorite leather sofa chair looking directly at the door leading into his apartment. An old, fairly worn, but very comfortable grey woolen blanket covered his one hand in his lap. In the other hand he held a shiny silver dollar coin which he turned back and forth between his thumb and forefinger. It went back and forth from heads to tails, head to tails. A few table lights placed on end tables around the room gave out an eerie illumination as if foreshadowing something that was about to happen. An old RCA phonographic record player in the corner of the living room played the song "Chances Are" by Johnny Mathis.

"Chances are, 'cause I wear a silly grin the moment you come into view."

It was an appropriate song, with appropriate words, for an appropriate moment such as this. For his entire lifetime Jonathon had prepared himself for this very moment. He knew what was coming. And it did.

His apartment door opened inward, and Timmy stood in the shadow and light from the surrounding hallway. The gun, a Glock 9mm semi-automatic with a silencer, which he had used so many times earlier this night, was held in his right hand that hung by his side. Jonathon sensed that Timmy was older than the age of 10. Not older in wisdom and maturity, but older in hatred. Timmy also had the look and smell of death, and now he was here, finally.

"Just because my composure sort of slips the moment your eyes meet mine."

"Please come in," Jonathon said without expression.

Was the spider inviting the fly into his parlor, or was the web of horror going to engulf them both?

"I've been expecting you," Jonathon continued.

"And I've been waiting to meet you," Timmy replied matter of factly. Almost too factly.

Jonathon did not verbally reply but nodded his head with a slight frown on his face, as if he had expected that answer.

Stepping into the room, Timmy closed the door behind him. He stood maybe eight or ten feet away from Jonathon, who still sat in his chair. Although the light in the room was mostly subdued, Jonathon had planned it that way. There was just enough light to illuminate both their faces. And now, Jonathon, although blind since birth, could finally see him in his mind, in the presence he felt – after all these years of his premonitions, his feelings, his sensations, his knowing. Yes, his knowing. That was what Jonathon did best, he knew. Finally, he could look this expected intruder full in the face, full in his eyes, and full into his soul. Even without sight, Jonathon could see. It was a gift that made him who he was. It was a gift that some would say was really a curse.

Whether it was a biological energy or aura of the person who stood before him that formed the images in his mind, or an uncanny awareness or consciousness, Jonathon's ability to see in his mind cannot be truly explained. And what he now saw was a physical manifestation of all the demons that had haunted him all his life, and culminated in this exact moment, this expected meeting. His nightmare was now a reality.

As Jonathon stared straight ahead, Timmy inched slowly closer. With each step, a big sardonic smile widened on the young boy's face. Yes, Jonathon thought to himself, this boy was older than the age of ten. He was actually as old as time could measure. This was not a 10-year-old boy in a 10-year-old body, this was not even a child, this was the devil himself. Jonathon knew this for sure, because through those eyes which he could not look into, and beneath the smile he could not see, he could feel there was no soul. Only evil. Pure evil.

Timmy stopped a few feet away from Jonathon who remained quietly in his chair while staring straight ahead. Jonathon stopped his hand movement with the silver coin, and without any hesitation or difficulty, gently placed it on the end table next to him as if he had done this a thousand-plus times before.

There was a long moment of silence, which was finally broken when Jonathon's empty hand reached upwards to his face and removed his dark sunglasses which he always wore. Where there should have been a set of matching eyes, there was, instead, a set of two dark holes. Most people never experienced seeing Jonathon this way without his sunglasses. The few who had were always shocked. Not Timmy. He just turned his own head slightly back and forth while looking expressionlessly at the psychic in the chair.

Both Jonathon and Timmy, or should I clarify, both Jonathon and the Devil Incarnate remained silent while looking at each other. Each studying the other's expression, or lack of expression, each looking into each other's hidden pasts, their immediate present, and whatever future possibly existed. Each knowing what brought them there for this very moment of truth. Truth, if there was such a thing. Truth, which supposedly holds all the answers to all the questions. Truth which reveals that which cannot be denied. This was, as it was now, a moment of truth between them. A moment, a long time coming.

Time stopped.

And then Jonathon spoke the truth.

"I'm not the last one," he said emotionlessly.

"Maybe," Timmy replied without any emotion also.

"No," Jonathon replied, as if thinking to himself, or talking to himself out loud. "No, there's one more." He paused, then continued, "No, there's actually two more," he concluded with a slight nod in his head as if he knew. "Actually, several more," he added satisfyingly to his last comment.

"What makes you think that?" Timmy said quizzically, as if this were a game of mind chess. ("*You move, I move, next move?*")

"I don't 'think' that. I know that," Jonathon replied quickly, and just as quick, paused, then continued, "And I know why you're here."

Timmy took another step forward, now cutting the original distance between them in half. His smiling expression changed to more of a boyish wonderment, or maybe one of intrigue. *"Does he really know why I am here? And if he does, why is he still here?"* Timmy thought to himself. *"Your move."*

"It was an accident. An unfortunate accident, nothing more, nothing less. It happened. Maybe it shouldn't have happened, but it was meant to happen. Everything is meant to happen," Jonathon spoke up, moving his head to have his empty eye sockets look directly at Timmy's widening eyes.

"Stop digging in my mind," Timmy responded with more than a hint of anger in his voice. "You killed my brother."

Checkmate. Or?

Jonathon wondered if the boy was hiding a secret that was yet to be revealed. This "killed-my-brother comment" made Jonathan feel very uncomfortable for the first time in a long time. Uncomfortable, because he did not sense this coming. For someone who thought he was all knowing, this was something he didn't know, and it caught him off guard.

"Your brother?" Jonathon replied in both a question and a statement.

"You and all the others killed my brother!" Timmy raised his voice even more, as a stinging statement.

Jonathon's mind raced in overtime. He tried to hurriedly put all the pieces of the jumbled puzzle together. *"What brother? Was there someone else there in the road besides this kid and his dog?"*

Jonathon always had a vision of a young boy and his dog. A vision that came and went over the years but became stronger over time. At first, just a repeating vision of a young boy and a dog catching a ball. The vision, or let's call it a premonition, eventually included a small gun, a hand gun, in someone's hand. And recently, the past few nights, the vision showed him looking at blood on his hands, smiling. He was definitely smiling at the blood on his hands. That was it. There was nothing more. There was no "dead brother" in any of the many visions. A boy, Timmy, and a dog, the cocker spaniel. Jonathon was on the bus; he was there at the accident. The shuttle bus hit a dog, just a dog. No one else. No one on the bus said anything about hitting a child. And he was certain that didn't happen. Everyone said that a dog was dead. Nothing else. No one else. *"A gun, now he's here holding a gun. And the blood on my hands, and the smile. It all adds up."* A frown came over his face. He knew what was coming next, he knew the outcome. He had even planned for it. But, the dead brother thing? It made no sense. His premonitions always added up, just like they did now in his mind. And the outcome would be in his favor. It had to be in his favor, it was always in his favor. Because he always knew. He always knew. But now, maybe he didn't. But, maybe...?

"There was no brother. There was only a dog. Just you, us, and the dog," Jonathon finally replied in a stern tone, as if he were a parent scolding his child, setting the record straight.

"No. No. NO! You killed my brother. You ALL killed my brother! You're all murderers, and this is the fault of all of you!" Timmy shouted back, no longer controlling his seething emotion, nor holding back his ready-to-explode anger.

"You're a fucking killer!" Timmy's voice was loud enough to echo through the small apartment. It was loud enough to drown out any semblance of the continuing words in the song "Chances Are" which played in the background.

"Guess you feel you'll always be the one and only one for me."

And then just as quickly as he yelled, he stopped. He stood there, slowly raising his one hand which held the gun.

Jonathon's body tensed while his mind raced with a mixture of thoughts. He needed more time to assimilate this. He was a psychic, not a psychiatrist. This revelation that the kid thought his dog was his brother left him confused. But if anyone was fucked up, it was the kid, not him. Jonathon had one more chess-like move to play, before the game would be over. He had to ask one more question, to buy one more moment of time, to be sure that the outcome would be just as he knew it to be or felt it should be. One more very important question that may hold the answer to all this madness.

"Your brother. Was he there when the bus hit the dog? Was he behind you? Next to you? In front of you?" Jonathan asked if as if trying to get the kid to understand that he was wrong, and maybe just imagining a dead brother.

As if hitting the nail on the head, Timmy appeared shaken, stunned. There was no immediate answer from Timmy. He just slowly, almost painfully, lowered his gun back to his side.

Jonathon's words made him realize that there was something, somewhere in this kid's messed-up mind, something that connected the dog and his dead brother together. Maybe Jonathon was a psychiatrist, too. Maybe he just hit the proverbial nail on the head, hit the home run over the fence, threw the glass of water into the kid's puzzled face to shock him enough and bring him back to some sort of reality, if he had any left at all.

Timmy stood there, probably thinking Jonathon's words over, probably beginning to see he was wrong, probably realizing that "Mr. Know It All" knew it all, and was right. Just like a kid's game, taunting each other, "Nyah, nyah, nyah, nyah, nyah!" For sure this was probably just psycho-therapy-babble trying to defuse and confuse this whole situation.

"Good move," Jonathon thought to himself. *"Checkmate, back to you."*

And then Timmy shifted his body under his growing discomfort. His eyes narrowed, his face twisted into an undeniable smirk, and his words were slow and concise, "You killed my brother...and you killed my dog."

"Here we go again," Jonathon said to himself. *"This kid really needs help. And it's up to me to help him. What else can I say that..."*

"Your mom and dad must be worried that you're not home," Jonathon blurted out without further thought. "Do your mom and dad know you're here? You don't want to make your parents upset with you?" Jonathan slowed it down and asked with a more compassionate voice.

"Yep, I've got the kid confused. Rethinking, realizing, believing that his parents are worried. The parents' concern will make him recognize that what he's doing is wrong. The parents' thing always gets any kid's attention. Christ, it always got my attention when I was a kid, when I was told I was wrong. Parents are always right," Jonathon smugly thought to himself.

There was no response from Timmy. There was another long pause between them. And then the pause ended.

Timmy's weird and twisted-looking devilish smile returned to his boyish face.

"You killed them, too," Timmy spoke softly.

Raising his arm again, this time Timmy pointed his gun directly at Jonathon's face.

Final checkmate, over your checkmate. Game over.

"No, not over. This isn't the end of this cat-and-mouse game," Jonathon quickly thought to himself. He already knew the outcome. This game of life and death wasn't over yet. It was all playing out the way his visions had put it together. A young boy. A dog. A gun. Blood on his hands. And a smile on his face.

Jonathon had one more move to make.

"You're not going to kill me." Jonathon spoke clearly in defiance. "No... I'm going to kill you."

From Jonathon's lap, his one hidden hand raised upward from underneath the wool blanket that covered his lap and pointed a small handgun of his own. A gun that was concealed from Timmy the whole time. A gun that Jonathon knew he had to have. His visions, his premonitions had always showed him a gun. A gun that he recently acquired, and had prepared himself for this very moment, and the moment that was about to happen next. His finger was on the trigger. It had been on the trigger the whole time. He knew what he had to do. His premonition told him over and over and over again. A big smile suddenly widened on Jonathon's emotionless face as the final words to the song played...

"And if you think you could. Well, chances are your chances are... awfully good."

He quickly pointed the gun directly at Timmy and pulled the trigger. Finally. Just as he predicted.

"Bang-bang. You're dead."

CHAPTER 33

AND SO, THE END BEGINS.

Mrs. Jameson swallowed a lot of pills. A whole lot of pills. And quite a mixture. Lots of little yellow ones, a few mid-sized pink ones, and some "really big" white ones. Most belonged to her, some belonged to her husband. She swallowed two, maybe three handfuls. The descriptions on the bottles were basically what every doctor prescribes: "a cure-all for all your ailments and all your troubles." Of course, the descriptions also said not to exceed a certain amount at any one time. That was a big "no-no." She must have missed that, or paid no attention to that, since she took a whole lot of pills.

After washing them all down with a glass or two of tap water from the bathroom sink, Mrs. Jameson looked straight into the bathroom cabinet mirror and nodded silently to herself. She knew what she did was wrong. She knew what she did was right. She just knew. And now she knew what she had to do next.

Leaving the empty plastic prescription bottles on the bathroom counter, she went into their bedroom and took out her best dress from the closet. It was a pink flowery one. But when she saw her wedding dress hanging there, enclosed in a protective bag, she knew that was the dress she had to wear.

Mr. Jameson never really complimented her much since he came back from the military. Before then, he always complimented her. Showered her with affection and adulation. They were childhood sweethearts, best of friends, and even great lovers when it came to the special time they would share under the sheets. She had always been a bit shy, and really didn't parade around much in her birthday suit. But he did. And what a "birthday suit" he had. Made her "all the more" hot and ready when he entered the bed and made love. But, all that was a long time ago. A long, long time ago. The past months were a nightmare. Or let's just say "hell on earth" for both of them.

Mrs. Jameson always believed in the path the Lord planned for them and never doubted or questioned why. Mr. Jameson always believed that the path ended a long time ago when he shot some "towel heads" in a remote country he was sent to defend but didn't quite understand why. But it was his duty, and it was her duty. But their spiritual and physical paths veered further and further apart with the death of their son. Mr. Jameson could live with the haunting specter of death he saw, and was part of, but the death of a child, his son?

Mrs. Jameson was the epitome of being a good mother. She loved her sons, took care of her sons, adored her sons. They came from her, and were a part of her. They were the most important part of her life. She would even give her life for her son's life if need be. That's the way it should be. That's what a good mother does, no questions asked. She was a good mother, and a good woman all wrapped up in one. Everyone liked her. Everyone said good things about her. Her family loved her so much that if Mother's Day hadn't already existed, they would have named it after her.

But underneath it all, she had trouble coping with the death of her son, as well. Neither she nor her husband ever faced it together, ever talked about it together, or ever held each other and cried together. They each lived through it alone, in their own way. It was an endless nightmare for both.

The death of a child cannot be explained in a word, a sentence, a paragraph, a chapter, an entire book, or an encyclopedia of books. Unless you've experienced it, you have no idea. You have no idea. That's the truth, if truth can be understood. Because there are no words, no sentences, no paragraphs, no chapters, no books, no encyclopedia of books that can define one's inner most feelings, the death of a child is almost a feeling without feeling. An emptiness with something unknown in it. A phony smile that hides a real loss. It is timeless. It never ends. It never stops. It is always there, no matter where you are, no matter what you do, it is always, always, always there. You live each breathing moment with it, and then you die with it. And for both Mr. Jameson and Mrs. Jameson, there were no answers to the question "why." And for all the psychological and made-up medical answers found in a word, a sentence, a paragraph, a chapter, a book, or an encyclopedia of books, they were all a lie. Words to comfort, words to hide, words to make it all better. Just a bunch of words. Meaningful but meaningless. All lies. Only the Jamesons knew what a loss of a child really meant, and maybe you do, too. And then, only then, can you understand.

Tonight, in the middle of a storm, in the middle of words of anger, in the middle of a slap across the face, and a feeling of hatred, pure hatred, that "meaning of loss" had somehow surfaced. It reared its ugly head and their two paths, which were once so joy-filled in the beginning and middle of their married life, were now to have a final tragic end. A final, very tragic, horrible end.

When he reached the top of the stairs, Mr. Jameson stood silently, almost wavering in his posture. His face showed lines of agony and sadness from all his years. There was no happiness in his eyes, just emptiness. Dazed, confused, decided, undecided. His body seemed to rock back and forth as he tried to catch his breath. When he was young like his sons, he could scoot up the stairs like nothing mattered. But now, tonight, each step had become more and more difficult. Old age catches up to everyone, admit it or not, it really does, but this, this was more than that. This was a complete breakdown of one's mind and body. And all the alcohol he had consumed.

As he stood there, for God knows how long, a minute, an hour, a day, a lifetime, the sound of rain against their house started to increase again. The storm had come and gone and was now back. It seemed to be circling the area, circling his life. A sudden crack of thunder added another crack in his heart, as he shook his head trying to rid himself of all his inner demons. But they wouldn't leave. They laughed at him. They mocked him. They made a fool of him. She had made a fool of him. She called him names. She hated him. She despised him. She spit at him. She. She. She. She was the enemy. The real enemy that gave his life real unbearable pain. And it had to end now. It had to end forever. As if back in the hell of what one calls war, his mind had one single thought, he was on a mission. A mission of undeniable death.

Blood continued to drip from his palm as he still tightly held the broken glass. He had carried it upstairs because he thought he had a plan for its use. But plans change. So do marriages. So does life.

He held his hand open and looked at the sharp, bloodstained glass. It was stuck partially into his palm. Not too deep, but deep enough. There must have been some form of physical pain; some, but not enough. How does one measure pain? It's almost like explaining death. You can't. It's an experience. Just another of all the experiences we all go through in our life. Yet, the secret to managing pain, the secret to managing death, is acceptance. And not everyone knows how to accept it. But he did.

For Mr. Jameson, Jesse James as he was called by those who loved him, the pain he experienced throughout his life was a lot, but not as much as right now. His eyes were glossed over, almost without expression. His breath was faster and heavier, as if he were about to explode from within. Maybe because of the steep set of stairs he had just climbed. Maybe because of the exhaustion in his heart. Maybe is not an answer, it is just another excuse. His mind was filled with mixed feelings. Or maybe his mind was blank. If only someone were there beside him to ask him, would we really know. But it wasn't for us to know. Knowing is understanding. But there wouldn't be any of that tonight, or ever again. No. His pain was all consuming. Too consuming. There were no boundaries. And what he would do next, no one would know, no one would understand. Not even himself.

From a nearby window, a flash of lightning from the outside illuminated the hallway he was standing in. It was not a pretty picture. His whole body was trembling. His face was turning red in color. A deep, dark, blood red. And if you were there and were a witness to this, you would not want to ever talk about it, nor would you want to ever remember it. It was complete madness.

He closed his hand into a fist and squeezed the glass deeper into his palm. Deeper and deeper it cut into him. But there was no feeling. Nothing. Blood started to flow again. Faster. A lot of blood. If he screamed, it was silent. If he cried, it was without tears. His eyes narrowed to a slit. His face tensed tightly into a snarl. Finally, he took a step.

Without a word, without a sound, he entered their bedroom.

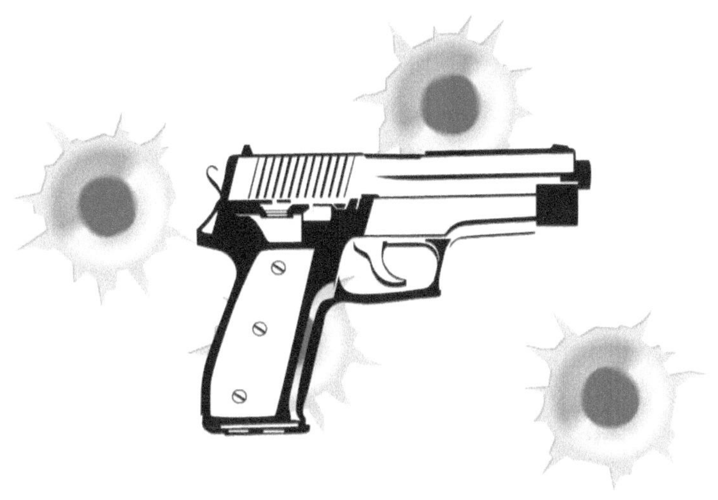

CHAPTER 34

2+2 DOESN'T ALWAYS EQUAL 4.

Ms. Judy Griswold was a very "happy-unhappy" older woman. She had reason to be. She had entered her 40th and final year of being, first, a school teacher, then a school team coach, a school student-security monitor, a school career counselor, and finally the school psychologist. Basically, she had seen it all, and she had enough. Enough! Her whole career was a roller-coaster-ride-like journey and she couldn't wait to get out. Retirement was just around the corner. Finally.

Simply put, public grade-school education had changed, collapsed, and was out of control in today's world of political correctness from the day she first entered the teaching profession. In the beginning, her young students would adoringly call her "Ms. G." and put fresh, red apples on her desk daily. In those early years, she enjoyed being a school teacher and enjoyed her children. She referred to her them as "her" children, as she had none of her own, being a lonely woman who never married. She was married to her profession. It came first and foremost. Ms. Griswold was liked, and loved, by just about every student and every member of the always changing faculty from year to year. It was a pleasure and a reward to her to be a teacher. That was then; unfortunately, this is now.

Over time, things change, and so did her career path. How she ended up being the school psychologist is a story in itself. With school budgets shrinking each year due to over-inflated administration salaries and teacher union pensions, the school's teaching staff faced what seemed like endless yearly cuts. But she was always one of the lucky ones to keep her job. She was moved around on the school employee chart and put into other academic roles, roles she never really did like, but roles that she performed well enough to keep her gainfully employed. Her tenure, and being a union member, always saved her from being put out to pasture in her later age. That, and her affair with Mr. Wilshaw.

Donald Wilshaw, was the handsome 25-year-old history teacher, who, at six-foot-two, and eyes of blue, had the most awesome sandy blonde hair that reminded her of a Beach Boy (one of her favorite bands that she grew up listening to). To say the least, she had "eyes for him" from the first day they met. Even though he was 25 and she was 50, to her, age didn't really matter. At five-foot-eight, and still keeping her weight in check, she was the most attractive of the "mature," that is, older women teachers in her school. She still had what she called "perky" breasts and had hardly any nasty old cellulite on her still shapely and slender legs. All that was on the plus side of her. On the negative side, she did have a big butt. Very big. Spread from here to there, probably from all the sitting at her desk over her 40-year career. That's a lot of sitting, and she did have a lot of butt. But, it did attract a lot of attention as she walked the school hallways, and the younger boys and many of the older teachers gave a look or two as it swished back and forth following her wherever she went. Although mostly a conservative person at best, she was also flirtatious when she needed to be, and wanted to be. This was apparent as she made it known to the young Donnie, as she called him playfully when she first met him. And he picked that up, as well as picking up her dress, in one of the school storage rooms late one afternoon, as they discovered and uncovered their passion for each other. She was naughty and nice. He was well endowed. He was also the guy she wanted to spend the rest of her life with. She dreamed it over and over again in her lonely bed at night. She imagined being a good wife and good mother to him and all the children she wanted to have with him, all rolled into one. Unfortunately, he was married and already had young children of his own. And, at her age, the "eggs" in her "hen house" were pretty much empty. Even though they had a clandestine, continuing affair over the years, she was content to remain a woman in waiting. He always told her that he was leaving his situation for her – that glimmer of "re-nesting" hope that a lot of old maids cling to – but he got promotion after promotion, made more children with his wife after his first few children, and was destined to stay in his existing life.

When Wilshaw became the vice principal, then school principal, then the district superintendent, he always continued to hold a special spot in his life for her. In his positions, he always found a way to protect her during any school staff downsizings. He found her new jobs to fill while other more qualified people were shown the school's front door. She was thankful for what he did, never gave up hope of eventually being together, and continued to love him for all the secret memories they shared. Because of this, she didn't mind the twice-a-month back-seat private romp they would have in his van while parked late at night behind the school gymnasium. She would always find a way to give him a "special raise," and he would always find a way to give her a special raise – 5% salary increase with each school year when hardly anyone else got a raise. But she hated her job – school jobs, that is, and became more "happy-unhappy" as time went by.

In the early years of her school teaching, discipline was one of the keys to the success of teaching a student. Students feared their teachers! God forbid if a note came home from a teacher to a parent about their child's bad behavior. The child may have gotten a spanking. In today's world, there is no meaningful school discipline, let alone a spanking at home. Today, it's reversed – every teacher fears his or her students. Teachers worry about the wrath they bring upon themselves if they have any missteps in guiding kids through a typical (if there was such a thing) school day – a day that Ms. Griswold referred to as "babysitting on a powder keg," while trying to teach some silly, outdated programs that nobody cared about anymore. Kids have more interest in what they find on the internet than in a schoolbook. So now, in her final year, final months, final weeks, before the golden ring of retirement that she, and so many other retiring teachers look forward to, 10-year-old Timmy Jameson became a problem. A big, unexpected problem.

Both Timmy and his younger brother Ryan had been mostly quiet, polite, and good students in their years at Parkland Elementary School. Both always did their homework, never talked back, always listened, and left the other children, or their classmates, mostly alone. Neither was a joker, a troublemaker, an attention-getter, or a problem child in any sort of way. They must have had some good parenting behind the scenes. And, of course, they did. Timmy had a few school friends; Ryan hardly had any, and preferred being with his brother. Timmy, being the older of the two, always seemed to protect his younger brother. Not that he really needed it, but it was the way Ryan followed Timmy around all the time, wanting to be just like him.

If you looked at the two brothers separately, one was ten and one was nine. Maybe the parents planned it that way, to be close in age. Timmy was just 10-year-old Timmy. And Ryan was just 9-year-old Ryan. Everyone referred them as the "Jameson boys," and sometimes kids and teachers got their names confused, as they began to look more and more like twin brothers as they grew through their years. Timmy never got many calls of Tim or T, or whatever other nicknames kids give to other kids. Just Timmy. Ryan was just Ryan, no nicknames for him either. Two easy names to remember, for two kids who really didn't stick out.

From the first time Ms. Griswold saw both boys in school, they seemed so nice. She hardly paid any attention to which one was which, as neither needed any previous counseling help. They appeared to be and were "just normal kids." But that was then, and this is now. How things quickly change, especially after a sudden and tragic, unexpected, life-changing death! Now in her role as school psychologist and recently added-on title as "grief counselor," little did she know that she was about to meet the "devil in disguise."

Some might have thought it was unusual for Timmy to return to school, soon after the passing of his brother. Mrs. Jameson, responsible as she was, called Mr. Wilshaw and asked his opinion and guidance on this. He recalled that she explained that her son needed some extra looking-after, as he was very withdrawn, and even imagined some strange things. He didn't ask what these "things" were, and rather just followed school-district protocol. A protocol that recommended the boy meet with Ms. Griswold, the school psychologist.

Wilshaw trusted her to be the one most capable person the Jameson family and their son could work with. Even though she had no background whatsoever to handle a situation like this, it didn't matter to him, nor did he clearly think about the possible repercussions of any unqualified, and uncertified, school psychologist's advice. Instead, he just fantasized about the way she rode him up and down in the back seat of his small van. That's all he thought about or cared about, in between his mundane tasks of balancing dwindling budgets and kissing politicians' asses for more school program money each year. Surely, she could find a way to take special care of some nameless and faceless kid, he never knew about before, didn't really care to know about now, and who had just supposedly witnessed his brother's death or killed his brother. Didn't really know the Jameson's full story. Didn't have time to. Just had to take care of this matter, this blip on his daily, working radar screen, and move on to the next. Like finding a way to pay for more classroom computers that the school board thought would be good for everyone. Everyone including the supplier of the computers, who was married to one of the school board members.

So, "happy-unhappy," old Ms. Griswold waited for Mrs. Jameson to bring her son in to her office early that Monday morning before school started. To Griswold, the meeting was just a waste of any real counseling time, not that she knew what that really was, but for her, it was just to meet him and greet him like some social hour at the local bar down the road, which she frequented most nights after another long, boring school day. Yes, she was definitely not the right person that a 10-year-old, potentially psychotic kid in his fragile state of mind, needed most, right now.

When Mrs. Jameson left her office after a long hug and sweet, short kiss on her son's forehead, Ms. Griswold looked at the notes she had jotted on a piece of paper in the women's bathroom stall about 15 minutes earlier. Yes, in her mind, she was well prepared, especially with the first question.

"So, tell me about your weekend," she asked the young boy as if she were a lawyer in a court room, instead of a qualified psychologist/grief counselor who knew what to do.

"Great first question," she smiled as a way of complimenting herself while waiting for his answer. *"The Jameson family had just buried his brother, and this shy-looking kid believed he had killed him. Good starting point."*

She certainly wasn't prepared for the answer he gave, and it certainly set the tone for the conversation to follow.

"My brother can't come to school today," he answered in a typical 10-year-old voice, not with any tone of emotion, or hint of tragedy. Just seven unexpected words. Words that, beneath each and every one, held a secret meaning.

He turned his head slightly to the right and left, as if studying her.

"Okay, that was strange," she thought to herself, while tightly puckering her lips.

Pausing before the next question, she looked down at her notes again to see what her next question was. In her hurried, uncaring preparation, she had written down, "Due you like school?" misspelling "do" as "due." *"Now how silly and stupid was that?"* she mused to herself.

There was a long continuing and awkward pause as she waited for a reply that never came. *"Silly question anyway,"* she thought to herself and decided to go on to the next.

"Okay," she said out loud, while exhaling a deep breath. "Why can't your brother come to school? Doesn't he like school?"

"He doesn't like you!" he shot back, catching her off guard, enough to make her sit up a bit from her aging, hunching posture older people like her exhibited.

"He's hiding. He can't ever come to school," he added quickly.

"Hiding?" she thought to herself. *"What?"* She cocked her head slightly thinking about this. Her one hand started to tap her wrinkled-looking, bony fingers on the pad of paper on her lap. His responses were not at all what she expected a typical 10-year-old boy to tell her. But then again, she had no clue what to expect, because at this moment he was anything but typical.

Ms. Griswold took another deep breath and let it out so they both could hear her. Not on purpose, but maybe out of frustration or just confusion. She stopped tapping her fingers and made her hand into a ball-like fist, tightening it like she was squeezing an imaginary rubber ball. She was, without a doubt, the most qualified unqualified person to be sitting in this room across from what appeared to be and what was really, a pretty mixed-up kid.

"Who's he hiding from?" she finally spoke, trying to establish some form of adult guidance and authority.

"The devil," he answered quickly without any thought, or hesitation.

"The devil?" she replied, more shocked than surprised from what she had just heard.

From the moment he came into her office that morning, to the moment she had just questioned his reply, this young boy had sat stone-faced, emotionless. But now, he slowly broke a smile on his youthful face. A very strange, almost disturbing smile. And it made her big butt squirm in her chair.

"Don't you believe in the devil?" he asked, almost teasing her.

"Well," she cleared her throat trying to come up with the right answer, as if there was one. "That is a very good question that you just asked." "*Come on, find an answer and a way out of this conversation,*" she said to herself. "The good book says..."

"Do you believe in God?" he quickly cut into her reply.

"Well, yes, I do," she both thought to herself and said out loud at the same time. "Yes. I do believe in God."

"Then you must also believe in the devil," he added, as if giving her the answer to his question.

"I believe in good and bad. Both good and bad." "*Okay,*" her mind raced in overtime, "*what the fuck do I say next? Got it.*"

"Do you believe in the devil?"

"Yes." His smile started to disappear as his eyes looked directly into hers and pierced deeper into her mind. "The devil is in this room."

"Didn't see that coming. Lordy, I'm gonna need to see a psychiatrist when this is over and done." Her mind and body shook slightly, as if a cold chill just came into the room.

There was another awkward pause. Then he continued.

"Ms. Griswold, can I ask you a question?"

"Yes," she said with a tinge of being uncomfortable in her one-word reply.

"Are you afraid of dying?"

"Well," she paused as her heart skipped a beat or two, and as she tried to sort out where this line of questioning was leading. "I don't think much about it, but if you want to know the truth, yes, I am somewhat afraid of dying, but remember, I'm older and old people are eventually expected to die," she concluded, pleased at what she believed was the right thing to say.

"My brother wasn't old," Timmy said, not as a question, but more as a fact.

"No, but..." she started to say.

"My mother says my brother still lives. Father O'Malley says my brother still lives. Do you believe he still lives?"

"Well, I guess what you say..." she started to answer, while stumbling over her words.

Again, he interrupted her. "He's waiting for me."

"Waiting for you?" she asked him, while asking herself how she could possibly respond to him correctly after this. *"Definitely didn't see this coming!"* she thought to herself.

"Yes. He's waiting to play with me." Again, the unnatural-looking smile from him, to match the unnatural words he spoke.

"Yes, of course," she said, as if finally putting 2 plus 2 together, just like they teach you to do in school. "Someday you will play with him again, when you join him in heaven."

"But what if he's not in heaven?"

"What do you mean?"

"What if there's no heaven? What if there's only hell?"

"Okay," her mind talked to herself again, as her eyes must have rolled back in her head. *"This is way above my pay grade. And a bit too spooky."* This was one road she definitely did not want to travel.

"Well, in time, I think you'll sort it all out. Remember, your mom and dad love you. Your classmates and friends love you. So, everything will be okay." *"Right,"* she questioned her own words, as she seemed to be grasping for magic straws that weren't there.

No answer.

Finally, she broke the silence. "Remember, I'm always here if you need me, Ryan. I'm your friend too," she struggled to say.

"You called me Ryan. He's dead. My name is Timmy. Timmy!" he replied in an angry tone, a shaken tone.

"I'm sorry. I thought..."

"Timmy!" he shouted at her, loud enough to be heard outside her small office room.

She didn't reply. She was too shaken, too scared, too disturbed by the entire conversation. She had made a mistake, she didn't know one brother from the other, and it brought out a lot of his hidden anger, maybe the feelings of suppressed guilt in him. She didn't know. She didn't really care. All her notes were a waste of time. All she wanted to do now, at this very moment, was get this kid out of her office and out of her life. Her retirement days were just around the corner.

"I'm sorry. I won't let that happen again," she apologized, nodding her head as if she meant it.

Again, the same stone-faced, showing-no-emotion, 10-year-old kid was sitting before her, looking at her curiously, just like he looked at her when he first entered her office. *"Curiosity killed the cat"* came to her mind, whatever that meant.

Timmy silently got up, and without another word, or another look, he turned away and started to leave. He was definitely in control, she was definitely not.

Stopping at her office door, he paused, as if thinking to himself, and slowly turned looking back at her, again emotionless, but this time with a very unusual, very different look in his eyes. A look that seemed to cut into the very fabric of her being. A look she would always remember and would always try to forget.

"Ms. Griswold..., don't be afraid."

She stared in silence, then very slowly, as if in a cloudy trance, spoke words to both him and to herself, "I don't understand."

There was another long pause, and he went again from stone face to smiling face, looking deeper into her eyes, and probably into the farthest reaches of her soul.

"You will."

And with those final, chilling words, final, chilling look, the young Jameson boy left her office, and she sat there, for a long, long moment. She sat in both a state of shock at what he said, and in a state of being scared "shitless" by what he could possibly mean by his last words, "You will."

Finally, she had enough nerve to compose herself. Her eyes looked at the piece of paper she had been holding through their entire conversation – the small piece of paper with the questions she had scribbled on before the meeting while sitting in the bathroom stall, her favorite place to think. She realized she had only asked one question from her notes. The rest were never asked. She failed to follow her thoughts, but she did remember having a good morning bowel movement when she wrote these.

Crumpling up the paper, Ms. Griswold let it drop on the floor beside her. She got up from the desk and walked to the office door that he had left slightly ajar. Students were all going to their classes, and the hallway was emptying. She felt empty, too. Closing the door slowly, she turned the latch, locking herself in her office. *"Maybe he had also 'locked' himself somewhere between heaven and hell."* Her mind was racing with the assorted thoughts and words she had just heard from him. They were jumbled, bumping into each other, racing through her mixed-up mind.

Sitting back down, she took a deep breath, and sighed. She thought to herself that she needed help; not just him, but she needed help, too.

Without hesitation, she picked up the nearby phone and dialed the private number to Mr. Wilshaw's cell phone. She didn't know what she would say, but she had to talk to him. She had to talk to him right now. This young kid needed help, a lot more help than she could ever provide.

The phone rang and rang, and finally his voicemail message came on.

"This is Don. Sorry I can't talk now. Please leave a message." Beep.

She hated all these goddamn sing-songy voices like all the other stupid cell phone messages most people thought were so cute on their phones. She hung up. "Shit," she muttered to her "happy-unhappy" self. "Shit, shit, shit, shit, shit!"

As her anger grew, she even stamped her two feet as if she were throwing a child's tantrum. One shoe came off her foot. She stopped and had to chuckle, her first laugh in a long time, even though she laughed at herself.

Letting out another deep breath, she tried to recompose herself. She needed to think what to do next. Her fingers on her right hand started to tap on the well-worn desk top. It was the only sound in the room. Again and again and again. She tapped hard enough for it to hurt and to finally make her stop. When she did stop, she opened the top, right drawer of her desk and took out a small little plastic bottle. It was hidden far back behind some papers in the cluttered drawer. It was one of those small bottles of alcohol that basically was just enough for a quick drink. And so, she did just that. She downed it quickly.

Putting the cap back on, she put the empty bottle back in the drawer. She then opened the drawer underneath that drawer, and her hand went directly into the very back of it, behind the hanging folders, and found what she as looking for. What she needed. What she wanted. She slowly and carefully brought it out. What she had just gone through in the conversations of a very mixed-up 10-year-old boy was too much for her to handle. The one shot of the cheap vodka in the plastic bottle only clouded her aging mind more. Without being able to talk to her boss, her lover, and without any more alcohol to help her forget everything, there was only one way out. And she had to do it now. For her own sanity. It was the only thing that could help.

She took a thick, six-inch long, two-inch round, pinkish color, plastic device from her drawer. She put her thumb on the switch and knew what she had to do. It gave off a low humming sound with a delightful vibrating feeling. It was the only way to forget what she had just been through, and to get her mind at ease, until the next time she could ride up and down on Mr. Wilshaw.

CHAPTER 35

SOMETIMES THE FUTURE CAN'T REALLY BE TOLD.

D o you know what it's like to kill someone? Let me back that up. Do you know what it's like to kill someone with a gun? Let me back that up. Have you ever pointed a gun and shot at someone? Let me back that up. Have you ever shot a gun? Let me back that up. Have you ever held a gun? Let me back that up. Have you ever wanted to kill someone? A lot of questions. Important questions. For Jonathon Stone, psychic extraordinaire, "Mr. All-Knowing," aka "Mr. Supposed-to-Know-It-All," the answers to all these questions were about to be revealed.

When he fired his hand gun, which he had pulled hurriedly from his lap during the emotional cat-and-mouse game with a 10-year-old boy who was holding a gun on him first, Jonathon didn't have time to take aim. He couldn't anyways, because he was blind. But his hearing was so acute, he knew where Timmy stood. And so, he fired directly at where he felt Timmy was standing. And, Timmy didn't have enough time to move out of the way of the flying piece of hot lead that was quickly expelled from Jonathon's gun.

The bullet struck Timmy at the same time Timmy's gun discharged and sent a bullet striking Jonathon. Even though Timmy fired second, his gun was bigger, faster, and more powerful. It was a killing tool. As so many times earlier in his crazy and spiraling killing spree, the gunpowder ignited and, before a second ticked away, the bullet rotated along the grooves of the gun barrel and propelled outward at a speed of over 450 feet a second. Jonathon was no more than eight feet away.

Jonathon's gun was a cheap handgun used mainly for possible self-defense. And that was part of the difference. The difference was Timmy knew what it was like to kill someone. Timmy knew what it was like to kill someone with a gun. Timmy knew what it was like to point a gun and shoot someone. Timmy knew what it was like to shoot a gun. Timmy knew what it was like to hold a gun. Timmy knew what it was like to want to kill someone. Timmy knew all the nuances of the words calm, cool, and collected. Jonathon didn't. And that made all the difference in the world, especially that very moment.

Jonathon's bullet hit Timmy in the left arm, cutting through his thin jacket and the short-sleeve shirt he wore, penetrating the young, boyish skin in a grazing manner. It hit him at an angle and pushed his arm back with the sudden thrust of the powerful bullet that it was, but only grazed him. Enough to sting him, enough to make him bleed, but not enough to really hurt him, wound him, kill him, or prevent Timmy from killing him. Which is basically what he did. The difference was Jonathon had never fired a gun at anyone before. He had bought the gun knowing he would need the gun to defend himself in this moment he knew was going to happen. He went to the gun store's target range and shot the gun a few times, both hitting and missing the paper target. He felt comfortable knowing how to pull the gun trigger and fire a bullet. He felt prepared. And he was. But the difference in this moment was he didn't know how to kill. Timmy did.

Although Jonathon surprised Timmy with the quick hand movement of pulling the gun from his lap and firing, Jonathon never took aim and never fired more than once. Timmy already had taken aim when he pointed the gun at Jonathon. When he pulled the trigger, he pulled it 4 times in a row. Rapidly. Bang. Bang. Bang. Bang!

All four bullets hit their mark. All those hours of target practice with his dad, and tonight's target practice with a lot of old people who had mostly lost their quickness in addition to their steadiness, paid off. They were all easy targets.

The first bullet hit Jonathon mid-chest, broke a bunch of bones, and punctured his left lung. Made him gasp for air. The second bullet hit him in the neck, going directly through his windpipe and out the back of his throat, lodging itself into the thick cushion of his sofa chair. The third bullet was close to the location of the first bullet, but was perfectly placed to go right into his heart, slicing all those little bitty arteries and veins and making them explode inside his already bloodied chest. That was pretty much the "kill shot." The fourth and final bullet hit Jonathon squarely in his upper part of his jaw, ripping through his bottom lip, shattering a whole bunch of pretty old, and somewhat loose, teeth from years of dental abuse. This bullet ripped apart the gums and remained lodged somewhere in the back of his head. That was the "disfigurement shot." From Timmy's viewpoint, the guy he just shot would not want to see what he now looked like in a mirror. Definitely a disfigurement shot. Not that it mattered; he couldn't see anyway.

Jonathon's head was slumped slightly forward, his empty eye sockets wide open. His gun had dropped to the floor after he was shot, and both of his hands rested on his bloodied lap, palms up. If Jonathon were still alive, he could see that he was right. In his premonition he was looking at bloodied hands. Unfortunately, his. He believed the premonition meant the "blood on the hands of the victim" he was going to shoot. Wrong. It was his blood. And if there was any hint of a smile on his face, or frown on his face, any satisfaction of congratulating himself for getting his vision mostly right, or dissatisfaction for getting his vision mostly wrong, well, you couldn't really tell. Since his jaw was shot half off his face, and fragments of blown-apart, old yellowish teeth were sticking out of the side of his head, well, maybe a smile, but actually, more the look and shock of unexpected and sudden death.

Timmy looked curiously at the dead man, fascinated by the two empty eye sockets. Just staring at them as they seemed to stare back at him. Quietly moving across the remaining distance between the two of them, Timmy stood directly in front of Jonathon, studying him. Bending slightly forward, and moving his own face to within inches away from Jonathon's, Timmy looked into each eye socket. Staring at them. Thinking about them.

Raising his left hand slowly, he brought his left index finger forward and put it directly into the empty hole. First one hole. Then the other. He brought his finger out just as slowly and looked at it, thinking about it. Without any indication of what he was about to do, he put the finger to his mouth and licked it, tasting it, thinking about it.

Turning his attention away from the dead man, he looked at the rip in the jacket where he was shot, and blood was flowing slightly, leaving a stain on his coat. *"Mom wouldn't be happy about this,"* he thought to himself. She always complained about how he and his brother always found a way to dirty or tear their clothes. Nope, she would not be happy. Neither was Timmy.

He took his right hand, while still holding his gun, and extended his right index finger to where the blood was coming out of his wound. There wasn't a lot of blood, since the bullet had only grazed his arm, but there was enough. Placing his finger into his bloody wound, he pressed it forward and held it there to help slow it down. After a long moment or two, he removed his finger and brought it directly in front of his face looking at it, thinking about it. Without any indication of what he was about to do, he put his finger in his mouth and tasted his own blood.

This man tried to kill him.

Without expression, Timmy raised and pointed his gun one more time at his adversary, placing it directly on Jonathon's forehead, and pulled the trigger one more time. The force of the gunshot sent the man's head backwards into the chair. The bullet went right between Jonathon's two missing eyes, creating a new hole in his head. A matching "third" empty eye socket. Blood and brain matter started to pour out.

Like a renown painter having just added the finishing touch to his masterpiece, Timmy smiled to himself. He was fully satisfied with this "additional bullet" he had put into his newest piece of "death art." There was a lot of death tonight, but this one seemed the most rewarding.

Tucking his gun back into his coat pocket, Timmy turned without another look at the dead man. As he walked way, he started to sing very quietly to himself, so as not to disturb the dead,

"You are my sunshine, my only sunshine. You make me happy when skies are *red*."

And, on that final note, with that twisted and ominous change in verse, Timmy left the apartment, leaving the door wide open.

Still sitting upright in the cushiony leather sofa chair was the dead Jonathon Stone. Sitting all alone, empty eye sockets still staring wide open but filling with the flowing red blood from the new hole in his head. Without a sound, Jonathon's limp body fell forward, and onto the floor.   His one hand outstretched, landing next to, and touching the gun he had dropped in his final moments before. Blood flowed from the wounds he had violently received, spreading out in all directions across the carpeting. For someone so knowing, you could take bets that he never "saw" this coming. Probably not. In his whole life, from the day he was born to today when he just died, he never "saw anything." Nothing. Blind to the real world that surrounded him, he only felt it, and imagined it. He lived and died in his own darkness.

Jonathon Stone was now just a dead, former psychic, not as great as everyone, even himself, thought he was.

CHAPTER 36

TILL DEATH DO US PART.

When Mr. Jameson entered his bedroom, he wasn't prepared for what he was about to see. His wife of eleven years laid peacefully on top of their several-year-old, Kmart blue-light special, gold-colored bedspread, an open and empty prescription bottle in one hand, and an open Bible next to her other hand. In the eerie room light, from the mixture of cheap, ornate lamps that adorned the room, along with two flickering and dying candles on the bed stand, she was as beautiful as beautiful could be. He hadn't seen her looking this way in a long time. A long, long time. Not since that special day eleven years ago. And now tonight. She was wearing her wedding gown.

He stood in silence, a silence only broken by the distant passing thunder and a few weakening flashes of lightning. He stood there looking at her and thinking how attractive she was in her peaceful state. He had originally expected to come into the room and continue their argument, which had been festering for a long time, ever since the death of their son, and maybe even before. A long time coming. But now, everything changed.

Tonight, their stormy relationship blended and climaxed with the storm outside. He had seen death before. Lots of death in the service he gave for his country, killing people in a faraway land. He had seen death at home with the sudden passing of their son. It's not that he was a hardened man and didn't have feelings. It's just that he was an exhausted man whose feelings engulfed him. Maybe that's why he hadn't shed a tear. He didn't know how anymore. He was a former killing machine, and that was still a part of him. He knew death was an inevitability for everyone, so it didn't matter to grieve; all that mattered was to move on. And that's what he did in his mind, as his body merely followed orders.

Slowly walking to the bed, he stopped next to it and looked at her again and again, finally leaning over and kissing his wife on the forehead. He opened his one hand which he had held so tightly, and the sharp, bloodied piece of glass he had carried upstairs fell onto the floor next to the bed. Blood dripped from his hand as he brought it back to his side. Peering at the open page of the Bible, he could see the words,

"Even though I walk through the valley of darkness, I will fear no evil." Psalm 23:4. She believed in the Bible. He did not. He used his bloody hand to close it shut, almost as if symbolically closing what was left of their life together.

Behind her, at the top of the bed were three ornate pillows used to brighten the old bedspread which was overdue for replacing. Just didn't have the funds this month, or last month, or the month before to do so. Money was always tight in the Jameson household. His disability pension from the service, along with the monthly social security he collected, paid most of the bills. The three or four local children she watched a few days a week gave them that little bit extra to buy their two boys some new clothes. They were growing quickly as young boys do, so there was always something they needed. The farm hardly produced any crops, as the summer was so dry. Thank goodness, she always found a way to stretch what they had, and make do without the things, the extra things she wanted.

He reached over her, and with his one bloodied hand, took the top pillow closest to him. He brought it forward to his chest, now holding it in both hands. Blood from the wound in his palm started to stain one edge of the pillow where he held it. Didn't matter, wouldn't ever be washed after tonight, wouldn't ever be placed back with the other pillows after tonight. Most likely would be thrown out like their lives had been.

He looked at her lovingly, and with one free hand, brushed the long, brown hair which covered part of her face. He ran his fingers gently across her brow, over her closed eyes and followed the contours of her lines and wrinkles that had become more prominent with the passing of each year. He leaned forward and let his lips meet hers in a short and final kiss. Standing back up, he finally spoke.

"I love you."

Without any emotion, he brought the pillow down onto her face and held it tightly with his two hands. Very tightly. There was no struggle from her. If she was already dead, it didn't matter. If she was still dying, it helped her find her peace. He pushed it harder and harder onto her face forcing her head into the mattress beneath her. He used all his strength, all his anger, all his passion. He used everything he had including a few drops of his blood, which flowed from his cut hand onto her wedding dress. He held the pillow tight on her face, for a long time, until all his strength was spent. And then, he stopped.

If you were there, you would have heard him finally let out a sound. If you were somewhere else in the house, you would have heard him finally let out a sound. And if you were outside the house, you would have finally heard him let out a sound. An ungodly, unholy sound of agony. Pure, unleashed, agony! A scream, a shriek, a wail. No words could describe this sound. It was just a sound of final release. For both of them.

With the end of the sound, a single tear came down his cheek. Just one, no more than that just one. It came down his cheek, across his lips, and fell onto her wedding dress. It was the first time he cried in a long, long, time.

He let go of the pillow, and let it rest over her face. He turned and left the room. He knew what he had to do.

CHAPTER 37

WHEN THE CHILD BECOMES THE MAN.

As Timmy returned to his house after burying his dog, the rain had come to a complete stop. He was wet and cold, but his body did not shiver. It did nothing more, nor nothing less, than move forward in a robot-like manner towards home. If he had any thoughts of what he just did, or was about to do next, he kept them to himself. But inside his heart, he was filled with pain. Lots of pain.

One last faraway lightning flash helped illuminate the darkness he left behind, and the darkness he was walking into. He dragged the shovel behind him, leaving a small snake-like trail in the wet grass and dirt path that he walked along. His plan was simple. He would return the shovel to the barn first, which was now within his sight, he would then sneak in the house and change out of his wet clothes, and…

He stopped.

Stopped, stood, and stared in disbelief, and quickly dropped the shovel and ran.

From inside the open barn door, seen in the mixture of fading, old fluorescent lights above *(put that on the "to-do list")*, he watched his father step off a chair that he was standing on with a rope strung high around the beam above, circling his neck, and hang himself.

"Nooooo!" Timmy exclaimed in complete and unbridled shock.

Running as fast as he could without falling on the slippery grass and mud that led to the barn, he watched his father's body struggle in the air, swinging back and forth. Back and forth. It was a race against time for Timmy, for his dad, for both.

Once inside the barn he quickly grabbed his dad's kicking legs. With all the strength a 10-year-old boy could muster, he held his dad up by lifting both legs to take the weight of his hanging body off the tight noose around his neck. His dad continued to kick. Whether it was to kick free, and continue to hang himself, or to try to help Timmy loosen the rope around his neck, Timmy didn't know. All he knew, all he felt, was that he was saving a 200-pound man, his dad, from death by hanging by holding him up. But for how long could he do this? Because the rope was now so tightly wound around his father's neck, there was no way he could receive any instructions from his dad to help him figure out a way to free him.

While continuing to hold up his struggling father, Timmy frantically turned his head in all the directions he could, looking for something to help him. There, on the barn floor, about four feet away, he saw the chair that his dad had been standing on, now laying on its side. When Mr. Jameson jumped off the chair, he had kicked it backward away from himself. Being an old barn chair, it was well worn from the dampness of the years it was used or left unused, and its one back leg had broken off when it hit the hard, dirt, barn floor. Still, Timmy thought to himself, if he could get the chair, maybe his dad could balance himself long enough to stop the hanging, and he could find another solution.

With both of his arms wrapped around his father's legs, his dad continued to struggle. Was he trying to kick free of his son and die, or was he trying to help Timmy save him? Maybe Timmy wasn't holding his dad up enough to prevent the noose from tightening even more by the weight of his hanging body. That had to be it. Timmy tried to physically lift his dad up higher. For a moment or two, it actually seemed to work, but it was only for a moment or two, as his dad's weight was just becoming too much to hold much longer.

The chair.

It seemed to be the only choice he had. Timmy knew he had to get the chair back in place under his dad's feet. But he knew he had to let go of his dad's body and let him hang while he did this. It was a choice he didn't want to make. A choice he had to make. And he did.

Letting go of his dad, he ran to, and quickly grabbed the overturned chair, hurrying back to his hanging father. Timmy hurriedly tried to put it back beneath him. Mr. Jameson's legs still were twitching, as his young son did the best he could to place the wobbly 3-legged chair under him.

Timmy grabbed his dad by his swaying legs again, lifting him upwards to take the weight off the noose around his neck, and struggled to replace his feet onto the chair. Finally, he was able to lower his dad's heavy legs onto the chair seat. For a moment or two it appeared as if this would work, and he would save his dad's life. But only for a moment or two. And then, the rickety old 3-legged wooden chair collapsed again, with another of its legs shattering and falling off.

For a 10-year-old boy, it was a battle with time, weight, and a horrible reality. Both of his young arms were as tight as could be around his father's thick legs, holding his life in his hands. But the weight was becoming too much. Too much. Timmy, exhausted and distraught, struggled as much as he could with the weight. But he was slowly, surely, losing the battle.

But Timmy wouldn't give up.

"Nooooo!" he screamed out loud again to himself, to his dad, and to whomever else in the world would listen, as he made one last exerted effort.

Timmy planned to hold him for as long as it would take, even if it would take forever. Timmy would save his dad; he had to! His dad was the one most important person he looked up to. His father had taught him everything a young boy needed to know as he grew into manhood. He certainly loved his mom, but his love for his father was a different love. In life, a parent watches their children grow, until one day they become old enough to let them go. It is the natural evolution of life. The boy becomes the man. He may leave home to start his own family, but he always carries his love for his father and mother with him. Timmy wasn't about to let his father die. Today or ever. Timmy had already experienced enough death in his 10-year-old life, and he wouldn't accept nor tolerate any more. He was determined to not let this happen. Timmy would never let go of his dad. Never!

But, he did.

Falling to the floor on his knees, with perspiration covering his hands and face, Timmy slumped forward exhausted. He had no more strength in his arms, his body, his heart, to hold his dad upwards any longer. He was just a 10-year-old boy. Ten years old. Timmy was breathing hard from all the exertion, and he was so tired, so exhausted, he could hardly lift his head up, but he did. And he watched his father's legs twitch, once, twice, three times. No more, no less, as his body continued to swing to and fro, until finally, it stopped.

He was dead.

Throughout the old barn, there was hardly a sound to be heard. Only a faint, howling wind came from the outside open barn door and wrapped itself around both of them. A cold, chilling wind. A wind of death.

When you're an older person, time always seems to go by so fast. When you're a young boy, especially a 10-year-old boy, time seems to take forever for things to happen. At this moment, time stood still. It was nonexistent. So was Timmy's mind. It no longer existed in the real world. It only existed in a world of its own. Somewhere between madness and insanity. And it would only become worse.

Timmy cried. A long, long cry. Not a lot of loud, childlike babbling and sobbing sounds, but more like how a man would cry. A very deep, and very sad cry. A very personal cry. The Bible says that God will wipe away tears and pain will be no more. But today, there weren't enough tears for Timmy's pain to be washed away.

Eventually, Timmy slowly got up from his kneeling position. With one arm, he wiped the remaining tears away. He was done crying. There would be no more crying. There were no more tears. He stood looking at his father's limp hanging body. Timmy looked at his dad's face. His eyes were partially opened, and partially closed. There were faint colors of black and blue creeping around the tight rope on his neck. His body swayed a little more, just a little more. Might have been the wind, or maybe the old barn just shifting in the earth. Whatever it was, Timmy reached out an open hand to stop the movement. Doing so, he touched his dad's pants leg, and could already feel the cold from beneath it. Or so he thought. It brought back the memory of how he once held his brother, and how the warmth of his body changed to the cold of being dead. Butch's body temperature also changed when he held his dog tonight after the accident and finally carried him home to his grave nearby. Timmy had no words to say out loud, nor prayers to say within. He was an empty shell of a boy turning into a man, taking the place of his father, just standing and staring.

Suddenly, and unexpectedly, a woman's soft voice called out from behind.

"You've been a bad boy, Timmy. A very bad boy."

Timmy turned toward the open entrance of the barn from where he heard the voice. Standing there, in a mixture of light and shadow, with the outside wind blowing through her long brownish hair, was his mother. She was dressed in her wedding gown.

CHAPTER 38

A MOTHER'S UNDYING LOVE.

She was beautiful. So very beautiful in her wedding gown. Timmy recognized it immediately from the photo of their wedding day, which sat prominently in an 8x10, cheap, black plastic frame on his parent's bedroom dresser. Even though the picture was only 11 years old, it had started to fade. Printed on Kodak paper, "Making memories last" was stamped on the back. How appropriate for the moment. And here she was, standing in the entranceway to the barn, alive, vibrant, beautiful, in a long, flowy white gown, just like in the picture. She looked heavenly. She looked like an angel. She looked so full of life. She brought a smile to Timmy's face. The first smile he had in a long time. She returned the smile.

"Timmy, you know I love you," Mrs. Jameson said in a warm and comforting motherly voice.

"Yes," Timmy replied, with a feeling of happiness and relief in seeing her.

"You know that you've always been very special to me," his mother continued in the same calming voice.

He nodded his head "yes," as if agreeing with her.

"Come closer, Timmy. Come closer to your mother." Her voice again spoke reassuringly to him. It contained a warmth he so needed from the long, wet, and traumatic evening he had endured.

He took a step or two closer to her, and a step or two further away from the hanging, limp, dead body of his father.

"Timmy." She paused, and with a soft sigh continued, "You've been a bad boy. Daddy and I are very sad about this, very sad."

He didn't quite know how to respond to her words. His brief moment of happiness was changing to disappointment. His brief moment of relief was changing to concern.

"Timmy, you've been a bad boy for a long, long time. You killed Ryan. Timmy, you know that, don't you? You killed him." Her words weren't filled with anger, or as a mother scolding a child for something he had done wrong. They were spoken more as if he needed to be reminded of what he already knew. Something that his mother knew too.

"Yes, Mommy." His head lowered as if he were ashamed. His words reflected that shame in the way he answered, not looking at her in the eyes, but realizing in his heart that she was right.

"You killed Butch, your dog," she continued in a knowing voice, adding more shame to his already hurt feelings.

"I didn't mean to," he quickly replied, as if trying to defend himself, cover up his actions, and escape the truth.

"You killed Daddy," she stated firmly and finally, while shaking her head slightly back and forth as a disappointed parent would do.

"I know. I know," he replied slowly, admitting to whatever the truth was that he believed it to be, even if it really wasn't.

"I'm so sorry, Mommy. I didn't want to kill Daddy. I didn't want to kill Ryan. I didn't want to kill Butch. I didn't want to kill anyone," he replied in a pleading tone, in a voice filled with his deepest and darkest emotional pain finally being released.

"I know you didn't, Timmy, but you did. You're a bad boy, Timmy. A very bad boy. And because you're so bad..." She paused, as her pleasant demeanor and motherly smile quickly turned into something else, something that was anything but polite.

"... you also killed me," she stated with a hint of anger. A hint of displeasure. A hint of the punishment he was about to receive.

Timmy slumped his boyish shoulders and shook his head back and forth, responding as if on the verge of crying, but not able to. All of his tears were already gone.

"No, Mommy. No, Mommy, please don't say that, please don't. I would never want to hurt you, Mommy."

"But you did. You hurt all of us, Timmy. And there's only one way to be a good boy now." Her voice resumed a more sweet and loving tone.

"I'll do anything, Mommy. I'll do anything to be a good boy. I don't want to be bad." Timmy straightened his posture and with these words became more cheerful, as if understanding she would help him find a way to make everything right again.

"Then you know what you have to do, Timmy, don't you?" his mother pointed out with a growing wicked smile and a voice that resonated a fearful truth about to be revealed.

There was another long pause, or maybe just a short pause that seemed long. It was starting to rain again outside the barn. The raindrops could be heard on the old tin barn roof above. A distant flash of lightning showed their house behind her. Without any further words from her, any instructions, or any direction, everything came together in his mind. Everything.

"Yes, Mommy," Timmy replied, as an obedient child understanding and accepting his punishment in a mature and willing manner.

He paused before continuing, and gave her the exact same wicked smile back.

"I know what I have to do."

And he did.

"And when you're done, Timmy, you know that Ryan, Butch, Daddy and I will be waiting for you.

Only then can we all be together again. Isn't that what you want, Timmy? To be together again, as a family?"

"Yes, Mommy, yes. I want us all to be together." He quickly nodded his head in agreement.

Her expression changed back to the same tone and voice of when she first entered the barn and spoke to him.

"I'm glad you understand, Timmy." She smiled and put one hand over her heart to express her gratitude in his knowing.

"But remember, you're a very sick boy, Timmy. Very sick. You're bad and sick. But Mommy will help you make the right choices to make it all better. To make all the sickness and bad things in you go away." She smiled again, as a mother would smile to a child who is wanting and needing help.

"I don't want to be sick, or bad, anymore, Mommy," Timmy replied with every bit of his voice feeling the importance of her help to make the right choices. He certainly couldn't make them by himself; he needed her to make them.

"I know you don't. And that's why you have to go now. Go and make things better for you, for me, for all of us." Her smile was the brightest of smiles he had ever seen or could ever feel. It brightened him from inside out and made him smile, too.

"Can I hug you, Mommy? Can I hug you before I go?" he asked with a pleading happiness in his eyes.

"Yes, Timmy. You can hug me now, and forever."

And he did.

Timmy went and hugged his mother tight. He hugged her so hard! He never wanted to let her go.

He hugged her like any loving son would hug his loving mother. And in that hug, he knew that everything she said was true, and what he needed to do to make it right with her help. As they hugged, she leaned closer to his face and whispered into his ear. Something secret, something private, something only he needed to know. And he nodded his head, understanding what she said. If he did everything his mother told him to do, everything would be alright. He would no longer be bad. He would no longer be sick. And that would make him happy.

She stroked his wet and wispy hair as he hugged her so hard.

It was a loving and touching moment between mother and son. And if his father were still alive, instead of hanging dead from the rope tied so tightly around his neck, he would have been happy, too. Happy to see his wife and son talking about all of them being together again as a family. Happy to see everything coming together the way it should be. And he would have smiled along with them. He would have also smiled seeing Timmy hug empty air. There was no one there. His young arms were wrapped around what he believed in his heart to be there. What he believed was right. But in his head, he was so wrong. So very wrong. So very bad, so very sick. So very, very crazy!

CHAPTER 39

THE RIGHT TOOLS, FOR THE RIGHT JOB.

A few minutes later, when Timmy entered his parents' bedroom, he knew exactly where to go, and exactly what to do. His dad's gun case was under their bed. Kneeling next to the bed, he reached his hand underneath it. He either didn't see or didn't pay any attention to his dead mother's body on top of the bed. Or maybe he didn't want to. The bed pillow, with the traces of Mr. Jameson's blood on one edge from the cut in his palm, still rested over her face.

Timmy pulled the metal gun case from under the bed. He knew that the rifles and shotguns were stored safely in a locked gun cabinet at the far end of the room, inside the closet. He didn't want those and, besides, he only sort of knew where his dad kept the key. But the handgun that was kept under their bed was very accessible. It was planned that way in case Mr. Jameson needed to get to it in a hurry, if he had to protect the family. In today's world, you never know what might happen next, and his military training had him prepared for anything and everything.

The gun case had one metal latch and quickly opened to his touch. Mr. Jameson had a revolver in it. A Glock 17 semi-automatic handgun. It was his favorite. With a short recoil and floating barrel, it is carried by most law enforcement officers for the high capacity of ammunition it can deliver, 17 bullets in one easy-to-load magazine. With a weight of 625 grams, it was light enough, yet heavy enough, for the two Jameson boys to learn to use. From his days in the military, their dad also knew how to make some personal modifications to the guns he used, including an attachable metal silencer for the front of the barrel.

"Sometimes silence is golden," he would say to his boys when squeezing the gun's trigger during their target practice.

It was a perfect weapon in the hands of a killing machine.

Both brothers had practiced with it a few times under the supervision of their father. Mr. Jameson had told Timmy and Ryan where the gun was and where all the extra magazines were, if they ever needed to use the gun, as a back-up plan, if he, himself, was unable to get to it.

"Always protect your family first, no matter what the situation."

He remembered his father repeating to him and to his brother, "You have to be ready in today's world; you never know when you might need to defend yourself."

And so, Timmy was now ready. Ready to protect his family from any more killings, to make everything better, as his mother told him. He knew he had a mission to do, just like his father talked about in the military missions he once had. Timmy would follow his father's instructions and "take care of business." There would be no regrets, no emotion, no remorse. His mother had told him the plan in "words he felt and understood" in how she looked at him in the barn, and the silent words she whispered in his ear. His father had prepared him with the training and gun instructions, and now it was "his turn" to hurt those who hurt him and had made him hurt his family.

In his bedroom, he grabbed his school backpack, and filled it up with several fully loaded gun magazines that he had carried with him from his parent's bedroom. He didn't have to count them, he knew he had enough.

Changing out of his wet clothes, he put on a dry shirt and a clean pair of pants that hung in his closet. In his closet, he also found and put on another jacket, since he had used his other one to cover up Butch in the earlier burial. It was his brother's jacket. He tucked the gun in his coat pocket, went over to his desk drawer, opened it, and pulled out a 7-inch, mean-looking hunting knife in its sheath and attached it to his side belt, hidden by his jacket.

His desk clock showed the big, bright red-colored numbers 9:19 p.m. Looking in the wall mirror next to his desk, he brushed back his still slightly wet hair with his fingers. He didn't have time to comb it, but he did want to look nice for what he had to do.

He left the room abruptly.

Down the stairs he went to the front door. Without closing it behind, he raced towards the small garage next to their house to find his bicycle.

The rain had stopped, and it was getting a bit colder, and maybe a snowflake or two was in the air. Weird Wisconsin weather. Always changeable, always had to be prepared for whatever Mother Nature brought.

His bicycle was just inside the open wooden garage. Even though it had been raining, the garage entrance was deep enough to not let much rain in. Timmy reached his bicycle, a used blue-and-gold Schwinn with a well-worn and adjustable hard plastic seat. His dad either bought it in a garage sale, or maybe found it alongside someone's thrown-out trash. Never really knew for sure. It had a flat tire and some bent spokes when he got it, but his dad was handy at fixing things like this.

Grabbing its silver metal handle bars, he rolled it out of the garage.

Before he did anything else, he checked his pants pocket to make sure he still had it. It was there. He pulled it out and looked at it. The Sunny Side Up

Retirement Home nametag badge with a small picture of an old woman, Dorothy Paine, Apartment 101, and the full retirement home address. He knew where it was, as his parents had passed it in their car a few times, and he remembered his father saying it was where old people lived "with one foot already in the grave," whatever that meant. The retirement home badge also had a small magnetic strip on the back to open doors. It was a way to get in. He smiled to himself and put this "secret pass" back into his pocket.

Tightening the straps on his backpack to make sure it was firmly attached to his back for the long bike ride to come, he paused once more to look at his home, as if to reassure himself that what he was doing was the right thing.

There in the open front doorway, lit with the soft and warm backlight from the home's interior, was his entire family. Mom in her wedding gown. Dad in his military outfit. And his brother in the nice new outfit they bought to bury him in. And Butch, his dog, holding his favorite ball in his mouth as if he wanted to play. They all looked so nice, so happy, so loving. It made him smile. Perhaps the biggest smile of all the smiles he ever smiled. There was no doubt in his fractured mind that he knew he was doing the right thing.

He waved goodbye and they waved back. He couldn't wait to do everything he had to do and come back and be with his family, all together, just like his mom promised. He turned his bike around and quickly rode down the driveway.

The doorway to the house stood empty and quiet behind him.

It was time for the killing to begin.

CHAPTER 40

SUCH A NICE PLACE TO VISIT, SUCH A NICE PLACE TO DIE.

When Timmy finally approached the retirement home, he slowed his bike down. He had been peddling very fast for about 30 minutes. Sweat, mixed with a few traces of that light rain that kept coming and going, rolled down his forehead. As he came to a complete stop, he used his hand to wipe it all away.

There it was, the Sunny Side Up Retirement Home. Tucked so nicely, and safely, amongst all the remaining apple trees atop all the dead bodies hidden in the ground from the days Fat Frankie Fantozzio owned the land. It was two stories tall, mostly a wooden structure with an accent of brick around the entrance, a long, winding, circular asphalt driveway in the front, some parked cars alongside the main building, and a mixture of lights seen from the scattered apartment windows.

Timmy knew the mission; he had played it over and over in his mind as he raced there on his bike. Everything that night was happening so fast. He didn't even remember much of the ride. He only remembered what his mother told him. Here he was, "Home to all the people who had made him kill." All the bad people who had made him believe he was bad, too. There were so many bad people there! All the people who were on the bus and who made fun of him and his dead dog Butch. His mother told him that when she whispered in his ear. Bad, bad, bad people. And, how convenient for his mission, they all lived right here together, all in one place, in a nice looking, easy-to-access building. A place that was about to become a bloody-looking funeral home.

It was close to 10 p.m. now. For most of the old people who lived there, it was probably bedtime. Or should we say "dead time," as Timmy prepared to make that happen next.

Timmy peddled his bike away from the main entrance of Building #7. Not wanting to be seen, he placed his bicycle alongside the resident building connecting to the main lobby. From his pants pocket he pulled out the name tag that had fallen from one of the residents who had gotten off the shuttle bus at the scene where the accident happened. It wasn't really an accident, Timmy recalled his mother whispering into his ear. They wanted to hit him and

Butch on purpose. They wanted to hurt him like he had once hurt his brother. Now it was his time to teach them a lesson, to make sure they would never hurt anyone else, ever again.

The ID tag that he held was in the shape of an oversized credit card. The magnetic stripe on the back of it would provide an entrance into the building. There was a side door not far from where he placed his bike, maybe it would work there too, but he decided to go towards the front entrance instead. Maybe his mother was giving him private directions in his mind, or maybe he just didn't know any better way to enter unseen. So, he approached the front entrance without thinking twice.

The sliding, double-glassed entrance doors were closed. Two signs were attached, one to each glass door, "THESE GROUNDS ARE PROTECTED BY SURVEILLANCE CAMERAS." The other sign said, "Visiting Hours 8 a.m. - 8 p.m." Timmy looked around the outside perimeter of the doors and then peered through them. There were no security cameras to be seen anywhere. He remembered how his father once told his mother, while driving in their family car, that a lot of homes had security signs only, no cameras, just fake signs to scare away trespassers or would-be robbers. Most people couldn't afford these systems. Apparently, this was the case here, too.

In order to cut expenses and to pocket more money for themselves, the owners put up fake security signs without ever intending to invest in an expensive security video system. They could have easily afforded it. But who in their right mind (clue

#1), would ever want to break into a retirement home and harm these old and frail people? They would have to be crazy (clue #2). So, Timmy swiped Dorothy Paine's ID card on a device attached to the wall next to the glass doors that proclaimed, "USE YOUR ID CARD TO ENTER AFTER 8 P.M." The doors silently slid open, and he walked into a foyer with a mixture of wheelchairs and walkers that the residents used when leaving the building. They were all placed so neatly in a row. Timmy used the ID card in a second entrance device on another wall that opened the main glass doors to the front lobby. *"Great security system so far,"* Timmy thought to himself.

In the lobby were several comfortable-looking couches and chairs for visitors to wait in, or maybe residents to fall asleep in. A large piano, placed in the center of the front lobby and a grand staircase, wide at the bottom, narrowing at the top that led to the 2nd floor, was directly behind all of this. To the immediate right, in the entrance way, was a reception area that visitors went to and signed in before seeing their family members or friends who lived there. During the daytime, there was always one person behind the reception desk; but now, after hours, why pay the help to sit there and stare at "ghosts?" That's what the retirement home management discussed and agreed upon, as they laughed out loud and figured out another way to save costs, and pocket even more money for themselves.

Timmy went to the open sign-in book, looked at it curiously, then closed it. There would be no more visitors after tonight.

What caught his eye next was very important. There was a large cork bulletin board mounted to the wall next to the reception desk. Attached with small silver push pins were a couple of pieces of paper advertising the dining room hours and the upcoming weekend church service hours. But one other item caught his attention, an item that was definitely clue #3 – a signup sheet for today's shuttle bus trip to the mall. Times to and from the shopping mall. And the names and apartment numbers of each of the passengers who planned to go on this trip. Timmy peered at the list and immediately found Dorothy Paine's name and Apartment 101 next to it. He looked at the ID tag he had been using, and it definitely matched with what he read. Here were the names and apartment numbers of the twelve people on the bus. And adding to this piece of information, near the board was a special display of photos of all the residents living in this wing of the retirement home with their names. Timmy stood looking at all the pictures from top to bottom. There was a picture of everyone who was on the bus today and a few others who weren't. Didn't matter. Timmy now had all the information he needed. It was almost too easy. Up to this point, from leaving his house to his arrival and entrance to the building, Timmy had shown no emotion whatsoever. That all changed now. A smug-looking smile filled his face. A sardonic, evil smile.

His focus returned to the list of names of residents who rode the bus. Without hesitation, he pointed one finger to the top of the list, touching the first name, while nodding his head in approval. Approval of what he knew he would do next. Moving his fingers very slowly across the names in a spider-like fashion, going from one name to the next, he started to sing very softly to himself, and everyone on the list.

"*The itsy-bitsy spider went up the water spout.*

"*Down came the rain and washed the spider out.*

"*Out came the sun and dried up all the rain.*

"*And the itsy-bitsy spider went up the spout again.*"

Twelve names, just like the exact number of people in a trial jury, twelve. And here he was, standing in the middle of their lobby with his roadmap of how to find each one. And that was the plan. He would visit them one by one, and he would do what he was sent here to do. He would be "their jury and their judge." For what they had done to him, it was his turn to do to them. And their verdict, would be all the same. Death.

CHAPTER 41

IT AIN'T OVER TILL THE FAT LADY SINGS.

1:11 a.m. Almost three hours had passed since Timmy entered the front lobby of the Sunny Side Up Retirement Home and stared at the pictures of those he intended to meet and kill. And he did. Three long hours of pure hell and death for those who lived here, with a lot of blood in between. And now, his mission was finally over, almost.

Timmy stood in the long retirement home hallway that led to and from the front lobby where he first entered. He stood catching his breath and nursing his wound. The bullet that hit him from Jonathon Stone, the now dead and "dearly departed" psychic, had definitely cut through his jacket and into the side of his arm. He had been emotionally numb to any pain all night, but now the wound was beginning to get his attention. Timmy touched the hole in his jacket and put his hand over the blood that was coming out of it. Not a lot of blood, but enough to make him think about it, and what he needed to do to stop it.

Taking off his backpack then jacket, he saw how bloodied his shirt sleeve had become. Timmy remembered how his father taught him and his brother the "tricks of survival" if ever the day would come to use them. Some fathers would probably just teach their sons some sort of sport, or maybe talk to them about their school work. Not Mr. Jameson; he wasn't like most fathers. Most fathers grew fat and lazy while watching TV, or playing video games, or looking at porn on the internet when their wives weren't looking. No, Mr. Jameson preferred his gun practice time, with or without the boys, and chopping wood with his ax behind the barn, to let his frustrations out and forget the killing world he had been part of in his military days. He would try to forget, but he would always remember. And those memories are what haunted him the most and defined him as he was.

Timmy recalled that his father told Ryan and him about applying a tourniquet to stop any bleeding until they could get medical attention. He knew he needed a tourniquet, but medical attention was not high on his list of other things to do. He hastily kicked off one of his sneakers and reached for and took off his sock. It was a long, white, tube sock. His mother always told both brothers to put on clean socks every day. "Cleanliness is next to Godliness," she told them with a smile. And so, they did. The socks were all the same – long, white, tube socks that she would buy on sale in a big package of ten at the local Kmart. He did have black dress socks, but he only wore those to church on Sunday. Wrapping the sock around his thin, boyish arm, it covered the wound. There was enough sock left to tie it into a knot. It would do until he could get medical attention, which, again, wasn't part of the plan. He grimaced a bit as he tightened it, but knew it had to be done, and remembered what his father told him, "Never fear pain. Face it like a man; it makes you a stronger person."

Picking up his jacket from the floor where he dropped it, Timmy put it back on somewhat gingerly, not to affect the positioning of the sock tourniquet. He picked up his backpack with his good arm and slung it over his shoulder.

It was at that point that he saw them.

All of them.

Each and every resident he had visited. Each and every one he shot and presumedly killed. They all stood in the hallway surrounding him. They were all alive! And they were all standing there quietly staring at him. And they all raised their hands together in unison and pointed at him. This time they were the jury. This time they were the judges.

Timmy frantically pulled the gun from his pocket and fired at each one, just like they were sitting ducks in a row in an amusement park game. No shots came from the gun. No bullets whizzed through the air to stop these ghosts. He heard only the click of the gun trigger, firing time and time again. And as quickly as Timmy turned in a circle to fire at every one, they were all gone. They were never there. Or, if they were, they were there no longer. Neither was his mind. "Snap, Crackle, Pop." Just like the cereal.

Breathing heavily, Timmy pulled his backpack forward, reaching into it, and pulling out another cartridge of bullets, and quickly reloaded. Didn't really need them at this point unless he wanted to shoot at empty air, but he would need them soon enough, especially as a voice called out from behind.

"No more death! No more!" a recognizable older man's voice cried out.

As Timmy turned toward the unexpected voice, he was suddenly struck in the face by a wooden cane, knocking him a few steps backwards, and down.

Dazed, on one knee, he looked up and saw a man charging forward in slow motion – Domingo Rodriguez. Timmy had left him alive when he met him earlier, somehow feeling sorry for him and the story he had told him. But now...

The cane was held high in the air above Domingo and ready to hit Timmy again.

The Glock 17 semi-automatic fired quickly. Two shots. "Bang-Bang." One into Domingo's upper chest. One directly into his face, between his eyes.

The cane fell from Domingo's hands, and his body was pushed two or three steps backwards from the sudden force of bullets. He teetered on his thin, long legs, back and forth, as if trying to regain his balance. But to no avail. He was already dead on his feet. As if in slow motion, Domingo fell forward onto the hallway floor, his crumpled body just inches away from Timmy. What was left of Domingo's bloodied head from the bullet that shattered his face was now cracked open like an egg, from having landed full force on the floor. Deep red blood and pieces of brain spilled out.

Slowly, Timmy stood up from the crouched position that he had fired from. *"The old man was wrong in his comments,"* Timmy thought to himself. There was "more death," his.

The blow from the cane left a slight cut on the side of Timmy's head from where Domingo surprisingly struck him. He touched his palm to the area to determine how bad it was. Not bad, but bad enough, as blood trickled down his face. That, with the pain in the arm from the bullet that hit him earlier, made him angry. Very angry. Or maybe it was the unseen, or unheard except to him, voice of his mother that seemed to make him do what he did next. He pointed the gun at Domingo's bloodied head and fired one last shot.

"Bang."

Like a fat watermelon being hit with a sledge hammer, large and small pieces of flesh flew in all directions.

Now they were all dead, all, except one, the bus driver.

But the killing wouldn't end right here, right now. The plan of killing each one in his or her apartment had been changed by Domingo. And that was a problem. The sound of the gunshots, although muffled by the silencer, was still loud enough, added to the screaming voice of the angry man attacking him, to get the attention of the residents who were still awake or lightly sleeping in the adjoining apartments. Previously, inside each apartment Timmy entered, the sound stayed in the room. Although the builders had cut cost corners with having no real security system, nor any nighttime front-desk supervision, money was allotted to, and spent on sound proofing each apartment. Didn't want to have complaints from noisy, old coots who either babbled to themselves as they slowly lost their minds with Alzheimer's or made too much noise with a loud TV or radio because they had forgotten to turn on their hearing aids. The hallway was different. The floor was tiled with some accents of thin carpeting, and the exterior doors were cheap plastic or filled with a thin balsa wood, so sound carried in and around the hallway. And old folks, as noisy (and nosey) as they were, and as deaf as they are in their twilight years, heard the shots.

First, one apartment door opened in front of Timmy, then another behind him, and one more next to him. Most of the killings tonight had taken place in the apartments up and down the long hallway in this one building. The few residents who were not on the bus trip were obviously spared, at least up until now.

Mrs. Williams, a nice-looking, 88-year-old, gray-haired lady was first to open her apartment door. She was very nearsighted, had forgotten to put on her glasses, or just couldn't find them, and stood peering out, then stepping out into the hall. Wearing a bright pink bathrobe with large, gaudy flowers from neck to toes, she stood out like a sore thumb.

"For gosh sakes, what's all the commotion?" she asked out loud to herself and to the blurry figure of Timmy she saw standing a few feet away.

Then she saw the dead body of Domingo on the floor. Not that she really could make it out as a dead body, but it certainly was someone lying there.

"Did someone fall down? Is that you, Dorothy? You know you'll fall down if you don't use your walker," she cautioned the body on the floor, as she turned her head back and forth, as if trying to get a clearer view of who it really was.

Mr. Klimowitz, a long-ago retired math teacher, and now a long-time resident of the retirement home, came out of his apartment in a pair of loud blue pajamas, barefoot on one foot, and a black sock on the other. He was also wearing a flannel night cap with the logo of the Minnesota Vikings on it. He held an almost-empty glass of scotch in his one good, but very shaky hand.

"For Christ's sake, it's 1:18 in the morning, and someone's throwing a party in the hallway? Come on folks, this ain't New Year's Eve!" he mumbled to himself and whomever else was listening. Not many people ever listened to him. He was a real "time management" person. That's why he wouldn't go on the bus trips. Always afraid of being late or being early. As a math teacher, he always went by the exact and correct numbers. He was also, at times, a recovering alcoholic.

Mrs. Nelson, a 91-year-old busybody, who knew everyone's business but couldn't remember anyone's name, came out of her apartment last. She was in her bra and panties. Besides forgetting people's names, she also forgot if she had clothes on or not. She had a very bad memory. At this moment, the way she looked at her height of five foot, two inches tall, and weight of over 300 pounds, someone should have reminded her.

"Oh my! Who's that on the floor? I don't think I know who that is? Do I?" she added to the other residents' voices. "And, for god sakes, whatever your name is," she scolded the remains of Domingo's half blown-away head, "quit bleeding all over our nice, clean, hallway floor. And, whoever you are, if you don't get up right now, I'm going to call the police!"

These last words stung Timmy. The police.

His mind raced frantically. He couldn't let her, or any one of these other old people call the police. *"It's not part of the plan,"* he thought to himself. His mother would be very mad at him if the police came. They might even go to his house and tell her what he did. He couldn't let that happen. He couldn't.

And then Timmy did the necessary "only thing to do" to prevent any further recognition of him, or anyone calling the police.

Three quick shots. "Bang. Bang. Bang." Just like in the movies. Three quick, and perfectly aimed kill shots. And kill they did.

All shots were aimed at their heads. That's what his father taught him. No need to waste extra shots on their body; unless they were hit in the vital organs, they might survive, just as Timmy survived the body shot that was aimed at him by Jonathan Stone. Always the head. Always shoot at the head for the quickest and certain kill.

Their heads blew apart like smashed pumpkins, and their thin, bony, old and frail bodies (except for and including the very fat Mrs. Nelson) collapsed to the floor, adding to the still-flowing blood of the already dead Domingo Rodriguez. Amazing how much blood old people had.

Each one of the "nosey" residents were nosey no more.

Timmy surveyed the hallway, up and down. Quiet. Empty. He had killed them all. The body count had just unexpectedly grown, and now it was over, or so he thought.

But he was wrong.

Suddenly, to his surprise, another apartment door opened up closer to the front lobby. A large and thick bee-hive shaped gray wig peered out, followed by a round concerned face of an older woman. It didn't matter what her name was, she was just the final resident in this wing of the retirement home. She really didn't play much of a part in this drama, other than her words of exclamation.

"What the hell is going on?"

A single shot from Timmy's Glock entered quickly into and out of her head, making her wig slide sideways and cover her eyes that were filled with horror and pain. The weight of her obese, freshly dead body made her fall forward, out of the open door and onto the hallway floor with a resounding thud. She was very fat, even fatter than the other woman he had just shot. *The food must be good here,* " Timmy thought to himself, maybe, or maybe he thought nothing. Didn't matter. There would now be a lot more blood to add to all the other blood on the floor and adjoining walls.

No more residents would stick their heads out or ask silly questions. Everyone who lived here in this wing of the Sunny Side Up Retirement Home was now dead. Everyone. No more nosey neighbors left to offer their heads as targets. No more witnesses to blame Timmy or tell his mother for all the bad things that happened here tonight. The only blame would be on themselves for what they did to him, to his brother, and to Butch his dog. His mother would be so proud of him for all the excellent work he did here tonight. And she was.

Standing at the far end of the "hallway of the dead," she stood there looking so alive, so beautiful. She smiled at Timmy. He smiled back.

And now it was time for Timmy to leave. Everything was calm and silent. Everything was just right. Just a lot of death throughout the blood-splattered hallway and into each adjoining apartment.

He had one more stop to make before he could go home and join the rest of his waiting family. He had to go to the bus driver's house.

Taking out the piece of crumpled paper that had guided him to each room, he reviewed all the residents' names and apartment numbers on the list. He nodded his head in agreement. They were all dead. At the bottom of the paper was the bus number, time, and location for the planned trip to the mall earlier today, and the name of the driver. Marvin Fox.

Timmy recalled him as being very mean. Very mean and angry to both him and to the residents on the bus trip. He yelled a lot, and he shook a lot, and he couldn't stand still, Timmy remembered. They were all bad people in Timmy's mind, but this name made Timmy frown and nod his head slowly. He tightened his hand on the gun he still held in one hand. Marvin Fox was next to die.

But not quite yet.

Down the hallway, the glass front-entrance doors to the main lobby suddenly opened.

CHAPTER 42

"GOSH DAMN!"

Ambulance EMT Lucy Johnson and Detective Ray McNail entered the Sunny Side Up Retirement Home through the same front lobby Timmy had come in earlier. After securing the lobby area with no one in sight and nothing more to see, Ray led the way towards the hallway with Lucy close behind. They proceeded slowly past the many wall photos of all the Directors and main financial contributors to the Home. They even passed the photo of Miles Patchwork, on-duty evening security guard. Lucy paused for a moment looking at it. *"Maybe he was making the evening rounds or fell asleep in some hidden place from the usual nightly boredom,"* Lucy thought to herself.

On another wall near the closed and silent entrance desk, Lucy watched the detective take notice of a smaller display of photos of all the residents living in this building. Next to it was a corkboard with information of various upcoming activities. Everything looked in place, even though unknown to them, the sign-up sheet for today's bus trip was missing.

They continued quietly and cautiously through the large lobby and approached the first main resident hallway just a few yards past the entrance sign-in desk. There was a huge grand staircase ahead of them which led to the 2nd floor. She watched Ray as he walked tentatively ahead of her with one hand on his gun. With his other hand, he gently touched all the nearby chairs and other lobby furniture as he passed them. They all looked in place and undisturbed. Lucy wondered what Ray was thinking. Maybe there was nothing wrong here. Maybe everything was alright; maybe they just forgot to lock the entrance door that she and Ray found ajar. *"Hmmm,"* she silently said to herself as she thought all this over, not knowing he was thinking it over at the same time in his analytical detective mind, *"The door ajar, that could be a clue. A puzzling clue."* And it was.

Lucy frowned while continuing to think to herself about the situation they were in. She knew she couldn't, nor wouldn't speak. That was protocol. They had to be quiet. Everything here was quiet also, too quiet. Almost "dead" quiet. *"That's funny,"* Lucy thought to herself, *"dead quiet. Most of the people here are knocking on death's door as this being their last stop, their home before ending up in the big home in the heavens above or the hells below."* A shudder went through her, as she reflected about that for a moment. She also thought about why she was even in this situation, which most certainly was way above the duties detailed in her pay grade. She was here because this is what she wanted to do, to be a part of an exciting situation like this, rather than sit behind a medical desk, drawing someone's blood to be analyzed. And, she was a secret admirer of Ray, ever since she first met him as a 12-year-old girl when he came to her school to give a lecture on the importance of police work. She liked his smile, his nice clean look, and the way he presented himself. A young school girl's "crush" that never went away. If only she had the courage to tell him her feelings. But she was too shy, and he was too busy being a 24-hour-a-day detective. Even though he was old enough to be her father, she secretly carried her feelings through the years and was happy to work as a lab technician in the police office close to his before she became an Emergency Medical Technician. Now, even with the unknown in front of them, she always felt safe around him. And with that security in her mind and feelings in her heart, she began to wonder, *"How bad could this situation here really be? Was the 911 call for help just a prank call by some teenaged local yokel hopped up on pot, or, would they be turning the corner and walking into a living nightmare?"* Whatever it was, she was thrilled to be a part of it because she was with Detective Ray, facing it with him. But the real thrill, if one could call it that, was yet to come, for both of them. As they turned the corner of the lobby and entered the hallway leading to the resident's apartments, the whole situation immediately changed. The nightmare became real.

What she saw was something neither she nor Detective Ray expected. Lucy, in a state of shock, stood and stared without words. And the surreal silence was finally broken by two words. Two famous words that had become his, and his alone.

"Gosh damn," Ray muttered out loud to himself.

The hallway was littered with dead bodies. A lot of dead bodies. In front of them and continuing all the way to the end of the long hallway. The floor was a flood of blood. Blood was also splattered and still dripping off the adjoining walls. Old people's bodies were laying in front of their open apartment doors throughout the hallway. An array of their gross-looking body parts and pieces of blown-off flesh lay scattered about, and all around them. It was a scene of unimaginable horror.

Lucy, shaken from this graphic encounter, tried to make sense of it all and started to count the dead bodies in her head. "*Three, four, five,*" or maybe more. Hard to tell at first shocking glance. Dazed and confused, while trying to hold her emotions together, Lucy's only thought now was that this whole situation, definitely, was, without a doubt, way above, way, way above her pay grade. She couldn't count the bodies anymore. She couldn't, and she didn't want to. She turned to look at Ray. Maybe he would be able to get the exact count. He was the consummate professional, nothing bothered him, not even death, and he would know what to do next. He always did. But if he did, in that horrific moment of their discovery, he would tally up all the dead almost correctly, but would miss one – himself.

"Jesus, Ray..." she shook her head as started to say something to him. But she never finished the sentence.

Without warning, suddenly out of nowhere, as if having been watched and targeted from the moment she and Ray entered the hallway, a lone, silent, gunshot sent a single bullet propelling down the hallway filled with death. It struck Detective Ray right smack in the middle of his throat.

"Nooooo!" Lucy screamed as she witnessed a stream of his blood come spurting straight out.

It was like someone squeezing a big, fat, plastic ketchup bottle, just like the type you use when you're at an outdoor picnic, pouring it all out on your freshly cooked hot dog. But this was no picnic. She watched in complete horror as Ray's blood shot right out of his neck, as his flailing hands reacted either by choice, or by instinct, to being unexpectedly shot in the middle of his neck. His hands furiously clutched at his bleeding wound.

Standing a mere few feet away from him, Lucy stood frozen like a deer in a car's headlights. She watched in complete terror as Ray tried to stop the flowing blood by sticking his finger right into the gaping hole in his neck. But to no avail. Way too much blood pouring out. Way too big of a hole. Way too bad of a wound for even Lucy to consider or try to bandage, even if she could. No, she knew he knew, nothing more could be done to help him.

His legs seemed to buckle like a tree twig snapping in half. Without any accompanying sound, Detective Ray's body collapsed straight down to his knees. He swayed back and forth like an accordion being compressed. There, he teetered for a moment. A long, long, moment, as Lucy would recall. His eyes turned to meet hers, and he started to make weird and horrific gasping sounds, almost as if he were pleading to tell her something. She finally came to her senses and tried to grab him.

"Ray. Jesus Christ, Ray. Hold on, hold on. I'll get help!" as his blood squirted onto her hands.

And with his last breath, he spoke just two, almost distinguishable words. Those words, his words, were the most fitting words to sum up this whole crazy nightmare that they just walked into together, and one that he would eventually be carried out of, alone.

"Gosh...Damn," Ray mumbled in a weak, whispery, blood-gurgling voice as he looked at her for one final time, not for help, but for a moment of letting her know that he, too, always had secret feelings for her, but now, he wanted her to leave, and be safe.

She would always remember this moment. She would always be haunted by it, and by his last two words to her, "Gosh damn," although it could have been, "Love you."

His body slumped forward face first into the blood-covered floor with the sound of his nose and teeth breaking apart.

Detective Ray McNail was dead. And that was the missing body in his earlier body count. The one clue he failed to see, and never saw coming: his own death.

Lucy, terrified, dropped her medical bag, screamed again, and ran as fast as she could with his blood on her hands, back towards and out of the front-lobby entrance door.

Stepping out of the silent shadows, midway down the hallway, Timmy slowly tucked his gun in his coat pocket, surveying the remnants of his work. Satisfied, he turned and, without hesitation, ran down the hallway away from the lobby, leaving behind one more kill with all the other bodies that already littered the blood-covered floor.

CHAPTER 43

CHILDREN SHOULDN'T PLAY WITH MATCHES.

At the end of Building #7's hallway, opposite from the main lobby, was a smaller circular sitting area with a few cheap-looking chairs and a couch, similar to the ones in the main entrance. All the furnishings throughout the buildings were bought in bulk at the same time to save decorating costs and, of course, enabling the owners to pocket the extra cash. A checkers board sat on a small table between the two large flowery-looking sofa chairs. A hand-written tent card was placed on the board, "Next Move Red." Timmy stopped his flight for a moment and looked at it.

"How interesting. The color red, like all the blood that was spilled tonight," Timmy thought to himself.

He picked up a red checker piece, was about to make a jump on the board, then put it back where he found it.

Timmy stood there and quickly surveyed the entire area. There were two separate long hallways, identical to the one he just came from, each leading in a different direction, each having the same number of apartments. It was obvious that all the Sunny Side Up Retirement Home hallways and apartments were made in a "cookie-cutter" style. Again, just another way to cut costs.

To his far right was a door with the sign "EMERGENCY EXIT" over it. Next to the door was a fire alarm.

Timmy thought about the front entrance he had come in through. It was now probably being watched by policemen or other types of armed guards. And he was not prepared to deal with another set of unknown circumstances down the two hallways to either side of this area. The exit door looked like the quickest way out, so he could get back home to his family. He recalled that he had placed his bicycle next to an outside door. Perhaps it was this one.

Reaching into his pocket, Timmy pulled out the pack of matches he had picked up earlier in the apartment with the "passing gas lady," DeeDee Lapinsky. He then pulled out the piece of paper that he had taken from the lobby bulletin board, listing all the names of the people on the bus that day, and all the information for the bus trip. After tearing a match from the matchbook and igniting it, he lit the piece of paper and threw it on the sofa closest to him. Being a cheaply manufactured sofa without any fire retardant built into it, the sofa immediately caught fire. Sparks shot in the air and landed on another couch next to it, which also immediately ignited. Within moments, the fire was growing in its intensity, and that's when Timmy went to the exit door and pulled the fire alarm.

A loud, wailing alarm sound, accompanied by flashing red lights, filled the hallways in all directions. The oldies, that is, the residents who still could hear, or who had slept with their hearing aids on, groggily started to come out of their nearby apartment doors, confused and scared as to what was happening. Both adjacent hallways, like the one he had come from, had 16 apartments, eight on each side. Those who didn't hear the alarm, or the commotion, were destined to die in the inferno that started to spread quickly through each hallway via cheap carpeting and cheaper wallpaper. It didn't take long to have both hallways engulfed in flames. This was part of the plan that his mother told him to do.

"Burn the place down, so there won't be any clues left behind to point to you."

That's what he was instructed to do and had to do. Burn the place down, to prevent these other bad people who lived here from ever harming him or any more of his family. Everything his mother had told him to do was proceeding on plan.

Timmy looked back and saw a growing group of older people screaming in the hallways. Lots of loud, terrified screams. Most of them had pajamas on and were either using canes or walkers, as they slowly tried to sort out what was happening, and, maybe for the few lucid ones, find an escape route. Some of the residents started to catch fire. One person stood totally upright, holding tightly onto a walker, while being completely engulfed in flames. Within a few moments, only a charred body would remain standing, before falling on the burning floor and turning into ash.

Timmy remembered the words the family priest spoke the day they buried his brother, "From ashes to ashes, dust to dust." Now he understood what those silly words meant. A smile crept across his face.

The raging fire quickly spread all around him, from apartment to apartment, up and down each new hallway, and back into the hallway he had left behind. He could see his previous "works of art," the dead bodies on the hall floor, starting to burn. Detective Ray, or what was left of him, burned the most. Must have been the alcohol in his system from drinking earlier that night.

Everything and everyone was on fire. Even Dorothy Paine's brand-new set of false teeth, which remained on her night table next to her burning dead body, melted from the heat.

But through this bizarre holocaust, Timmy seemed impervious, unaffected, untouched from all the flames that licked the surrounding floors and walls. The growing flames seemingly danced around him in a rhythmic and frightening glow. He appeared to be in the center of it all. It was as if he were the conductor. It was as if he were Satan incarnated.

And this inferno was his own living, orchestrated hell.

Amused. Crazed. Completely insane. He started to laugh an evil, horrible laugh. A laugh that resonated with the licking sounds of the flames that continued to spread even more, even faster, up and down the hallways. A laugh that rose even higher above the screams from all the many trapped, slow-moving, old people flailing about on fire. It was like a slow-motion dance of death. His laughter grew louder. It was an all-encompassing, maddening laugh. One that was everything and nothing...simultaneously.

What a wonderful place to live. What a wonderful place to die.

The Sunny Side Up Retirement Home was totally ablaze as Timmy pushed open the exit door and slipped outside into the remaining shadows of night.

His work was done here. Now to leave this place behind and find and kill one more bad person.

CHAPTER 44

ON THE ROAD AGAIN.

His bicycle was just outside the retirement home's side entrance door, exactly where he left it. Timmy stood it upright from its leaning position against the building wall. Throwing one leg over it, he settled comfortably onto the plastic seat. It crossed his mind how he got the bike on his 7th birthday. A Super Flyer, 25-inch Schwinn, deep red color, like the "red blood" he left behind in the burning building. Pausing for a moment, he recalled how it was his first bike and it didn't have training wheels.

"If you want to learn how to ride a bike, then you need to know how to fall off a bike," his dad told him.

And, in those early days there were many spills and a few scars of his battle with the pavement left on his knees and arms. Made him "all the more tough," Mr. Jameson would say. Whether he learned that in his military stint or before, Mr. Jameson's word ruled the house and set the tone for his growing up. Both he and his brother enjoyed riding their bikes very much. It was their own personal time of freedom, as they rode up and down the quiet neighboring roads and lonely dirt trails in the woods around them. It was a special time he would always remember. A very special time. But that was then, and this was now. Timmy half nodded to himself, wondering if there were bikes in heaven, and if his dead brother was up there riding one also. That would be special, too.

Before biking away from the burning retirement home, Timmy looked to the front of the building to see several police cars with flashing lights, an ambulance with interior bright lights on, and four or five uniformed people scurrying between them. In the distance, he could hear the siren sounds of the approaching fire trucks. He also could make out another police car with flashing lights coming fast behind it.

With so much commotion going on, it was a perfect time for him to leave. Adjusting his backpack, he then tucked the gun deeper into his jacket pocket, turned the bike away from the front area of the retirement home and quietly peddled across the lawn, keeping hidden into as much darkness as possible.

He remembered his dad once telling his brother and himself after a practice shooting session, "Don't ever let your enemy know where you are, but always know where they are."

Timmy smiled to himself. Not the smile of a crazy lunatic, but the boyish grin of a 10-year-old kid who knew he was getting away with something. Something very, very bad.

Recalling the name of the driver on the mall bus trip sign-up sheet, Timmy knew where he had to go next. As he peddled his bicycle along a dimly lit road, the horror of the retirement home was left further and further behind, as he planned another horror yet to come.

After being about a mile or so away from the burning retirement home, Timmy coasted off the roadway and into the entrance of a nearby gas station which had recently closed. He had overheard his mom and dad talking about how sad it was that this station was closing just because it didn't have the typical donut shop or convenient store attached to it, as the one that was just built close by, up the road.

Alongside the vacant building was a worn-looking, upright, enclosed plastic-windowed phone booth that people would use to make private phone calls. That, too, had become outdated with so many people having cell phones these days. The Jamesons did not. They were old school, preferred a land line, one of the last ones in the area, as a matter of fact. Neither Timmy nor Ryan were given a cell phone, even a toy one just to play with. Wasn't a priority in their household, and, most likely, his parents couldn't afford one. Didn't matter much, though. Hardly anyone ever called. But Timmy saw his dad stop here once or twice for gas and use the phone. He recalled his dad looking up a name, number, and address in the phone book which was attached to a metal chain inside the booth to prevent it from being stolen by some troublemakers. But they did write graffiti on the plastic windows, and some pretty nasty words, before and after the gas station closed.

Leaning his bike against the phone booth, Timmy opened the metal folding door. It creaked a bit, as it was rusting on its track and hinges. The worn, leather-bound, phone book was still there, attached by a chain to a metal pole under the phone.

He opened it up, went to the alphabetized names starting with the letter "F", and without much difficulty found what he was looking for. This was a small town and neighboring community so there weren't a lot of names and addresses. Just enough, and just the right one he was looking for. Marvin Fox, 2914 Grassmere Parkway. He knew where that was. His mother visited a lady friend on that street once or twice. He remembered the word "parkway" and recalled asking his mother why it wasn't named street or drive? She really didn't know the answer to his question, so she just said it "sounded better." 2914 Grassmere Parkway. Not far, but far enough. Maybe 20 minutes or so at a fast-peddling rate.

Timmy looked at his watch. Another few hours or so before the sun would start to rise to begin another day. He touched his arm where he was shot. It felt warm through the hole in his jacket. He could feel a trickle of blood from underneath the makeshift tourniquet he had created and applied to himself. It was starting to hurt even more. He applied a bit of pressure using his other hand and rotated his arm once or twice to keep the circulation going. Before he got back on his bike, he looked over his shoulder from where he had come from. Although he couldn't directly see the fire, he did see the light from bright flames of the burning retirement home extending upwards into the nighttime sky. Still burning. Probably would burn for a long time. The longer the better. He didn't want anyone to follow him, look for him, or interfere with him. The retirement home fire would keep everyone busy and away from looking for him. Not that they even knew who to look for. All the better. He took care of everything there he had to.

Time to finish what his mother had told him to do. Time to kill again. And then finally, finally time to go home and be with his family.

CHAPTER 45

WELCOME TO HELL.

It was starting to rain again. There were a few flakes of wet snow mixed in; not much, just a few. It was more of an early morning drizzle. Not like the storm the night before. But weather and storms are unpredictable; so is the mind of a madman, or should we say, "mad-boy."

On his ride to 2914 Grassmere Parkway, Timmy thought of what he had to do, and how he would do it. The words, *"That dog almost killed us,"* still echoed in his mind from earlier that day. The words haunted him, over and over again, and filled him with rage.

Killing had come so easy to Timmy, so that wasn't what bothered him. What concerned him was how he could make this person, this Marvin Fox, who was responsible for the death of his dog Butch, suffer the most. After all, he made Timmy suffer. He made Timmy's family suffer. It was only fair that he got a taste of his own medicine.

A month or so ago, Timmy overheard his mother discussing a story with his dad regarding a very bad killing on the other side of the town. Apparently, some immigrant fellow who worked on the local farms had murdered a newly married couple while robbing them. Not only did he kill them, he cut off their heads and drove around town with the heads rolling around in his car trunk. His mother was so upset, she kept telling Mr. Jameson that this person, who she referred to as low-life scum, a "sicko," deserved the same, if not worse. Because he loved his mother so much, he knew she was right then, and was right now, as her voice whispered in his ear to do the same.

Timmy smiled as he finally approached the house where the bus driver lived.

It wasn't much of a house. One story, grey clapboard siding, probably built in the mid-1950s. It was small sized, with a bedroom, a bathroom, a kitchen, a living room, and maybe some closets. It was nestled in between two slightly bigger houses. They both needed painting; so did this one. Grassmere Parkway was basically a mixture of old and new. A neighborhood in revitalization. The old, and even older people who lived here were either dying in their homes or being shipped to retirement and nursing homes to die. The younger millennial types were taking advantage of the low real-estate costs, government loans, and city tax help. It was a nice place to find a starter home, fixer upper, and play house until a baby arrived and a bigger home in a nicer neighborhood was needed.

Marvin Fox lived alone. He had acquired the house from his Aunt Martha, who lost her husband Fred in a freak car accident a few years back. While driving home from work, Fred had a major stroke, lost control of his hands and feet, and drove his one-day-old Ford Fiesta into the back of a two-ton garbage truck at 70 miles an hour. The accident report said his foot somehow got stuck between the accelerator and the floor mat. The Fiesta crumpled like an accordion. A whole lot of garbage came pouring out of the back of the open garbage truck and covered what was left of him and his car, like a meat sauce covering a bowl of spaghetti. Martha lived two or three years after the accident, drowned her sorrows in drink, and drowned herself, one night, as she fell asleep in her bathtub after a few too many glasses of cheap wine. Without children of their own, Marvin, a distant relative who showed up before Fred died and who did some small fix-up jobs for them, was awarded the house after a contested battle without a real will. A handwritten note with the signature of Aunt Martha, which looked an awful lot like his signature, showed up in court and said the house was his. And so, he inherited it, along with the two cases of left-over cheap wine that were found in the bathroom closet.

So, here it was rapidly approaching dawn, almost 12 hours since the bus accident that started or, let's say, added to Timmy's downward sanity spiral, and Marvin was still awake. Marvin was seated in his underwear at the small, wooden kitchen table snorting one last line of cocaine. He sat there all alone, illuminated by the overhead kitchen fluorescent light that also shone out and into the remaining morning darkness.

On his way home that night from his unhappy job as a "baby sitter" bus driver for the oldies, Marvin had met his drug dealer friend, a big, black, burly guy with the one-word name "Coco." Certainly, a name like that would never give away the fact he was the local cocaine kingpin. Marvin scored another bag of that wonderful white powder he so needed, especially after the accident. A snort or two, or maybe three or four, would make him shake happily while his eyes spun in his head like ping-pong balls. It was the only thing he could think about, the only thing that gave his life some sort of purpose. He was hooked. Very badly hooked. However, as cheaper stuff, which is all he could afford, it had been cut over and over again, till god knows what was in it now. But it didn't matter what was really in it, it made him feel so "fuckin' good," as Marvin would exclaim out loud after every snort. And, it also kept him wide awake with no chance of slumberland in sight. At least he had his well-worn porn magazines to keep himself entertained until it was dawn. After all, he had to be wide awake and alert for his other part-time job as a kindergarten school bus driver. His two jobs were at both ends of the spectrum, carting around young ones to old ones, while sneaking one more sniff or two until he could get home and continue enjoying himself and his naughty magazines.

Timmy watched him, studied him, thought about him, as he peered through the kitchen window. Hidden in the darkness, Timmy stood close to the house, next to some overgrown evergreen bushes that badly needed trimming. It was drizzling rain again, and even the old rusted gutters on Marvin's house couldn't hold the water from being sprayed and splashed all over. The rain didn't bother Timmy. His sore arm did. He lightly touched his arm where the pain was now throbbing. The gunshot wound would need some attention sooner or later.

Reaching into his pocket, Timmy pulled out his gun. Checking the magazine to make certain it was fully loaded, and it was, Timmy smiled faintly to himself. For a moment or two, Timmy thought about heaven above him, and hell below him. Maybe he had one foot in each. His smile disappeared as he proceeded to the front door of the house.

Inside the kitchen, Marvin laid out the last line of cocaine he had on the table. With his face closely parallel to the dirty table top, he sniffed it down, and down further, until it was well within his system. A small trickle of blood came from his nose.

"Fuck yeah!" he exclaimed out loud to himself, slapping his knees gleefully like a child getting a present he had longed for.

"Good shit. Real good shit," Marvin proclaimed to the empty kitchen, nodding his head in agreement to himself, as his eyes continued to spin in his head, round and round, just like the wheels on a bus. Shaking his whole body like a wet dog trying to dry off and letting out a deep breath, Marvin picked up an empty can of beer. Holding it high above his wide-open mouth, he poured what was left in it downward, to get the last drop that still had to be somewhere in it. Licking his lips, Marvin took another snort and sat back in the chair. Done for the night. Well, not quite.

Timmy entered the kitchen with his gun pointing directly at Marvin.

"Holy shit!" Marvin exclaimed as if he were suddenly snapped out of a bad dream, only to be placed into a worse dream.

"Who the fuck are you? And how did you get in here?" Marvin continued, trying to make sense of it all.

"You left your front door unlocked. You killed my brother," the young intruder replied without any emotion.

"What the fuck are you talking about? Killed what brother?" Marvin blurted out almost in a scream, but more dazed and confused.

Timmy responded in a whispering voice, almost as if he wanted no one else to hear his reply. "Last night, with your bus."

That startled Marvin, along with the cocaine and alcohol that raced throughout his half-numb body.

"Wait a minute. Last night, some dumb dog ran in front of my bus, and…and, hey, you're that kid, that kid with the dog. What the hell are you doing here in my house?" A moment of clarity took form in Marvin's rapid reply.

"I've come to kill you," Timmy stated with a tinge of foreboding authority.

As if surprising Timmy, as if surprising himself, Marvin quickly jumped up from his chair and took an awkward step towards Timmy. The chair fell backward striking the floor with a loud noise.

Unfortunately, in his drug-induced state, the movements he made, and the movements he thought he was making, didn't quite connect.

But Timmy's reactions did. Quickly and without hesitation, he shot Marvin in his right shoulder. Not a kill shot, as he could have – more of a warning shot of what's to come.

The impact from the bullet forced Marvin to stagger backwards, yelling in pain.

"Jay-zus Christ! You shot me! You fuckin' shot me!"

"And I'm going to shoot you again," Timmy responded matter of factly.

As he finished the sentence, Timmy pointed his gun again, this time at Marvin's other shoulder, and pulled the trigger. All it takes is five pounds of pressure and the bullet is on its way. Same as before, not a kill shot, just another wound to make him "suffer" as he made Timmy suffer earlier that night.

Blood was now squirting out of both of Marvin's upper arms as he screamed in pain again. He even did a two-step type of dance with the pain he was in. Marvin's hands grabbed frantically at the holes in both of his shoulders as he tried to stop the bleeding.

"Why? Why are you doing this? It was just a dog. A fuckin' dog! Are you fuckin' crazy?" he screamed at

Timmy and at himself at the same time, not knowing that Timmy was indeed crazy – very, very crazy.

"You killed my brother," Timmy calmly repeated again. "You're a very bad man, and my mom told me that bad men deserve what they get."

Timmy's words echoed within, and bounced off of Marvin's mixed-up and drug-numbed brain. Marvin's eyes started to spin in his head again. As the blood came out of his two wounded shoulders, he tried to find some sense of clarity as he sized up the kid in front of him. Even though he was wounded, he was bigger than the kid, stronger than the kid, smarter than the kid, and he could, and should, easily overpower the kid. So, he thought. This was his plan. Not that it was a good plan.

Marvin charged forward at the young boy who stood a mere few feet away. He yelled at the top of his lungs with a mixture of pain and out-of-control emotion. Yelling like a charging Indian would do when attacking a cowboy. Just like in a game of cowboys and Indians, like Ryan and Timmy used to play. Except this was no game. This was life and death.

Timmy pulled the gun trigger again, this time shooting Marvin in his left knee.

Screaming in even more indescribable pain, Marvin quickly fell to the floor, inches away from the boy. He landed on his one good knee, while grasping onto the kitchen table. It was the only way to keep him from falling down completely. His bony kneecap was completely shattered from the bullet, as torn pieces of skin and bone were exposed. Blood poured out and all over his naked leg.

"You son of a bitch," he screamed at Timmy, clinging to the table for whatever was left of his life.

Marvin's head spun around looking for a weapon or anything to use in his defense, or to throw at the kid. All he could see on the table was just a half of a plastic straw that he had cut and used to snort the coke, and his favorite nudie magazine, *Big Boobs Bonanza*.

"You shot my fuckin' kneecap off! You shot it off!" he screamed at Timmy as he clawed at the table surface, slowly losing his grip from the weight of his body and sinking backwards towards the floor.

"Here, let me help you," Timmy said smugly, aiming his gun directly into the top of Marvin's hand, which was desperately gripping the table.

He fired the gun again.

The bullet went smashing through Marvin's knuckles and part of his wrist, through the cheap wooden kitchen table, and down into Marvin's left foot on the blood-soaked floor beneath the table.

More screams; more pain.

Marvin's hand no longer resembled a hand. What was left of it slowly fell apart, as he lost his struggling grip and fell to the floor. The bullet that struck his foot by chance did some nice damage, too. From the angle it entered through his ankle, it was apparent that he would never be able to dance that "coked-up two-step" he did a few minutes ago in his underwear, let alone stand and walk. Besides, he no longer had a kneecap to hold his weight up.

Marvin tumbled backward, landing in the ever-growing pool of his blood. His brain was fried on drugs, just like the TV commercial advertised, and his pain had no further way to escape from the screams he made.

He started to sob, then cry. Death was definitely "knocking on his door."

It was beyond pitiful to see a grown man, even a bad man, look and act this way. With whatever strength and reflexes he had left, even with the bullet hole in the arm he used, Marvin attempted to pull himself up from the floor using his one good hand. He almost made it, too. But Timmy did the humane thing. If you can call it that. He shot Marvin in that hand also, again at close range, blowing off three of his fingers in different directions and adding even more squirting blood to what seemed like an overflowing river on the kitchen floor.

Marvin landed full on his back. No knee cap, no foot, no hands, and a hole in each of his shoulders. Ping-pong eyes filled with tears of extreme horror and suffering. Only the complete numbness from all the cocaine he snorted kept him from passing out.

"No more, please...no more," Marvin pleaded, completely exhausted, and with what would be his last remaining breath.

Timmy stood over him and aimed his gun directly at where Marvin's heart would be under his blood-soaked white tee shirt. Wasn't sure if this bad man really had a heart. How could he, after what he did to his dog, his brother, to the people at the Sunny Side Up Retirement Home, and everyone else who he fucked over and hurt in his measly life.

Timmy fired again. And again. And again, into Marvin's chest. If there was a heart, it was surely no more. Marvin died immediately, but his cocaine-filled body twitched a few more times.

Timmy stood there looking at what was left of Marvin. His twitching finally stopped, and he was most certainly dead. Beyond dead. He was being checked into Hell.

Timmy remembered the news story about the man who killed the two people and then cut off their heads. He recalled his mother saying how very bad that man was, and how he deserved the same fate. Marvin Fox was also very bad, and Timmy knew he also deserved it. That's what his mother wanted him to do. And that's exactly what he knew he had to do.

Reaching behind his jacket, Timmy pulled out his hunting knife. He had used it twice before, earlier tonight. It still had some dried blood on it. It was time to use it again.

Timmy leaned over Marvin's dead body and knelt behind his head. Timmy didn't want to get any blood on his pants from the many large red puddles already on the kitchen floor. He didn't want his mother to be mad at him if he got his clothes any dirtier than they already were. Unfortunately, he would. Timmy looked at Marvin's face and smiled.

He slowly made a deep, sharp cut into Marvin's neck and throat.

CHAPTER 46

"A TISKET, A TASKET, LOOK WHAT'S IN MY BASKET."

Timmy left the house the same way he found it. Sort of. Marvin remained in the kitchen. Sort of. The few traces of the white powder Marvin so enjoyed were still spread across the kitchen table, and one of his favorite girlie magazines was still laying on it, open to a posed picture of a very naughty girl with a very naughty smile. Everything else remained the same, except for his head. It was no longer on his body. Timmy had carried it out with him. He was taking it home to show his mother. He knew his mother would be happy with what he did to Marvin, and he wanted to make his mom proud of him for thinking all by himself to bring the head home to show her.

Holding Marvin's head by the long greasy hair attached to the top of it, Timmy left through the same front door he had entered earlier. He had never carried a head before. He didn't know how much it would weigh, or if he could actually carry it. When he first picked it up after his sort-of-skillful, mostly sloppy surgery that he performed, he realized it was heavier than the basketball that he tossed in gym class, but lighter than a bowling ball that he once held when the family went to a local bowling alley after Sunday church. He liked bowling but didn't really like basketball. Marvin's head weighed about the same as the big orange pumpkin he and his brother selected from a nearby farmer's field the last time they shared Halloween together. They even drew and cut out the face on the pumpkin together. Best one they ever did. They had "family fun" making the pumpkin look scary with its crooked pumpkin teeth and broad pumpkin smile, which glowed eerily from the burning candle inside it. He and his brother even attached two small potatoes with toothpicks as its ears. And, after the holiday, they even had fun smashing it behind their barn with dad's sledgehammer. Hey, kids are kids, and Halloween was a big deal to them.

By the time he reached his bike parked next to the house, Timmy had already planned out the way he would carry home the cut-off head. Obviously, it would be too awkward to hold and ride with it. It certainly wouldn't fit in his backpack; and if it did fit, it would make a big mess with the dripping blood and guts, which still hung out from it. But he remembered that he had a small bungee cord strapped to the back of his bike that he occasionally used to attach and carry some school books, which were too heavy for his backpack.

Timmy placed Marvin's decapitated head on its side on the ground while he unstrapped one end of the bungee cord from his bike. Carefully, but not too carefully, he picked up the head of Marvin by the hair again. Proceeding to stretch and wrap the bungee cord across the front of Marvin's face and across the back of his bike, Timmy secured it tight, like it was being held in an imaginary bike basket. If the head was alive, which of course it wasn't, Marvin would have been able to look out at the road as they traveled away from his house. Marvin, in his drugged state of mind, probably would have enjoyed that.

Adjusting his backpack, Timmy surveyed the area to make certain no one had seen him, or Marvin's head. Feeling it was safe to leave, he started to peddle away back towards his home. He was looking forward to seeing his family and being with them again, and, of course, introducing Marvin to them.

Wanting to avoid being seen with a severed human head attached to the back of his bike with a bungee cord, Timmy decided to take some less-traveled streets and roads. He basically knew the way home, so it was just a matter of time to get there.

As he peddled in and out of the last vestiges of darkness, in and out of streetlight shadows, and through the on-and-off drizzling rain, only a bright set of car lights could show off the unique item he was transporting. Timmy started to whistle a favorite tune of his. It was something he and his brother took turns whistling to each other when they were by themselves, *"Zip-a-dee-doo-dah, zip-a-dee-ay. My, oh, my, what a wonderful day."* It was certainly a "wonderful day" for him with all the new and wonderful people he met and killed. And the memory made him happy as he rode his bike towards home with his new friend Marvin.

Even though Timmy was very smart and adapt at killing, he did not fully understand the logistics of transporting a sweaty, severed head that was becoming more and more loose in the bungee cord with each rotation of his bike wheels. The cord slowly slipped from around Marvin's mouth, where he had originally wrapped it, and moved upwards, now tugging on his nose. The force of the bungee cord pushed the nose straight up like a "piggy nose." Timmy recalled how he and his brother once joked about a piggy nose when seeing their first live pig at the local state fair a summer or two ago. The boys had quite a laugh over it. The way Marvin's nose looked now made Marvin's appearance quite comical, and the boys would have surely laughed at it, too.

With a few more bumps in the road, sprinkled in with the pesky rain that was still in the air, plus a few sharp turns Timmy made when changing streets, it was just a matter of time before Marvin's head fell off the bike. No big thud, or large sound to get Timmy's attention, just a few gushy bounces on the road, followed by a long, awkward-looking roll before it came to rest, face up. By the time it stopped, Timmy was long gone from where it fell. Marvin's head had stopped its rolling about and ended up "smack dab" in the middle of the road. If Timmy were bowling, you could call that a perfect "strike." Sadly, he didn't even realize it was no longer on his bike until he got home. And when he did, no big deal, he would just tell his family about it, and they all would share a laugh or two.

For Marvin's head, it wasn't so funny. And it certainly wasn't anything to laugh about. It just lay in the road undisturbed for quite some time. The early morning cars either dodged the strange, unknown thing in the road, or just flat-out missed it. Remarkedly, the severed head remained untouched for exactly four hours and seventeen minutes. Then, it was finally hit.

A school bus filled with screaming kindergarten kids "ran" over the head.

As luck would have it, and certainly Marvin seemed to have all the luck in the world in the predicament he ended up in, the bus was the same bus that Marvin was supposed to drive that morning in his other job. But when he was late, someone else was assigned to the bus and off it went, at a higher speed than normal to make up lost time. With hyperactive kindergarten kids yelling as they normally do, the new bus driver wore headphones to tune them out. He was blasting some Led Zeppelin tune, tapping his hands on the wheel, and singing along to himself. He didn't see the object – that is, Marvin's head in the road – until he was just about upon it, and tried to artfully dodge it. Because the roads were still wet from the overnight rain and the continuing sporadic drizzle, the bright yellow, shiny school bus slid a bit to the center and went directly over the head. The weight of the bus squashed it just like the big orange pumpkin Timmy and his brother had once squashed after Halloween. The bus squashed and flattened the head right then and there, and all over the road. One might comment and say it was "road kill," but it was already killed, that is, dead. The weight of the two-ton bus put so much force on Marvin's decapitated head as it drove over it that Marvin's two eyes popped right out of their sockets. They actually "flew through the air with the greatest of ease" – you know the rest – and landed, separately, a foot or so apart on the edge of the road.

After spinning around in dizzying circles, the eyeballs finally came to a stop. One of Marvin's eyes looked directly upwards to the sky above, while the other eye looked directly downwards to the ground below. Both eyes stayed there, just like that for quite some time. More cars, trucks, and buses continued to drive over whatever was left of Marvin's head, which was now very much squashed and splattered all over the road.

A lone crow, from the nearby farm where Timmy and Ryan had once gone with their parents to pick out their pumpkin, circled above, looking at the two round objects below. With no immediate vehicles in sight, it landed cautiously between the two eyes, looking curiously back and forth between them. The crow cawed a few times, then stopped, and just stayed there. A silent morning breeze made some of its dirty black feathers bristle as it stood silently, turning its head, eyeing the two separate eyeballs. The bird finally made a choice, hopping over to the one eye that was staring upwards. It pecked at it for a moment, then opened its beak, and picked it up in its mouth. Without hesitation, as if it were meant to be, the crow flew upwards into the morning sky as if taking the eye to Heaven. Marvin's other eye remained alone, staring downward at the ground, as if staring at Hell.

CHAPTER 47

HOME SWEET HOME.

When Timmy arrived home, everything looked exactly the same as before – the front door was still open, and all of the lights in the house remained on from last night. He parked his Schwinn bike near the front porch and immediately walked toward his house. Halfway up the front porch steps he paused, turned, and walked back towards the bike. Timmy looked at the loose bungee cord that had once held Marvin's decapitated head. It hung loosely with some fresh blood still dripping off it. Frowning, he casually wiped the blood off it with one bare hand, then wiped his hand on his pants. Without any further emotion, he turned and hurried into the house. Disappointed he didn't bring his new friend home, he could, at least, show his family the blood from Marvin's head that now stained his pants.

Hungry from a hard night's work of killing, and with his arm still very sore from where the bullet struck him, without hesitation, he entered the kitchen where he had seen his parents argue the night before. Pieces of glass from Mr. Jameson's broken beer bottle still littered the floor. Stepping on the glass made a sharp crunching sound, breaking the otherwise "dead" silence. Not too loud, but loud enough. Didn't matter much to him, as he made a beeline to the cookie jar on one of the kitchen counters. He loved his mother's fresh-baked cookies, and he knew there had to be one or two left from her baking a few days ago. And there was. Chocolate chip cookies, with lots of chocolate chips. Two left. Eat one now; save the other for later. If his brother was here with him, he'd give him one. He remembered how their mom would give them some of the left-over cookie batter to eat, and how his dad would want some, too. Her cookie baking was always a fun family time. With a few quick bites, the cookie was now in his tummy, and Timmy proceeded upstairs.

His mom still lay on the bed in her wedding dress, undisturbed, exactly where Mr. Jameson left her. But the pillow he used to smother her had slipped off her face onto the bed. She looked so peaceful, so angelic. Timmy stood in the doorway looking at her. A smile crossed his face. He was glad to be home. Timmy was glad to see her again.

"Doesn't she look beautiful?" A voice came from behind him.

Timmy turned, and his father was standing next to him. He put his one hand on Timmy's shoulder, not far from where he had been wounded.

"The wedding dress was her mother's. It meant a lot for your mom to wear it. Her mother, your grandmother, died years before, when your mom was young. She always said, by wearing her mom's dress on her wedding day, that she'd feel that her mom was with her. She even said she felt her mom's presence when we said our vows. Amazing how you can feel that your loved ones are still with you even when they're gone," his dad concluded.

"You and Mom will never leave me, will you?" Timmy asked, looking quizzically at his dad.

"No, we will never leave you, and you will never leave us," a woman's voice replied from behind him.

His mother was now sitting upright on the edge of the bed, her bare feet barely touching the floor from beneath the long wedding gown. She moved her feet back in forth as if playing with the air.

"We will always be together, as a family, just as we need to be." Two voices from behind suddenly caught his attention and made Timmy turn back towards the hallway.

His dad and mom now stood together holding hands. Mr. Jameson was dressed in his wedding day rented tuxedo, and she in her gown. Both looked so happy to be together, and so happy to be with Timmy.

"And now it's your turn to join us," his mom said so lovingly, so gently, as her one free hand touched Timmy's forehead, brushing aside his hair.

Timmy smiled even more from the comfort of her warm hand. He closed his eyes, and a small boyish tear came gently out, and rolled down his cheek.

When he opened his eyes, his father was kneeling on one knee in front of him with his hand on Timmy's wounded arm.

His father's reassuring voice made him feel comfortable again.

"You're the man of the house now. You know what you have to do. Just as I trained you for this moment. You must not leave any trace of what happened behind. Nothing. No one must ever know what you did, what we did. It will be our secret, our family secret."

His father's hand moved down the arm to where Timmy had been shot and he carefully touched it.

"And once everything is done, there will be no more pain. There will be no more anger. There will be no more hatred. There will only be the four of us together again, together forever as a family."

"I want that so much." Timmy's one hand reached upwards and touched his father's hand that was still on his arm.

"I know what I have to do. Momma told me when I saw her at the barn. She whispered a secret into my ear. I've done everything she told me to, and I'll do everything you told me to do, too," Timmy replied confidently.

"I love you, Timmy," his father said softly, but sternly as he embraced him. "You're a good boy.

You've always done everything a good son would do, and now it's time to finish what remains..."

"And I love you, too, Timmy," his mother's voice added, from where she now sat again on the edge of the bed, still dangling her bare feet in the air.

"Come, let me hold you, Timmy." She opened her arms for him to embrace her.

He ran to her and wrapped his arms around her. He held her tight, knowing that this would be the last time he would hold her, until the next time. The final time. It would be so wonderful to be laughing and smiling and hugging altogether as a family should. Timmy held her so tight and didn't want to let go. Didn't want the next time to ever come. He only wanted this moment to last for all time. He held her so tight, like the first time she had held him when he was born into this world. And now this world was coming to an end. Another tear, or two, or three, came down his face from his open eyes, as they met with his mother's eyes. She had such beautiful eyes.

As they looked at each other, her eyes said it all. Her voice filled his mind and his heart with what he knew she would say, and what he wanted her to say.

"It's time."

And it was. He slowly let go of her and looked at his mother one more time. One last time. Moments, minutes, hours, days, weeks, years, time seemed to stop. Soon, they would be together for all of whatever time is. They would be together forever. Time would never keep them apart again. But first, he had to finish what she had told him to do. What his father had told him to do. He was such a good boy, and he would do just as they said. Only then could they all embrace, and all be together again.

Timmy quickly left the room, never looking back. The hallway was empty. His father was no longer there. His mother's dead body still lay on the bed in her wedding gown. The tears that fell from Timmy's eyes rolled slowly down her now-revealed, cold, dead, smiling face.

CHAPTER 48

A NICE NIGHT FOR ANOTHER FIRE.

In the family barn, Timmy knew exactly where to find what he was looking for. A spare can of gasoline that was used in the lawnmower. It was full. Mr. Jameson prided himself on having enough gas available to always finish the lawn cutting. Timmy grabbed the can with his one good arm and passed by the body of his father, still hanging from the rafters. It was as if he wasn't even there. But if he was, he certainly would be proud of what his son was about to do next.

The young boy started to squirt the gas throughout the entrance of the barn, while recalling his instructions, *"Use only half of the can. Save the other half. Do everything just as Mom told me to do."* He placed the can outside the barn door and had to get one more item. The shovel. Timmy had replaced it exactly where it belonged after he buried Butch. Mr. Jameson made it a rule to put things back exactly where they belonged, or else. Or else you couldn't find them, Timmy smiled to himself. His dad was always right.

Placing the shovel outside, a safe distance away from the barn, Timmy picked up the half-empty gas can and went directly into the house. He went into the kitchen and immediately started pouring the gas around the room. He used both of his arms in holding the gas can upside down and pouring out the last drops of liquid. The gunshot wound on his arm no longer hurt since his dad had touched it. Amazing what a parent's comforting touch, or comforting words, can do to ease the pain. Timmy was pleased that his dad had taken the pain away, and now, it was his turn do the same. There would be no more pain for any of them. But first, the other cookie. After all, he was a growing boy, and he loved his momma's cookies.

Tossing the empty gas can into the middle of the floor, a few pieces of the remaining broken glass shattered even more. Reaching into his jacket pocket, Timmy pulled out the pack of matches he had used at the retirement home. Two matches left. Just enough. One here, one there.

As he left the house, the fire quickly spread.

The barn was next. There was a lot of old, dry wood inside. The rain may have kept the outside wet, but the inside would burn quickly, and it did.

Standing in the yard between the two buildings, Timmy pulled the gun from his backpack and checked how many bullets were left. Two. He thought about it for a moment. That would be enough. The rest of the gun's magazines that he used that night were empty and remained in the backpack. He had shot a lot of bullets that night. But he still had what he needed. Two. Where he was going next, he wouldn't need anything but the gun and the shovel. Timmy threw his backpack into the fire. He tossed the bloody hunting knife, as well. "Leave nothing behind." Those were the instructions. That was how to keep the secret.

Picking up the shovel that he had taken from the barn, he looked at his home for the last time. Timmy now had another home he had to go to. That was the other part of the secret his mother had whispered to him. Without any expression, hesitation, or reservation of what he had just done, Timmy turned and abruptly started to walk away from the burning house and barn.

Inside the house, his mother's beautiful wedding gown caught fire, as the flames had now worked their way up the stairs. The gown that her mother had given to her, the gown that made her look so beautiful had started to burn, and so did she.

Inside the barn, the fire had also spread quickly. The flames burnt through the hanging rope attached to the rafters and his dad's dead body fell onto the floor. His clothes caught fire, and so did he.

Both the house and barn were totally consumed in flames.

Timmy was over the backyard hill that led to the woods when he stopped and turned to look back. There were so many bright-colored flames blending into the morning sky, so many flames dancing across the yard and consuming both the house and barn. The fire was growing in its intensity. Big, tall flames that seemed to grow higher and higher with each passing moment. So tall were the flames that they appeared to kiss heaven above.

The crackling wood sounds of the barn and house blended together and seemed to scream an eerie sound of laughter. Such a big fire. So many flames. Bigger than the fire at the retirement home. So much fire; a raging inferno. You'd think this place was really Hell. And from where Timmy stood, and from what Timmy felt, it really was.

CHAPTER 49

THE FINAL DESTINATION.

Dawn had finally arrived when Timmy reached his destination. His final destination. He used the shortcut through the surrounding woods behind his house, following the creek across the field beyond, through another set of woods, and finally into an area that was so peaceful, so restful, so undisturbed, except for what was to happen next. The Wood View Cemetery. His journey into madness which began months ago with the death of his brother was about to end.

Timmy traced his path from his last visit here to where he was now instructed to go. His mother was guiding him. He knew that she would continue to guide him as he completed his task. And now he was almost there. Just past a few old towering trees that were still shedding the last remaining dying autumn leaves before winter. Just beyond a few of the older monuments that rich people had paid for when their so-called dearly beloved left this earth for the great beyond.

It was exactly where it was the last time he had visited it, before Butch was killed. A small granite stone in the ground with the name of his brother on it. His brother's grave. His brother's home.

Timmy stood quietly, holding his father's shovel and looking at the grave marker beneath him.

"Hello, Brother," Timmy spoke to the earth below.

It was the resting place of his brother – the brother he had killed.

The surrounding silence of the early morning was broken by a slightly strange wind that seemed to come from beneath him, from above him, and from all around him. A wind that would have put a chill in most normal people. But Timmy wasn't "most normal people." The wind seemed to caress him, to answer him, to beckon him. And as suddenly as it started, it was suddenly gone. An absolute silence. Nothing more, nothing less.

"It's time," he whispered into the silence, which abruptly changed with his spoken words.

The early morning peeks of sunshine were now turning into an overcast sky. Dark clouds were in the distance. Another storm was approaching. Whether it would be as big a storm as last night, he would have to wait and see. No one could accurately predict the weather. It didn't matter to Timmy. He knew what had to be done. He knew how long it would probably take, and so he started. He put the blade of the shovel he had carried there into the ground in front of the gravestone and began to dig.

A sound of thunder could be heard in the not so far away.

Being early morning, the graveyard was empty of any visitors. There were set hours for visiting, and he was here well before those hours began. The front gate was still closed to visitors by car. A groundskeeper opened the gates at 10 a.m. and closed them at 5 p.m. If he didn't have to cut or trim the lawn, he went off and did other things in between. Timmy came through the surrounding woods so none of this mattered to him.

As he dug into the ground, his arm began to hurt again. He thought about how his father's touch had made the pain go away. He would just have to work through the pain until he saw his father again. Because of last night's rainstorm, the ground was very soft, so the beginning of the digging came easy. But he had to go six feet under. That's where his brother was.

It started to sprinkle, then started to drizzle. That was good for his digging. As he got deeper into the ground, it softened and made it easier. Sweat and rain mixed together and poured from his forehead. The shirt beneath his jacket was mixed with perspiration and last night's blood. He knew his mother would make him take a bath when all his work was done. A nice warm bath, just like every Saturday night when he and his brother were younger. Playing and laughing in the tub full of bubbles. A nice warm bath. Yes, that's what he looked forward to, that's what he thought about, and that's what kept him preoccupied as his digging continued.

He was deep below ground level when the shovel finally hit the top of the coffin. He had dug quite a hole, and there was quite a pile of dirt that he had thrown out and about. He shoveled faster. The top of his brother's coffin was now completely uncovered. Timmy was standing on top of it. He had to shovel out some more dirt from the sides of it. It had become more difficult for him to throw the dirt out of the deep hole he had shoveled himself into. But he did. He had to. This is what his mother told him to do. There could be no excuses. It had to be done. In order for them to be a family again, he had to be with his brother.

The coffin was smaller than a full-size man's casket, but it was still big enough. Timmy stopped his shoveling and, without taking a rest, or taking a moment to wipe the dirt, rain, and sweat that covered his face, he knelt down looking for a latch, and a way to open it. He remembered when they closed it at the funeral parlor, his mother cried so hard, so very hard. There was the sound of her crying and a clicking sound. He remembered both. But it was the clicking sound he remembered most, the clicking sound. It resonated in his head. There had to be a latch or something like a latch. He got down on his knees and felt around the sides of the casket until...there, he found it. Some type of latch, but there it was, and he was in an awkward position to open it. He leaned against the wet ground he had dug into. Some of the dirt from above started to fall back in.

"Not good," he thought to himself. He had to be careful, he didn't want to fill the open hole back in yet. The ground was still getting wet from the continuing rain, so it was being held somewhat in place, kind of mud-like.

He dug a little more to the side of the latch.

He had to toss this new dirt out of the hole above, adding to all the other dirt, and be careful it wouldn't fall back in. After a few tries, he got it right, and continued to dig at the side wall.

Within moments, he dug out enough of a space to fit himself into, just enough. He leaned down again, keeping his weight and back to the dirt wall, and tried to open the casket top. It wouldn't budge. He tried again. It still wouldn't open.

He took his shovel and hit the locked latch with the blade. He hit it once, twice, then more times than you could count. It snapped. Or was that the sound of thunder? Or was it both?

Outside of the open grave, the storm started to intensify. So, did his efforts. He hit the casket latch again and again. A bolt of lightning illuminated the interior of the grave. Worms and ugly little bugs were burrowing in and out of the surrounding dirt walls.

Rain started to pour down on him as he used the shovel blade to try to pry the casket top open. The latch had snapped; it should have opened. What he hadn't anticipated was that it had rusted from being in the wet ground. The cold, damp ground made the coffin so tight, so hard to open, that one would have thought that it didn't want to be opened. It probably didn't. But then it did.

The casket top suddenly sprung upward, and slowly opened.

Another flash of lightning revealed the body and face of the dead boy inside, now starting to decay. The dead body of a boy who had died too early. A boy who had brought so much pain and suffering to his brother who believed he killed him, and to his family who loved and missed him so very much. The rain fell into the casket, licking at the now gray-colored face that was starting to shrink from time and lack of life while entombed.

Another bolt of lightning, another sudden clap of thunder.

Rain, or maybe tears from heaven fell onto the face of the dead boy. And it wasn't what one would have expected. It wasn't the face of his Ryan in the coffin. It was the face of Timmy. It wasn't Ryan in the grave; it was Timmy in the grave.

CHAPTER 50

"WHAT THE HELL JUST HAPPENED?"

The local fire department had quite a busy night. Not only did it try to save the burning Sunny Side Up Retirement Home, but it also tried to save the burning Jameson home and barn. It failed at both.

The local town's fire and police were stretched beyond what it could do. Other fire departments, police, and ambulances were called in as quickly as they could arrive from nearby surrounding towns. No one was prepared for this. No one expected this. The sprinkler system inside the retirement home never went off to prevent the disaster from happening.

Little did anyone know, except the builders of the retirement home, that more costs were cut with the installation of a cheap, faulty, and a mostly non-working sprinkler system. Both this fire and the Jameson fire raged out of control for hours. The morning storm helped bring some of it under control but, by then, so much was destroyed. There wasn't much to save.

It was also an unpredictable night filled with unimaginable and unaccounted for death. The survivors of the retirement home from Buildings #1 through 6 of the octagon-shaped facility huddled outside, sitting in their wheelchairs or standing with their walkers. Those still trapped inside in Buildings #7 and 8, whether injured by fire, or shot, were all dying or already dead.

Lucy Johnson and Deputy Sheriff Alonzo Gonzalez stood in a state of shock outside the burning buildings. County Sheriff Stanley Robach had just arrived to see the losing battle between firefighters and the growing flames. He watched two firemen try to enter the main lobby hallway to retrieve Detective McNail, but the flames were already consuming his body. Besides, Lucy had already told the first responders that McNail took a direct hit, did not appear to be moving, and, most likely, was not alive.

There was an uneasy feeling surrounding the entire scene, as no one knew what to do next. The firefighters were told to stand down, as this tragedy was the result of an active shooter, or possibly more shooters, in the building, until the police cleared the scene. No one wanted to take any unnecessary chances.

Sheriff Robach took off his police hat and wiped the sweat from his brow. His middle-age stomach pressed tightly against his leather police jacket. He was in his late 50s, a good father and family man nearing his last few years of a stellar career in law enforcement before retirement. He was also a very respected police officer in the community, and one who could take control of any situation at any given time. However, this was a situation for which he was not prepared. He was both stunned and shaken to see his dead friend's body lying in the hallway of the burning building, totally engulfed in flames and covered by falling burning building debris.

"Jesus Christ. What the hell just happened?" he mumbled out loud to both himself and anyone else in the immediate area who was listening, or didn't want to listen.

"Did anyone see or get a description of the shooter?"

"No, it happened so fast," Lucy answered tentatively, while shaking her head to match her words. "I think there was just one shot, maybe more, but there were bodies all over the hallway. Blood everywhere. It was a massacre. A horrible massacre."

"Don't rule out terrorists," Gonzalez added. "We've had a bunch of them transplanted here under the damn federal immigration law. They could be behind it."

With anger in his tone, Robach faced his deputy.

"Watch what you're saying, and no one, but no one, talks to the press but me. We've got to get the facts, and some straight facts before we spread shit rumors that make us out like fools."

"But it could be," Gonzalez shot back at Robach.

"Shut up, Alonzo!" he barked quickly at the deputy. He never liked Gonzalez from the very first day he met him. And he was right. Nobody really liked this guy. He knew that this "wanna-be" macho cop got his promotions due to the mayor's diversity initiatives. There was a big difference between a real cop and a clown in a cop's uniform.

"It could also be someone from the retirement home," Robach injected, while trying to piece it together. "We can't rule out anything or anyone. But for now, no more talk, just keep the onlookers and families out of harm. If there was a shooter in the building, he or she is hopefully dead from the fire."

"Unless they escaped," Lucy added hesitantly.

There was a pause in the conversation. The Sheriff looked around to see that it was just the three of them together, and far enough away from any other listening ears.

"Whether the shooter is dead or still alive, whether it's a he or a she, the person or persons that did this are crazy or mad. No person in their right mind would do this. They're fucking insane. By the grace of God, we'll find out what their motive was and we'll catch the son of a bitch." Robach took a pause while letting out a deep breath. He slowly shook his head back and forth thinking as he watched the flames spread even higher into the nighttime sky. Then he made another connection. "But what I do know – what happened here tonight was the work of the devil himself."

County Sheriff Robach's words weren't far from the truth. This very night, this very moment was the result of both a mad and a crazy person. An insane person. Perhaps, as Robach stated, "the devil himself." Who else could unleash so much horrible, frightening, and traumatic hell? It was an unbelievable, unexpected, and unforgettable nightmare that came to life, only to leave so much death behind. No words can define what hell really is. Or who the devil really is. One can only understand it when one lives it. A lot of people were living it tonight. A lot of people.

Lucy Johnson stared sadly at the scene in front of her. Blocking out what she had just heard, and thinking of what she lived through, what she saw, and what she now felt, a cold chill went through her entire body. She wrapped both of her arms around herself as if to warm her and to comfort her. She was lucky to be alive. She watched even more of the building collapse from the fire. *"This really was Hell,"* she thought to herself, and acknowledged that by making the sign of the cross.

Local residents and family members of those who lived here were arriving to locate and help their family, their loved ones, their friends. Many retirement home residents were huddled with fire-department blankets wrapped around them. Some were being attended to by all the ambulance crews. Quite a few were being transported to the local hospital or other area facilities to get immediate care, or to get far away from the damaged and still-burning, smoke-filled buildings.

The retirement home fire was at full intensity now. The flames grew in all shapes and sizes and seemed to dance in front of them. Laughing at them, taunting them. A few faint screams could still be heard from within the collapsing remains of the burning structures. Adding to the horror of this night, was the foul and permeating smell of still-burning flesh. A lot of burning flesh.

There were no more words from the three of them, as they stood silently and watched the on-going confusion of everything that was happening. There was a lot of crying, moaning, babbling, hugging, and questions going around all at once. Confusion owned the moment. And from all the living horror that had unfolded tonight, the basic and most repeated question was, "What the hell just happened?" They got part of it right. "Hell" just happened.

Death had certainly come to a lot of people that night. A lot of people. But death wasn't quite over yet. Death was still waiting to claim one more victim. A victim that was supposed to be already dead, but who was really alive, and wanting to die.

CHAPTER 51

BROTHERLY LOVE.

Ryan looked into the coffin that held his dead brother's body. There were no more tears that he could cry. They had all been washed away with tonight's rain, and all he had suffered since his older brother's death. His heart was beyond broken; his soul was beyond empty.

"Hello, Timmy," he said in a soft, almost whispering voice.

"I've missed you so much. So very much. I'm sorry I killed you." He paused, choosing his words carefully, but knowing what he had to say next.

"I should have died, rather than you. You were my big brother, and I looked up to you so much. Every day I wanted to be just like you. Every day I watched you and followed you and wanted to be you.

You were more than a big brother, you were my best friend. You were my world, and without you, my world was empty." A sound of thunder seemed to abbreviate what he just said.

Rain continued to fall on him as he stood inside the open grave, tightly squeezed next to the open coffin.

"I didn't mean to kill you. I know the doctors told Mom and Dad that you had a sudden illness, they called it an aneurism, whatever that is, but you and I know the truth. The real truth. I was mad at you. Very mad. Because you said I couldn't be like you anymore, and you told me that we couldn't play games anymore, that I had to grow up. I was so angry at what you said, at how you hurt me that I wanted to hurt you, too. I picked up that rock on the ground and hit you on the head from behind. Just to hurt you. But I hit you real hard. Too hard. I killed you. I killed you!" Ryan raised his voice in anger as a quick bolt of lightning and a roar of loud thunder punctuated his grief.

He paused. The only sound was the falling rain splashing on him and the open coffin. Some distant thunder finally broke the silence.

"I didn't mean to. But I did. And when you fell on the ground, I got scared and put the rock underneath your head where you fell. I told everyone you tripped and fell. They believed me and then told me that you fell because of something else. But you and I know the truth. Mom and Dad know the truth. And now I'm here, so we can be together again."

Ryan slowly pulled the gun out of his jacket pocket. He looked upward into the open sky.

Whether it was the rain, or the few remaining tears he somehow summoned, didn't matter. It all blended together in a face of complete sadness. All that mattered were the words.

"I'm sorry."

Ryan climbed into the open coffin and started to lie down next to Timmy. It was a tight fit, but there was enough room for them both. Maybe he thought about doing this from the very day they closed the coffin in the funeral home, or maybe he just thought about it now. Maybe.

Once inside the open coffin, lying on and next to his decaying dead brother, Ryan used his one free hand to grab the inside top lid. He slowly pulled it downwards and entombed them both. Together.

Rain continued to fall softly on the top of the closed coffin. It was as if a grieving, crying mother was running her hand gently across it. The dirt on the side walls he had dug around the coffin were turning into mud from the continuing rain, and began to slowly slide downward.

It started to rain harder. For a moment, the sound of the falling rain resembled the sound of a hammer nailing a coffin shut. And then as quickly as it started up, it slowed down. The sound became the steady rhythmic pitter-patter of rain drops again. And that's all that was heard until the sudden muffled sound of a gun being fired inside the coffin.

A loud echoing sound. A loud, unearthly sound. A sound that was heard from heaven to hell and back.

And then silence. A long silence. A strange silence. Until suddenly the silence was broken. A second gun shot rang out from inside the coffin.

The mud walls of the freshly dug grave seemed to collapse as if on cue. Mud, dirt, more mud, more dirt, all fell down onto the closed coffin, sealing the brothers inside. Together. Forever.

CHAPTER 52

AFTERMATH OF AN EVENING GONE CRAZY.

The FBI arrived at the remnants of the Sunny Side Up Retirement Home later that afternoon as the fire still smoldered. Because of the scope of this situation, it was necessary for their involvement. Three agents arrived together in one official government black SUV. They had driven from their office in the state capitol. A lot of media, both local and national, were already there, interviewing witnesses, neighbors, or anyone who could add some facts to what had happened.

Last night's storm was long gone, and the cool, late autumn sun was peeking in and out of the clouds, as if it was keeping watch of what was going on there. The entire area that encompassed the destroyed buildings and the remaining attached structures was barricaded and roped off from the onlookers. A few firemen were still spraying water on smoldering debris. Clean-up crews in hazmat suits and large machines for moving and digging debris were busy at work looking for, and hoping to find any survivors. There would be none. The body count, or what resembled bodies, was growing by the hour. There were a lot of dead people. A lot.

Sandra Brunell stepped out of the black vehicle first. She was the leader of the three FBI agents. Sandra was younger than the other two agents who were males in their early to mid-50s. She was all of 33. Tall, blonde, athletic looking, she could have been mistaken for a model, except for the way she carried herself. Assurance, Authority and Ass-Kicking tough. Five years of military service, then direct enrollment in the FBI training facility at Quantico. Head of her class in both academics and fire arms. Just assigned to the midwestern office near Milwaukee. Not the biggest and best fun spot in the U.S. of A. It didn't matter to her where her assignment was, she was all-business 24 hours a day, times seven. Whether this situation here was an act of terrorism, or some sort of mass killing by a psycho, she would find out. That was her job, and that's what she did. She was good at it. Real good.

Sheriff Robach and Lucy Johnson were waiting to meet them. He extended a handshake as they approached him.

"I'm County Sheriff Robach, and this is Lucy Johnson. She's the lead paramedic and was witness to the shooting."

"Agent Brunell, Agent Fedyk, and Agent Thompson," Sandra led the introductions. They all shook hands, not out of politeness, but out of protocol.

"What did you see?" Brunell inquired, setting the tone that was all about being serious. No time for "chit chat" or other local banter. Just the facts.

Lucy repeated everything from the moment she received the call of "a situation in progress" and concluded with her escape from the building after Detective McNail was killed. There were no interrupting questions. She rattled it all off without any emotion. Lucy was a professional, first and foremost, and she acted as expected, no matter how affected she was by everything that happened, especially losing the man she had a secret crush on, McNail.

Brunell listened intently, as her team took some notes as they, too, wanted to hear everything first.

"Thank you, Ms. Johnson," Sandra replied, then turning to Robach, "Sheriff, what did you see?" Robach also related everything from the moment he got summoned from his out-of-town family event, through the events of last night, and what was happening as of today in the aftermath.

"Thank you, Sheriff. We'll need a copy of your reports when available." Agent Brunell took a moment to survey everything going on in front, around, and behind her. She let out a brief,

"Hmmm," as if thinking about something, and she was, and then she took control.

"Agent Fedyk will be assembling a forensic team. Any bodies recovered will be looked at by his people working with your people. Agent Thompson will start interviewing the firemen and other first responders who were here last night and are here today. I'll be leading all investigations and communications. Anything you say to the press, please discuss with me first. Evidence and facts are the keys we need to uncover as quickly as we can. This obviously isn't the norm for any of us. So we have to work as a team."

Without waiting for any response, she turned and surveyed everything again, then turned back and looked directly at both Robach and Lucy. "Off the record, what do both of you think happened?"

Robach nodded his head sideways to Lucy to answer first.

"I think it was a lone shooter. I heard only one shot. It was done by someone who knew how to handle a gun. Direct hit on Detective McNail. It wasn't random shooting. It was aimed. It was meant to stop us from coming in." As Lucy paused to collect her thoughts, a slight tear came from her eyes. "Why him, and not me, I don't know?"

"Consider yourself lucky," Brunell added without any compassion to Lucy, not caring nor wanting to know about her feelings. All she wanted to know was the facts, which would lead her to the evidence, which would reveal the truth, and help her find the killer.

She nodded her head and looked to Robach, indicating it was his turn. "Sheriff?"

"I don't think it was a resident. There haven't been any reports or calls regarding any problems here. Wouldn't expect it from a bunch of elderly people in a retirement home. Not sure if it was a terrorist or some terror group. There haven't been any messages to my department taking claim. I'm thinking it was someone who had a problem with these people or the owners of the place. Maybe revenge."

"Or maybe just a crazy person," Brunell added.

They all stood in silence. On-going rescue machinery was the only sound disturbing their moment of reflection.

"Okay. How many have been accounted for, how many missing?" Brunell jumped back into the "on-the-record" mode as she surveyed the destroyed buildings.

"Fifty-two residents lived in both wings that were damaged. Eighteen bodies or skeletal remains of bodies have been recovered so far, plus Detective McNail. Another twenty missing. We're finding a lot of bones here. A lot. But there's more," Sheriff Robach replied with a deep frown on his face.

"More?" Brunell turned to the County Sheriff.

"Possibly. There was another fire, about three miles west of here, that started shortly after this fire. Their home and barn burned completely to the ground. Nothing left. A local family of four. Two parents and two kids – sorry, make that one kid, the other died last summer. Jameson family. Kept to themselves, nice people, no problems that were reported. Kinda secluded. Used to be a working farm in the old days. We have some people there examining the cause of the fire and looking for them. Hopefully they were away on vacation or something."

"Any ties to here? Family, friends?" Agent Fedyk asked as he continued to take notes.

"Nothing I can think of. We'll check into that. Maybe the fire was just a coincidence. There was a lightning and rain storm last night, big storm. They had an old barn. Maybe it got struck by lightning," the sheriff concluded.

"Nothing else?" Brunell asked as if looking for something more.

"People once reported gunshots from or around there. Jameson had a gun permit and practiced behind the barn. A lot of people up here have gun permits, a lot of hunters, especially with the deer population. Being secluded and all, there were never any disturbances for us to investigate."

Agent Brunell thought about this for a moment. Made a mental note, and turned back to the still smoldering destroyed buildings, then returned to Robach.

"When we're done here, I'd like you to drive me out to their property." Her eyes again turned away slowly from Robach and back to the horrific devastation before them. "Twenty people missing, maybe more. Add that to the dead ones already found. That's a lot of people. Let's hope there aren't any more."

But there was. The dead body of Marvin Fox was still undiscovered, laying on its back, headless, on a blood-covered kitchen floor.

CHAPTER 53

ALL THE PIECES OF A MIXED-UP PUZZLE.

Old Man Jenkins was the groundskeeper for the Wood View Cemetery. He was sort of grandfathered in, having been a relative of a relative who first developed the cemetery in the early 1900s. Since the plots were mostly full and somewhat outdated, there wasn't much to do these days except cut the lawn, trim the bushes, and pull the weeds from and around some of the gravestones. He opened and closed the cemetery gates everyday like clockwork, either puttered around or went back to his nearby trailer home where he watched the daily game shows or "soapy operas," as he joked about them. He didn't have cable TV, so he stayed on the local stations for most of the day. He was approaching mid-seventy, didn't have children, and was finally contemplating retirement. He hadn't saved enough money yet, but, even if he saved his entire paycheck, he couldn't afford a fancy and expensive place like the Sunny Side Up Retirement Home, so his retirement kept getting pushed off.

A newer cemetery, Hill Haven, opened a year or two ago, and most people were buried there now. It had some fancy buildings where people could be buried inside. Jenkins never liked that idea. Felt everyone belonged in the ground, not stacked on top of one another with plush sitting chairs and calming music played all day long. Besides, it was cheaper to be put in a hole in the ground than placed in some fancy-looking metal rectangle box with your name and picture on it. Felt God wanted everyone to follow His commandments and abide by the Bible's words, *"Dust to dust, ashes to ashes, put me in the ground, don't spread me around the town,"* or however it went. Jenkins wasn't very good at religious stuff; he just enjoyed his TV and a few cans of beer between morning and night. So, it was because of this that Jenkins didn't tour and check the cemetery grounds each day.

The Jameson grave that was dug out by Timmy had filled in quite a lot by the sliding pile of dirt from the intense storm. It wasn't perfect, and any casual observer might have said it didn't look right, but as days passed, it snowed, and the grave was covered and stayed covered, and stayed hidden from any prying eyes. It became forgotten. The disturbed grave of the Jameson boys remained a secret, until a brief thaw a month or so later when all the clues finally led back there.

During that month, Agent Sandra Brunell went back and forth to her Milwaukee office. There were other cases that began to take precedent and were overwhelming the bureau and police departments throughout the state and the entire nation. Prank calls, missing people, death threats, terrorist threats, kidnappings, strange packages in the mail, police shootings, a church shooting, a school shooting, just plain old shooting at each other and, of course, bank robberies – several times a week. It was enough to keep all the local and state law-enforcement offices very busy and sometimes spinning in circles looking for all the clues. Evidence, evidence, evidence. It always leads to the truth, that always leads to the answer.

The entire country was plagued by something crazy every day, in every imaginable or unimaginable place. No one, no place was safe anymore. It was as if the whole world was filled with crazy people. And it was. You know that, and so did Agent Brunell. And that's where she was narrowing her focus in the Sunny Side Up Retirement Home murders. It had to have been done by a crazy person. A real crazy person. Or so she thought.

Just as the case was growing cold, cold as the approaching winter weather, the pieces of the puzzle finally started coming together. All the pieces were there, obvious or not. Some led to dead ends, some almost tied things together. Almost. But there was one missing piece that would make everything fit together. A dog. A stray dog. A brown cocker spaniel that sat day in and day out next to a grave that held the bodies of two brothers who had become one.

It was exactly one month to the day that Agent Brunell decided to return to Brentville and pay a visit to Parkland Elementary School. She had talked on the phone with the principal about one of the children, Ryan Jameson, who was presumed dead in the Jameson family fire. The fire was so intense that the retrieved bones held few clues, as they were mostly destroyed in the collapsing structures or burnt to ash. There wasn't any DNA available on the family to support any clear evidence of who was who, although it appeared that the bones found were of adults, not of any child. Besides, the murders and associated deaths in the nearby retirement home were taking all of the main focus of the investigation. But there was something odd about the Jameson family.

Throughout the month that passed, Agent Brunell had a strange feeling that haunted her about the Jamesons. In her research, she learned that Mr. Jameson was a military man, and most of his records were classified as secret, but he was capable of being an expert marksman from what she could find out. But it didn't make sense that he would be the killer. The few remnants that looked like bullets at the retirement home fire had melted beyond recognition. It was one hell of an inferno, to put it mildly. She couldn't tie the forensic findings of the bullet fragments to any gun he had registered. Besides, he may have also had unregistered guns, which he did, but which she didn't know. But, in her investigation, she heard stories in some of the interviews that their surviving son, Ryan, the younger of the two brothers, had trouble in school and that bothered her. She remembered that her first case involved a young child who hated his parents and actually shot them to death. It left a string of nightmares in her, as this case was doing also. So, she couldn't rule out anything. The world was filled with crazy people, and even some crazy kids. But even so, what would be the motive? Why? The principal suggested that she talk to the school psychologist, Ms. Griswald.

It was her last day after a long career of teaching and babysitting, as she sometimes referred to her job. Surrounded by a few cardboard boxes filled with special mementos and letters from her favorite students, Ms. Griswald was counting the few remaining hours till she would shut off her office light for the last time. A long, planned winter break in a rented Florida condo outside of Ft. Myers was on her horizon, with a lot of margaritas, morning, afternoon, and night, waiting for her.

Just a few more hours. She couldn't wait. *"I deserve it."* She always kept that thought to herself as her retirement time grew closer. And today was finally the day. And what a day it was! It was like a revolving door of students and faculty stopping by to say their goodbyes and wish her well. She could care less. Just a few more hours. Not a care in the world, nothing could possibly go wrong. Or could it?

Her office door was slightly ajar when a sudden knock caught her attention. Principal Barnes, an attractive, well-dressed woman in her late 30s entered first, followed by Agent Brunell.

"Judy, this is FBI Agent Brunell."

Ms. Griswald's eyes opened wide in a gesture of complete surprise. She extended her hand awkwardly, never having met an FBI agent in person, or had planned to meet one, let alone in her office on her last day of work.

"Agent Brunell has a few questions regarding the Jameson boys. I recall you were seeing one of them recently for some school- and home-related problems, so I'd like you to share that information with her," Principal Barnes concluded as she stood between the two of them throughout the introduction.

"Ahh, okay. Please sit down, Agent…" Ms. Griswald gestured with her one hand to a nearby chair, while trying to figure out in her spinning thoughts what this was all about.

"Thank you, Ms. Griswald. This shouldn't take too long," Sandra said, in a polite, business-like manner. She then turned towards the principal.

"Principal Barnes, I'd like to talk to Ms. Griswald in private."

"Sure. I'll be in my office if you need me for anything else," Barnes replied politely, although also interested in what could possibly be going on.

"Judy." Principal Barnes nodded to Ms. Griswald, with a look of "just take care of business and no problems."

She turned and left the office, closing the door behind her.

"Retiring. Must be nice," Brunell began the conversation with a friendly and professional smile.

"Forty years, five weeks, three days, and counting the hours to the end of today," the soon-to-be-retired woman answered in a happy, but exhausted tone.

"Probably have a lot of interesting stories to tell," Brunell added, not so much as a question, but more or less as a comment.

"A lot," Griswald replied, warming up to her.

There was a pause as if both women were studying each other before continuing the conversation. Agent Brunell spoke first.

"Tell me about the Jameson kids. You knew them both?"

"I didn't know much about the older one, Timmy, but I saw the younger one, Ryan, a few times in the past few months," she replied.

"Why was that?" Brunell cocked her head as if interested in knowing more, much more.

"Well, ever since his older brother died, Ryan became more of a recluse. Kept to himself, not that he had that many friends, but he was becoming more withdrawn and paid less attention in class. I only know this because, after any of our students have a traumatic experience, whether at home or here at school, it was my job to document it," she replied smiling, pleased with her answer, and proud of her role and having been involved in the matter.

"Do you have a file on him?"

"Sure, I've left everything in this filing cabinet for my replacement, whoever that will be." She pointed at the lone tan-colored, three-drawer cabinet behind her. "School budget hasn't allowed any new hires, so everything is still being jostled around. But, not my concern."

"May I see the file?"

"Sure." She got up from her desk chair and opened the file drawer. Everything was alphabetized. "Right...here."

Opening a typical hanging file folder, Ms. Griswald pulled out a folder with a few pages of paperwork and handed it to the agent.

Without any conversation, Brunell sat quietly, turning the pages while taking a long moment looking at them.

"How did the older brother die?" she asked, without looking up from the folder.

"It was some sort of aneurism. Totally unexpected. Sad, he was so young. Happened during the summer months before school started. His younger brother was with him at the time. They were playing in the field behind their house."

"Do you think Ryan died in the family home fire?" Brunell asked, changing the subject from Timmy to Ryan.

"Gosh. I haven't kept up with all the news. Mostly everything has been about the retirement home. How awful was that? Shortly after the fires, the Retirement place and his family home, Ryan didn't show up in school, so I'm assuming from what the principal told us, he must have perished with his mother and father."

"Quite a fire. Investigators are still trying to figure out how it happened," Brunell added without much of a pause between their dialogue.

"Same night as the retirement home, if I recall," Ms. Griswald added to that.

"Yes. Quite a coincidence." The FBI agent slowed her response down, as if looking for something more.

"Yes, I guess so," Ms. Griswald concluded.

"Is this a game of cat and mouse?" Griswald thought to herself. *"Or is she just asking standard FBI-ish questions like they do on the TV shows I watch at night? Or, is there something more? What is she after? Is there something she's looking for that involves me?"*

Brunell scribbled some notes on her pad and then looked back at her. "Were there any significant problems or situations with Ryan after his brother's death?"

"You mean, how he handled it?"

"You said he was withdrawn. Can you explain that?"

"Well, at first I remember that he wouldn't say much. Sort of just sat in class, that's what his teacher told me. There's a note in the file from one of his teachers."

Brunell nodded to her. "Go on."

Griswald shrugged slightly with her reply, "It was my job to see him and talk with him."

"So, you've been the lone school psychologist, that's your title, for how long?" Brunell again switched the conversation.

"Well, actually only about a year or so."

"Have you always been a psychologist?"

"Well, I've been a teacher most of my life, but with school budget cuts and all the teacher layoffs, my career took some changes and I ended up in the role," Griswald stated somewhat hesitantly in her defense.

"Hmm." Brunell smiled at her, then looked at the file again.

"How did Ryan relate to the other kids in his class? You said he didn't have many friends?"

"Actually, he didn't have any."

Brunell paused, and looked up from the file.

"What do you mean?"

"His brother was his best friend, so I'm told, and Ryan never had any friends other than his brother. His classmates were just that. He was a loner. Until he got a dog. Strangest thing, the dog would follow him to school and sit outside the classroom window all day waiting for him, rain or shine. His teacher thought it was good for him to have a pet. That it probably helped him cope. So Principal Barnes decided to let the dog stay on the school grounds as long it was leashed and didn't bother anyone."

"What kind of dog?"

"I think it was a brown cocker spaniel. Had a funny name, I remember the kids making fun of it. Butch, yes, that's the name, Butch. Kinda odd name for a dog."

"Is it still around?"

"Come to think of it, no one's mentioned it, or seen it, since Ryan stopped coming to school, I mean, since his death."

"What makes you so sure he's dead?" Brunell lifted her eyebrows with the question, as if she finally was getting somewhere.

"Well, he disappeared. Hasn't been in school in over a month. Probably died in the fire – that's what I read in the papers."

"So, the dog also disappeared after Ryan disappeared?"

"What is she looking for?" Griswald thought to herself. *"This is my last day of work and I have a goddamn FBI agent asking me questions about some damn kid who probably died in a fire and his missing dog."*

Brunell made a few notes on her pad while waiting for an answer.

"I guess." Griswald frowned.

Brunell resumed her questioning. "What peculiarities did Ryan exhibit, if any?"

"Well. There was one – a bit strange, but probably a part of his grieving."

"And what was that?"

"Well," she slowed down her response and was careful in choosing her words. "He didn't respond to being called Ryan anymore. He said Ryan was dead. He told everyone to call him Timmy."

"Call him Timmy!" This immediately caught Agent Brunell's attention.

The FBI agent leaned forward in her chair and looked directly at Ms. Griswald with a stern expression. "You said Timmy was his older brother. He's the one who died last summer. And you didn't think this was odd, calling himself by his dead brother's name?"

Griswald squirmed uncomfortably in her chair from the agent's comment.

"Well," she stumbled for the right words again, "apparently Ryan always looked up to his brother, wanted to be just like him. Guess that's what happens with a lot of young siblings."

"Guess?" The FBI agent smirked.

"Well, from what I've read, sometimes siblings have rivalries or sometimes they have fixations."

"So, this was a fixation?" Brunell's question took on a very sharp tone.

"OK, let me put it this way. Ryan would only respond to being called Timmy. Wanted only to be called Timmy. Maybe that's all he heard when his name was called. Maybe he was pretending to be his brother. Sometimes kids do funny things when someone close dies."

"And you didn't think this was strange?" Brunell's lack of patience with Griswald's answers was starting to show.

"Well, a lot of young kids take on the identities of other people, comic book superheroes, movie stars, popular singers, friends, and sometimes family. A lot has to do with social media," Griswald replied, as if she knew the answer, or at least felt comfortable with her answer.

"It's always about social media, isn't it?" Brunell added with a half-fake smile.

Griswald seemed to stumble for the right answer, if there even was one. "I guess."

"So, this kid, Ryan, the younger brother, assumed his dead brother's name, and everybody went along with it?"

Griswald fidgeted in her seat again, seeming to run out of answers, and just making them up as she went along. "Well, he called himself Timmy, and he responded to being called Timmy. So, I guess that was his way of handling it."

"You're quite a guesser," Brunell said sarcastically.

"Well, I guess I am," Griswald replied, as if what she heard was a compliment.

Brunell wouldn't even answer her last response. *"This person is apparently stupider than shit,"* she thought to herself while scribbling the words "Ryan = Timmy = Ryan" on her notepad and then circling it. She stared at it for a few long moments trying to fit all the pieces to this weird "kid-changing-identity" puzzle together. Finally, she looked up.

"Did you discuss this with his parents?" she asked calmly.

"I met with the mother after a school meeting and discussed it with her." Griswald was getting tired of all this. She had enough with the questions. She started to fidget even more in her seat, tapping one hand on the side of her wooden arm chair, then looking at her watch. *"You'd think I was on trial. I didn't do anything wrong,"* she thought to herself, wanting this whole FBI interrogation to end. *"Obviously, the kid was a nut job; so are most of the kids around here,"* she continued in her mind as she agreed with herself. *"This is nonsense. Who cares if this kid is dead? I gotta finish packing up."*

Brunell finally cut into Griswald's "lost-in-her-thoughts" expression. "What did she say?"

Griswald let out a silent sigh and started to answer. "Pretty much what I just told you. The kid adored his older brother and was traumatized by his brother's death and was probably coping with it by calling himself Timmy."

"And this didn't bother you? Or bother his parents?"

"Listen, I wasn't trained to be a psychiatrist," Griswald replied, almost pleading.

"Or a school psychologist," Brunell quickly added.

That stung.

There was another moment of silence between them as Griswald struggled to compose herself. Finally, she continued.

"His mom seemed okay with it. But she also seemed a little distant. Like she was distracted by a lot of things. Must have been emotional for her to lose a son so young."

"So, everyone – parents, teachers, friends, and you were okay with Ryan taking on the name of his dead older brother?" Brunell asked forcibly.

Griswald thought about this for a moment, her expression growing solemn as she tired from all the agent's questions. She shrugged, almost in defeat, let out a deep breath, and replied with a genuine regret in her eyes, "I guess."

I'm sure you did," Brunell added very quickly and again, very sarcastically.

There was another awkward pause between them. Either it was very warm in her office with the door closed, or all of this was making Griswald sweat. She reached for a tissue on her table and wiped her neck.

Brunell continued her questioning. "Did he take on his identity, too?"

"I'm not sure how to answer that. I never had any interaction with Timmy before his death. I only saw

Ryan a few times. That's all I was required to do. He was just a mixed-up kid."

"Just a mixed-up kid." Brunell mulled it over. It was her time to pause and think to herself. *"Mixed up, or maybe something else? What? He became his brother. Why?"*

Brunell's cellphone suddenly rang, interrupting the silence and their meeting. She looked at her caller ID; it was the sheriff.

"Excuse me, I have to take it."

She turned her back to Griswald as she answered it.

"Brunell." There was a long pause. "Okay. I'll be there as soon I can. Hold everything till I get there."

Ending the call, she turned her attention back to Ms. Griswald.

"Something important?" Griswald asked, as if it were her turn to do the questioning or maybe because she was just nosey.

Brunell didn't answer her directly; instead, she just flashed a brief smile before changing back to her FBI-ish look.

"I'd like to borrow this file. If I need to talk to you some more, where can I reach you?"

Griswald didn't really want to tell her that she was packing her office and home and leaving soon for that long-deserved vacation to a condo in sunny Florida, but she did.

"You can call me by my cell, 534-723-8055. I'm taking a few months to go to Florida. I hate the winters here."

"Should be warm there. I like Florida. Nice place to retire. Thank you for your time." Brunell got up from her chair and turned to leave, then stopped, and turned back.

Griswald got up slowly from her chair.

"Just one more thing," Brunell paused, seemingly on purpose.

Ms. Griswald waited for the FBI agent's words. *"Hopefully she's going to wish me happiness in my retirement and never talk to me again."*

"Just don't plan on leaving town soon."

"What? Oh shit!" Griswald thought to herself. *"Shit, shit, shit. Why did I tell her I was leaving town?"*

Without extending a "thank-you handshake," Agent Brunell flashed her a final smile she'd never forget, one of those fake "F-You" smiles. The FBI agent turned and left the office, leaving Griswald standing alone with several packed, and still-to-be-packed, opened cardboard boxes on her office floor.

She slowly sat down in her chair and let out a long deep sigh. This was not how she imagined her last day would be. This conversation with this "F'n Sherlock Holmes" FBI agent had her rattled and left her heart pounding. *"What did I miss in the Ryan kid? What didn't I see? What is this all about?"* She shook her head, thinking of everything. Everything. *"He was just a mixed-up kid. Shit, all the kids today are mixed up. All the teachers are mixed up, too. Everyone is mixed up; it's a mixed-up world!"*

Griswald got up from her desk dead went to her half-open office door. She closed it, put the lock on it, and returned to her chair, sitting quietly, tentatively, for a long moment. Her decision was made. She opened one of the previous packed boxes and put her hand in it, searching for something. It didn't take long to find it. She knew where it was. She knew what she had to do next. And she needed it badly now. She needed to be calmed down, so she could finally leave the school and her office, and all the "shit" she put up with for years in this job, behind her.

She found it.

Griswald carefully took out the pink vibrator and brought it toward her wrinkled and waiting legs. With her one free hand, she hiked up her long over-the-knees, plain-Jane dress and opened her legs wide. She smiled to herself with anticipation. It wouldn't take long. She knew the drill, if you want to call it that. With her other hand she flicked the switch on.

Nothing!

She tried it again. Nothing. And again, still nothing. The battery was dead.

"Shit, shit, shit." This was not the way she wanted to end the last day in her job. "Shit, shit, shit."

Discouraged, she opened her hand while closing her legs and let go of her pink friend. It fell to her now-closed lap, and she started to cry.

CHAPTER 54

DEAD-ALIVE.

On her way to the cemetery, Sandra thought about the call from Sheriff Robach that interrupted her conversation with the school psychologist. He told her about an out-of-town family visiting the local cemetery and seeing a half-opened grave. They notified the caretaker who, in turn, notified the police. Robach got the call and drove there to meet with the family at the caretaker's office. They were a bit shaken as they described what they saw. A limping, brownish-colored dog (wasn't sure of the breed) was pacing back and forth around a gravesite, which was partially dug open. At first, they thought nothing of it, as it could have been just an imminent burial site. The mother of the family, being a dog lover, went to see if the dog was alright. The dog looked mangy and wet, and could have been a stray, but he was staying around the grave like he belonged there. What caught her attention most was that the dog was also digging in the ground between its pacing. As if it were looking for something. When she went closer to the gravesite, the dog's demeanor changed, and it started to growl, menacing her. The dog's growl emitted a strange and bizarre sound as it showed its fangs and appeared ready to defend the open grave. Spooked by this, the family of four quickly got in their car and drove to the front entrance where they alerted the caretaker. He asked to be shown the site on a map, and after they left, he drove a cemetery-owned golf cart to the grave. When he got there, hoping that it was nothing to be bothered about, he witnessed the exact same sequence of events as described by the family. He took notice that it was the gravesite of the Jameson kid who had died and was buried last summer. He was aware of the recent fire, and deaths of the Jameson family, and decided this was nothing he wanted to deal with, and he called the police.

When Robach arrived, he also witnessed the same thing.

As he approached the gravesite, the mangy-looking dog growled menacingly at him. It bared its sharp, fang-like teeth and stood in front of the partially opened grave, preventing him from coming any closer. It looked like it had been injured in an accident, as it limped on a leg that must have been broken at one time and had healed badly. It also had splotches of old dried blood matted in its fur. He was tempted to pull his gun and shoot the animal to put it out of its misery, and perhaps prevent it from attacking him, but he hesitated.

He knew FBI Agent Brunell was in town again. She had called him earlier and mentioned that she was going to a local school to learn more about the Jameson kids. Since this was the gravesite of one of the kids, and since it appeared to have been disturbed, and it was now being protected by a strange growling dog, he thought he better call her now. So, he did. And now, she was almost there.

As she approached the entrance to the Wood View Cemetery, her thoughts focused on Griswald telling her about the young boy Ryan, taking Timmy's name, maybe more. Griswald also said that Ryan had a spotted brown-colored dog who waited for him patiently every day at school. And now a dog matching that description was waiting at the brother's grave, digging in the ground.

"Was the dog trying to tell them something, or maybe trying to protect something, or maybe trying to hide something?"

She thought about this and decided this might be the "clue" to help her put all the final pieces of this strange puzzle together. Maybe the Jameson kid wasn't just a mixed-up kid. Maybe he was somehow connected to the fire at his family home and maybe even to the fire and deaths at the retirement home. Maybe. As far-fetched as that might have sounded to the average person, she was not an average person. She was a trained FBI agent, a profiler, as her job description read. And as such, she had to look at all the clues, analyze all the options, determine all the connections. There was something here at this cemetery that she needed to see. One thought started to fill her mind. *"Maybe he was more than a mixed-up kid. Maybe he was a crazy kid? Maybe he was..."* And with that thought, a shiver went through her body as she drove into the cemetery grounds.

As she parked her car, it was starting to rain, just a light drizzle. The weather was always so unpredictable here in northern Wisconsin. If only she would have gotten the FBI assignment in Florida instead. Then she could have met with the retired Ms. Griswald, and shared a margarita or two, in between a laugh or two.

Right now, this was far from being a laughing matter. There was an odd feeling surrounding her every step as she followed the directions to the Jameson gravesite. Something was not right. Something was very wrong. Very, very wrong, and she would soon find out what that was.

A low rumble of thunder gave her another chill. Sandra grabbed her open coat collar with one hand and held it tighter, as if to protect herself. Her other hand went inside the coat and touched her holstered gun. She didn't really think she would need it, but just knowing it was there was enough of a "security blanket" at the moment.

A man's voice came from the standing tombstones ahead of her.

"Agent Brunell, over here." Robach's voice grabbed her attention.

She could make him out in the distance as she passed a tall grey monument with a family name on it that she wouldn't even try to pronounce. Some names were just too difficult to say, not that hers was the easiest either.

Next to Robach was a short, balding, elderly man, wearing a black plastic-looking old raincoat and holding his hands behind his back. *"Must be the cemetery caretaker,"* she thought. *"Who in their right mind would want to work every day surrounded by the dead?"*

Another chill went through her, but not as big as a chill that was about to come.

About twenty feet ahead of the two men was the half-open grave. What looked like a hastily dug grave was now being rained on, turning the open earth into a mound of dark mud. That was fairly shocking to see. But it was the dog that shocked her the most. It was digging at the ground around the grave, then pacing in a circle, limping, then digging again. It paid no attention to her, or the two other onlookers.

"Agent Brunell, this is John Jenkins, the cemetery caretaker." Sheriff Robach started without offering a handshake.

"He called in to my office and told me about the family who was here earlier and what they saw. I gave you that part of the story on the phone and what I saw when I arrived, but the part I didn't tell you everything about..." He paused. "...was the dog. I didn't know how to describe it. You have to see it for yourself."

Even though they were a short distance away from the dog, she was close enough to see what Sheriff Robach had wanted her to see and experience it without explaining it to her. Actually, he thought that if he had told her, she wouldn't believe him anyway. And so, she turned her attention to the dog, and she saw it.

When the dog turned to circle where it was digging, one side of his body was partially exposed. It was obvious that the dog had been in some sort of horrible accident, or something had happened after whatever that accident was. This part of the dog's body revealed rotting, decaying flesh. Sandra had seen a lot of horrible things in the two years of the Afghanistan military missions she lived through, and she had seen a lot in the short time she was an active FBI agent. She had seen dead bodies, both adults and children, and dead animals of all types, when they had been just killed or were dead for some time. She knew what happened over "some time." There was a difference. And that difference was evident in what they were looking at, as if it were something that was "dead, but still alive." This dog was certainly alive, it was moving and digging, but from what she witnessed of its injury, it should have been dead, a long time ago.

Another deeper chill went through her body. Another closer roll of thunder snapped her back into the moment.

"Oh, my God!" she muttered to herself out loud.

"Yeah, pretty strange. Real strange," Robach added.

Sandra turned to him as if to agree, but her look said it all.

Was this the clue she had a premonition about? Was this dog Ryan's dog? And was this dog buried alive here and dug its way out? How close to the truth was she? How far from the truth was she? She had to know the truth. And there was one way to find out.

She turned towards Robach and the caretaker.

"Stay here."

And she turned away from them and began to walk slowly towards the dog.

Robach put his hand on his holstered gun. He quietly pulled the strap away from it if he needed to get access to it in a hurry.

After a few steps towards the open grave, the dog stopped its digging and turned to look at her. It started to growl. As it was heard before by the family that came here first, and then by the caretaker and then Robach, it was a strange growl. A menacing growl. A growl that didn't belong to what one would assume to be a gentle cocker spaniel dog. As the growl grew louder, the fangs of the dog were exposed. Rotting teeth, a mixture of dirt and blood.

"*Jesus, what is going on here?*" Her mind raced.

Sandra stopped.

Now was the time to do what she remembered from the conversation with Ms. Griswald. Sandra stood perfectly still and spoke directly at the dog in a calming voice.

"Butch."

The dog's fangs and rotting mouth began to relax and return to some semblance of normal. The growling continued, but at a lower frequency.

"Butch, it's okay. Good dog, Butch, good dog," Sandra calmly continued.

Sandra knew she had the attention of the dog. Whether this was Ryan's dog or not, it was reacting to the name Butch. The growling stopped. It relaxed its aggressive stance and almost looked like a normal dog would look when it was called by its name and feel non-threatened. Almost, except for the half-rotten, open side of the dog.

Sandra felt more comfortable as she started forward again, but she still walked with caution. The soft and gentle rain started to intensify.

Robach took a step forward also, very slowly, and with his hand still on the holstered pistol.

The caretaker took a step backward. For sure, the whole thing that was unfolding was way above his pay grade and what the job description was.

Sandra was a foot or two away from the dog. It just stood there looking directly at her. Not wagging its tail, not giving any indication of what it was going to do next.

She slowly reached out one hand. Open. Towards it.

Robach stopped about ten feet behind her, his hand wrapped tightly around his pistol, ready to draw it out if he had to, ready to use it, as he was preparing himself to do.

Sandra's open hand stopped inches from the dog's face.

"Butch, it's okay, I won't hurt you. Good dog." Her words seemed to comfort the dog. A comforting it hadn't experienced for some time now. A comfort the dog needed and hopefully would react to.

And it did. It licked her hand.

Sandra let out a slow deep breath that she had been holding while waiting for the dog's reaction. As the dog licked her hand, it looked up at her, studying her, analyzing her, finding a peaceful comfort in her.

And she saw close up what had shocked her from afar, what had shocked everyone. Half of the dog's right side was hanging skin and open flesh. It definitely had an injury for some time or more. Whatever happened to the dog, it definitely shouldn't be alive looking like this. The dog had the stench of rot. The smell of death. It was dead-alive, if that could even be a possibility.

Using a calm voice, she spoke again to the dog.

"Where's Timmy?"

No response. The dog looked at her curiously.

"This was Timmy's grave, and had his name on the headstone. But..."

Sandra knew she had to say what she had to say next. It would be a telling point in this heart-stopping moment. She whispered the next words, just loud enough for the dog to hear and maybe understand.

"Butch...where's Ryan? Where's Ryan?"

And the dog reacted. It turned its head away from her as if it understood her, which it really did. It understood the question, and it was now giving her the answer. The dog turned to look at the half-open grave, then turned back to look at her.

She repeated again, "Butch, show me. Where is Ryan?"

The dog moved away from her. and limped to the open grave. It started to dig in the rain-soaked ground.

CHAPTER 55

IT ALL COMES TO AN END.

The rain started to come down harder. Thunder echoed throughout the cemetery, seeming to bounce off the old and crumbling grave monuments. Sandra watched the dog dig into the wet ground. She turned back towards the sheriff and the caretaker.

"Get some tools. Get some men out here. We're going to help the dog dig."

"Are you kidding me?" the old caretaker grumbled.

"You heard her. Let's get this done, now." Sheriff Robach picked up his walkie talkie and called the town police station for additional manpower.

It didn't take long for two other police officers to arrive. Two other maintenance workers from the cemetery also showed up at about the same time. In the meantime, the caretaker had picked up four large shovels from the main entrance storage shed.

It was too wet for the large backhoe to be used, so it all had to be done with manual labor.

Sandra gave them instructions, all the time keeping an eye on the mysterious dog who was limping, digging, and periodically pacing around Timmy's gravesite.

With Sandra leading the way, they approached Timmy's grave. And that's when all hell broke loose.

No more than ten feet away from the dog, it suddenly turned to them, stopped its digging, and started to growl.

"Butch, it's okay, it's okay." She tried to calm it.

But it wouldn't stop its growling, even after hearing her calm voice. It started to snarl. Started to bare its rotted teeth and fangs and took on a whole different appearance. And then it started to bark, loud barks, louder than the thunder which came and went with the now pouring rain. Its eyes seemed to grow wider, and its pupils turned red. Blood-colored red.

"What the fuck!" one of the maintenance workers said out loud, hardly being heard over the dog's growls.

Sheriff Robach drew his gun.

Sandra again tried to calm the dog down.

"Butch, it's okay. We're here to find Ryan."

And that's when it attacked. Leaping in the air directly at Sandra.

And that's when Robach fired his gun.

One, two, three quick shots. Hitting the crazed animal, maybe once, maybe twice, maybe all three times. It fell to the ground, dead.

"Holy shit," another of the maintenance men uttered after having lifted his shovel up to protect himself.

"That fucking dog wasn't human," another cop added to the unsettling moment.

Robach looked at him.

"Of course, it wasn't human; it was an animal!" he shouted at him in frustration and shock, but even he thought, whatever the dog was, it wasn't like anything he had ever seen or experienced in his lifetime.

Shaken, but still trying to maintain some sort of FBI composure, Sandra looked at Robach.

"Thanks."

One simple word. One important word. He may have saved her life. He probably did.

They all stood looking at the body of the dead dog. One of the other policemen took his shovel and touched the carcass. They all saw the same thing.

"There's no blood."

The caretaker had seen enough. He made the sign of the cross, dropped his shovel and turned away.

One of the other policemen yelled at him, "Hey, where're you going?"

"Let him go," Robach quickly spoke. If he could, he probably would have left with him. Definitely, all of this was above his pay grade, too.

A flash of lightning illuminated the entire graveyard. With a backdrop of tall, crumbling, weather-worn tombstones, and twisted, old tree limbs without leaves, it looked like a scene from a scary horror movie. Actually, it was worse. It was real.

Wet. Shocked. Confused. They all took a moment to shake off what had just happened, though they would always remember it. Sheriff Robach finally broke the silence as his eyes caught Sandra's.

"Why do you think it attacked us?"

"It was probably protecting the grave," she answered as if knowing, but not really knowing.

"From us?" The sheriff frowned.

"Maybe, or maybe protecting us, from what's in it," Sandra concluded, as she turned away from him, and looked back towards the open grave.

Those words sent a chill through all of them at the same time. The rain had been steady for over an hour-plus now and twilight was rapidly approaching. They had work to do. They were going to dig open the rest of the Jameson boy's grave. They were going to learn whatever secret there was, and whatever reasons there were that made all this madness happen in the first place.

It started to thunder again.

Within thirty minutes of digging, and about four feet into the ground, they found a buried shovel.

"Not one of ours," a bearded maintenance man stated, matter of factly.

"Whoever was digging this hole, left the shovel inside the ground," Sandra answered as she looked at it in the continuing pouring rain. "Too wet, too dirty to find prints, but leave it above ground."

"About a foot or so to go," another of the diggers added.

It was getting more difficult for all of them to be inside the hole at once. They used a ladder that the maintenance workers brought with them so that they could climb in and out as necessary, as the hole got closer to the six-foot-under grave requirement.

The rain had made the ground very soft, and some mud was sliding back in for every two or three shovelfuls of wet earth they took out.

Ten minutes later, there was a clanging sound as one of the metal shovels struck the object they were looking for. After a few more minutes of work, three of them stood on the top of the now-exposed coffin. Sandra, Robach, and one of the other officers were above ground looking down.

Robach turned and looked at Sandra. She looked back at him with a slight nod of her head. Without asking her, he knew what he had to tell them.

"Open it up."

"Don't we need a court order?" one of the policemen in the open grave shouted up.

"We got a half-open grave, a missing kid, maybe a dead kid in the fire, 22-plus people dead from a retirement home fire that could be connected or not, and a dead dog without any blood that was guarding whatever is in the ground beneath us. Let's just say the court order is in the mail. Now open it up," Robach yelled as the wind started to increase and made more disturbing whistling noises through the surrounding standing tombstones.

"Carefully," Sandra added, "Very carefully."

One of the two maintenance workers and the remaining officer climbed out of the hole. There was only room enough for one person to do what had to be done. It would be different if they were bringing the coffin out of the ground. They weren't. They were opening it inside the ground.

The maintenance man felt for the latch on the side of the coffin. Finding it, he stopped and looked upwards, all the while getting some of the continuing rain directly onto his face. He tried to shield his eyes with his gloved hand.

"Someone has already opened it. Looks like it was opened with a blunt instrument. Lots of dents and scratches. Maybe done by the shovel we found buried in the dirt."

"A half-opened grave, with a shovel buried half-way into the ground, which covered the coffin, which had been previously opened, and protected by a half-dead dog." All of this raced through Sandra's analytical mind. The pieces of the puzzle were coming together for her. This would be the moment she knew would unlock the answer she was looking for. She looked at Robach and looked back down into the grave.

"Do it. Open it up," she yelled down to the maintenance man inside the grave.

And no one was prepared for what they were about to see next.

Inside the coffin were two bodies hugged tightly together. One was the decaying body of Timmy Jameson who had died months ago. The other was the body of the Jameson boy, Ryan, who had been missing for a few weeks. Dried blood was splattered throughout the inside of the coffin. There was a bullet hole in the decaying chest of Timmy. There was a bullet hole in the chest of Ryan. Both bullet holes were exactly where their hearts would be. Both had been shot in the heart. One bullet for each boy. Bang-Bang. They're both dead.

Perhaps a symbolic ending of the love they both shared for each other. Perhaps. They were together again, finally in death. Two dead brothers, buried as one.

Endgame.

And then, they all saw the gun.

It was clutched tightly in the decomposing hand of Timmy, his partially exposed skeletal finger wrapped tightly around the trigger.

Outside the grave, in the traces of the first signs of moonlight, could be heard the distant barking, then the howling, then what sounded like the fading, crying voice of a sad, lonely, lost dog.

There would be no further clues to be found.

Author's Notes and Acknowledgements.....

The Hardy Boys, Joe and Frank, are two young teenage sleuths, sons of the renown Chester Hardy, one of America's top fictional detectives. It was May 1958, on my 10th birthday, when I received my first Hardy Boy book, *The Case of the Disappearing Floor.* Reading my first mystery novel opened the doorway to my imagination. And I was hooked. Over the next few Christmases and birthdays I received and read 39 Hardy Boy mysteries. And I still have them today.

Sixty years later, after a successful career at Eastman Kodak Company writing TV and Video programs and scripts, Kodak publications, newsletters, advertising and marketing campaigns, I have now embarked on the "second chapter" in my life.

The first few years of my retirement were spent enjoying my family and grandchildren with some travel in between and renewing my lifelong hobby of collecting comic books. And that's where another doorway was opened in my imagination. I wrote and published my first comic book, **BLACK MAN WHITE MAN,** a murder mystery about a black police detective who unknowingly transforms at night into a white serial killer. That was followed by my second comic, *DREAMER,* about a teenage boy who, while trapped in a coma, travels into the dreams of disabled children and helps them find the "hero" in themselves. Even with a few more comic book projects in the works, I decided to challenge myself and attempt to write my first novel. And what a challenge it was! And what a journey it was! There was no outline, no planned ending, just an idea. I started to write in chapter sequence, not knowing where it would go, or how it would conclude, but somehow it all came together. It became an unknown roller coaster ride for me, and an intended roller coaster ride for you, the reader. And here it is...***BANG-BANG, YOU'RE DEAD***.

There are several people who gave me the encouragement, advice, and the push to help me complete this book. Without them, it may not have happened.

First and foremost, Debbie, my wife of 44 years. On my daily retirement "honey-do list" there were a lot of "to do's," but Debbie gave me the time and encouragement to follow my writing passion. I thank her for her patience and understanding, and most importantly, her love and wisdom. She has been a "blessing" in my life, and I am so lucky to have her as my wife and life-partner. Now that this book is printed, I have a lot of those honey-do projects to get caught up on before I start my next novel.

When working in Kodak Publications, I had the opportunity to collaborate with an amazing editor, Elly Stevens. She always made sure all my "t's" were crossed and "i's" were dotted. Not only did she come out of retirement to work with me on this book, but she offered her writing knowledge and guidance, and helped me add important elements in the story to pull it together. She is a great friend and I couldn't have finished this story without her talent and support. I thank her for that, and look forward to working with her again.

Megan Parker is the designer behind this book. She is a renown author of several award-winning novels including her *SCARLET NIGHT* series. I admire her writing ability and design skills, and when I asked her to help me, I was so pleased that she agreed and became part of my team. It meant a lot to me when, after she read a preview chapter of this book, she told me she couldn't wait to read the whole book. I hope you feel the same.

And of course, the one person who made this story come to life in my imagination – my 92-year-old mother-in-law, Dorothy Payne, who recently moved into an independent living facility similar to the one in the story which sparked the idea. Yes, an important character in this story has a similar name, and yes, she does become a victim. But I would never kill my mother-in-law; I love her and respect her so much. So, I want to "dedicate this book to her," otherwise, she said she just might kill me!

And finally, I thank you, the reader, for purchasing this book, and I thank all my family and friends for all their support and love throughout an incredible lifetime. Never forget that, every day, everyone in your life plays a part of the journey that helps to shape who you are. Enjoy each "chapter" in your life, challenge yourself, let your imagination lead the way, and always follow your dreams. And at the end of each day, be proud of yourself for all you have done and all that you leave behind for others to remember you by. I am.

Joe Janowicz

COMING SOON

From the creative team-up of USA Today bestselling author Nathan Squiers, and *BANG-BANG YOU'RE DEAD* writer, Joe Janowicz

BLACK MAN WHITE MAN, perhaps one of the most controversial stories you will ever read.   Set in today's racially explosive world, ***BLACK MAN WHITE MAN*** is an edgy mystery/horror thriller in which a black police detective unknowingly transforms color and personality at night into a white serial killer who is murdering the family and friends of the black detective.

Both are obsessed and driven to kill each other, with neither knowing they are one and the same….or are they?   Both are conflicted by their prejudices against each other. And with each murder, the clues left behind point to the black detective as the killer. To prove his innocence, he must uncover the hidden truths of his past, as he looks into his soul, to face the demons within.

Available in bookstores and online Spring 2019